*"What is required of us now is a new era of responsibility—
a recognition, on the part of every American, that we have
duties to ourselves, our nation, and the world, duties that we
do not grudgingly accept but rather seize gladly, firm in the
knowledge that there is nothing so satisfying to the spirit, so
defining of our character, than giving our all to a difficult task."*

—President Barack Obama, Inaugural Address

THE OBAMA REVOLUTION

THE OBAMA REVOLUTION

Alan Kennedy-Shaffer

The author is grateful for permission to include the following previously published material: Excerpts from
Alan Kennedy-Shaffer, "Taking a Stand," Patriot-News, August 10, 2008. Reprinted by permission of the
Patriot-News. Excerpts from various columns by Alan Kennedy-Shaffer published by Scoop08. Reprinted by permission of Scoop Media.

The opinions expressed in this book are those of the author of this book
and do not necessarily reflect the views of the publisher or its affiliates.

ISBN-10: 1-59777-638-6
ISBN-13: 978-1-59777-638-7
Library of Congress Cataloging-In-Publication Data Available

Cover Design by Sonia Fiore
Book Design by Marti Lou Critchfield
Cover Photo by AP Images/Rick Bowmer

Printed in the United States of America

Phoenix Books, Inc.
9465 Wilshire Boulevard, Suite 840
Beverly Hills, CA 90212

10 9 8 7 6 5 4 3 2 1

In loving memory of my grandfather,
the Hon. Rev. Dr. William Bean Kennedy,
this book is dedicated to my grandparents.

CONTENTS

INTRODUCTION

PRESIDENT BARACK OBAMA

Tears of joy streamed down my face on Tuesday, November 4, 2008, when the television networks proclaimed Barack Hussein Obama the next president of the United States. Dazed after a long day of precinct visits with Democratic congressional candidate Bill Day, I stared at the screen and knew that the eighteen-hour days and the stressful phone calls had all been worth it. The work of my fellow campaigners in the Tidewater region of Virginia had paid off, and we were finally able to bask in the glory of knowing that we had contributed, in some small way, to the Obama Revolution.

Two weeks earlier, I had watched the 47-year-old Democratic senator from Illinois address a full house at the Richmond Coliseum, less than two blocks from where he launched his campaign in Virginia nearly two years ago with the endorsement of Governor Timothy M. Kaine. Technicians had splashed "Change We Need" across electronic display screens and dangled theater lights from the ceiling as an overflow crowd of 13,000 Virginians packed into bleacher seats to hear the Democratic presidential nominee talk about how his candidacy would change the future of the nation.[1]

Media coverage took center stage at the event, occupying more than half of the floor space in the vaulted auditorium, as well as reserved risers and tables. Like a basketball game or a circus, loud music blared and vendors sold everything from T-shirts to cotton candy. Spectators chanted and did the "wave," always with one eye on the podium. Staffers covered their ears and yelled into cell phones as they waited for the man Senator John McCain had once called "That One"[2] to arrive.

After striding briskly to the podium, Obama proclaimed a message of positive, collective change emphasizing that "we can't let up and we won't let up.... Here's what John McCain doesn't understand," he said. "When the economy's in turmoil...Americans don't want to hear politicians attacking each other. They want to hear what we're going to do." Amid broad applause, the presidential nominee built to a crescendo with notes of unity: "We'll rise and fall as one people, as one nation."[3]

Nearly two years earlier, on February 17, 2007, Obama had stressed his belief that the nation needed a "politics that brings us together rather than a politics that breaks us apart." He concluded in his speech to Democratic Party loyalists gathered at the Richmond Convention Center that it was time for the American people to "pay attention."[4]

Fast forward to election night 2008, 143 years after the Civil War relegated the slavery of African Americans to history, and the nation was definitely paying attention. Obama's televised victory speech, which followed a gracious and principled concession speech by Republican nominee John McCain, summed up the dreams of a nation eager for change.[5]

"If there is anyone out there who still doubts that America is a place where all things are possible; who still wonders if the dream of our founders is alive in our time; who still questions the power of our democracy, tonight is your answer," Obama began. "It's the answer spoken by young and old, rich and poor, Democrat and Republican, black, white, Latino, Asian, Native American, gay, straight, disabled and not disabled—Americans who sent a message to the world that we have never been a collection of Red States and Blue States: we are, and always will be, the United States of America.[6]

"It's the answer that led those who have been told for so long by so many to be cynical, and fearful, and doubtful of what we can achieve to put their hands on the arc of history and bend it once more toward the hope of a better day." Obama added, "It's been a long time coming, but tonight, because of what we did on this day, in this election, at this defining moment, change has come to America."[7]

Humbly recognizing that he was "never the likeliest candidate for this office," the president-elect expressed gratitude to all the "working men and women who dug into what little savings they had to give five dollars and ten dollars and twenty dollars to this cause." He channeled President Abraham Lincoln in thanking the "millions of Americans who volunteered, and organized, and proved that more than two centuries later, a government of the people, by the people and for the people has not perished from this Earth."[8] Acknowledging that uniting a nation torn apart by partisan smears and eight years of incompetence will not be easy, Obama reminded the 125,000 Americans assembled at Grant Park[9] that "it was a man from this state who first carried the banner of the Republican Party to the White House."[10]

"As Lincoln said to a nation far more divided than ours, 'We are not enemies, but friends...though passion may have strained it must not break our bonds of affection.'" Obama continued, "And to those Americans whose support I have yet to earn, I may not have won your vote, but I hear your voices, I need your help, and I will be your President too." He extended an olive branch not only to those in the United States who did not vote for him but also to those citizens of other nations who could not. Reaching out to an international audience yearning for a break with the failed policies and deceptive rhetoric of President George W. Bush, the first-term senator told "all those watching tonight from beyond our shores" that "our stories are singular, but our destiny is shared, and a new dawn of American leadership is at hand...."[11]

"To all those who have wondered if America's beacon still burns as bright—tonight we proved once more that the true strength of our nation comes not from the might of our arms or the scale of our wealth, but from the enduring power of our ideals: democracy, liberty, opportunity, and unyielding hope,"[12] Obama assured the citizens of the world. And the citizens of the world assured Obama that they believed in him and in the enduring power of democracy, liberty, opportunity, and hope to lift up the downtrodden, to give voice to the ignored, and to reestablish diplomatic relations with nations spurned by the worst president in American history (with the possible exception of President James Buchanan).[13]

The citizens of the world echoed Obama's sentiments that night. For millions, possibly billions, of citizens of foreign countries, the 2008 presidential election concludes what a French editor termed the "glorious epic of Barack Obama" and "brings the narrative that everyone wants to return to—that America is the land of extraordinary opportunity and possibility, where miracles happen." "It allows us all to dream a little," a Venezuelan activist told the *New York Times*. A British barrister said that "people feel he is a part of them because he has this multiracial, multiethnic and multinational dimension" which creates "a personal connection." An African scholar lauded Obama for being "a successful negotiator of identity margins," and an Indian official praised Obama for promising "genuine multilateralism."[14]

In his victory speech, Obama also emphasized that the "union can be perfected,"[15] a remarkably optimistic statement that summed up the feelings of those who needed hope after losing their jobs and homes, those who took to the streets when the networks projected a winner, and those who wept "tears of joy"[16] because an extraordinary African and American man had just been elected the next president of the most powerful nation on earth. More than a century after Lincoln led the nation through the bloodiest war in its history, proclaimed the abolition of slavery in rebellious states, and was fatally shot on the eve of the nation's greatest triumph over oppression, another ambitious Illinois lawyer proclaimed victory over those who sought to prop up a house divided.

The climax of Obama's victory speech, however, arrived in the form of the compelling story of Ann Nixon Cooper, a 106-year-old woman born not long after the demise of slavery. Punctuating the centenarian's ringside view of American history with refrains of "Yes We Can," Obama described how Cooper came into the world at "a time when there were no cars on the road or planes in the sky; when someone like her couldn't vote for two reasons—because she was a woman and because of the color of her skin." He described how "at a time when women's voices were silenced and their hopes dismissed, [Cooper] lived to see them stand up and speak out and reach for the ballot." He described how "she was there for the buses in Montgomery, the hoses in Birmingham, a bridge in Selma, and a preacher from Atlanta who told a people that 'We Shall Overcome.'"[17]

Obama continued, "In this election, she touched her finger to a screen and cast her vote, because after 106 years in America, through the best of times and the darkest of hours, she knows how America can change."[18]

It was an *e pluribus unum* moment.

For millions of African Americans, Obama's election represents the lifting of a racial barrier that had barred black Americans who came before him from reaching the pinnacle of national power.[19] The election of the son of a white Kansan and a Muslim Kenyan represents all that is right about a country where every child born on American soil can grow up to become president. The election signals the reclamation of the American Dream and the reaffirmation of that "fundamental truth—that out of many, we are one...and where we are met with...those who tell us that we can't, we will respond with that timeless creed that sums up the spirit of a people: Yes We Can."[20]

For millions of young people, the words "President Barack Obama" conjure up the dreams of a generation longing for change, longing for a voice in the democratic process, and longing for a leader who will speak truth to power. Our generation—perhaps best described as "Generation Change"—has proven that we are capable of breaking down the racial, gender, and social barriers that have kept so many from living out their dreams. That is what the 2008 election was all about and that is what Obama's presidency will be all about.

On a personal level, Obama's victory speech struck home when he recognized the "young people who rejected the myth of their generation's apathy—who left their homes and their families for jobs that offered little pay and less sleep."[21] Traveling from Virginia to North Carolina to Pennsylvania and back to Virginia to serve as one of Obama's lieutenants in the most organized campaign the world has ever seen, I kept going because I believed that the politics of hope would someday triumph over the politics of fear. To a generation of grunts who worked the phones late into the night, gulped down day-old coffee, and recruited volunteers, the reward lies in the knowledge that we were part of something larger than ourselves. And with the election of President Obama, we still are.

President Barack Obama faces many pressures as he enters the White House: from an unnecessary war in Iraq to a struggling war in Afghanistan to an economy in the midst of recession to an environment wrecked by climate change to a Washington accustomed to pork-barrel spending and mudslinging. It will be up to each one of us to remain involved and invested in politics in order to support Obama in his quest to change the world. We have won the first battle in the war for change. But as Obama said on election night, "the road ahead will be long."[22]

The Obama Revolution is just beginning.

ALAN KENNEDY-SHAFFER

THE OBAMA REVOLUTION

The Obama Revolution is more than a revolution of policy and proposals, although it undoubtedly involves new policies and new proposals. The Obama Revolution is more than a revolution of strategy and campaign tactics, although it certainly required new strategies and new campaign tactics. The Obama Revolution is more than a revolution of rhetoric, although it thankfully includes new rhetoric and a return to eloquence. The Obama Revolution is, first and foremost, the story of how a generation of believers and the politics of hope won the presidency and changed the world.

Like the American Revolution, the Obama Revolution asks the nation to break away from the repressive policies and hubris of a leader named George in order to reclaim the American Dream of liberty and justice for all. The Obama Revolution asks the nation to reject the politics of fear and the efforts of the current regime to divide us along racial, religious, and sectional lines, in favor of a new order based on need, ability and bipartisanship. The Obama Revolution asks the nation to throw off the chains of a ruler who came to power under dubious circumstances and to support a new leader determined to unite the country behind the politics of hope. To truly understand the revolution, however, we must first examine the improbable rise of Barack Obama.

THE AUDACITY OF OBAMA

The audacity of Barack Obama! Some people think that they deserve to occupy the Oval Office just because they sit in the august halls of Congress, take potshots at an increasingly unpopular president, and have a vision for America that transcends racial, social, and partisan divisions. Just who do these people think they are?

With the publication of Obama's second book, *The Audacity of Hope*, the junior senator from Illinois claimed his position as the rising star of the Democratic Party—for good reason. Unlike former presidential nominee John Kerry of Massachusetts, disgraced former vice presidential nominee John Edwards, or former front-runner Hillary Clinton, Obama does not have any baggage from failed national campaigns, did not vote for the Iraq War, and escaped the wrath of right-wing reactionaries relatively unscathed.

xvi

"Why Barack Obama Could Be The Next President" read the cover of *Time* magazine on October 23, 2006.[23] "Why Not Obama?" asked columnist Richard Cohen of the *Washington Post* on October 24th of that year.[24] "Barack Obama should run for president," declared conservative columnist David Brooks of the *New York Times*.[25] Oprah Winfrey even chimed in, asking Obama to appear on her show, which he did.[26]

As Bush's approval ratings plummeted, the Republican pork machine destroyed every last shred of integrity that Congress ever had, and Iraq waded deeper into civil war, the nation cast about for a political savior. Americans longed for a charismatic leader who put principles above politics, who preferred the long view to the myopia of the moment, and who opposed the Iraq War before it began.

Enter Barack Obama, an untested, relatively inexperienced newcomer who instantly reminded people of President John Fitzgerald Kennedy. With a father from Kenya and a mother from Kansas, Obama knew what it was like to straddle the divide between privilege and poverty. Obama reminded those in power not to forget "the world of immediate hunger, disappointment, fear, irrationality, and frequent hardship of the other 99 percent of the population."

After graduating from Columbia University, Obama migrated to Chicago to work as a community organizer. After graduating from Harvard Law School, Obama returned to Chicago to work as a civil rights lawyer. He served seven years in the Illinois State Senate before becoming only the third African American—employed loosely since Obama is the son of an African and an American—since Reconstruction to be elected to the United States Senate.

Obama became a household name after delivering the keynote address at the 2004 Democratic National Convention in Boston, Massachusetts, that summer. Proving that he knew enough about politics to hold his own while remaining ideologically inclusive, Obama declared that "the pundits like to slice-and-dice our country into Red States and Blue States; Red States for Republicans, Blue States for Democrats. But I've got news for them, too. We worship an awesome God in the Blue States, and we don't like federal agents poking around our libraries in the Red States."[27]

Obama posed the quintessential question directly: "Do we participate in a politics of cynicism or a politics of hope?"

Looking always to the future but never ignoring the past, Obama entered an already "crowded Democratic field"[28] on January 16, 2007, forming an exploratory committee and preparing for his formal declaration of candidacy, which he delivered in Springfield, Illinois, on February 10, 2007.

Significantly, Obama had the courage to speak out against the war in Iraq six months before the invasion in 2003. "I am not opposed to all wars," he remarked at the time. "I'm opposed to dumb wars."[29]

I first met Obama on May 18, 2005, in the Hart Senate Office Building in Washington, D.C. Meeting Obama convinced me that he truly believed what he was telling the nation. He made me promise that I would do everything in my power to bring about positive change.

Obama's campaign brought a renewed sense of purpose to our nation. And Obama brought a new sense of urgency to the podium whenever he called on his fellow citizens to put their faith in a rising star with a vision of liberty and justice for all.

OVERVIEW

This book seeks to provide a thorough look at the Obama Revolution, beginning with the new leader's policies, proceeding to the campaign strategies that brought the nation to this point, followed by an in-depth rhetorical analysis, and concluding with some thoughts on the American Dream and America's future. I will make the case to you that this is a transformational moment in the history and future of our country—a revolution in politics and policy, campaigning and involvement, rhetoric and vision. It is a curious tale of how a generation of people young and old took to the streets and made believers out of our fellow Americans.

As we proceed, keep in mind the rhetoric of hope that Obama employed throughout the campaign and that he promises to employ as the 44th president of the United States. Ask yourself how the 2008 presidential race has changed the way that candidates campaign, how the rhetoric of hope has changed the way that politicians talk about change, and how Obama's call to serve others has changed the way that we talk about America. Go out into the streets once again and proclaim the gospel of hope to others, providing them with a renewed faith in their ability to change the world.

If there is an underlying theme to this book, it is that no one man or woman, no one president or voter, and no one strategy or speech, has a monopoly on the American Dream. Uniting our fractured nation will take much willingness to empathize with others and walk hand in hand toward the rising sun. We will have to rededicate ourselves to the cause of liberty and the pursuit of happiness. We will have to recommit ourselves to overcoming the injustices that tear us down and the bigotry that tears us apart.

We will have to follow the immortal advice of Mahatma Gandhi and be the change we wish to see in the world.

CHAPTER ONE

CHANGE WE STILL BELIEVE IN

When was the last time three Virginia governors, two prominent United States senators, and scores of other elected officials appeared on the same stage to herald the "march of victory"? When was the last time they were all Democrats?

On February 17, 2007, thousands of Democrats from across the state—including myself—convened in the former capital of the Confederacy to hear speeches by Richmond Mayor and former Governor L. Douglas Wilder, Senator Jim Webb, former Governor Mark Warner, and Governor Tim Kaine, followed by the keynote address by the latest entrant in the presidential race.

Barack Obama, endorsed earlier in the day by Governor Kaine, drew a standing ovation as he ascended the steps to the stage with his wife Michelle. The couple looked young and vibrant, the perfect picture of a presidential pair. Decked out in a black suit with a white shirt and blue tie, the presidential candidate looked dashing with the governor on his left and his wife on his right.

Obama began his address simply, thanking Kaine and the rest of the Democratic leadership in Virginia for inviting him to the biggest Democratic dinner in the country. He talked about Virginia as a potential swing state. Acknowledging the nation's troubles, Obama suggested that "maybe, just maybe, I can help you get through these difficult times." Confronted with a mismanaged war, a misguided president, global warming, rising oil prices, and out-of-control deficits, America needs a "politics that brings us together rather than a politics that breaks us apart."[1]

Pointing out that the United States started with a Constitution "stained by slavery," Obama reminded the audience that inequality has often given way to hope and progress. "Somebody noticed," Obama explained, "Somebody agitated, somebody pushed...people marched and agitated until we arrived at a more perfected union."[2]

1

Because a few courageous Americans have had the "audacity to hope," Obama continued, our nation no longer lives half slave and half free. Over the last few years, however, "we seem to have lost the capacity to dream big dreams." America must regain the audacity of hope, Obama said; this challenge will help the country come up with creative ways to provide all Americans with basic medical care, ensure that all children have access to high-quality schools, and find new sources of energy so that Americans no longer "fund both sides of the War on Terrorism."[3]

The presidential hopeful challenged Bush's plan to escalate the Iraq War by sending more troops to Baghdad, declaring the conflict a "war that should never have been authorized and that should have never been waged." The nation needs a national security strategy for the 21st century, Obama said, and that means "bringing our troops home." With "unfinished business" in Afghanistan, Obama remarked, the nation can ill afford to continue fighting a losing battle in Iraq—a battle with no end in sight. "What sets America apart is the power of our ideals and projecting those ideals all around the world," Obama asserted, stirring the crowd to passion.[4]

"The easiest thing is to conclude that the world, as it is, is the world as it must be," Obama said. While the Iraq War has diminished America's moral standing in the world, the nation can still recover its moral compass by leaving Bush's failings behind and putting our trust in the nation's next president. Guided by the audacity of hope, Americans have a unique chance to "transform [the] nation"[5] into an ever brighter land of opportunity.

EIGHT IS ENOUGH

On September 11, 2001, Americans watched in disbelief as hijackers turned commercial jets into deadly weapons, caused the World Trade Center towers to implode, and struck fear in the hearts of millions of ordinary citizens. Widows grieved, lawmakers called for blood, and priests warned us that the end was near. Millions of people took to the streets to memorialize friends, relatives, and strangers who died in the 9/11 attacks. Partisans in Congress put aside their differences long enough to express their shared outrage and to authorize the Pentagon to pursue Osama bin

Laden through the mountains of Afghanistan. Al Qaeda sought refuge in caves; Vice President Dick Cheney sought refuge in an "undisclosed location." President George W. Bush promised to be patient and focused, and the nation believed him.

Americans again listened to Bush, Cheney, former Secretary of State Colin Powell, former Secretary of Defense Donald Rumsfeld, and former National Security Advisor Condoleezza Rice in 2002, when they advocated invading Iraq on the grounds that Saddam Hussein possessed weapons of mass destruction and intended to use them against the United States. White House officials repeatedly asserted that Iraq's "weapons of mass murder" posed a "grave and growing danger" to our national security and raised the specter of mushroom clouds in order to drum up support for the seemingly inevitable invasion. For six weeks in 2003, bombs over Baghdad consumed the country's attention. Troops marched into the Iraqi capital and Karl Rove staged a "MISSION ACCOMPLISHED" photo-op on the deck of the U.S.S. *Abraham Lincoln.* President Bush promised the nation that "major combat operation in Iraq [had] ended," and most of the nation believed him.[6]

Americans cheered in 2003 when the Bush Administration announced the capture of Saddam Hussein and released photos of the former Iraqi dictator in his underwear. Thinking that the worst was over, the country rallied behind the White House and the man who kept saying that he wanted to be remembered as a "wartime president." With Saddam Hussein behind bars, investigators hunting for weapons of mass destruction, and contractors beginning to rebuild Iraq's essential infrastructure, Americans lost interest in the Iraq War and turned their attention to other pressing matters, such as unemployment and global warming. Republicans in Congress began talking about abortion, assisted suicide, and gay marriage, and Capitol Hill returned to business as usual. President Bush promised swift justice for Saddam Hussein, and Vice President Cheney declared that the insurgency was in it "last throes"—and some of the nation believed them.[7]

Americans reelected Bush in 2004 by a narrow margin in an election marred by allegations of fraud, intimidation, and disenfranchisement. By bashing gay and lesbian relationships, Republican operatives put Democrats on the defensive and routed proponents of peace with claims that citizens either supported the president or were supporting terrorists. With all three branches of government dominated by Republicans, a new wave of not-so-compassionate conservatism washed through the corridors of power. Halliburton and other contractors with connections to the Bush Administration made off like bandits. The torture at Abu Ghraib embarrassed and saddened the nation. President Bush promised to win the "war on terror" and to turn Iraq into a self-sustaining democracy, and few people believed him.

Americans recoiled in horror in 2005 as Hurricane Katrina displaced hundreds of thousands of residents of New Orleans and other coastal areas in Louisiana and Mississippi. Destroyed homes, abandoned shopping malls, and vacant office buildings serve as a lasting testament to the destructive power of Mother Nature and the problem with incompetent government officials. While Bush ate cake on a landing strip with Senator McCain, and Rice went shopping for shoes in New York, senior citizens died in nursing homes that were never evacuated, and poor black residents died because bridges to rich white neighborhoods were closed. Instead of demanding accountability from the Federal Emergency Management Agency or apologizing to the victims of Hurricane Katrina for ignoring early warnings, Bush toasted FEMA Director Michael Brown, saying, "Brownie, you're doing a heck of a job."[8]

Twelve years after the Republican Party seized control of Congress during President William Jefferson Clinton's first term in office, the Democrats took back the House and the Senate in a 2006 electoral realignment that stands as a tribute to the power of democracy to move America in a new direction. With the help of millions of Independents and change-minded Republicans, the Democrats gained dozens of seats in the House of Representatives, half a dozen seats in the Senate, and half a dozen governor's mansions. Former Navy Secretary (and former Republican) Jim Webb even defeated GOP Senator George Allen, made infamous because of his "Macaca" moment, by 7,231 votes.[9]

Unfortunately, the 2006 election did not end the national nightmare. The residents of New Orleans continued to suffer from FEMA's sluggish and inadequate response to Hurricane Katrina. The brunt of the cleanup work done in the city has been handled by volunteers from across the country. Many of the trailers that FEMA promised never arrived, and many of the trailers that were provided turned out to be contaminated with formaldehyde and other toxins.

The Iraq War became increasingly unpopular, human rights deprivations and mass misery continued in Darfur, and many of Bush's core staff members fled the White House like rats from a sinking ship. But Bush continued his race to the bottom, sending even more soldiers and money to Iraq while ignoring the Taliban and Osama bin Laden. The Bush Administration's misguided Iraq adventure, having already cost the nation over a trillion dollars according to a congressional report titled "The Hidden Costs of the Iraq War," caused many former soldiers and officers, such as Ret. Lt. Gen. Ricardo S. Sanchez, to switch sides and oppose the war.

When President George W. Bush stepped to the podium to address the nation on January 23, 2007, he was quite literally overshadowed by House Speaker Nancy Pelosi, the first female to raise the gavel in our country's history. Paralyzed by the resounding repudiation of the Republican agenda in the midterm elections, Bush sounded conciliatory as he described how our government must "spend the people's money wisely," "balance the federal budget," and "uphold the great tradition of the melting pot that welcomes and assimilates new arrivals."[10]

Trying to capture some of former Vice President Al Gore's success, Bush acknowledged for the first time that we must "confront the serious challenge of global climate change." He also mentioned the need to "awaken the conscience of the world to save the people of Darfur."[11] Behind Bush's revamped rhetoric, however, lay a lot of inconvenient truths. Maybe Bush figured that the American people had forgiven him for squandering billions of dollars on tax cuts for millionaires. Maybe Bush figured that no one had noticed the national debt skyrocket to double what it was on January 19, 2001, when he was inaugurated. Maybe Bush figured that if he mentioned global climate change, he would never have to explain why the White House had rejected a request from 10 major chief executives for binding caps on greenhouse gas emissions.

More likely, however, Bush probably figured that by talking about domestic issues, he could avoid any serious discussion of a failing war in Iraq. Faced with an increasingly unpopular war, the increasingly unpopular president did not even mention Iraq until near the end of his speech. When Bush finally got around to talking about the war, he sounded like ousted Defense Secretary Donald Rumsfeld, saying that "this is not the fight we entered in Iraq, but it is the fight we're in." Woefully ignorant of reality, Bush warned that failure in Iraq would result in a "contagion of violence" and a "nightmare scenario," but ignored the nightmare scenario that already existed in Iraq, a nightmare that has ravaged our military and left more than four thousand American soldiers dead.[12]

Bush bet his presidency on swift victory in Iraq, an obsequious Congress, and a sleeping citizenry, and he lost. He got himself trapped in the war in Iraq and wondered why he could not seem to find a way out. A *Washington Post*-ABC News poll conducted in early 2007 found that sixty-four percent of Americans believed that the Administration's unilateral decision to invade Iraq was a mistake, while three out of four Americans disapproved of Bush's handling of the war. Only 45 percent of Americans still thought of Bush as a strong leader, only 42 percent of the public said that the president could be trusted in a crisis, and only three in 10 Americans felt that Bush understood the problems of people like you and me.

Webb summed up the general feeling in America toward the Iraq War during the Democratic Party's response speech when he quoted President Dwight Eisenhower's question about the Korean War: "When comes the end?" Webb emphasized that "this country has patiently endured a mismanaged war for nearly four years." He astutely noted that "many, including myself, warned even before the war began that it was unnecessary."[13]

"The majority of the nation no longer supports the way this war is being fought; nor does the majority of our military," Webb explained, "We need a new direction."[14]

A NEW DIRECTION

Obama's campaign offered unity after eight years of divisiveness and fear mongering. Adopting "eight is enough"[15] as a slogan to represent the nation's dissatisfaction with Bush's failed policies and embarrassing rhetoric, Obama promised leadership for a new era of progressive change. The president-elect even showed his commitment to unity by working with Bush during the transition, although he promised to break with Bush on most policies upon assuming the presidency.

On the campaign trail, Obama demonstrated his willingness to listen to concerns of people whose voices were drowned out by moneyed interests with closer ties to the Bush Administration. He recognized that millions of Americans had been left out of Bush's attempt to re-create the failed economic policies of President Ronald Reagan. He understood that Americans do not want a president wedded to a peculiar notion of good and evil that does not permit debate and that does not tolerate dissent.

Promising to end the culture of corruption that pervaded Congress for much of Bush's tenure and the culture of denial that pervaded the Bush White House, Obama railed against corporations that stiff the middle class whenever possible and then beg for bailouts whenever needed. He railed against policies that favor the wealthy, policies that make the rich richer and the poor poorer. And he railed against an insular political culture that has ignored working families for far too long.

The economy and the Iraq War overshadowed all other issues in the campaign and election. Because Obama spoke out against the Iraq War before it began and voted against granting Bush the authorization to pursue war without a defined mission, without an honest motive, and without a foreseeable end, he possesses the fortitude and moral authority to finally end the war. Although opposed to "dumb wars"[16] like the war in Iraq, Obama has said that he is not necessarily opposed to all wars. In fact, he wants to enhance the nation's security by shifting soldiers and resources from Iraq to Afghanistan, the central front against the people who attacked New York City and the Pentagon on September 11, 2001. Ending the go-it-alone, cowboy attitude of Bush, Obama has said that he will reject the doctrine of preemptive war except in cases of genocide, preferring instead the politics of peace. He will bring back diplomacy, permitting the United States to restore its reputation as one nation among many, and to regain lost alliances and friendships.

Obama has striven, and will continue to strive, to unite all Americans behind a new kind of politics. In his book *Change We Can Believe In*, which came out before the election, Obama presented a vision of a new era of progressive change in America. The campaign's policy analysts discussed a New New Deal that would include progressive reforms on ethics, education, energy, economics, and environmental protection.

Contrary to the right-wing pundits' fears that an Obama presidency will raise everyone's tax dollars, waste money on pig-iron projects, and bankrupt the state, Obama's policy proposals are grounded in his own values. "The people I've met know that government can't solve all our problems, and they don't expect it to," Obama wrote in the foreword. "They believe in personal responsibility, hard work, and self-reliance. They don't like seeing their tax dollars wasted."

Obama emphasized the shared values of Americans who "also believe in fairness, opportunity, and the responsibilities we have to one another. They believe in an America where good jobs are there for the willing, where hard work is rewarded with a decent living, and where we recognize the fundamental truth that Wall Street cannot prosper while Main Street crumbles—that a sound economy requires thriving businesses *and* flourishing families." Obama also reiterated his belief that "we can create five million new green jobs that pay well and can't be outsourced by investing in renewable sources of energy like wind power, solar power, and the next generation biofuels."[17]

For the president-elect, policies are always personal. Discussions of policy proposals and positions can sometimes become highly technical and get lost in the details, and every politician knows that voters want to know how specific policies will affect them or others like them. Without a story to explain the policies, the details make it difficult to understand their true significance. For this reason, Obama described his general positions in ways that make it easier to decipher between policies that favor the wealthy and policies that favor the middle class. He makes it clear to folks reading his platform that the national government makes lots of choices, often with working families on one side and corporate executives and wealthy individuals on the other.

"We can choose to let families who aren't sure if their next paycheck will cover next month's bills struggle on their own, or we can decide that if you work in this country, you will not want," Obama explained. "We can give energy rebates to consumers who are having trouble filling up their gas tanks. We can give tax breaks to middle-class families and seniors instead of to Fortune 500 CEOs. We can lower health care premiums for those with insurance and make coverage affordable for those who don't have it," he wrote. "And we can provide working families with a nest egg and make it easier for them to save for retirement."[18]

The remainder of this chapter discusses four key elements of Obama's policy proposals: rebuilding the old economy, inventing the new economy, reengaging with the world, and embracing America's values. Critical to overcoming the economic failures, the international crises, and the internal strife of the last eight years, these four elements provide a basic framework for Obama's presidency and would also provide a means to break with the past in order to create a brighter national future.

REBUILDING THE OLD ECONOMY

In order to strengthen the middle class, Obama proposed to "create bottom-up growth that empowers hardworking families to climb the ladder of success and raise their children with security, opportunity, and hope for a better future," as opposed to the Bush Administration's "economic policies that protect special interests and the privileged few and ignore the working families that are America's backbone and the engine of our economic growth."[19] With millions of jobs lost since the beginning of the Bush presidency, the numbers of foreclosures approaching the number of foreclosures during the Great Depression, and global competition for new jobs, the United States government would need to find creative ways to both maintain the jobs that have not disappeared and create new jobs.

First, Obama planned to implement an emergency economic plan as an antidote to "one of the worst economic crises in a generation." He wanted to "jump-start the economy" by mailing $1000 rebate checks to American families, relief checks worth $500 for an individual and $1,000 for a married couple. He would pay for the relief checks by taxing the windfall profits raked in by big oil companies due to wild fluctuations in the price of crude oil. He planned to "establish a $25 billion Jobs and Growth Fund to replenish the Highway Trust Fund; prevent cutbacks in road and bridge maintenance; and fund new, fast-tracked projects to repair schools." This would be in addition to $25 billion in temporary funding to state and local governments in "the areas hardest hit by the housing crisis."[20] Because the Highway Trust Fund had nearly been depleted, a Jobs and Growth Fund, or something like it, would be critical in keeping our highways maintained, our bridges safe, and our schools asbestos-free.

Second, Obama planned to assist American families with their short-term tax troubles and their long-run economic security. He wanted to "create a new 'Making Work Pay' tax credit of up to $500 per person, or $1,000 per working family." Obama also hoped to "eliminate all income taxes for seniors making less than $50,000 per year," which would entirely eliminate the income taxes for 27 million seniors on fixed incomes. In order to ease the burden of rising gas prices, Obama wanted to "crack down on speculators by fully closing the 'Enron loophole.'" He also wanted to help American workers by retraining and educating workers left behind as more and more jobs move overseas. Having advocated successfully for the Illinois Earned Income Tax Credit, Obama wanted to do the same at the national level, giving a much needed boost to lower income workers. He wanted to "raise the minimum wage to $9.50 an hour by 2011 and index it to inflation," while also supporting labor rights and workplace safety. To help family farmers, Obama planned to cap payments so that small farmers are not forced to compete against government-subsidized agribusinesses.[21]

Third, Obama planned to make health care affordable for all Americans by lowering costs, improving quality, guaranteeing coverage, and promoting prevention. Health care premiums continue to rise while jobs disappear and wages stagnate. "In 2006, 11 million insured Americans spent more than a quarter of their salary on health care," and there are now nearly 50 million uninsured Americans. There is also "massive waste and inefficiency" in the industry, with high administrative costs, high numbers of medical errors, and high numbers of prescription drug errors, swallowing up large sums of money that could otherwise be used to prevent illness and disease. Obama wanted to lower costs by $2,500 per family by investing $50 billion in new technologies, reimbursing employers for reducing workers' premiums, and tackling disparities in coverage and treatment. For those without health insurance, Obama wanted to establish a National Health Insurance Exchange, "similar to what members of Congress have," and an affordable national health insurance plan available to anyone. He also wanted to lower prescription drug costs by opening up the markets to generic drugs, and promote preventive care across the board.[22]

Fourth, Obama planned to empower families to succeed by making it easier "to get an education, put away a nest egg, own a home, start a business, and provide a better way of life for their children." In order to encourage students to excel, he wanted to "recruit, prepare, retain, and reward a generation of new teachers." This would make students more likely to receive the attention they need from the moment they start school until the moment they graduate. Unlike No Child Left Behind, Obama's plans would include the funding required to actually raise standards. He would also put more money into after-school programs and early childhood education programs, such as Head Start. He wanted to make college affordable for all Americans by covering $4,000 worth of tuition payments in exchange for 100 hours of public service each year.

On the working family side, Obama would require transferable workplace pensions, expand the Savers' Tax Credit, and save Social Security from those who want to hand it over to Wall Street. He wanted to protect homeownership by reducing mortgage interest rates by 10 percent and making mortgage obligations easier to understand. He also wanted to "expand the Family and Medical Leave Act to cover more employees," and promised to fight for pay equity between men and women.[23]

Finally, Obama planned to restore trust in government and return to fiscal responsibility in the wake of "the most fiscally irresponsible Administration in American history." He promised to "pay for all of his proposals and reduce the deficit," "return to conservative budget practices," and accomplish "immediate deficit reduction." With a national debt that effectively doubled on the Bush Administration's watch and budgets that have morphed from "a surplus of $236 billion at the end of the Clinton Administration" into "a deficit of more than $400 billion today," Obama faces severe fiscal challenges as he enters the White House. But through careful spending, which will necessitate ending the Iraq War, reforming farm subsidies so that the nation is no longer subsidizing large agribusinesses, and holding the line on earmarks, Obama planned to reduce the deficit and the national debt.

Obama also wanted to lower health care costs by promoting prevention, while at the same time making Medicare solvent again. Because he did not want to create new burdens with new taxes on the middle class, he vowed "to not increase taxes for any household making less than $250,000 a year," which included 98 percent of all American households and more than 98 percent of small business owners. Hoping to end the tax abuse of the last eight years, Obama planned to start "cracking down on [offshore] tax havens," close "offshore tax loopholes," and simplify the tax code, all of which would save ordinary taxpayers money in the future.[24]

INVENTING THE NEW ECONOMY

In order to invent a new economy here in the United States, Obama proposed to invest in the technologies and the industries of the future, rather than clinging to the boundaries and the jobs of the past. "We must make sure that the American people have the tools they need to thrive in a world that is more tightly linked, has more economic competition, and is facing new global challenges," read Obama's plan. "Barack Obama will pursue a competitiveness agenda built upon education and energy, innovation and infrastructure, trade and reform that will create jobs and prosperity for all Americans."[25] Globalization has forced the nation to transform itself from a nation of fields and factories to a nation of fiber-optic wires and fuel-efficient vehicles. The nation must turn the challenges of global competition and interconnectedness into opportunities for growth and development. Obama's policy proposals have always aspired to do just that.

First, Obama planned to promote energy independence and to create five million green jobs. He recognized that "as our climate warms and scientists predict more severe storms and severe weather that ruin crops, devastate cities, and destabilize whole regions, we must act now to wean ourselves off the fossil fuels that produce the greenhouse gases that cause global warming." He wanted to "double fuel economy standards within eighteen years," while helping automakers pay for it with "$4 billion in retooling tax credits and loan guarantees." He pledged to invest in research and development of gasoline-electric and plug-in hybrid vehicles and to provide a "$7,000 tax credit for the purchase of advanced technology vehicles, as well as conversion tax credits."

On a more controversial issue, Obama would require oil companies to use their offshore drilling leases or risk losing them. In order to encourage the creation of new, green jobs, Obama planned to "double federal science and research funding for clean-energy projects," help industries adapt to cleaner technologies, and encourage the use of biofuels, "clean coal technology," and nuclear energy. He wanted to implement a national cap-and-trade program to reduce carbon emissions and reengage with the world on environmental issues.[26]

Furthermore, Obama planned to give every American the option of getting a "world-class education from cradle through to adulthood."[27] By requiring federally funded schools to set goals and expectations, encouraging more parental involvement in their children's education, and making community service part of every child's education, Obama would help to bring responsibility and community values back to the classroom. He would invest $10 billion more each year in early childhood education through his Zero to Five plan. He would also reform No Child Left Behind and create Teaching Service Scholarships that would "completely cover training costs in high-quality teacher-preparation or alternative-certification programs at the undergraduate or graduate level for those who are willing to teach in a high-need field or location for at least four years." He wanted teachers and administrators to have opportunities for continuing education so that they can remain up-to-date on teaching methods and programs. As part of a new $200 million program, he would provide grants to schools willing to provide "additional learning time for students to close the achievement gap." He also wanted to make college affordable to every qualified student and to improve workforce development programs.[28]

Additionally, Obama planned to put the United States at the front of the pack once again in scientific research and technological innovation. It is a sad fact that "among industrialized nations, our country's scores on international science and math tests rank in the bottom third and bottom fifth, respectively," even as "more than 80 percent of the fastest-growing occupations are dependent upon a knowledge base in science and math." Obama wanted to remedy those discrepancies by expanding access to broadband Internet access through the Universal Service Fund. This would help bring broadband access to every community. Obama was similarly committed to network neutrality, often called "net neutrality," in order to "preserve the benefits of open competition on the Internet." He would also double funding for basic scientific research, double funding for cancer research, and "allow greater federal government funding on a wider array of stem cell lines." Obama's most direct initiative in the area of science and technology would be to "appoint the nation's first Chief Technology Officer (CTO)."[29]

Moreover, Obama planned to build the infrastructure of the 21st century, just as "fifty years ago, Republican Dwight Eisenhower and Democrat Al Gore, Sr. worked together to build the Interstate Highway System." Because of a lack of strategic planning and infrastructure maintenance, many of the nation's highways, railways, bridges, and airports are falling into disrepair. As a result, there have been more traffic jams and accidents, derailments, bridge collapses, and flight delays than there would have been with proper investment in the infrastructure that drives the modern economy. To correct these problems, many of which stem from the flawed earmark system that provides much of the funding for transportation infrastructure, Obama wanted to create a National Infrastructure Reinvestment Bank with "an infusion of federal money, $6 billion per year." He wanted to update air traffic control systems and tighten federal safety guidelines and enforcement. Most importantly, he wanted to invest in public transportation, specifically the development of high-speed rail transit.[30]

Obama also planned to help small businesses and manufacturers survive and thrive by eliminating "all capital gains taxes on start-up and small businesses." He would provide a new 50 percent tax credit for small firms that offer quality health care to their employees. Additionally, he wanted to encourage minority-owned businesses and rural economic development, two areas traditionally left behind. He planned to offer further tax credits for investment in family businesses and tax breaks for "landowners selling to family farmers just starting out." Through matching grants, Obama also planned to encourage states and cities to invest money in "innovation clusters—regional centers of innovation and next-generation industries—across the country." He wanted to encourage manufacturers to "improve efficiency, implement new technology, and strengthen company growth," as part of a broader plan to move toward more sustainable economic growth.[31]

Finally, Obama planned to encourage Americans to "embrace the global economy and open markets for our goods and services, while ensuring that we can compete on a level playing field." While not wanting to "initiate a race to the bottom that compromises the environment, the wages and rights of workers, and the competitiveness of our country," Obama wanted to use the World Trade Organization (WTO) to open up markets through trade agreements. He wanted to eradicate offshore tax havens for corporations and to expand the amount of money and types of assistance available through the Trade Adjustment Assistance (TAA) system to workers whose jobs moved overseas. He also wanted to protect American jobs by negotiating trade agreements that would "benefit American workers and that have strong and enforceable labor and environmental standards in the body of the agreement." Specifically, Obama planned to amend the North American Free Trade Agreement (NAFTA) to meet these goals.[32]

REENGAGING WITH THE WORLD

In order to restore the nation's standing in the world, Obama proposed to end the war in Iraq swiftly and safely, pick up the pieces in the fight against Al Qaeda in Afghanistan, restore the morale of the nation's military, prevent nuclear proliferation, and renew international alliances that will help the United States in the future. He recognized that the nation would have to "rebuild our alliances and rally the world to tackle [the] truly transnational challenges [posed by global terrorism], replace despair with hope, and keep America secure, prosperous, and free." Choosing to reject the "failed ideology and tired thinking of the past," he planned to transcend the politics of fear that have paralyzed the nation's international interactions over the past eight years.[33]

Initially, Obama planned to end the war in Iraq as quickly as safely possible through a phased withdrawal within the first year and a half of his presidency, replacing combat soldiers with diplomats. He pledged that he would "not build permanent bases in Iraq." In order to prevent further harm to Iraqi civilians, Obama planned to "dedicate $2 billion to help the more than five million Iraqi refugees throughout the region," and to "work with Iraqi authorities and the international community to hold accountable the perpetrators of potential war crimes, crimes against humanity, and genocide."[34]

After dealing with Iraq, Obama planned to turn the military's attention back to Al Qaeda and the central front against global terrorism, which "is not Iraq, and it never was. That's why ending the war in Iraq is essential if we want to finish the job against the terrorists who attacked us on 9/11—Al Qaeda and the Taliban in Afghanistan and Pakistan." Believing that "it is unacceptable that seven years after nearly three thousand Americans were killed on our soil, the terrorists...are still at large," Obama planned to put more troops, resources, and nonmilitary aid into Afghanistan. He also planned to increase funding for multinational intelligence efforts, support the "moderate majority against the extremist minority" in the Muslim world, and strengthen the ability of the United States to prevent, or respond to, future attacks on American soil.[35]

These major proposals were accompanied by related proposals to restore the military's morale and capabilities after years of war, plans to prevent nuclear proliferation, and plans to restore the nation's international alliances. On the military side, Obama wanted to reduce the strain on military families from multiple and frequent tours of combat duty, ensure that ground forces go into battle with adequate training and protective equipment, and "end the 'Stop-Loss' program of forcing troops to stay in service beyond their expected commitments."[36] He also wanted to make sure that veterans receive fully funded medical care, mental health care, and assistance with the transition back into civilian life. On the diplomatic side, Obama wanted to secure vulnerable nuclear materials, take steps toward nuclear disarmament, and rally the world with aggressive diplomacy, global health aid, and debt relief for developing countries.

EMBRACING AMERICA'S VALUES

Embracing what he perceived to be America's shared values, Obama proposed to "restore the faith of the American people in our most important institutions." Beginning with the government, Obama planned to "eliminate waste, streamline bureaucracy, and cut outmoded programs." He wanted to "invite the service and participation of American citizens" in both government and civic institutions, and to "hold true to the obligations we have as stewards of our precious national resources." Finally, Obama wanted all Americans to "strive to be good neighbors and good citizens who are willing to volunteer in our communities—and to help our churches, synagogues, and community centers feed the hungry and care for the elderly."[37]

First, Obama planned to restore trust in government and clean up Washington, a goal exemplified by the fact that "no registered lobbyists [were] employed by his presidential campaign." Moreover, the campaign did not accept contributions from lobbyists. Obama wanted to close the revolving door between government and K Street lobbying firms by barring gifts from lobbyists, forcing agencies to certify that they "will not take political affiliation into account as they make hiring decisions for career positions." He also planned to let anyone with Internet access track lobbyist reports and pork-barrel spending.[38]

Second, Obama planned to increase voluntary citizen service opportunities in order to enable new generations of Americans to serve the nation in both military and nonmilitary service branches. Specifically, he wanted to "expand AmeriCorps from 75,000 slots today to 250,000," which would permit the creation of a Classroom Corps, a Health Corps, a Clean Energy Corps, a Veterans Corps, and a Homeland Security Corps. Obama also wanted to double the size of the Peace Corps from 8,000 to 16,000, provide $4,000 toward college tuition in exchange for 100 hours of service, and expand "service-learning" programs in the public schools.[39] Obama promised to create more opportunities for senior citizens to serve by "expanding and improving programs like Senior Corps to connect seniors with quality volunteer opportunities."[40]

Third, Obama planned to "promote partnerships between government and faith-based and other nonprofit community groups to provide services to the needy and underserved." He also planned to create a President's Council for Faith-Based and Neighborhood Partnerships and a Train-the-Trainers program "to empower thousands of local faith-based social services organizations to train other local faith-based organizations on best practices...and compliance with federal laws and regulations."[41]

Fourth, Obama planned to promote stronger and healthier families through the Responsible Fatherhood and Healthy Families Act, the Nurse-Family Partnership, Earned Income Tax Credits, the Family and Medical Leave Act, and the Child and Dependent Care Tax Credit. Funding and expanding these initiatives would, respectively, encourage "men to be involved in their children's lives," provide better health services to "low-income first-time mothers," reward supportive parents, and "help families with their daily juggle."[42]

Fifth, Obama planned to support initiatives that would equalize opportunities for all Americans, specifically for those Americans who have traditionally been victims of discrimination. He wanted to ensure pay equity between women and men, enforce and expand civil rights protections, end racial profiling in all states, and protect voting rights for new voters, student voters, and minority voters. He also supported reproductive choice, opposes violence against women, and planned to "end discrimination in our armed forces based on sexual orientation by repealing the 'Don't Ask, Don't Tell' policy."[43]

Sixth, Obama planned to cooperate with local officials on the nation's borders to promote sensible border control measures, while holding accountable companies who hire undocumented immigrants. He also wanted to create a "pathway to citizenship that puts the undocumented at the back of the line, behind those who came here legally."[44]

Seventh, Obama planned to safeguard the environment for future generations by restoring the Clean Air Act's protections, resuming enforcement of the Clean Water Act, and making polluters pay for their hazardous waste dumping. Significantly, he planned to "strengthen the EPA Office of Environmental Justice" in order to combat localized environmental problems.[45]

Eighth, Obama planned to protect gun rights for hunters and preserve lands for fishing, hunting, and boating. He also planned to oppose efforts to drill in the Arctic National Wildlife Refuge and to ramp up conservation efforts in national forests and parks.

Finally, Obama planned to fight crime and promote public safety by hiring 50,000 new police officers and 1,000 new FBI agents, and by restoring funding for anti-drug and anti-gang programs. He also planned to create federal drug courts and end the "cycle of youth violence."[46]

These diverse policies crafted an Obama platform that embraced the dignity of humanity. He respected the rights of all Americans and the importance of the environment, the economy, and education. Barack Obama's values-centered proposals did not alienate anyone, but invited everyone to join his movement.

CHAPTER TWO

A GREEN DEAL

Barack Obama's policy positions and proposals suggest that the 44th president of the United States has the potential to create a Green Deal for the 21st century, similar to the New Deal of the 20th century. Focusing specifically on Obama's bottom-up economic ideas, climate change, and Darfur, this chapter explains exactly what a Green Deal might look like. Not all of these ideas are new. In fact, many of the ideas and initiatives that could create a Green Deal for America were formulated during the last eight years, but the Bush Administration ignored or destroyed them. The Obama Administration has the opportunity to resurrect these ideas and begin to solve the problems of economic injustice, climate change, and genocide.

Renewing, rebuilding, and reinventing the nation's economy are steps one, two, and three. Because economic downturns affect the poorest and most vulnerable first, followed by the middle class, and finally the wealthy, shifting from trickle-down government policies to bottom-up government programs must be at the top of the agenda. To Americans struggling to pay the rent or the mortgage, struggling to buy bread, milk, and fruit at prices that continue to creep up, and struggling to fill their gasoline tanks, economic change is urgent. Helping those who are working hard to help themselves is one of the government's primary roles. It is time for the nation to give the working poor and the middle class not a handout but a hand up. It is time for an economic Green Deal that creates new, sustainable jobs for those Americans willing to work.

Green jobs are jobs that cannot be downsized or outsourced. They are jobs that would be open to any American willing to work hard to make the country a leader in the global economy. Massive downsizing and outsourcing in recent years have left many workers without employment or without employment that pays a living wage. As Japanese automakers, such as Honda and Toyota, moved aggressively to produce hybrid vehicles, for instance, American automakers dug themselves deeper into debt by ramping up production of sport utility vehicles (SUVs) and other kinds of trucks. As a result of domestic resistance to greening the automobile industry, consumers desiring to purchase hybrid vehicles have had, at times, to put their names on waiting lists and look overseas for the cars of the future.

Renewing the economy will require a national commitment to economic policies that invest in those who invest in America. This will mean putting money into programs to make the domestic automobile industry more sustainable and environmentally friendly—investments that will ultimately permit the automobile industry to hire more workers and to continue to employ those workers who still have jobs. Other industries, such as the coal industry, also need to bring their technologies up-to-date in order to compete in a global economy. With environmentalists emphasizing cap-and-trade programs as a means of reducing carbon emissions within a free market framework, it will be even more critical in the future for industrial plants and major polluters to take measures to cut back their greenhouse gas emissions.

Rebuilding the economy will require a national commitment to education and employment. In a global economy, it is increasingly critical for all Americans to have the opportunity to attend a four-year college or a community college. Obama's proposal to provide $4,000 in tuition credits to every student who donates at least 100 hours per year in national or community service would go a long way toward making higher education affordable and accessible for all Americans. Similarly, putting Americans back to work immediately through new conservation and public works programs would also revive the struggling economy and make all Americans feel like they have a stake in the nation's future. Harking back to the Civilian Conservation Corps and the Works Progress Administration of the 1930s New Deal, a Green Deal could easily incorporate elements of these programs into a massive new program to put unemployed or underemployed Americans back to work.

Reinventing the economy will take a new emphasis on serving the community and saving the environment. Restoring our commitment to each other and to the world will help end the culture of individualism and greed that brought America the Savings and Loan crisis, the Enron fiasco, and the recent mortgage-market collapse. Prominent economists now agree that speculation, deregulation, and policies tilted in favor of large corporations and the richest of the rich contributed to the financial meltdown that culminated in public buyouts of private insurance companies in September 2008. But efforts to renew, rebuild, and reinvent the economy will not be successful in the long run without a firm commitment to making the New Deal of the 21st century a Green Deal.

Following the consciousness raising of Al Gore and his Academy Award-winning documentary, *An Inconvenient Truth*, Obama will have the opportunity to reinvent the economy in a way beneficial to the planet. Putting the federal government squarely behind alternative energy development would create jobs that cannot be outsourced. Wind, solar, and hydroelectric power sources are already being developed but need more support from the government to be economically viable in the short term. In the long run, alternative energy technologies will pay dividends on the nation's investments, replacing the need to drill for oil in hostile lands or environmentally fragile regions. What it will take, however, is a commitment to long-term goals, not instant gratification. Band-aid solutions, like the national gasoline-tax holiday supported by Senators John McCain and Hillary Clinton, must be avoided, since they blind us to the root of the problem.

Obama wisely rejected the national gas-tax holiday in spite of public clamoring for immediate relief from high gas prices. Obama instead followed the economic model made famous by freshman Senator Mark Warner of Virginia, a former governor lauded for his commitment to balancing the budget and crafting business-savvy solutions. Warner's success as governor stemmed from his belief that environmentally friendly policies will ultimately benefit everyone. A similar ideology will be very useful for President Obama. Obama has already indicated that he is committed to halting the trend of global warming. One of his first acts as president-elect was to speak publicly in favor of efforts to combat climate change, including proposed international agreements rejected by the Bush Administration.

As part of a broader Green Deal, the nation must get serious about securing energy independence so that we are no longer dependent on Middle Eastern dictators and monarchs who suppress human rights and democratic reforms. No more wars for oil, no more reliance on countries with proven records of human rights violations, no more ties to volatile and violent regimes who once received money and guns from the United States but have since turned on the world's richest superpower. Additionally, the nation must get serious about stopping genocide. Turning a blind eye to genocide exacerbates the problem, allowing ruthless regimes, violent warlords, and leaders of ethnic factions to murder millions and propagate incessant rape, pillaging, and destruction across vast regions of the world. At least as important as restoring America's military and economic hegemony is restoring America's moral leadership. Leaders and citizens of the United States of America must stop ignoring places like Darfur, where senseless acts of violence continue, and start contributing to global efforts to stop the genocide.

ISSUE SPOTLIGHT: OBAMANOMICS

In exit polls conducted on November 4, 2008, more than half of Americans voting "chose the economy as the most important" issue affecting their choice for president.[1] Because economic downturns affect everyone, starting with the poorest and most vulnerable, Americans often perceive the economy as the most important issue in times of hardship. At critical junctures in American history, the people of the United States, especially those struggling to survive, have demanded more from their government. "In 2008, as in 1932, a long era of Republican political dominance came to an end in the face of an economic and financial crisis that, in voters' minds, both discredited the GOP's free-market ideology and undermined its claims of competence."[2]

The middle class is both shrinking and suffering, the ranks of the poor are swelling, and even the wealthy are feeling the pain of "the worst stock market crash since the Great Depression."[3] Americans understand that rising unemployment and underemployment diminish the nation's ability to provide for its citizens and to compete in an increasingly competitive, global economy. Americans understand that something must be done. Even conservative columnist William Kristol acknowledged that the "worst financial crisis in almost 80 years has happened on [Bush's] watch.... If Republicans and conservatives don't come to grips with what's happened—and can't develop an economic agenda moving forward that seems to incorporate lessons learned from what's happened—then they could be back, politically, in 1933." Following this ominous warning, Kristol proceeded to criticize the Bush Administration and the Republican Party for repeatedly deregulating American corporations, racking up record deficits and national debt, and "letting free markets degenerate into something close to Karl Marx's vision of an anatomizing, irresponsible and self-devouring capitalism."[4]

As Barack Obama wrote in *The Audacity of Hope*, doing nothing is not an option. "Over the long term," he predicted, "doing nothing probably means an America very different from the one most of us grew up in. It will mean a nation even more stratified economically and socially than it currently is: one in which an increasingly prosperous knowledge class, living in exclusive enclaves, will be able to purchase whatever they want on the marketplace—private schools, private health care, private security, and private jets—while a growing number of their fellow citizens are consigned to low-paying service jobs, vulnerable to dislocation, pressed to work longer hours, dependent on an underfunded, overburdened, and underperforming public sector for their health care, their retirement, and their children's education."[5]

Wracked by war, recessions, and rising inequality, our nation stands at a crossroads in history. Will Americans make the smart decision to replace trickle-down economics with bottom-up economics? Will Americans finally replace Reaganomics with Obamanomics?

Obama placed significant emphasis in his position papers and policy proposals on shifting from the "discredited philosophy of trickle-down economics"[6] to bottom-up government programs. "The trickle-down economic theory says that we should give those at the top more, and they will start and expand businesses and provide jobs and income for all," explained one prominent economist. "This is not a theory; it is propaganda put out by a Congress controlled by the wealthy to justify giving fully one third of the Bush tax cuts to the top 1 percent of earners in America."[7] Obama understood the urgency for economic change to Americans struggling to meet the rising costs of food, shelter, and transportation. Condemning the "'winner-take-all' economy, in which a rising tide doesn't necessarily lift all boats,"[8] he made it clear that one of his priorities would be to help those who are already working hard to help themselves. By his plan to create "green jobs"—sustainable jobs that cannot be outsourced—Obama recognized the need to give both the working poor and the middle class an economic boost.

The next generation of green jobs will be open to any American willing to work hard to make the country a leader in the global economy. Although many green jobs will focus on environmental protection, sustainability, energy production, and other areas linked to making the earth figuratively or literally greener, other green jobs will be in the service industry or in manufacturing. Just because a job requires heavy labor or involves repetitive work does not mean that it cannot fit into the new economy. The new economy will be about what even conservatives admit works: "decentralized networks, bottom-up reform and scalable innovation." In the short-term, economic policies must "mitigate the pain of the recession and...change the culture of Washington." These policies should be followed by "middle-class tax relief and an energy package" that would "transform this country's energy supply."[9]

Obama was forced to create major economic stimulus plans and tax credits to help Americans deal with rising costs and declining incomes. Downsizing and outsourcing trends in recent years have left many workers without employment or without employment that pays a living wage. Domestic resistance to greening the automobile industry, for instance, created severe problems for American automakers as soon as demand for hybrid vehicles and small cars began to outpace demand for sport utility vehicles and pickup trucks.

The current financial crisis requires a new approach to government spending and regulation. Implementing bottom-up economic policies that put more money into programs to make the domestic automobile industry more sustainable and environmentally friendly, with stringent requirements for the automakers to formulate long-term plans to keep their workers on the job, would be a great way for the government to both rebuild and reinvent the automobile industry. Other industries, such as the coal industry, also need to bring their technologies up-to-date in order to compete in a global economy. In past years, regulators have frequently looked the other way while coal-fired power plants continued to spew excessive amounts of pollutants, toxins, greenhouse gases, and radioactive coal ash into the atmosphere. With environmentalists and Obama publicly in support of cap-and-trade programs to reduce carbon emissions within a free-market framework, polluters will soon be forced to take measures to cut back on their greenhouse gas emissions.

Making the federal government fiscally sustainable would go a long way toward freeing up funds for environmental cleanup and conservation. Obama proposed to restore trust in government and return to fiscal responsibility in the wake of "the most fiscally irresponsible Administration in American history," promising to "pay for all of his proposals and reduce the deficit," "return to conservative budget practices," and accomplish "immediate deficit reduction." With a national debt that effectively doubled on the Bush Administration's watch and budgets that have morphed from "a surplus of $236 billion at the end of the Clinton Administration" into "a deficit of more than $400 billion today," Obama faces severe fiscal challenges as he enters the White House. But through careful spending, including ending the Iraq War, reforming farm subsidies so that the nation is no longer subsidizing large agribusinesses, and holding the line on earmarks, Obama could reduce the deficit and, eventually, the national debt.[10]

What makes the current financial crisis so scary is that it may have only just begun. According to a prominent economist who predicted the bursting of the mortgage bubble several years ago, "1) the problem is much bigger than it is being made out to be, and final losses will be in the multiple trillions of dollars worldwide, 2) we are not yet halfway into the national housing price decline, 3) this crisis did not happen by accident, but was a direct result of the lack of regulation in the finance industry that occurs when Wall Street is the biggest dollar contributor to your elected representatives' campaigns, and 4) it will take all the wisdom of our President and our Congress to extricate us from this financial disaster without causing a lengthy worldwide recession."[11] Solutions to the economic crisis should focus not on next year's stock prices but on the long-term ability of Americans to find good jobs and to compete with workers in other countries.

Rebuilding the economy will require a commitment to bottom-up education and employment for all Americans, especially America's youth. The young people of today are the economic engine of tomorrow. From Head Start to high school, young Americans deserve a first-rate education. It should not matter whether a person grows up rich or poor. Obama's proposals to make college more affordable and accessible to young people who might otherwise have to postpone or forgo it for financial reasons will help ensure good jobs. Similarly, putting citizens back to work immediately through new conservation and public works programs would also help get the economy back on track and make all Americans feel like they are involved in America's future. When young people graduate from high school, college, or graduate school, they need to be able to find decent jobs at decent wages. When all else fails, the government should partner the unemployed with areas where work needs to get done.

The Green Deal for the 21st century should look to the New Deal of the 20th century for creative ways to create jobs immediately. President Franklin Delano Roosevelt, for instance, established, in 1933, the Civilian Conservation Corps (CCC), an emergency agency whose mission was "to reduce unemployment, especially among young men; and to preserve the nation's natural resources.... Many CCC projects centered around forestry, flood control, prevention of soil erosion, and fighting forest fires."[12] My grandfather Will used to tell me about how his brother Mac worked for the CCC during the 1930s at a time when it was nearly impossible for a young man of Mac's age to find employment. He recalled Mac leaving home for long stretches to reforest and refurbish the national parks and national forests that many Americans today take for granted. Similarly, the Works Progress Administration (WPA) "offered work to the unemployed on an unprecedented scale by spending money on a wide variety of programs, including highways and building construction, slum clearance, reforestation, and rural rehabilitation."[13]

Economic reinvention will require the dedication of all Americans to the community, to the country, and to the global environment. It will take a firm commitment to making the New Deal of the 21st century a Green Deal with an emphasis on education and employment. With innovation and creative implementation of bottom-up economic principles, the United States can pull through the current economic crisis and come out stronger for it.

ISSUE SPOTLIGHT: CLIMATE CHANGE

After former Vice President Al Gore finished a lecture on global warming at Yale University in the spring of 2004, he stepped down from the podium, waiting for the hordes of students who attended the lecture to rush up to him. The hordes never came. Thirty seconds later, I was alone with the man who was once almost the next president of the United States.

As I approached Gore, shook his hand, and asked him what steps we could take to reduce global warming, I wondered why so few people cared about one of the most significant issues facing our planet. Did they not grasp the implications of what Gore had said about melting glaciers, shifting weather patterns, and rising carbon dioxide levels? Did they not understand the potential devastation of climate changes that could lead to hurricanes, flooding, or another ice age? Did they not understand the consequences of our actions?

Three years later, I cheered from home as Gore stepped to the podium to accept an Oscar for his documentary, *An Inconvenient Truth*. I could not help but admire the man for persisting in his quest to educate the world about global warming, giving the same slide show that I had seen in New Haven, Connecticut, again and again and again. While Gore's stiff manner prevented him from coming across as genuine during the 2000 presidential campaign, that same solemnity lent him credibility as he lectured Americans on the problem of climate change in the years since leaving the Vice President's home at the Naval Observatory. He has been working diligently to clean up our planet. But Gore cannot do it alone.

If ecology has taught us anything, it is that each person's activities may have little effect on the environment, but our civilization's collective actions affect the environment tremendously. Burning fossil fuels releases carbon dioxide and other greenhouse gases into the atmosphere, causing a buildup of gases that traps the sun's rays, which in turn raises temperature levels. By destroying the protective ozone layer around the earth, the earth both receives and absorbs more of the sun's heat. "The vast majority of scientists agree that global warming is real, it's already happening and that it is the result of our activities and not a natural occurrence." Moreover, "we're already seeing changes. Glaciers are melting, plants and animals are being forced from their habitat, and the number of severe storms and droughts is increasing."[14]

Scientists have correlated the rise in global temperatures to an increase in powerful hurricanes, the spread of insect-borne diseases such as malaria to higher altitudes, the melting of glaciers and ice shelves, and unusual animal migration patterns. If we do not act to reduce the rate of global warming, the world could face devastating flooding, droughts, wildfires, heat waves, and species extinction. Scientists have found incredibly strong correlations between carbon dioxide concentration and atmospheric temperature levels, suggesting that burning fossil fuels has contributed greatly to the climate change taking place all around us. Alarmingly, the carbon dioxide and temperature levels today are swiftly approaching the highest levels on record, with today's temperatures and carbon dioxide levels approximating those found on earth 100,000 years ago.[15] If current trends continue, global temperature levels may soon exceed these historic highs, leaving us to speculate about the future of civilization.

What makes global warming so difficult to tackle is the tendency to consider only the immediate costs of changing our habits while ignoring the long-term costs of adhering to the status quo. While developing more fuel-efficient vehicles, such as gas-electric hybrid cars, may impose higher research and development costs on automakers in the short term, the long-term reduction in greenhouse gas emissions will likely save consumers billions by lowering air-conditioning bills, reducing flooding, and depressing gas prices. The nation's addiction to gasoline, the price of which has fluctuated in recent years from under two to over four dollars per gallon, is a major culprit in carbon dioxide emissions, along with coal-fired power plants and oil heating. While most developed countries have imposed stringent fuel efficiency requirements on automobile manufacturers, the United States has lagged behind. The Environmental Protection Agency estimated that gas mileage for American vehicles has stagnated over the last twenty years, with cars averaging only 24.6 miles per gallon and light trucks averaging only 18.4 miles per gallon. Considering the explosion in the number of SUVs on the road, which fall into the light truck category, our nation has actually lost ground in the last two decades.

The good news is that by going green, the United States can rapidly become a "global environmental leader, instead of a laggard." Three-time Pulitzer Prize-winning columnist Thomas Friedman described the greening of America and of the world as "geostrategic, geoeconomic, capitalistic and patriotic." He wrote that the environmental problems that the world faces "are so large in scale that they can only be effectively addressed by an America with 50 green states—not an America divided between red and blue states." To that end, Friedman proposed that government foster innovation by imposing "steadily rising efficiency standards for buildings and appliances," "steadily rising mileage standards for cars," "a steadily tightening cap-and-trade system for the amount of CO_2 any factory or power plant can emit," and "a carbon tax that will stimulate the market to move away from fuels that emit high levels of CO_2 and invest in those that don't."[16]

As a nation, "we need a Green New Deal—one in which government's role is not funding projects, as in the original New Deal, but seeding basic research, providing loan guarantees where needed and setting standards, taxes and incentives."[17] With an emphasis on creatively combating climate change, a Green Deal would have the potential to create "a new cornucopia of abundance for the next generation by inventing a whole new industry."[18] By going green, we can simultaneously reduce our greenhouse gas emissions and our dependence on foreign oil. Reducing our dependence on foreign oil would benefit our nation in a variety of ways, most notably by lessening our reliance on autocratic regimes like Saudi Arabia and wiping out one of the motivations behind the Iraq War. In this way, the Green Deal would not only improve the environment, but also make America safer.

Fortunately, Barack Obama has already signaled an interest in pursuing policies that would reduce carbon emissions in the United States and combat climate change across the globe. In Obama's second major policy statement since his election on November 4, 2008, the president-elect told a bipartisan "gathering of governors and foreign officials"[19] that "my presidency will mark a new chapter in America's leadership on climate change that will strengthen our security and create millions of new jobs in the process.... When I am president, any governor who's willing to promote clean energy will have a partner in the White House," Obama said. "Any company that's willing to invest in clean energy will have an ally in Washington. And any nation that's willing to join the cause of combating climate change will have an ally in the United States of America."[20]

Although stopping short of promising to sign the Kyoto Treaty or to negotiate a stronger treaty that would commit the nations of the world to reducing nonrenewable energy dependency and greenhouse gas emissions, the president-elect implicitly rejected the Bush Administration's lack of interest in creating any federal or international standards that would reduce greenhouse gas emissions. Obama promised that "the United States will once again engage vigorously in these negotiations, and help lead the world toward a new era of global cooperation on climate change." And he made a point of noting that "the science [of climate change] is beyond dispute and the facts are clear. Sea levels are rising. Coastlines are shrinking. We've seen record drought, spreading famine, and storms that are growing stronger with each passing hurricane season. Climate change and our dependence on foreign oil, if left unaddressed, will continue to weaken our economy and threaten our national security."[21]

Obama's public stance on climate change echoes the policy positions that he laid out during the campaign. In his platform, he adressed global-warming issues and the need to reduce the nation's dependency on fossil-fuels in order to reduce greenhouse gases. As discussed in Chapter One, Obama's plans include stricter fuel-economy standards, vehicle tax credits, and the development of new, green jobs through increased funding of research for clean-energy projects, as well as aid to industries adapting to cleaner technologies. He also proposed a Global Energy Forum to "complement—and ultimately merge with—the much larger negotiation process underway at the UN to develop a post-Kyoto framework."[22]

Perhaps most importantly, Obama promised to implement a "market-based cap-and-trade system to reduce carbon emissions by the amount scientists say is necessary to avoid catastrophic change—80 percent below 1990 levels by 2050."[23] Because a cap-and-trade program is designed to force companies to internalize costs by paying for "the right to pollute each ton of CO_2 emissions they create,"[24] it "draws on the power of the marketplace to reduce emissions in a cost-effective and flexible manner."[25] As a result, "American innovators and entrepreneurs will have a direct incentive to find new ways to reduce pollution."[26] Although "many consider such an imposition on producers to be a new tax," and some environmentalists have argued that a market-based cap-and-trade system "is nothing more than allowing polluters to pay for the right to pollute,"[27] it seems likely that cap-and-trade systems will allocate the burden of paying for carbon reductions most efficiently. Considering the lack of attention to climate change in the past, Obama's proposals to combat climate change are remarkably progressive.

But in order to accomplish what he has proposed, Obama will need the support of millions of Americans willing to rally their neighbors, call their Senators and members of Congress, and, ultimately, sacrifice for the greater good. "The fundamental reason why each of us is driven and motivated to act morally is that we are not alone. We inhabit this planet with six billion other people and countless other species of animals, all of whom wish to be treated well."[28] Job creation and national security aside, environmental protection is at the heart of why America needs a Green Deal. More than economic productivity and military might, moral leadership is what has distinguished America in the past and what the nation must exercise in the future. If we don't look out for our planet, who will?

Although it may already be too late to prevent all of the effects of global warming, as evidenced by the devastation of New Orleans by Hurricane Katrina, it is not too late to try. We owe it to ourselves, to our descendants, and to our planet to do what we can to undo the damage that human activities have already caused. Because the environmental destruction wrought by one generation may not have a visible impact for one or more generations, climate change is atransgenerational issue as well as a transnational issue. Borders, ethnic differences, and generational gaps pale in comparison to the weighty significance of protecting the only planet—the only home—that we have. Al Gore has been talking about the threat of global warming for an awfully long time—does the election of Barack Obama mean that we are finally listening?[29]

ISSUE SPOTLIGHT: DARFUR

Blood streaked down Kaldoum Adam Ahmed's face and bruises covered her back, but the soldiers did not stop.

"You must tell us where he is!" one of the soldiers yelled angrily.

"I don't know," Ahmed answered calmly.

"I don't know." Wearing the green camouflage uniforms and caps of the Sudanese army, the soldiers kept whipping the pregnant woman until they were convinced that she was telling them the truth.

"If you want to kill me," Ahmed whispered, "you can kill me." The soldiers did not kill Ahmed. She was one of the lucky ones.[30]

Ahmed's husband, Adouma Ahmed Khames, also survived the brutal attack on their village in the Darfur region of Sudan that day in July, hiding under a pile of rotting grass. Knowing that the soldiers were likely to return again the next morning, Khames headed west during the night with other survivors. Ahmed stayed another day before leaving the destroyed village of Deker. She walked east with her five children, seven months pregnant and distraught from the horrors that she had just witnessed. She left behind mass graves hastily dug to bury friends and relatives who had not fared so well with the gun-toting, truck-driving messengers of death. She also left behind four friends who had been raped the day before.[31]

Attacks by government soldiers and their allies pushed the violence in Darfur to a new level. Nearly half a million Sudanese people have already died in bombings, militia attacks, and firefights between government and anti-government forces. Two million people have been forced from their homes and are scrounging for shelter, food and medicine any way they can. Refugee camps are overcrowded and international aid is scarce. Villagers live in a perpetual state of fear as militiamen shoot men in broad daylight, rape women without hesitation, and loot civilian homes across the land. Seven thousand African Union peacekeepers stand by as the killing continues, afraid to enter "no-go" areas of Darfur. Each week, 10,000 people are dying in Darfur. They need help in order to achieve peace in the region.[32]

Officially labeled "genocide" by the Bush Administration years ago, the conflict in Darfur has caused ten times as many civilian deaths as the war in Iraq and more than twice as many deaths as the genocide in Bosnia in the late 1990s. In human rights terms, the genocide in Darfur is a big deal. Bush and other world leaders dragged their feet, however, pinning their hopes on the chance that the Sudanese president, Lt. Gen. Omar Hassan al-Bashir, would accept United Nations peacekeepers into the country. After Bashir's government signed a peace agreement in May, 2006, with one of the rebel groups, Bush welcomed Minni Minawi, the rebel group's leader, to the White House.[33]

Not long after meeting with Bush, Minawi joined Bashir's government and helped the Sudanese army navigate the harsh terrain. The peace deal completely failed and many experts said that the successive rounds of killings were attempts by the Sudanese government to wipe out as much of the opposition as possible before the prospective arrival of a major force of African Union peacekeepers. Where the Sudanese army had previously depended upon Janjaweed militias to fight the rebels, government soldiers planned and executed many operations themselves. It has not been uncommon for besieged villagers—most of whom are nonviolent and simply want to live peaceably—to see government soldiers clad in green camouflage intermingled with police in brown uniforms and masked militiamen.[34]

If there were ever a time when the rampant killing of civilians by government-sponsored hit men justified international intervention, Darfur was it. And Darfur is it. The genocide in Darfur has gone on far too long while the rich and powerful Western nations have stood by and waited for the Sudanese government to accede to their demands. Former Secretary of State Condoleezza Rice's prediction that there would soon be a breakthrough proved incorrect, and Bush failed to act on his administration's official stance on Darfur. Bush's hesitancy to commit United States troops as peacekeepers in Darfur belied the hypocrisy of his claims that the war in Iraq was justified by humanitarian gains. Bashir's regime has caused far more deaths, rape, pillaging, and looting, than Hussein's regime ever caused, but Bush refused to advocate regime change where it was needed most.

In March of 2006, I wrote a letter to the *New York Times* in which I offered to "serve as a peacekeeper in Darfur... Mass murder is being committed in Darfur and the world doesn't seem to care," I wrote. "While I refuse to join President Bush's misguided Iraq adventure, I will gladly serve as a peacekeeper in Darfur."[35] In January of 2008, I wrote a similar letter to the *Washington Post*, noting that "tragically, the United States has largely ignored the genocide while the United Nations looks elsewhere for troops.... The United States should send an all-volunteer force [to Darfur] immediately—I would be the first to sign up."[36] Bush never took me up on my offer to serve as a peacekeeper in Darfur. Meanwhile, the "hoped-for total of 26,000 blue helmets [have tried] desperately to bring peace to a war zone in which hundreds of thousands have died."[37] The United States and other major powers, in a stunning display of appeasement, have waited for the Sudanese government to agree to international intervention. This is simply unacceptable.

Barack Obama did not mention Darfur or genocide in *The Audacity of Hope.* Nor did he mention the genocide that has occurred, and continues to occur, in Darfur in *Change We Can Believe In*. He did, however, raise the issue twice in his internationalist speech in Berlin, Germany, on July 24, 2008. "The genocide in Darfur shames the conscience of us all,"[38] he remarked. Later in the address, he posed the critical question: "Will we give meaning to the words 'never again' in Darfur?"[39] The world may never know why Obama did not discuss the genocide in Darfur in his second book, a book which mentioned everything from ex-felons to Al Gore, or why Obama omitted the issue from the laundry list of proposals in his platform. There are signs, however, that Obama is paying more attention to the issue. A recent *Washington Post* story, for instance, said that Sudanese leaders expect a "major shift in U.S. policy."[40] Hopefully, Obama will talk about genocide prevention and Darfur more often in the future.

Because Bush dropped the ball on Darfur, a major policy address on genocide would permit Obama to contrast his predecessor's position with his own. It would allow him to take a stand on an issue with deep moral implications for our nation and for the world. Moreover, it is not too late to send an all-volunteer force to Darfur, preferably under the auspices of the United Nations. By creating an American peacekeeping force separate from our nation's military, the United States would eliminate the hazards of sending troops trained to kill into a region where what is needed most is peace. It is also not too late to enforce a no-fly zone in the region. When the goal of a regime is genocide, there can be no compromise. Will we allow the beating of pregnant women, the rape of young girls, the shooting of unarmed men, and the looting of helpless villages to continue unabated, or will we fulfill our commitment to prevent genocide by sending peacekeepers to Darfur? If we wait too long, there may not be any "lucky ones" left.

As president, Barack Obama faces extreme challenges from some of the most pressing issues of the day. The collapse of the economy, the ruining of the environment, and international genocide will have disastrous consequences if allowed to continue. Fortunately, a new Green Deal can solve the economic and environmental problems by investing in environmentally friendly technology and putting people back to work in green jobs. And by sending peacekeeping troops to Sudan and working multilaterally, the United States can help end the atrocities being committed there. It is up to Obama to act and us to support and implement his policies.

CHAPTER THREE

50-STATE STRATEGY

The incessant ringing of the telephone jolted me upright in bed. Groggily, I stumbled to the phone and picked up the receiver.

"Hello?"

"Hi, this is a reminder that Tuesday is Election Day. Please vote for [insert presidential candidate here]..."

I hung up.

The mechanical, pre-recorded voice on the other end of the line reminded me why robocalls are one of the worst inventions of modern campaigning. I would have preferred to read about Senator John McCain in the newspaper or to watch Senator Hillary Clinton's television commercials. I had already received three pieces of mail from Senator Barack Obama, and that did not include the DVD that the campaign sent to my mom ("or Current Resident").

Pennsylvania voters are used to playing a large role in national elections every four years. But not in April. For the leading contender in the Democratic presidential contest to make a whistle-stop train tour from Philadelphia to Harrisburg three days before the Commonwealth's closed primary was unprecedented. The fact that Clinton and Obama appeared at Messiah College, in the tiny town of Grantham, a week before the primary election, spoke volumes about what made the 2008 race different.

A list of the most Republican areas in Pennsylvania, printed in the Harrisburg *Patriot-News* a few years ago, said that the Mechanicsburg area (including Grantham) was almost 90 percent Republican. In the primary for an open seat in the 88th State House district in 2008, there were seven Republicans on the ballot and only one Democrat. Central Pennsylvania is the part of Pennsylvania traditionally counted upon by the GOP to balance out heavily Democratic Philadelphia. It is a part of Pennsylvania traditionally written off by the Democratic Party.

Down on the farm where I used to pick strawberries and drive a rickety blue truck, however, my former co-workers seemed unusually enthusiastic about the upcoming election. Scott Lesh, who graduated with me from Mechanicsburg Area Senior High School and hopes to become a teacher, asked me if I planned to attend Obama's "Road to Change" rally in Harrisburg that night. Jogging home, I noticed a handful of new yard signs and bumper stickers.

Because both Obama and Clinton had visited Mechanicsburg a week earlier, and Chelsea Clinton had appeared at a local Little League field that week, talk of the presidential race was starting to surface, even though some people had more urgent concerns on their minds. The co-owner of the local farm where I used to work seemed more worried about rising prices on fertilizer and gasoline than on the outcome of the election. The politics of Washington, D.C., can seem awfully far away to a struggling farmer or to a student facing mountainous debt.[1]

On Wednesday, April 23, 2008, the presidential candidates moved on to North Carolina, where they bombarded residents of Charlotte, Durham, and Asheville with glossy brochures and carefully cropped photos of the candidates with members of target demographics. Like many others in the United States, local residents in Mechanicsburg went back to the strawberry fields, to their offices and to their desks, worried about whether the Iraq War would ever end and whether they would be able to afford to fill up their tanks the next week.

But the unusually early focus on Pennsylvania did not go unnoticed. Pennsylvanians increasingly began to discuss the race. They began to organize. They signed up on campaign Web sites to receive e-mails about upcoming events. And they lamented having to set alarm clocks again—there would be no more automated presidential wakeup calls until November.

BEFORE BARACK OBAMA

Barack Obama's victory on November 4, 2008, was not inevitable. To many political analysts, it was not even conceivable. The rise of a black Democrat from Chicago to the White House within a few years is a story at odds with the conventional wisdom that prevailed before the 2008 presidential election. But it is also a story foreshadowed by the return of populist rhetoric in the 2000 and 2004 presidential races. It is a story of a Democratic Party that ultimately recognized the necessity of transcending the political limitations of the "20-state campaign."[2]

In the late 1990s and in the years immediately following the 2000 and 2004 elections, political scientists, journalists, and partisan operatives talked frequently about "the rise of a new 'Solid South.'"[3] Noted one prominent scholar, "Just as the mighty Democratic Party once held sway with only insignificant opposition, the Republicans are now the coming dominant force [in American politics]."[4] Envisioning a "one-party country," a pair of journalists wrote that "like a dominant sports franchise, the Republican Party has put in place a series of structural and operational advantages that give the GOP a political edge for the foreseeable future." Moreover, they predicted that even "if Democrats are successful in 2006, there are few signs that their party will be prepared to turn those victories into a winning movement."[5]

A former political writer for the *Washington Post* stated unequivocally that "the Democratic Party can no longer be described as the bottom-up coalition it was from the start of the Great Depression through the end of the 1960s." Pointing to the Republican Party's seemingly monolithic base and "unrelenting...drive to control national policy and debate," the same writer claimed that "no one could argue that the GOP has captured a solid majority of the electorate."[6] On the heels of the Republican congressional sweep in 1994, Republicans began to "view their ascension as rightful and inevitable as the vanquishing of evil at the end of a fairy tale."[7] In the period between Bush's election in 2000 and Bush's re-election in 2004, Republican Party operatives predicted that "the Democratic party will be forever doomed."[8]

Left-leaning political strategists, concurring, asked: "Does representative democracy have a future, or is it just a phase we've been going through?" Assessing the democratic process from the depths of defeat, they concluded that "the era of mass-movement parties is waning almost everywhere." Moreover, they were convinced that "electoral disengagement— or, to use a less delicate term, voter ignorance...[had] reached such disturbing heights one had to wonder how many people had the remotest idea what they were voting for."[9] Democrats looked at the election of Bill Clinton in 1992 and saw a popular-vote loser who only won because "Perot's disproportionately white 19 percent delivered the election to the Democrats."[10] They took little solace in Senator John

Kerry's loss in the 2004 general election, an election in which "the most aggressive mobilization effort ever mounted by Democrats failed to produce a base bigger than the GOP's."[11] Thomas Frank envied the "structure of conservative 'movement culture,' a phenomenon that has little left-wing counterpart anymore."[12]

Especially painful to progressives across the country was the failure of Howard Dean's bid for the nomination in the 2004 Democratic primary. Spurred on by a sense that it would take a mass movement built on progressive populism to defeat Bush, thousands of young people joined Dean on the campaign trail in Iowa and New Hampshire. I traveled, for instance, with several of my college classmates to join the campaign in Manchester, New Hampshire, where we made thousands of phone calls, knocked on thousands of doors, and stood on blustery street corners holding giant rally-sign "totem poles" until the frigid January air numbed our fingers. Dean's strategy in the Democratic primary was simple: recruit enough volunteers to talk to enough voters and electoral victory would follow.

Considered by Washington insiders to be an unwinnable, insurrectionist candidacy from the start, the Dean campaign miraculously managed to take the lead in New Hampshire polling shortly before the Iowa caucuses, only to lose New Hampshire after cable news programs replayed Dean's infamous post-Iowa caucus speech over and over again. What the Dean campaign brought to the table, however, was an understanding that field operations still mattered. Contacting voters directly brought Washington issues to the doorstep of each voter, and brought voter concerns back to the campaign's strategists. Since Dean became chairman of the Democratic National Committee in the wake of his failed presidential bid, the lessons learned in 2004 became the tenets of the Democratic Party's strategy in 2008 and ultimately played a major role in Obama's victory.

In the aftermath of Kerry's loss in the 2004 general election, Democratic Party operatives looked longingly at the Republican Party's "'ground war' strategy to counter the Democrats' traditional advantage in getting out the vote in the closing days of a campaign." The Republican Party had learned how "to find prospective voters for Bush wherever they were located...[and] tailor messages to the issue concerns of each person instead of using bland mail and recorded phone messages from popular figures using generic appeals." Not surprisingly, "the ability of the Republican Party to target their voters—not only in such large areas as exurbia and in sprawling suburbs but also within black and Latino churches, in unions, and in overwhelmingly Democratic college towns— stunned Democratic Party leaders."[13]

"Instead of spending the usual 75 to 90 percent of their money on undecided voters, Republicans spent half of it on mobilizing sympathizers who had seldom or never voted,"[14] journalists discovered after the election. "Bush's strategists studied commercial databases for correlations between buying habits and political sympathies. They learned to target people who drank Coors, watched college football, or had caller ID. They analyzed this audience and tailored messages for each of 32 subgroups." Moreover, the Republican Party had "locked up 27 states worth 226 electoral votes," before a single ballot was cast, whereas "Kerry began the 2004 general election with 10 states in the bag and aspirations to compete in 20 more.... By Election Day, he could count on only 13 states worth 186 electoral votes and was competing seriously in 10 others."[15] Kerry's decision to ignore most southern states allowed Bush to win as soon as he won Ohio and Florida.

Under the new leadership of Chairman Dean, the Democratic Party began to analyze what had worked in the past and what had been inefficient or ineffective. Although belittled by the pundits, many Democratic activists intuitively understood the strong potential of "populist appeals, such as those made by Gore in 2000 ('the people against the powerful') or in primary contests—Howard Dean in 2004 ('the Democratic wing of the Democratic Party'), John Edwards in 2004 ('Today, under George W. Bush, there are two Americas, not one')."[16] Democratic activists also realized that the Dean campaign's strategy of identifying where voters stood on a scale from one through five had enormous potential to compete with the Republican Party's targeting techniques. Implementing a targeting strategy on a large enough scale to do any good, however, had proven impossible for the Dean campaign.

But with sufficient preparation, strategic planning, and new technology, Dean believed that the Democratic National Committee could put into place an identification, persuasion, and mobilization program built around principles similar to those that had guided the Republican Party's 2004 targeting program. With the 2006 midterm elections approaching, Dean rolled out what he called the "50-State Strategy," a strategy that centered on inclusion and competition. It would require, however, thousands more staff members and volunteers than had ever been mobilized by the Democratic Party. To be implemented in 2008, it would also take a candidate willing to implement the strategy at a level of magnitude never before attempted by a presidential nominee. Fortunately for the Democratic Party, Barack Obama was that kind of candidate. And fortunately for Barack Obama, Obama for America and, later, the Campaign for Change, would generate the outpouring of volunteers and donations needed to successfully implement the 50-State Strategy.

HOWARD DEAN'S 50-STATE STRATEGY

"Election by election, state by state, precinct by precinct, door by door, vote by vote...we're going to lift our Party up and take this country back for the people who built it,"[17] Democratic National Committee Chairman Howard Dean explained in announcing his 50-State Strategy. According to the Democratic Party's Web site, the original goal of the 50-State Strategy was to have "an active, effective group of Democrats organized in every single precinct in the country." To achieve that goal, the Democratic Party "hired organizers chosen by the state parties in every state— experienced local activists who know their communities," "brought those organizers together for summits where they learned from each other the best practices for getting organized to win elections," and sent them out to recruit "more leaders and volunteers."[18]

Dean, a medical doctor who counted among his achievements as Vermont's governor the statewide expansion of health care and the legal recognition of civil unions, took the helm of the Democratic Party at a time when Democrats were more divided and disoriented than ever. Grounded on a philosophy of outreach to Democrats across the nation, even those alienated or disaffected from mainstream politics, Dean's campaign had made impressive inroads into the Internet grassroots, or "netroots," and had raised record sums online. By expanding that philosophy to every state, Dean created a 50-State Strategy that promised to rejuvenate and enlarge the Democratic Party's base. At its core, Dean's 50-State Strategy emphasized the hiring of local activists for the purpose of building, or rebuilding, local and state organizations.

Describing the 50-State Strategy on "Meet the Press" in 2005, Dean said that the Democratic National Committee was "putting...local people on the DNC payroll in every state in America. And that is going to be really what's going to create the opportunity for us to win.... We cannot run 18-state campaigns,"[19] Dean said, in an apparent reference to Kerry's unsuccessful presidential campaign. "We've got to be everywhere. We've got to be in Mississippi. We've got to be in Oklahoma. We have to be organized. By the end of this year, we have a goal of having a Democrat in every precinct in America, not every county, but every precinct in America, four paid political organizers in every state in America in 2005." Echoing Obama's 2004 convention speech, Dean emphasized that "there's no such thing as a red state and a blue state. There are purple states."[20]

Just like his campaign for president, Dean's 50-State Strategy encountered opposition from Washington insiders, including Representative Rahm Emmanuel, Senator Charles Schumer, strategist James Carville, and Clinton consultant Paul Begala. Emmanuel, chairman of the Democratic Congressional Campaign Committee, and Schumer, chairman of the Democratic Senatorial Campaign Committee, actually stormed out of a meeting with Dean in 2007 with "a trail of expletives."[21] Begala derided the organizing project as "just hiring a bunch of staff people to wander around Utah and Mississippi and pick their nose."[22] Dean, acknowledging his status as an "outsider,"[23] responded that "the fact is that our 50-state strategy has already laid a nationwide foundation for victory this year, in 2008 and beyond."[24]

In spite of the heavy criticism from other Democratic Party officials, Dean spent millions hiring organizers in every state in order to "rebuild the Democratic Party from the ground up." He recognized that the effort to put organizers and other staffers in states and counties which the Democratic Party had long ago written off was a "huge shift," but argued that "since 1968, campaigns have been about TV and candidates, which works for 10 months out of the four-year cycle. With party structure on the ground, you campaign for four years." The effort by Dean, a man who had been ridiculed on FOX News for listing 13 states and screaming, in a room full of screaming volunteers, after coming in third place in the

Iowa caucuses, was lauded by journalists and local organizers as nothing short of "revolutionary."[25]

Stories surfaced of volunteers who had offered to help years earlier but had never been contacted by the Democratic Party—until Dean's 50-State Strategy came along. "'I've been trying to contact the party since I moved back here in 1992,' [said] Harold Terry, 43, a Jackson [Mississippi] native who volunteered last week at a phone bank. 'Someone finally got back to me three weeks ago,'" read one July 2006 news report, indicative of many similar stories.[26] First-time volunteers tried their hand at door knocking at the behest of organizers, who urged them to hone their skills in preparation for 2006, 2007, and, finally, 2008. As the program gathered steam, columnists began to call Howard Dean's 50-State Strategy "one of the brightest ideas the DNC has had in its undistinguished history," a "belated catch-up effort [that] has exponentially multiplied grassroots party involvement," and an effort to win votes in areas where "a lot of Democrats think of the national party as the devil itself."[27]

Following the 2006 midterm elections, there developed a broad feeling that Dean's 50-State Strategy was working. Rebuilding local Democratic Party organizations in traditionally Republican states and counties, sometimes from the ground up, paid dividends in future election cycles as local organizations established themselves within their local communities. "In 'purple' states like North Carolina, where Democrats dominate most local and statewide elections, it's helping to turn red counties purple and purple counties blue, uncorking a new strain of progressive populism—the kind that won Senate races in Virginia for Jim Webb, Montana for Jon Tester and Ohio for Sherrod Brown," wrote one journalist. Significantly, "eight-term GOP Congressman Charles ['Chainsaw'] Taylor was dethroned by Heath Shuler, a social conservative, but one with a feisty pro-labor and environmental bent."[28]

"In a scene playing out this year all across 'red America,' from these lush hills to the craggy outcroppings of the Mountain West, previously unfathomable crowds of Democrats are streaming up the steps of the old county courthouse, past bobbing blue balloons and 'Welcome Democrats!' signs," one writer reported from "Bible-thumping, economically slumping" Wilkes County, North Carolina. Scenes like the one he describes occurred everywhere: "They're hopping mad about the national state of things but simultaneously giddy with a new-found hope—finally!—for their party. Inside...symbols of the new spirit bustle around. There's trim old Clyde Ingle, a onetime Hubert Humphrey campaigner who 'finally just got tired of sitting up there in Deep Gap and complaining.'... [And] there's Mark Hufford, a young, towheaded bundle of energy who's been helping Democrats win breakthrough elections as a field organizer."[29]

The Democratic National Committee, meanwhile, did not hesitate to take credit for having "expanded the number of targeted races for the 2006 midterm elections." In an e-mail to party loyalists, the Democratic National Committee noted that "races that no one could have predicted would be even remotely close are now within the margin of error. A race for an at-large U.S. House seat in Idaho is now being flooded with money—on the Republican side—as GOP strategists try to protect what was once considered a safe seat. This is exactly what the 50-state strategy is all about."[30] State party chairs went out of their way to praise the 50-State Strategy for helping them "turn it around,"[31] and for helping them "become part of the fabric of [the Latino and Native American] communities."[32] And at least one Republican operative admitted that "Dean could wind up looking like a genius eventually."[33]

With each successive election, Dean looked more and more like a genius. He had created a strategy to win red states and blue states, rich states and poor states, mountain states and coastal states. He had funded an operation that was finally bringing local, state, and national Democrats into close coordination—and not just on Election Day. State parties adopted the Democratic National Committee's 50-State Strategy as a way of funding their annual coordinated campaigns. The coordinated campaigns kept the Party going all year long. Reaching out to local activists through e-mail, organizers expanded the base in rural areas beyond the local chairman or chairwoman, mobilizing people to volunteer who had long been inactive. They knew that if they could collect more and more e-mail addresses for their mailing lists, assemble more and more Democrats for "Vote Blue" meetings, and continually plan for the next big election, the likelihood of success at the polls would go up.

To his credit, Dean understood that "to succeed, a new progressive politics must be grounded in an organized citizenry rooted in specific communities and at the same time linked together in larger networks with the capacity to deliberate about, develop, and carry out local, state, and national strategies.... Only through mobilization across localities and levels of government will citizens begin to develop broader understandings of common interests as well as the capacity for coordinated political action on behalf of those interests."[34] He also recognized that "in the long run, Democrats would be better off with an expanded electorate in which the median voter was closer to their position than with a smaller electorate in which they moved closer to Republicans—better off because even if they chose to make tactical moves toward the center, the electorate would be weighted further to their side."[35] In other words, the Democrats needed to do more than move to the center and hope to pick up votes from Independents. They needed to stay with their base and ensure that every potential Democratic vote went to the polls and cast a ballot for the Democratic ticket.

Dean's 50-State Strategy implicitly built upon the increasingly popular notion among political scientists that "like the old progressive Republican majority, the emerging Democratic majority reflects deep-seated social and economic trends that are changing the face of the country.... Today's Democrats are the party of the transition from urban industrialism to a new postindustrial metropolitan order in which men and women play equal roles and in which white America is supplanted by multiracial, multiethnic America."[36] The new Democratic majority would be a coalition of voters that defied the stereotypes about rural voters and that transcended the stereotypes about race and religion. Leaning heavily on young people to do the heavy lifting—round-the-clock organizing, volunteer recruitment, canvass leading—Dean's 50-State Strategy called upon Democrats across America to stand up and make their voices heard.

As the 2008 presidential primary campaigns got underway, the Democratic National Committee continued to fund and support the organizers hired as part of Dean's 50-State Strategy. Although not particularly well liked and never fully recognized by either Obama for America or the Campaign for Change, Dean's 50-State Strategy employees gradually folded into the Obama campaign. Fifty days before the election, in fact, Dean sent a personal plea to Democratic activists, explaining that "for the first time in decades, we

Democrats have a true 50-state operation on the ground. Over the last year and half, we've invested in building the infrastructure for a permanent Democratic Party—one that doesn't need to be rebuilt from scratch for every election.... We're transforming our 50-state strategy into a 50-state voter turnout operation for candidates up and down the ballot everywhere.... For the next 50 days it's up to us to come through with a 50-State Turnout operation to win elections in every state. The future of our party—and our country— depends on it."[37]

BARACK OBAMA'S 50-STATE STRATEGY

Turning the dream of competing in all 50 states into a reality, Barack Obama's presidential campaign drew strength from the Dean legacy, a prior campaign for change filled with youth and flush with online revenues. Obama's campaign drew strength from the 2006 Democratic sweep in races for the United States Senate and House of Representatives. And it drew strength from the unusually high levels of interest and activism leading up to the 2008 presidential race. The Obama campaign drew staffers and volunteers from across the nation, encouraging state-hopping by young women and men dedicated to changing the world. Without the efforts begun by Howard Dean years earlier, the Obama campaign would not have had local committees and party structures across America to build upon in the general election. In the primary election, of course, Dean's 50-State Strategy organizers remained neutral, but they recognized the need to unify Democrats as soon as one candidate clinched the nomination.

With an audacity of strategy that far surpassed the relatively modest aims of Dean's original 50-State Strategy, Obama sought to be competitive in every state of the country. Obama put time, money, and staff into rural areas in traditionally Republican states, making the South a particular focal point of the campaign. Campaigning in rural Virginia, my fellow organizers and I kept telling ourselves and our volunteers that the campaign would be won in Virginia. It would not be lost in Virginia, we knew, because Obama could still have won (and would have won) without Virginia. But the fact that Obama would be reasonably assured of winning the election if he took Virginia spurred those of us in the field to work just a little bit harder. Conscious that a victory in the historic capital of the Confederacy would be highly symbolic, we took to the streets with an expectation that we were making history.

Obama for America, Obama's primary campaign, did not implement a recognizable version of the 50-State Strategy. The nature of the caucus and primary schedule made a simultaneous campaign in all 50 states impossible. But critical elements of Obama's primary campaign would be included within the broader 50-State Strategy implemented between June and November. For example, the general election Campaign for Change concentrated on voter registration in much the same way that Obama for America had focused on voter registration until the final registration deadline. Taking a cue from Dean's philosophy of expanding the base, Obama for America registered millions of new voters, including hundreds of thousands of new voters in the critical swing states of Pennsylvania and Ohio, and the new battleground states of Virginia, North Carolina, and Georgia. Where Dean's 50-State Strategy lacked sufficient emphasis on registering new voters, the Obama campaign filled in the gap.

Throughout the campaign, the Obama campaign encouraged state hopping by staffers and volunteers, constantly creating paid and unpaid positions in every state. Where there was an office, organizers and volunteers worked out of the office. Where there was not an office, the campaign explored the possibility of opening one. During the primary season, for instance, I helped the Obama campaign in Virginia, North Carolina, and Pennsylvania, moving on as soon as the citizens in each state voted. During the general election season, I started in Pennsylvania and ended up in Virginia. Nearly all of my co-workers at the regional field director level and above had previous campaign experience, either from another campaign or from the primary season. Only field organizers, hired to work for regional field directors in particular counties, came in without "war wounds" and memories of past campaigns gone awry. Even some of the Campaign for Change field organizers, however, arrived with substantial field experience, having already helped out during the primary season.

Unlike the Democrat National Committee field organizers, Obama's field organizers were almost exclusively under 30 years old. The majority of field organizers, in fact, were under 25, with the 25-30 crowd filling the regional field director and statewide positions. A veritable young people's movement (see Chapter 5), the organizers fanned out across states during the primary season and across every state once Obama became the nominee. The campaign assigned large groups of counties to regional field directors and smaller groups of counties, sometimes only a single county or less, to field organizers. Intensely committed to uniformity, the campaign developed an established hierarchy and stuck with that hierarchy throughout the campaign. Shakeups were few and far between and replacements extremely rare. The extensive field staff developed a sense that the field campaign was the central front in the campaign.

Organizers in traditionally Republican areas, in particular, often felt like independent and autonomous organizers setting up outposts far from the Chicago campaign, with minimal support from the Democratic Party or the Obama headquarters. As late as September, 2008, for instance, the Obama campaign even had "a few paid staffers in Salt Lake City, despite the fact that Utah is the reddest of red states." The campaign defended the decision to "reshape the political landscape of a country deeply divided between red and blue," arguing that "the approach not only expands the playing field and aids down-ballot candidates, but...also helps with fund-raising and adds to volunteer efforts in neighboring states that are more in play—such as, in the case of Utah, Colorado, New Mexico and Nevada." Only after McCain selected Governor Sarah Palin as his running mate did Obama think about "redeploying its North Dakota staff— estimated in some press reports to be more than 50 people," as well as the staff in Alaska, Palin's home state.[38]

Organizers in small towns and rural outposts, while isolated from their colleagues and teammates, validated Obama's commitment to the 50-State Strategy. Every day from morning to night, they met with local Democratic activists, civic and community leaders, registered voters, and spread the word that Barack Obama had arrived to reinvent the Democratic Party. They understood from talking to beleaguered Democrats that "it's hard to get your supporters ginned up for a national campaign if they see no infrastructure, especially local get-out-the-vote operations."[39] Small town organizers made Obama offices hubs of political activity that would not only draw volunteers but also local media. Opening an office where no presidential candidate had ever opened an office before was a big deal to organizers eager to stake out a legacy for both the candidate and the organization. In the reddest of the red states, any new voters registered, any voters swayed, and any Democrats mobilized, were votes that could swing an incredibly close race.

To a large extent, the Obama campaign's 50-State Strategy hinged on registering huge numbers of new voters in every state. The campaign devoted much of the primary season and most of the summer before the general election to registering voters, an effort that gave the campaign the ability to compete in many states that would otherwise have been written off. Because the campaign was able to register "more than 400,000 new voters" in North Carolina, for example, the campaign made the state a competitive race by redeploying more and more staffers to the "southern state with a large African American electorate that has seen one of the highest levels of voter registration this cycle."[40] The extraordinary numbers of newly registered voters across the nation put red states everywhere back on the table. Southern states, in particular, long coveted by Democrats looking to expand the Electoral College possibilities of the party's presidential nominee, became a hotbed of Obama activism.

"There was no question that Democrats throughout the South were energized in ways unthinkable in the four decades since LBJ signed the Voting Rights Act," wrote one observer. "In every Southern primary, even the early ones when the Republican race was every bit as competitive as the Democrats', more Democrats voted in the primaries than in their counterparts." In states with large African-American populations, Obama won the cities handily, and made significant inroads into the predominantly white suburbs and rural areas as well. "While Obama racked up huge margins— often three to one—in the swelling 'postindustrial metropolises' of Dixie, he was also besting his white opponents on some of the most conservative white terrain remaining in the region."[41] Obama made a point of competing in not just every state, but also in every county and in every precinct.

Recognizing the growing irritation with the do-nothing politics of the past, Obama approached Democrats, Independents, and Republicans alike with the do-something politics of the future. He approached voters who felt left out, ignored, or taken for granted, and offered them a piece of the action. The efforts that Dean took, expanded by Obama, quickly showed results: "a multiracial, post-religious right generation of Southerners [began] to emerge, with precious little patience for the politics of the past. This new generation [was] joined by millions of middle-class and working-class boomers who have lived through too many false economic dawns to keep believing the same old lines.... Together, these Southerners are rebelling against the religious right's narrow definition of what 'values' mean in politics."[42]

In the final days leading up to the 2008 elections, when the "Republicans [were] having to spend precious dollars on ads" in the South and the West, pundits and activists began to debate the helpfulness of Dean's 50-State Strategy and the legacy of Obama's 50-State Strategy. "When Obama announced that he was implementing a 50-state strategy, he was laughed at," CNN commentator Roland Martin noted. After the Republicans were forced to go on the defensive in states like Virginia, North Carolina, Montana, Colorado, Nevada, Iowa, and Missouri, however, the critics stopped laughing. "Obama deserves a lot of credit for this because his 'change' campaign theme, along with the horrible leadership of Republicans nationwide, [helped] his candidacy," Martin concluded. "But changing the attitude among the nation's Democrats was also vital, and that's where Dean played a role."[43]

After Obama's election, the pundits and Democratic Party strategists applauded both Obama and Dean for the 50-State Strategy, which "was essentially vindicated during the presidential election, with Barack Obama investing heavily in, and winning, states such as Indiana, North Carolina, Virginia and Colorado." Donna Brazile, a Clinton Administration official who managed Al Gore's 2000 presidential campaign, went even further in complimenting the head of the Democratic National Committee. "Dean helped Obama and other Democrats prepare for this day," she told Salon.com. "While others lamented our loss in 2004, Dean got to work in devising a 50-state strategy that eventually laid the groundwork for Obama and others to harvest votes in 2008." "Daily Kos" blogger Markos Moulitsas even announced a personal goal "to make sure that Howard Dean gets his due props, and, by extension, all of us who fought to make Dean's vision a reality."[44]

Other journalists, such as Adam Nagourney of the *New York Times* and the *International Herald Tribune*, gave nearly all of the credit for the success of the 50-State Strategy to the Obama campaign, which "relied almost completely on its own staff money and organization in making incursions into Republican states." Moreover, Nagourney and others made the case that credit for Obama's 50-State Strategy should go to David Plouffe, Obama's campaign manager, who "made the case [throughout 2008] that the Obama campaign would compete in, and could win, states that Democrats had written off for years for reasons that were very particular to the nature of the Obama campaign and the dynamics of the 2008 race."[45]

AMBITIOUS GOALS

The debate over whether Howard Dean or Barack Obama should receive credit for envisioning and implementing the 50-State Strategy is an exercise in futility. Without Dean's strategic decision in 2005 to rebuild the Democratic Party's infrastructure, upgrade and improve the Democratic Party's technological capabilities, seek out small donors, and hire organizers in the West, the Obama campaign would not have been able to come in after clinching the nomination and build a 50-state, modern, grassroots campaign as quickly as it did. Without the Democratic National Committee's staffers already on the ground, the Obama campaign would have had to start completely from scratch in every state. Instead, the Campaign for Change was able to take Dean's dream and make it a reality in just a few short weeks.

"Using person-to-person contact as a chief persuasion tool to recruit new voters,"[46] the Obama campaign built the most organized campaign in American history, a campaign focused on reaching voters directly rather than bombarding them with negative ads. The field operation also cost less than Washington wisdom dictated, leaving Obama with substantial amounts of cash-on-hand as November approached. Reaching out to voters on the phone and in person turned out to be a winning strategy, turning traditionally Republican states and counties Democratic for the first time in decades. In the Middle Peninsula and Northern Neck of Virginia, for instance, Obama won four counties—Westmoreland, Essex, Caroline, and King and Queen—that Kerry lost in 2004.[47]

Young people defined the ground game, creating a movement for change built on relatively independent outposts in the far reaches of traditionally Republican territory. Here the ground game changed the tone of the campaign, challenging Republican candidates and operatives on their home turf. Here was a movement for change built on the backs of the organizers who set up, staffed, supplied, and ran their own offices and organizations. These efforts paid off handsomely. Competing in every state, county, and precinct, forced the Republican Party to play defense, which it did. Holding a theoretical advantage over McCain's "just enough" plan, despite the risk of stretching resources too thin, the Obama campaign set ambitious goals for a northern Democrat and won in previously unwinnable states.

Eschewing the strategy of focusing exclusively on holding the base and competing in a handful of must-win states, the campaign fought to win rural, win Southern, and win Republican. The Obama campaign narrowly won Florida, Indiana, North Carolina, and Ohio, all states that Kerry lost, and nearly won Missouri. By wider than expected margins, Obama won Colorado, Nevada, New Mexico, Iowa, and Virginia. Obama also received a respectable 45 percent of the vote in Arizona, losing McCain's home state by only nine points. By contrast, Obama won 62 percent of the vote in Illinois and nearly tripled McCain's numbers in his childhood home state of Hawaii. Garnering nearly 67 million votes and 365 electoral votes, Obama won a record number of popular votes and more than doubled his opponent's electoral vote total.[48]

In the end, Obama's decision to win as many states as possible and compete across the nation proved that a 50-State Strategy could be implemented on a national scale and could turn out victories in previously unwinnable places. Drawing on Dean's vision of deploying organizers to every state, every county, and every precinct, Obama won more states than he needed to reach 270 electoral votes, the magic number.

CHAPTER FOUR

COMMUNITY ORGANIZING

During the final days of the campaign, Nancy Pfotenhauer, a senior adviser to Senator John McCain, derisively distinguished between the "real Virginia"[1]—namely, the areas more rural, Republican, and "Southern in nature"[2]— and the rest of Virginia, fake Virginia, perhaps—namely, northern Virginia and the big cities, full of Democratic voters. Pfotenhauer's distinction between the real Virginia and the rest of Virginia belied the Republican nominee's claim that he wanted to put "country first." The reality is that McCain clung to the dying view that electioneering requires tearing down one's opponents and dividing our nation along sectional, partisan, and racial lines.

President Barack Obama proved that it is possible to put the country first by uniting Democrats, Republicans, and Independents. He proved that it is possible to put the country first by registering millions of new voters, turning forgotten states into competitive states, and creating the largest volunteer outreach effort in American history. Backed by hard-earned financial contributions from over three million Americans, Obama took his Campaign for Change to states and counties that the Republican Party had long taken for granted and that the Democratic Party had long written off. Knocking on millions of doors and calling millions of voters, Obama's army of volunteers breathed new life into the democratic process.

At my office in Gloucester County, in the heart of what McCain's advisers and Governor Sarah Palin so condescendingly referred to as the real America, we redoubled our efforts to put someone in the White House who would represent the interests of all Virginians and all Americans. In this rural county with 38,293 residents, Obama volunteers canvassed or called more people than there were registered voters. At the doors, Americans from all walks of life were saying that they wanted tax policies that would benefit the middle class, health care policies that would benefit

Americans struggling to keep their jobs, and national security policies that would improve the nation's standing and reputation in the world. In short, they wanted change.

While canvassing one weekend, I met a man with a Confederate flag on his pickup truck who felt so strongly that the country could not afford eight more years of failed economic policies that he put an Obama-Biden sign in his yard. The fathers and mothers in Mathews County who head to the shipyards at four o'clock every morning told me that we needed a president who would create millions of new jobs and provide health insurance for all Americans. They told me that we needed a president who would protect the right of workers to earn enough money to feed their children. They told me that we needed a president who would invest in energy independence so that we would no longer have to fight dictators for oil.

Obama's dream of an America where we look not at the color of one's skin, or the exercise of one's religion, or the expression of one's sexuality, but at the content of one's character, is the centerpiece of the American Dream. It is a dream of a nation where there are not red states and blue states but the United States, where the real America is everywhere that there are good schools and decent jobs. It is a dream of a nation where Republicans and Democrats send their children to the same schools, worship God in whatever way they choose, and unite under the same flag.

On November 4, 2008, Americans seized the opportunity to put our country first by overcoming the politics of fear and electing a president who believes that every Virginian has a stake in the American Dream. But it did not happen without organizers knocking on millions of doors and calling millions of voters. Rather than waiting for someone else to fight for the change we need, we realized that we must act to foster that change. We showed the world that even the real Virginia believed in change—and would vote for Barack Obama.[3]

TAKING IT TO THE STREETS

When Barack Obama announced on February 10, 2007, that he had made up his mind to run for president, he called on a generation to rise up and join him on the campaign trail. He also made it clear that his campaign would be different from any ever run before "Each and every time, a new generation has risen up and done what's needed to be done," he said. "Today we are called once more—and it is time for our generation to answer that call. For that is our unyielding faith—that in the face of impossible odds, people who love their country can change it."[4] Obama's call to organize, a call heard in the suburbs of Washington, D.C. and in the backwoods of Appalachia, put the nation on notice that the lanky lawyer from Illinois was serious about reaching the White House. He wanted hundreds, thousands, even millions of people to join him in the most ambitious organizing effort in American history. He enlisted college students and senior citizens to assist him in reaching out to every state, every county, and every precinct.

Like the machine bosses of an earlier era, Obama wanted precinct captains to walk their turfs and knock on doors in order to squeeze every possible voter out of their precincts. Unlike Boss Tweed, however, Obama did not dangle jobs to faithful partisans as a reward for loyalty. To volunteers, he offered his appreciation and gratitude. To a nation desperate for change, he offered hope. To poorly paid organizers who ran the offices emblazoned with the Obama logo, he offered an opportunity to make history.

Drawing on my experiences as the first organizer, Republican or Democrat, to set up shop in the Middle Peninsula and Northern Neck of Virginia, the story that follows is an insider's view of the campaign from the bottom up. At once intensely complex and astonishingly simple, it is a story of community organizing at its best.

When the Democratic Party of Virginia hired me to serve as a regional field director for Barack Obama, Mark Warner, and Bill Day in the Middle Peninsula and Northern Neck, I could not fathom the scope and magnitude of the job that needed to be done. Driving south on Interstate 95 from my home in Mechanicsburg, Pennsylvania, I could not have conceived how much I would learn over the coming months about rural organizing. My primary focus in Pennsylvania had been registering voters in public housing projects and neighborhoods where Spanish outranked English as the dominant language. My primary focus in Virginia was to turn a region long ignored by the Democratic Party into a region that could reverse the electoral fortunes of the state. Although I went to law school only 17 miles from my future office, I initially felt like a carpetbagger.

The truth is that I didn't know the first thing about organizing in rural Virginia. Sure, I had heard rumors of pig roasts and Rebel flags, but I had never spent much time outside the Brooklyn sidewalks of my childhood and the Mechanicsburg strip malls of my teenage years. Chris, a British student who had come to America to intern for the Pennsylvania Democratic Party for the summer, treated me like a departing missionary. Having spent many hours walking on opposite sides of the street through parts of Harrisburg where the police routinely warn white people not to go, we knew the corners and alleys where we would find the most votes. We knew how to turn 19-year-old punks into campaign recruiters. For a few red, white, and blue Obama stickers, we could draw a crowd of children, none of them older than the age of 10, willing to run up and down fire escapes to tell their parents that Barack Obama was at the door.

So when it came time for me to hit the road, Chris gathered my colleagues together for a group photo and told me to send him a postcard when I wasn't too busy getting shot at by folks who hadn't heard that *the war* was over. Of course, rural Virginia—like southwestern Virginia and the mountains of western North Carolina—is no longer filled with racists who wouldn't vote for a black man for president if he were the only candidate running. Columnist Frank Rich predicted before the election that although the pundits frequently wailed that "a black guy is doomed among Reagan Democrats, Joe Sixpacks, rednecks, Joe the Plumbers or whichever condescending term you want to choose," the "racists for Obama" far outnumbered the racists for McCain-Palin in the 2008 election.[5] At the end of many back roads and dirt driveways in rural America live a lot of people who, with the nation's future on the line, voted for change.

At eight o'clock in the morning after I arrived in Virginia, my supervisor Victoria drove me to the town of Mathews, where I would spend a great deal of time over the next few months. While Victoria's black SUV idled as we waited for the drawbridge over the York River to close, the deputy field director for the rural regions briefed me on my mission: reach out to local committee chairs, mobilize local activists, train and manage staff and interns, plan and set regional goals, and report nightly and weekly numbers both in an online spreadsheet and on increasingly frequent conference calls. An hour later, we were listening to Warner deliver his stump speech to a crowd of 35 local Democrats, activists, and elected officials at Lynne's Family Restaurant. Eating my Reuben sandwich and ketchup-smothered French fries with local folks excited about the prospects of Warner and Obama, I thought to myself: "So *this* is Virginia."

Cynthia, the vice chair of the Mathews County Democratic Committee, graciously offered me the guest bedroom in her home on Rural Route 626, which was recently renamed Ridge Road so that emergency vehicles could reach people more easily. Not long ago, the houses on Route 626 did not have street numbers, and some local residents still pick up their mail at the branch post offices that dot all of the counties in the region. Cell phone service is sporadic at best and Mathews residents grumble often about the lack of high-speed Internet access in the area. The options for Internet access in many rural areas, I soon learned, are limited to overly slow dial-up or exorbitantly expensive satellite. Because e-mail was not a viable option in reaching out to large numbers of local activists on a daily basis, the local political committees continued to rely heavily on phone trees as a way of contacting members.

Organizing the Middle Peninsula and Northern Neck of Virginia for Barack Obama and the Democratic Party would prove to be one of the most challenging things that I had ever done in my life. When Obama first became an organizer for the Developing Communities Project in Chicago, he was told that "communities had never been a given in this country, at least not for blacks. Communities had to be created, fought for, tended like gardens."[6] What he learned, however, was that organizing requires not only dedication to the cause but also planning and recruiting and persistence. "For the [first] three weeks," Obama recollected, "I worked day and night, setting up and conducting my interviews. It was harder than I'd expected. There was the internal resistance I felt whenever I picked up the phone to set up the interviews, as images of Grampa's insurance sales calls crept into my mind: the impatience that waited at the other end of the line, the empty feeling of messages left unreturned."[7]

Especially at the beginning, I found myself constantly comparing my own experiences to Obama's experiences as a community organizer in Chicago. Like Obama, I had graduated from an Ivy League university but had always felt like an outsider peering into the stained glass windows of Yale

University's august classroom buildings, structures that could have been castles in old Europe, and the library that more closely resembled a cathedral than a book depository. Like Obama, I had a grandfather who had spent much of his life in the insurance business, trying to turn a buck so that his children and his grandchildren would be able to attend the best schools in the world and have opportunities in life that he never had. And like Obama, I became an organizer in my mid-twenties for the "promise of redemption,"[8] in addition to becoming a bit player in the revolutionary movement for change that is sweeping America.

Obama described his first foray into organizing as a "small disaster." After spending weeks working the phones, interviewing community members, and planning for a big meeting with the police, "only thirteen people showed up."[9] My first event in Virginia, a two-day phone bank at Cynthia's home office in Mathews, was worse. Only four people showed up—and that included me and Cynthia. On the second day of the phone bank, we had the same turnout, but this time Cynthia had to prepare for a conference and could not make telephone calls. My second event, a walking canvass leaving from a shopping center near Gloucester Courthouse, went much better. I ensured higher turnout by spending the better part of the week calling every known Democrat and progressive activist who lived within 20 miles. Thirteen people showed up. And in spite of sweltering heat that day, every single person went out to knock on doors.

Those 13 volunteers—Dianne, JP, Suzanne, Shannon, Joe, Arnold, Tina, Sylvia, Deloris, Diane, Anthony, Carl, and Larry—not only completed the first walking canvass in Gloucester's collective memory but also signed up to knock on more doors and make phone calls. That day, I learned how valuable volunteer recruitment and retention can be. That day, 13 people began to turn a red county in a red state blue for the first time in decades. And because 13 people committed to volunteering regularly in order to transform their community—their neighborhood, precinct, county, and state—something truly amazing started to happen. Neighbors and friends heard about the effort and decided to get involved. A small walking canvass became a regular Saturday canvass, which became a community movement for change. That is how community organizing works—and how the Obama Revolution began.

By taking to heart the mantra of the field campaign, "respect, empower, include," a small group of paid and unpaid organizers went out into the streets and the suburbs and started a movement powerful enough to overcome Senator John McCain and Governor Sarah Palin's television attack ads, robocalls, and smear tactics. Field organizers revived machine politics in the cities, but without the kickbacks of the old political machines. Field organizers registered young people to vote in record numbers, going from house to house and dormitory to dormitory. But where the campaign made the most surprising inroads was in rural Virginia, North Carolina, and Indiana. In states where acerbic talk show host Bill O'Reilly encouraged residents to cling to their guns and show the new generation of community organizers the door, community members started talking to their neighbors about how this country desperately needed change.

Howard Dean, after failing to win the Democratic nomination in 2004, encouraged progressive partisans to organize at the grassroots level, "running for office and taking power back into their own hands.... We can't do this alone,"[10] he reminded activists. He was right. If I had driven to Virginia, knocked on a few doors, and made a few phone calls without trying to build relationships with local Democrats, my efforts would not have changed many minds in Mathews County or sparked a groundswell of Obama volunteerism in Gloucester. Instead, I started reaching out to the community, and community members started reaching back. When I arrived, I had no office, no cell phone, and an outdated list of Democratic committee chairs. Within two weeks, I had organized a phone bank, launched the first canvass in Gloucester County, and opened an office in Gloucester Point in partnership with a field organizer named BJ.

The Gloucester-Mathews *Gazette-Journal* reported that it was "the first time that the Democratic Party of Virginia [had] opened a field office on the Middle Peninsula during a presidential campaign." The "large crowd that gathered for the ceremony" included Democratic activists and committee members from four counties. They all signed up to volunteer.

CHANGING THE RULES OF THE GROUND GAME

"So let us begin," Barack Obama told the assembly of thousands who braved the cold at the freshman senator's official presidential launch. "Let us begin this hard work together. Let us transform this nation."[11] Obama's reliance on community organizing to win elections goes back to the earliest days of the campaign, when pollsters predicted that he would lose "71% to 26%"[12] to front-runner Hillary Clinton. Through Obama's incredible Web site, the campaign invited supporters in some states to attend "Camp Obama."[13] Camp Obama consisted of multi-day training sessions for people young at heart and eager to join the campaign before the campaign had opened many offices or hired many organizers. The campaign created the Obama Organizing Fellows program to serve similar objectives, mobilizing thousands of volunteers—mostly under the age of 30—to pack their bags and move to the nearest battleground state.

Shooting for the viral model of popularity discussed by Malcolm Gladwell in *The Tipping Point* and *Outliers*, best-selling books that explain why certain ideas, people, and movements become wildly successful while others languish in oblivion,[14] the Obama campaign sought to drum up business among those most excited about the campaign and eager to volunteer for a candidate who had hardly begun to fight. Camp Obama and the Obama Organizing Fellows program drew in budding community organizers who saw in Obama the next John F. Kennedy or Franklin Delano Roosevelt. BJ, the organizer who worked out of my office in Gloucester and who expertly managed area operations after I left to serve as political director for congressional candidate Bill Day, got his start at Camp Obama in California. Similarly, I started working for the campaign as an Obama Organizing Fellow, vetted and trained in Harrisburg, Pennsylvania.

Sustained from the beginning through November 4, 2008, the Obama campaign's intensive focus on grassroots organizing and direct voter contact paved the way for Obama's extraordinary victory on Election Day. Drawing on the systematic, political science research of professors Donald Green and Alan Gerber at Yale University, the Obama campaign emphasized direct voter contact as the most effective method of campaigning. The Obama campaign office in Fredericksburg even posted a flyer highlighting Green and

Gerber's conclusion that "contacting six households per hour produces one additional vote every 107 minutes." Likewise, volunteer phone banks have long been viewed as a useful part of get-out-the-vote efforts but rarely a central element of national campaigns—until Obama changed the rules. With Green and Gerber pointing to a study that found that "one vote was generated for every twenty-two contacts,"[15] the Obama campaign made a point of complementing door-to-door effort with phone calling.

Obama's experiences as an organizer in Chicago with the Developing Communities Project undoubtedly shaped the field plan for the campaign. Inheriting the received wisdom of "Saul Alinsky, a Chicago native regarded as the father of community organizing,"[16] the Obama campaign sought to incorporate Alinsky's elaborately conceived and controlled methods on a much larger scale. In Obama's personal organizing, "the roles of the residents were scripted and the organizer was a quiet, inconspicuous presence."[17] In Obama's campaign, nearly everything was developed centrally and scripted for organizers and local volunteers to follow. Although the sheer volume of training manuals, scripts, and reports was often intimidating to people on the outside looking in, organizers did an impressive job explaining the fundamental, numerical objectives to volunteers. Only reporters were not allowed in—they had to call Chicago.[18]

Saul Alinsky's ideology—which, incidentally, Clinton studied as a senior at Wellesley—emphasized "a belief that if people have the power to act in the long run, they will, most of the time, reach the right decisions." Best-selling author David Sirota explained that "the belief that people—not dictators, not elites, not a group of gurus—should be empowered to organize and decide their destiny for themselves seems so simple, and yet is far and away the most radical idea in human history."[19] This is not a new idea. It is not even an untested idea. It is just a largely untried idea. Howard Dean attempted to create a campaign based on empowering idealistic young voters, bloggers, and volunteers to work locally to win globally, but he failed to garner a broad-based following among the kinds of voters who have historically decided most elections. John Kerry never espoused a belief in community organizing, relying instead on the largesse of law firms, labor union field operations, and last-minute get-out-the-vote endeavors.

What made the Obama campaign radically different from so many other large institutions, oversized bureaucracies, and activist organizations was the dedication, at least in theory, to the goals of sustainable community organizing—respecting, empowering, including—rather than the top-down, one-size-fits-all management style that has permeated far too many campaigns. Although the Obama campaign's centrally directed outreach effort sometimes fostered resentment from local committee members and activists who felt that the folks in Chicago did not appreciate their efforts over the years to organize traditionally Republican areas, the underlying philosophy of the campaign cannot be questioned. The Obama campaign turned that philosophy of community empowerment into a volunteer-driven organization dedicated to reaching out to every person in America without regard to race, religion, or political affiliation.

Hardened journalists, normally not given to excessive accolades, agreed after the election that "the story of Mr. Obama's journey to the pinnacle of American politics is the story of a campaign that was, even in the view of many rivals, almost flawless."[20] It is the story of a campaign that continuously focused on the fundamentals while never losing sight of the overriding organizational philosophy of outreach and inclusion. Nearly a year after announcing his candidacy, Obama won the Iowa caucuses in the first big test of community organizing as the primary method of campaigning. That night he "delivered what even skeptics called one of the great political sermons of our time," a speech that mocked those who "said this country was too divided, too disillusioned to ever come together again around a common purpose. But on this January night—at this defining moment in history—you have done what the cynics said we couldn't do."[21]

Winning the Iowa caucuses in spite of the long odds put Obama on the map and generated enormous momentum for his campaign. Obama's disappointing and unexpected loss in New Hampshire, however, did not kill the feeling of hope that brought in even more millions of dollars and thousands of volunteers after Iowa. One analyst concluded that "while Iowa's momentum is measured traditionally, a portion of Iowa's extra jolt of technological momentum has an impact New Hampshire cannot stifle."[22] In other words, the loss in New Hampshire did not kill the party because the gains from Iowa were already flowing past New Hampshire, to swing states and beyond. In an intriguing way, that is one reason why nearly all of the field directors, deputy field directors, and regional field directors assigned to the critical swing states started as field organizers in Iowa and worked their way up the totem pole by state-hopping in later primaries.

Returning to the ground game, it was clear well before the general election that the Obama campaign was not going to play by the usual rules of presidential combat. The campaign refused to focus exclusively on the early primary states and refused to stay out of the traditionally Republican states in the general election. The campaign refused to relinquish control over field operations to outside consultants and pollsters and refused to turn over field operations to the pre-existing Democratic Party power players. The campaign refused to accept only traditional Democratic voters and refused to ignore the hopes and dreams of a generation of young people exuberant about the prospect of broad changes in what passes for representative democracy in Washington. In so doing, the Obama campaign changed the rules of the ground game and set a precedent in presidential politics that will be remembered for years to come.

Essential to Obama's version of the ground game was the constant pressure on everyone working for the campaign to knock on more doors, make more telephone calls, register more voters, and report numbers to superiors more and more frequently. Although the level of oversight from Chicago could be nearly suffocating at times, it certainly kept organizers motivated and volunteers on task. Focused on strategically employing tactics to hit specific goals—such as 10 voters registered, 50 calls made per person, or 25 doors knocked—the campaign's field plan called for "mobilizing resources through specific tactics to achieve an outcome that builds towards a larger goal." In what the Democratic Party of Virginia defined as the rural Tidewater region of Virginia, for instance, there were 150,837 registered voters, 112,987 of whom the campaign expected to vote. To get a majority, we needed to win 56,494 of those votes.

Of course, a simple majority of expected voters in the region would not have been a workable goal because it ignored the number of voters that the campaign hoped to register, the boost in voter turnout that the campaign expected would be generated by Obama's presence in the race alone, and the Democratic base present in the region. Some counties and some precincts were not likely to go for Obama no matter how much direct voter contact we did. In those areas, the goal was not necessarily to win a majority of expected voters but to win enough votes to allow the next larger jurisdiction—county, region, or state—to go for Obama. In this way, no precinct, county, or region was excluded from the ground game. Local organizers had to organize every precinct in order to have a shot at winning in every county, region, and state. Rather than hopeless turf, Republican areas presented the chance to win Republican voters to Obama's side.

Changing the rules of the ground game, moreover, meant steadily building toward Election Day by starting with local relationships and infrastructure, building capacity, absorbing and deploying volunteers, identifying and persuading voters, and finally getting voters out to the polls. From this perspective, "strategy trumps resources" and "organization trumps random action."[23] The Obama campaign did not want to leave anything to chance. The general election calendar for each state specified when organizers would meet with volunteers, when new offices would open, when new organizers would arrive, when the campaign would push voter registration above everything else, and when get-out-the-vote efforts would begin. Significantly, the training and planning manuals for each state said almost exactly the same thing, with changes in vote goals to reflect local numbers and changes in dates to reflect local events of interest.

One of the most widely repeated mantras of field organizers on the campaign was that while we could always raise more money and recruit more volunteers, we could not recoup our time. The greatest nonrenewable resource of the campaign, time represented a clock ticking down to Election Day. Maximizing the efficiency of volunteer recruitment, training, and retention was therefore critical to building the largest and most effective volunteer army in presidential history. Every time a staff organizer or volunteer picked up a telephone or knocked on a door to speak with a voter or potential voter, the campaign wanted to know that the staff organizer or volunteer would close the deal—whether that meant identifying the person's preferences, persuading an occasional voter to vote, or scheduling someone to volunteer.

In short, the 2008 presidential election changed the method and style of presidential campaigning forever through effective community organizing. The Obama campaign took advantage of early interest by giving thousands of local organizers a chance to make history. By renewing interest in registering voters, recruiting volunteers, and persuading voters to make a point of exercising their right to vote, the Obama campaign rewrote the rules of the ground game.

WINNING RED, WINNING RURAL

There is a warm rotund man named Perry Mason who lives on one of the rural routes in Mathews, Virginia, and who voted for Barack Obama. In fact, for the first time ever, he voted right down the Democratic ticket in 2008. A lifelong Republican, Perry finally got fed up with the Republican Party's slide away from working class Americans and into the pockets of Big Business and Big Oil. "We've been forgotten," he told me one sunny afternoon when I arrived, clipboard and walk-list in hand. "The working class has been put aside, the jobs are gone." Lounging in a lawn chair while a pig roasted on a spit, and fried apples steamed on a pan, Perry reminded me that the Republican Party used to be the party of balanced budgets and small government. Sure, he had a Confederate flag on his pickup truck, but he had nothing against black people. Before I left, he put up three Obama signs in his yard—and wanted more.

Meeting Perry and others like him helped me to understand that in the 2008 presidential race, a significant number of white Americans who might have been tagged as racist in the past—and held up for public ridicule as backwards, or worse—voted for Barack Obama when their country was on the line. What I found, in driving a thousand miles a week on the rural routes of the Middle Peninsula and Northern Neck, was that there were a lot of white people "whose distrust of black people in general crumbles when they actually get to know specific black people, including a presidential candidate who extends a genuine helping hand in a time of national crisis."[24] All the right-wing pundits who harped on racial animosity as a reason why Obama would definitely, absolutely, positively not win forgot that overt racism is less popular today than at any time in American history. If anything, there might have been a "reverse Bradley effect—Obama's primary vote totals more often exceeded those in the final polls than not."[25]

One reason why interest in Obama surged across America, from the deep blue states in New England to the traditionally solid red regions of rural Virginia and Appalachia, was because an extraordinarily high number of African Americans volunteered their time at campaign offices, registered to vote, and turned out to vote. Over half a million people voted by absentee ballot in Virginia alone, an indication that supporters wanted to do everything possible to ensure that their ballots were cast and counted. Similarly, lines snaked around polling places at six o'clock in the morning on Election Day, with large numbers of African-American voters going out of their way to vote early. In my region, some of the most dedicated volunteers happened to be African Americans, including Dianne, a local teacher who ran the field office on Election Day; Larry, who put four-foot by eight-foot Obama-Biden signs on the highway; and Debbie, who registered scores of people to vote.

Another reason why Obama won the ground war so decisively was because McCain faced stiff competition in areas where the Democratic Party had traditionally conceded to the Republican Party without a fight. Overall, exit polls showed that McCain emerged from the campaign with only 53% of the votes in America's rural areas, compared to Obama's 45%.[26] In closing the gap, Obama disproved some of the oldest myths about rural Americans. He also demonstrated that politics does not have to be about race; it can be about issues, or rhetoric, or judgment. Although there were times when voters asked to identify themselves would say, "Barack Obama is not fit to be president in a white man's world," twice that number disparaged McCain and his surrogates for playing the race card again and again. As long as Obama could get his message across—without it being distorted on the nightly news or in fear-mongering robocalls—we knew that we would win on hope and change. We also knew that we had to be Obama's messengers.

Due to the difficulties of canvassing in counties such as Mathews, I formulated and implemented a rural action plan to complement general directives coming down the pipeline from Richmond and Chicago. Ultimately deployed in rural areas across Virginia, the rural action program was a comprehensive voter outreach effort designed to overcome the challenges posed by low population density and a lack of urban centers. By building on community networks, relying on volunteers to call their neighbors, and supplementing traditional phone banking with phone calling from home, the rural action program both expanded the base and built volunteer capacity in preparation for get-out-the-vote efforts. Fundamental to the rural action program were the basic principles of empowering, respecting, and including local Democratic activists and volunteers for the Coordinated Campaign—a joint campaign for Democratic candidates in Virginia—and the Campaign for Change. By working in cooperation with local Democratic committee chairs, the rural action program prompted precinct captains and precinct teams to lead efforts in their respective precincts.

From August through November, a group of 12 interns from the College of William and Mary and two interns from Rappahannock Community College assisted me in implementing the rural action plan in all 11 counties in the region. Systematically calling through lists of Democrats, activists, and potential volunteers, the interns successfully recruited local volunteers to fill three-hour shifts between the hours of four o'clock and nine o'clock every weekday evening. Those volunteers, in turn, made over 25,000 calls to prospective voters, identifying their preferences and nudging them toward Barack Obama, the first name on the ballot. Volunteers who preferred canvassing knocked on several thousand doors, primarily on weekends. Molly, a student intern for the campaign, told William and Mary's student newspaper that "we hear about the decline of interest in politics, but these organizations reverse that."[27]

Tyler, another intern and college freshman, described his experience as an intern for the Democratic Party of Virginia as both challenging and rewarding. "I volunteer just my open time and use the rest of the time to complete my school work, though it does occasionally lead to conflicts. I compensate by staying up later, but I'm willing to do this in order to help my community."[28] Like the other interns, Tyler felt like he was part of something larger and more important than himself. He connected the campaign's goal of building communities across America with his own personal experiences entering data, knocking on doors, and recruiting volunteers for Obama. Tyler told me after the election that he was "proud to have been a part of it.... I think [Obama's] victory is the start of a new style of politics, and the end of the 'old boy' system. He knows he has the loyalty of the people and the momentum to jump-start things here at home."

In order to recruit more volunteers and retain the volunteers who came out every week, or even every day, BJ and I hosted debate-watch parties at the office for each of the presidential debates and the vice presidential debate. Before the final debate, congressional candidate Bill Day spoke to a crowd that spilled out onto the sidewalk by the front door. Inside the office, chairs of all shapes and sizes covered every inch of floor space and home-cooked food piled up on a table along one wall. The owner of a sandwich shop franchise in Gloucester, a soft-spoken young man named Michael, catered the event, donating hundreds of dollars to the party because, as he put it, it was "time for a change." Representative of the rural communities in Gloucester and Mathews, the final debate party—the only debate party hosted at a Democratic campaign office in Virginia that night—brought together volunteers black and white, working poor and middle class, Christian and Jewish. Squeezed into the office, I felt a little pride—here, in one room, were the great-grandchildren of slaves and the great-grandchildren of slave owners.

From coast to coast, the Obama campaign spurred Americans to organize. Obama called on his fellow Americans to begin the hard work of transforming a nation into something better. And the volunteers poured into Obama offices in states like Virginia, dedicated to winning red and winning rural. Even Perry came into the office to make some calls and to change the world.

THE POWER OF COMMUNITY ORGANIZING

Reaching out into traditionally Republican areas, Obama field organizers and volunteers traversed rural Virginia and the Appalachian mountains looking for sympathetic and persuadable voters. Unlike McCain and Palin, they believed in the power of community organizing to change the world. They believed that every knock and every call meant something to the people with whom they spoke and that every vote won had the potential to put Obama over the edge. In traditionally red states that were trending blue for the first time in 44 years, predictions of a historic victory played out on November 4, 2008, when Obama won Virginia by seven percentage points and even eked out a victory in North Carolina. For community organizers everywhere, it was a night to remember, a night that made all those 18-hour days, endless call lists, and incomprehensible canvassing maps worth it. Obama won.

But the regional field directors, field organizers, committee members, and precinct captains did not commit months of their lives to the cause just for one election. They wanted to turn Virginia blue for the 44th president for the first time in 44 years so that they would be able to tell their children and grandchildren that they helped to turn the tide where it mattered most. They wanted the communities where they organized to be a little better after the election than they were before—more respected, more included, more empowered—and to remember a time when people of all colors and creeds came together, sat at the same table to call their neighbors, and walked together from house to house, door to door. The Obama Revolution includes all of the people who fought for change so tirelessly, persistently, and without fail.

Through community organizing, the Obama campaign contacted people like Perry and had the opportunity to ask them what they saw in that lanky lawyer from Illinois. The campaign promulgated the methodology developed by Saul Alinsky and Obama in Chicago decades ago. Knowing that communities needed to be connected to one another and to their own members, the model of community organizing focused on the belief that the people will rise up and demand accountability from Washington and democracy for all. In rural Virginia, organizers, interns, and volunteers made tens of thousands of phone calls in order to identify the strong Obama supporters, the leaning Obama supporters, those neutral or undecided, those leaning toward McCain and those strongly supporting McCain. What the volunteers who brought furniture for the office, food for fellow volunteers, and hope for the future had in common was a shared belief in the power of the people to seek and achieve change. Building communities is not easy.

Like my uncle Billy in Boone, my aunt Emily in Durham, and my cousin Amber in Los Angeles, the volunteers in rural Virginia understood the need to build communities of hope by learning about people's concerns. The organizers understood the need in rural and urban areas alike to establish an office or a street corner where people could gather to talk about the change they wanted to see in the world, the change that the nation needs. And the organizers understood the need to empower community members to become leaders in their own right, recruiting more volunteers to the cause and running campaign operations with an eye toward the future. Obama's energetic outlook brought all sorts of new people into the political process, giving people reasons to be hopeful again. From organizing communities to changing the rules of the ground game to winning red and winning rural, organizers and volunteers brought Obama's message to even the most rural parts of the country, proving that the real America is also Obama's America.

CHAPTER FIVE

GENERATION CHANGE

Less than an hour apart, Senator Hillary Clinton and Senator Barack Obama rallied 6,000 screaming supporters at the Democratic Party of Virginia's annual Jefferson Jackson Dinner in Richmond on Saturday, February 9, 2008. Competing neck and neck for the Democratic nomination, the leading candidates addressed the assembled throng of legislators and political activists from the same podium in a final swing through the state before the primary.

"With Senator McCain as the likely Republican nominee, the Republicans have chosen more of the same," Clinton said, directing her wrath toward President George W. Bush and Senator John McCain. "I am so ready to see Virginia in the winning column in November." But the former first lady irritated some Obama fans when she used the word "audacious" to describe the suffragettes who fought for women's rights at Seneca Falls in the late 19th century. "No she did not," one young African-American woman said, visibly shocked that Clinton would reference the title of Obama's best-selling book, *The Audacity of Hope*.[1]

With 10-foot tall "OBAMA" paper letters dangling from the bleachers reserved for members of the public, the strong-lunged junior senator from Illinois countered Clinton's jabs by heralding his wins that day in Nebraska, Washington, and Louisiana. "We won north, we won south, we won in between, and I believe we can win in Virginia," Obama said. "There is a reason why the last six polls in a row showed I'm the strongest nominee against John McCain."[2]

Obama also responded to Clinton's criticism that he was too idealistic and too inexperienced to manage the country from the highest office in the land, saying that "there's a moment when [the] spirit of hopefulness has to come through.... It's true I talk about hope a lot—I have to," he said. "The odds of me being here are not very high." Pointing to the crowd, which included national and state officials seated at banquet tables and thousands of young people jammed into bleacher seats high above the stage, Obama reiterated that change was coming.[3]

Like the rest of the country, the sold-out crowd at Virginia Commonwealth University's Alltel Pavilion appeared nearly evenly divided, although Obama's supporters certainly seemed younger and more vociferous in support of their candidate. Chants of "Yes, we can," one of Obama's slogans, interrupted the speeches repeatedly, and hundreds of teenagers and college students rushed the barricades in front of the stage in an effort to shake hands with Obama. Whereas Clinton posed for photographs, Obama seemed nonplussed by all of the attention.

Student volunteers from the University of Virginia ran the coat check as legislators, aides, and a host of lobbyists poured through the metal detectors into the ballrooms for cocktails before the speeches. Ben Schultz, a junior at the College of William and Mary, said that it was a "rare opportunity" to see Clinton and Obama speak the same night. An Obama supporter, Shultz summed up the general sense that the youthful energy heralded a new generation of political activism. "It's important for young people to be involved in the political process," he said.

Delegate Brian Moran, chairman of the Democratic caucus in the House of Delegates, said that he had never seen so many people come out for the annual dinner. Although Virginia became a battleground primary and swing state for the first time in 2008, Moran said that "there was some belief that we wouldn't play the role that we're playing.... We've never had anything this large," Moran said, adding that the sheer level of excitement boded well for Barack Obama.

State Senator John Edwards, a natural fan of former Senator John Edwards of North Carolina, joked about how he would show his support for his new choice for president. "After Edwards dropped out," he said, "I decided I was going to change my name to Obama."[4]

EXPANDING THE VOTER ROLLS

"No, man. I don't have time." The young man, mildly irritated, waved me off. "Come on, it only takes thirty seconds," I shot back, pulling out all the stops. "Your vote can make Barack Obama the next president." Angling my clipboard with the half-page voter registration form toward the man, I waited. A few seconds later, the short-haired African-American man reached for my pen and wrote his name on the form. "Don't forget your social security," I said. "The elections bureau won't process your registration without it." Less than a minute later, the man signed his name and started walking away. I thanked him and told him to check his mail in a couple weeks for his voter registration card. "By the way," I followed up, "do you know anyone else who might want to register?" He pointed to a house across the street and a particular door. I thanked him again and headed toward the house, eager to register another new voter.

In a scene that played out millions of times across the country, my successful effort to register a new voter in the Allison Hill section of Harrisburg, Pennsylvania, was part of the biggest voter registration drive in recent presidential history. A central element of the Obama campaign's strategic vision, "a massive voter registration effort which helped to increase the overall number of registered Democrats, including large numbers of blacks," gave Obama the boost he needed to overcome hesitancy among older voters—especially southern white voters—to fill in the oval corresponding to the first black presidential nominee of a major party.[5] Led by an impressive team of field organizers dedicated to rapidly expanding the voter rolls, especially in low-income, minority neighborhoods, interns and volunteers changed the face of American politics forever and made a name for a generation coming of age—Generation Change.

Ultimately turning out for Obama by a margin of more than two to one, Americans between the ages of 18 and 29 not only voted in record numbers but also mobilized people young and old to support a candidate who defied expectations.[6] By registering record numbers of young people, African Americans, and Latinos to vote, the Democratic Party and the Obama campaign were able to "flip" many counties from having a Republican majority to having a Democratic majority, first by registration and then by getting out the vote. Seniors in many high schools and students on many college campuses also registered to vote in record numbers, pursuing their right to vote in spite of challenges from local registrars afraid that student voters would dilute the strength of older local populations. In some localities, such as Williamsburg, Virginia, students—including my friend Aaron Garrett—successfully sued voter registrars in order to win the right to vote locally.

In Gloucester, Virginia, the voter registrar nearly brought the full weight of the Obama campaign's legal team against her after she arbitrarily questioned dozens of voter registrations personally collected by Debbie, an extremely kind-hearted, middle-aged black woman who volunteered regularly at my field office. Debbie had devoted many tanks of gasoline to crisscrossing the county in search of unregistered, eligible voters, keeping track of each new registrant in a worn, spiral notebook that she carried with her at all times. Debbie was known around town as a boisterous and generous advocate for Barack Obama, frequently bringing baskets of food and juice boxes to the office to support the hungry staffers and volunteers. So when the registrar, who happened to be white, challenged Debbie's new registrations, most of which came from residents who happened to be black, we knew that the situation could easily get out of hand. Fortunately, the registrar ultimately backed down and Debbie's new voters had their voices heard at the polls on Election Day.

Like Debbie, most of my new voter registrations came from young African Americans, one of the largest segments of new registrants in the country. At the end of the day, a whopping 95 percent of black voters between the ages of 18 and 29 supported Obama, compared to 69 percent of first time voters and 53 percent of the general population.[7] Consequently, it did not come as that much of a shock on Election Day when the four counties in my region in rural Virginia that went Democratic for the first time in over a decade turned out to be four of the six counties in my assigned territory where the black population exceeds 25 percent.[8] Nationally, those counties where the black population exceeds 25 percent produced more than one-sixth of Obama's total votes, demonstrating the awesome electoral power of the black community when voting for the same candidate.[9]

First time voters, moreover, made up 11 percent of the electorate, casting nearly 14 million votes—mostly for Obama.[10] Voting for the Democratic nominee for president in greater proportion in 2008 than at any time in the past two decades, the newly registered and newly energized voters overwhelmed election bureaus not accustomed to massive numbers of new registrants.[11] "It's kind of incredible,"[12] Harry A. VanSickle, the Pennsylvania elections commissioner, told the *New York Times* a month before the Keystone State's primary. "We've told [election officials in local counties], whatever [turnout] you're expecting [on Election Day], increase it by 30 or 40 percent."[13] In the months leading up to the April 22 primary, both Barack Obama's organizers and Hillary Clinton's field workers worked hard to register new voters. The two campaigns registered 120,000 new voters in Pennsylvania during the first three months of 2008, and convinced 86,000 others to become Democrats. Only 12,000 Democrats reregistered as Republicans.[14]

During my sojourn as an Obama Organizing Fellow in Harrisburg, the Obama campaign team—composed at that point of one regional field director, four Fellows, two full-time interns, and hundreds of volunteers—flipped Dauphin County by registering thousands of new voters in a relatively short period of time. In order to turn Dauphin County Democratic for the first time since the Civil War,[15] the Obama campaign used street fairs, music festivals, and other community events, as opportunities to reach out to young, African-American, and Latino residents. Although the local Democratic committee and the Democratic Party of Pennsylvania had conducted voter registration drives in the past, no recent voter registration effort compared to the Obama campaign's intensive and sustained push to expand the voter rolls. By late June, "there were 81,489 Democrats and 81,340 Republicans in Dauphin County."[16]

Armed with the knowledge that newly registered voters were far more likely to vote for Senator Obama than Senator McCain on November 4, 2008, organizers and volunteers fanned out across all fifty states as part of the Vote for Change registration and mobilization drive. Registering millions of new voters, the Obama campaign's voter registration efforts swung the election in many counties and states. The number of newly registered voters in Virginia, for instance, exceeded Obama's margin of victory. In Dauphin County, Pennsylvania, Obama won by a little more than 11,000 votes, reversing the margin by which Bush beat Senator John Kerry in 2004.[17] Many of those votes came from first time voters who campaigners had accosted at bus stops, train stations, and other transportation hubs, and community events, encouraging them to register. Significantly, the gains made by the Obama campaign will not disappear anytime soon.

One of my Dauphin County colleagues nicknamed me "the god of voter registration," but there was really nothing magical about my techniques. I simply walked around the city of Harrisburg until I found new voters to register. The key to registering voters in both urban and rural settings is to go where few organizers and activists have gone before. Of course, high density residential areas and high traffic commercial areas often yield more registrations than isolated houses and empty parking lots. One of the Obama field staff manuals provided some basic pointers: "Be creative. Don't be discouraged by the need for trial and error. One thing is clear about voter registration drives—while there are certainly best practices to follow, there are few activities that will always be successful in every community across the country; there are also few activities that will never be successful. It often requires a bit of trial and error in a state or a specific community to discover what works well and what doesn't."[18]

Following the Obama manual's "obvious (but important) goal of registering likely Obama voters who would not otherwise register to vote," I focused on low-income and predominantly African-American or Hispanic neighborhoods. Almost every afternoon during the summer of 2008, I grabbed a clipboard, a stack of voter registration forms, a couple of pens, a few "Obama '08" stickers—which featured the much-lauded Obama 'O'[19]—and walked or drove to a housing project, a street of row houses, a park, a bar, or a mall. Sometimes with a partner but often alone, I walked the streets, approaching 18-year-olds hanging out with their friends, middle-aged immigrants on their front stoops, and elderly African Americans watching the evening news programs on televisions that glowed blue after the sun went down. Sometimes, I would get lucky and make a friend who would show me around the neighborhood.

On one afternoon, I met Nikita, an African-American woman who was probably in her thirties, who registered to vote after I climbed a rickety wood staircase to her upstairs apartment. Wedged between dozens of other apartments with their own rickety wood staircases, the young woman's apartment had a narrow balcony where an elderly woman sat on a metal folding chair watching the woman's two young children play tag. Every so often, the elderly woman—who I later found out was the children's maternal grandmother— cautioned the children to stay back from the edge of the balcony, which had a guardrail but only a couple of crossbeams. Reminded of the tiny, sixth floor Upper West Side balcony in Manhattan where my own maternal grandmother used to grow African violets, the Uptown Harrisburg balcony had that same allure of being at once dangerous and homey. After registering the grandmother, who had lived long enough to remember being told to sit at the back of the bus, I registered Nikita to vote and asked her if any of her neighbors might want to register as well, hoping to find more Obama supporters.

Sporting the Obama sticker I had handed her when she finished signing the registration form, Nikita took me from door to door, and we entered each house or apartment and spoke briefly with the occupants. Half a dozen of the neighbors, Nikita told me, were related to her and inevitably signed up to vote after discerning that I worked for Obama. Teaching me the virtue of persistence, the young woman hounded her father, her aunt and uncle, her cousins, and her niece, until they either registered or reregistered, depending on whether they had never registered before or had registered before but had recently moved to Harrisburg. The newly registered residents of Harrisburg then inquired as to what a young, white man in dress pants and a button-down shirt was doing in that part of town. Young white college graduates, it turned out, rarely stopped in that neighborhood—and certainly not on that block—even though the state capitol was less than two miles to the south.

Unlike Barack Obama, who complained that working in a lily-white company fresh out of Columbia University made him feel "like a spy behind enemy lines,"[20] my job as a 24-year-old community organizer in predominantly African-American and Hispanic neighborhoods made me feel included in the fabric of urban America in a way that most people of my skin color and upbringing never get to experience. But that is changing, just as the composition of the multinational corporations has probably changed to reflect the nation's rich cultural diversity and the shift away from the segregation embedded in America's history. And just as Obama found on the south side of Chicago, I discovered many residents at the top of rickety staircases who took "some measure of satisfaction"[21] in how they have survived, raised their children, and improved their communities—one vote at a time.

GETTING OUT THE VOTE

Field organizers and volunteers for Barack Obama and the Democratic Party not only went door to door in order to expand the voter rolls but also to convince registered voters to select Obama's name on their ballot and to remind them to vote on November 4, 2008. Remembering that until this election, some pundits and political scientists had called "today's youth...the 'know-nothing generation,'"[22] the young canvassers, phone callers, and data entry volunteers for the Obama campaign doubled and redoubled their efforts with each phase of the campaign—earning the moniker Generation Change. Turning voters out in extraordinary numbers, the youthful campaigners defied former Senator John Glenn's concerns "about the future when we have so many young people who feel apathetic and critical and cynical about anything having to do with politics."[23] They also met Al Gore's challenge in 2000 to "try to fight through that."[24]

The cynics and the statisticians recalled a Boston City Council election in 1989 in which Traci Hodgson, who was admittedly "not very familiar with the candidates running,"[25] was the only person who voted in her precinct and declaimed that "the political involvement of young people is at an all-time low."[26] Meanwhile, the Obama campaign looked to the future and saw an opportunity to turn out the most voters of any presidential race since 1968.[27] Relying primarily on young people to serve as organizers and interns, with middle-aged and older Americans making up the majority of neighborhood team leaders, precinct captains, and office managers, the campaign capitalized on the "correlation between the rise of major political movements and the surge of new voters into the electorate."[28] Recognizing that the only way to turn out all of the newly registered voters was to start a movement, Obama began a political revolution.

In rural Virginia, Obama organizers and volunteers won previously ignored counties one voter at a time. Suzanne Hood, a volunteer from Gloucester, related to me how tough it can be to turn out voters: "I was canvassing with Emily one Saturday in a neighborhood in Gloucester with a lot of apartments. We knocked on one woman's door, and she wasn't home, but by the time we finished other apartments in the area she was pulling into the driveway. She was a young black woman, and she was dressed in scrubs, having just come back from work. We introduced ourselves and asked the usual question about who she was planning on voting for in the Presidential race. She said that she didn't plan on voting and that she had never voted before. I asked if she was registered to vote and she said yes, but that someone had told her that her vote didn't really count so she had never bothered. She said she wasn't all that interested in politics."

Just when persuading the woman to vote seemed hopeless, Suzanne told me how she turned the situation around: "I told her why I believe it is important to vote—that I believe our votes really do matter, especially in a conservative place like Gloucester, where it is important for people to know that there are a number of different voices. She said she would think about it, and we bid her good day. When I went to vote, that woman was two people behind me in line! She remembered me, just as I remembered her. It was amazing to see that our canvassing had had an effect. She voted for the first time in her life because Obama's campaign believed that we should all be out there talking to each other, not just in big cities, not just in places where the vote was likely to be swayed Democratic, but in every county."

Spurred into action by knocks at the door, seemingly endless phone calls to voters who still had not made up their minds, and door hangers left in the wee hours of the morning on Election Day, Obama supporters turned out en masse, proving that Generation Change could live up to its name and deliver the change the country needed. Nearly a third of voters reported to Gallup a week before November 4th that they had either cast their ballots already or would do so before Election Day, allowing Obama to lock "in place a higher and higher percentage of votes tilting in his favor, making that portion of the overall electorate impervious to any last minute campaign trends."[29] Moreover, the early voting was "concentrated in the Western states, and to a lesser degree in the South,"[30] a disparity that permitted Obama to easily win Colorado, Nevada, and New Mexico, while spending more time in the final days in eastern pickup states: Virginia, Ohio, and Florida.

Because the campaign urged as many people as possible to vote early in states such as Georgia, or by absentee ballot in-person in states such as Virginia, long lines actually developed at many county or city election bureaus before Election Day proper. "Early-voting lines in Atlanta were 10 hours long," *Time* reported, "and still people waited, as though their vote was their most precious and personal possession at a moment when everything else seemed to be losing its value. You heard the same phrases everywhere. *First time ever. In my lifetime. Whatever it takes*" [emphasis in original].[31] Everyone wanted to ensure that their vote would count and be counted. No one wanted to miss out on what the campaign continually told them would be the most important election in their lifetime. Volunteers and local residents had all heard rumors that the predicted long lines at the polls might prevent some potential voters from voting, so folks showed up early, either before or on Election Day.

When I arrived with Bill Day and a stack of campaign literature at the Dare precinct in Yorktown, Virginia, at half past five in the morning on November 4, 2008, it was pouring. But there was already a line that snaked a hundred feet out from the entrance, doubled back and then twisted out toward the parking lot, where a hardy crew of partisans waited with sample ballots highlighting either the Democratic or Republican candidates. Most of the Virginians waiting to vote clutched umbrellas and talked quietly with spouses, neighbors, and friends. They frequently glanced toward the entrance, as if the double doors might slam shut at any instant. Deep in the heart of Republican territory,[32] Obama supporters—beaming with excitement at the prospect of turning Virginia blue for the first time since 1964—seemed to outnumber McCain supporters at that ungodly hour. So many Obama supporters arrived early, in fact, that by 10 o'clock, more than 50 percent of eligible Virginians had cast ballots,[33] out of a final statewide turnout of 74 percent.[34]

A fervent Obama supporter and elections official from Virginia Beach described in an e-mail to local volunteers how "we had many first time voters and, outside of the long lines at the beginning of the day, the rest of the day went smoothly. I know there were many out there who waited in line for a while and maybe even had to visit more than one precinct to vote (especially if you had moved and not updated your voter information) and I am glad that many persevered. It has been well worth it!" Students especially contributed to high turnout in many states, including Virginia. For example, students from the College of William and Mary loaded into school-sponsored vans and waited in lines two blocks long in order to vote. For those students, the ability to vote in Williamsburg was a major victory; 2008 was the first presidential election in which Williamsburg permitted students to vote locally. Even the city registrar was moved, attributing Obama's victory to Williamsburg's more than two thousand new student voters, the highest percentage of new registrants in the state.[35]

Aside from universal get-out-the-vote efforts, which emphasized increasingly frequent phone calls to those on the fence and knocks on the doors of those who had not voted in a long time, the campaign targeted young people, African Americans, and Latinos. Long before the general election, Obama's top lieutenants knew that "enthusiasm among black voters was so high...there was a chance that the campaign could help put into play states that no Democrat had won in decades: Indiana, North Carolina and Virginia."[36] The campaign's overseers also knew, however, that extraordinary registration efforts and turnout among African Americans might be necessary to overcome latent racism among the 29 percent of white Americans who, according to *Newsweek*, still believed that a black candidate could not get enough support from white voters to be elected president.[37] Such prognostications ultimately proved false, but the campaign could not be certain until the voters actually pulled the lever.

Latino voters, like African-American voters, supported Obama by an extremely wide margin, "despite idiotic and widespread pundit commentary [prior to the election] that insisted Latino voters wouldn't vote for an African-American candidate."[38] Voting for the candidate who represented a break with the politics of exclusion by a two-to-one margin, Latinos formed a symbolic "black/brown coalition"[39] with African Americans and "provided Obama with his victory margin—both in the popular vote and in the key swing states that flipped from red to blue."[40] A former staffer for Representative Dennis Kucinich's presidential campaigns and the director of Moving America Forward pointed out in a provocative analysis that substantial majorities of Latinos cast their ballots for Obama in California, Virginia, Illinois, Texas, and Arizona, and helped to flip Nevada, Colorado, New Mexico, Indiana, and Florida.[41]

Even though Bill Clinton won a slightly larger portion of the Latino vote when he ran for reelection, "helping the 1996 Democratic presidential candidate to carry Florida for the first time since 1976,"[42] Obama's ability to effectively garner the votes of most Latinos combined with his nearly unanimous support from African Americans suggest that "Latinos could be a leading edge of a long-term, center-left political realignment."[43] Because of the rapidly growing Hispanic population in the United States, there exists little doubt in the mind that "the rise of Latinos appears likely to help the Democrats considerably over the long term."[44] It is also intriguing to consider the similarities between the Obama campaign's organizing strategies and the organizing strategies of Cesar Chavez and the United Farm Workers movement. Obama even translated Chavez's "Si Se Puede" into his most famous slogan, "Yes We Can!"[45]

Americans polled immediately after the election agreed that Obama's extraordinary levels of support from African Americans and Latinos, coupled with Obama's landslide electoral vote victory, marked "either the most important advance for blacks in the past 100 years, or among the two or three most important such advances."[46] With nearly as many McCain voters as Obama voters viewing the election as a major milestone in America's racial history, more than two out of three Americans "say a solution to relations between blacks and whites will eventually be worked out, the highest value Gallup has measured on this question."[47] Obama handled the historic nature of his quest—as self-identified black son of an African and an American—beautifully throughout the campaign, always refocusing attention on his race to the historic nature of his quest as a leader of a political movement committed to hope and change.

The Obama campaign's highly structured efforts to get out the vote among all demographics, especially young people, African Americans, and Latinos, worked wonders, turning out all three traditionally Democratic, low turnout groups in numbers roughly proportional to the population of each demographic in the general population. Gradually shifting from registering voters at bus stops and during street festivals to knocking on a million doors every day in a single state during the final stages of the campaign, field organizers and volunteers demonstrated direct voter contact can be implemented on a national scale with great success. By rapidly and drastically expanding the Democratic Party's base and then turning out the expanded base in record numbers, the Obama campaign developed an all-encompassing strategy that reached out to as many Americans as possible in as direct a manner as possible.

Direct voter contact—the millions of door knocks, phone calls, door hanger placements, and sample ballots— from organizers and volunteers drew tens of millions of American voters into the political process, many for the first time. New voters received lots of attention from volunteers eager to increase turnout. But it was the volunteers who really made the movement.

VOLUNTEERS OF AMERICA

Young people signed up in record numbers to work for Barack Obama's presidential campaign as low-paid organizers and unpaid interns, forgoing school work, more lucrative employment opportunities, and the comfort of their own beds. Quitting jobs, taking leaves of absence from colleges, and saying goodbye to their friends and family, the organizers who formed the backbone of Obama's campaign for president sacrificed much in order to devote more than 100 hours per week to the campaign trail. At the same time, older folks eagerly volunteered to call their friends and neighbors, bring food for the office workers, manage the offices, knock on doors in every precinct, enter data, and put up more yard signs than the campaign had in stock.

Taking to heart the advice of Yohannes Abraham, Virginia field director and a classmate of mine from college, not to "wake up on November 5th wishing you had done more," the organizers, interns, and volunteers dug in their heels and did everything possible to win as many votes for Obama as possible. Eager to serve and to change the world, young people invested everything they had into the campaign—their time, their money, and their unyielding devotion—and created a new movement unprecedented in the history of presidential politics. Abraham frequently talked about how the organizers had to keep going, keep going, keep going, and he was right. Because of the strenuous nature of the campaign, it was easy to get sidetracked by personal hardships and distracted by instantly gratifying activities. Some of the best organizers in the field—including a supervisor and a coworker—suffered deaths in the family, but kept going.

Emily Hogge, an earnest, unemployed volunteer from Gloucester, recounted to me the poignant story of why, and for whom, she devoted her life to the campaign: "I was teaching in the Altgeld Gardens housing project in Chicago, the same place where Barack Obama got his start as a community organizer, when Obama announced his intention to run. All of my fourth graders were excited about his candidacy, but I remember one in particular who would stare at the newspaper clipping of the announcement, which was posted on our classroom wall. Keyonta was fascinated, and when I assigned my students the task of selecting a future occupation, he ignored the lure of pro-basketball player fame and said, 'I want to be Barack Obama.' One of the driving forces behind my initial support of Obama was that if he won, my former students would have an example of someone like them in the highest office in the nation."

Emily's personal story of connection and inspiration paralleled the stories I heard from dozens of organizers and hundreds of volunteers who felt drawn to Obama by his personal moral fortitude, his background as a community organizer in Chicago, and a sense that this man would prove to every American child who dreamed of becoming president that all things are possible in the United States. Emily witnessed in Keyonta's fascination and admiration for Obama "the first revolution—the internal one that comes from an awareness of self and self-worth."[48] She saw the rumblings of something to which Keyonta could aspire, not just for himself but for his community and his country. She recognized the budding temperament of a community organizer: the complete dedication of himself or herself to achieving a goal that will benefit those excluded from power. In that way, Obama's victory was just the beginning of the Obama Revolution.

Activated, networked, and mobilized by text messages to cell phones, an online networking site geared toward Generation Change, and incessant e-mail reminders from all levels of the campaign hierarchy, the youthful generation who filled the ranks of organizers, interns, and volunteers deployed the latest technology in innovative and exciting ways. As Joe Trippi, Howard Dean's 2004 presidential campaign manager put it, "what we're really in now is *the empowerment age*" [emphasis in original].[49] With the unlimited nature of the Internet, there really could be something for everyone, as the Obama campaign sought to prove. The campaign's main Web site, for instance, provided traditional content: position papers, biographies of the candidate and his spouse, upcoming events, and contact details. Employing the latest fundraising techniques, a splash page requesting donations preceded the main page, big red "DONATE NOW" buttons adorned the main page, and an "Obama Store" with campaign paraphernalia flooded the bottom of the main page.

Taking Obama's online presence to a much higher level, the campaign hired one of the co-founders of Facebook, the popular social networking site, to build "MyBO,"[50] a networking add-on to Obama's standard Web site.[51] With a functionality very similar to that of Facebook, MyBO offered supporters their own pages, friend and group connectivity, blog space, a way to fundraise for the campaign, a searchable calendar of global and local events, and an electronic method of calling voters in swing states or finding local doors to canvass. In conjunction with the creation of MyBO, Obama's Facebook profile registered "hundreds of thousands of 'friends' on the social networking site."[52] A prominent blogger enthusiastically described the phenomenon as part of "Obama's broad, wide, mainstream appeal, and he's bringing in new people...people who aren't necessarily political junkies who follow the blogs."[53] Instantly attracting volunteers, MyBO became a hub for external communication, internal coordination, and scheduling for the duration of the campaign.

For a candidate who was once criticized as a "candidate who lacked a long-term strategic view of the Web,"[54] the online revolution sparked by Obama and reported by students on *Scoop08* gave new meaning to "word-of-mouth, [which] in the Internet age embraces peer-to-peer contact through e-mail, blogging, text messaging, viral messaging as well as personal contact."[55] News of events spread swiftly and without the logistical nightmare of finding recipient addresses or a stamp for the envelope. Compared to telephone calls, MyBO, along with text messages and e-mails, reduced time demands and permitted distribution to many more recipients with much less effort. The campaign maintained control even as groups flourished and expanded. And by encouraging networking within Generation Change, the campaign promoted a dialogue between Americans that bodes well for the future of participatory democracy.

Most organizers on the Obama campaign came from somewhere outside their assigned turf and returned to some place they call "home" after the election, except for the high-level campaign staff members who joined the transition team in Chicago, angling for a plum job in the administration. On one of our occasional trips to the local watering hole in

Gloucester after a particularly strenuous week of organizing, BJ and I used to talk about the future—where we would go if we had the means, what we would do if we had the opportunity. BJ expressed interest in serving as a diplomat, an ambassador, or possibly secretary of state (a position, unfortunately, already taken). I, on the other hand, usually said that I would willingly serve in the civil rights wing of the Department of Justice, or possibly attorney general (again, unfortunately, already taken). Insomnia-induced, our dreams of grandeur remain ephemeral.

It is axiomatic that "most young people who participate in community organizing will not select this field as a career."[56] According to a couple of social workers, "a different perspective is in order: every youth who gets involved will benefit personally and also will become a more informed and active member of society."[57] Youth-led community organizing must focus on the community, not the organizer. The organizer will benefit from the experience of empowering others to mobilize and meet goals, but will likely leave to pursue other ventures before long. On the Obama campaign, that point of departure for most organizers was fixed in advance: November 4, 2008. The challenge of local communities across the nation is to pick up where the organizer's leadership left off, inspiring other community members to become organizers.

THE GENERATION THAT CHANGED

By recruiting a generation of young people and people young at heart to serve as organizers, interns, and volunteers, Barack Obama's presidential campaign unintentionally coined a term for a generation dedicated to changing the world— Generation Change. Through a 50-state voter registration drive called Vote for Change, the Obama campaign took the fight for voters to every street and every city. Recruiting and training thousands of potential field organizers through Camp Obama and the Obama Organizing Fellows program, the campaign challenged traditional notions of field organizing. Young staffers and interns led thousands of volunteers in voter registration efforts that yielded millions of newly registered voters across the nation. Mixing voter registration and outreach, the campaign created communities of hope.

Undertaking the most extensive get-out-the-vote operation in presidential history, the Obama campaign sought to turn out all the newly registered voters, in addition to base voters and persuadable voters, on November 4, 2008. Deploying a tightly controlled campaign staff, the Obama campaign set goals for door knocking and phone calling that numbered in the millions. The campaign also expected organizers to organize their own teams to the point of self-sufficiency by recruiting hundreds of volunteers each who could be groomed as team leaders and precinct captains. These dedicated campaigners registered voters, organized house parties, recruited neighborhood team leaders, groomed precinct captains, and culminated by directly contacting voters in order to win every vote.

Targeting youth voters for recruitment, African-American voters for mobilization, and Latino voters for activation, the Obama campaign developed an all-encompassing program of outreach that could focus on multiple specific audiences at the same time. Hiring a Facebook founder to design a social networking site to augment Obama's traditional Web site, the campaign recruited and mobilized people young and a little older through MyBO. After MyBO took on a life of its own, the campaign maximized its utility by deploying the site as its prime scheduling tool, for both field staff and volunteers. Combining high-tech communication and networking technologies with low-tech direct voter contact, the campaign registered and turned out one voter per contact, but millions in the aggregate.

Winning more votes than any presidential campaign in history, the Obama campaign mobilized a generation willing to fight relentlessly for change.

CHAPTER SIX

THE RHETORIC OF HOPE

A small but dedicated group of Barack Obama supporters from William and Mary piled into a car bound for Charlottesville late in the afternoon on October 29, 2007, hoping to catch a glimpse of Obama at the Pavilion. They got even more than they hoped for when Obama gave one of the most decisive speeches of the presidential campaign. Evoking the scene from the Barry Levinson film *Man of the Year* in which Robin Williams rapped at a political rally, the "Countdown to Change" rally had the trappings of a rock concert. Flashing lights swept the covered arena as speakers blasted Gnarls Barkley's "Crazy." Thousands of young people screamed when their hero emerged from the shadows with outstretched arms and pumping fists. And that was just the beginning.

Recognizing that Senator Hillary Clinton was leading Obama and John Edwards in the polls, Governor Tim Kaine introduced Obama as an underdog. "Underdogs win races," he said. "When you're the underdog, you work harder, you work smarter." Facing a rowdy crowd excited about the prospect of electing a Democratic president who would not be afraid to reject old backroom Democratic politics, if that is what it would take, Obama said that the next president would need to have "courage and conviction" and "judgment and character." Responding to Republican attacks, Obama called himself a "hope mongerer.... I stand guilty as charged," he said.[1]

Because the next president would have the tough job of bringing the country together after eight years of divisive fear mongering, Obama talked about how his campaign had brought together blacks and whites, Christians and Jews, Democrats and, um, Independents. After the laughter subsided, Obama pointed out that he had Republican supporters as well. "I know there are Republicans because they whisper to me and say, 'Barack, I support you.' I say, 'Thank you. But why are we whispering?'" Obama's jokes about his distant relation to Cheney, however, provoked the most laughter. "It doesn't help when you put my cousin Dick

Cheney in charge of energy policy. You know what they say, 'Everyone's got a black sheep in the family.'"[2]

Turning to more substantive matters, Obama drew loud applause when he denounced the Bush Administration's persistent disrespect for Constitutional rights and principles, as well as the ill-conceived war in Iraq. "You're tired of an Administration that treats the Constitution as an annoyance. Most of all, you're tired of a war that should never have been authorized, that is costing us billions, and that is not making us safer," he said. "We need to end the war [and to] start bringing the troops home," Obama declared, vigorously poking the air with his index finger. "It will be the first thing I'd do."[3]

Gathering momentum, Obama promised to combat AIDS in Africa, to stop the violence in Darfur, and to close the infamous military prison at Guantanamo Bay, Cuba. "We are not a nation that turns a blind eye to slaughter," he said to cheers and shouts of support. "And while we are at it, we are going to close Guantanamo...because we are not a nation that locks people up without charging them.... We need to break the fever of fear that has come to dominate our politics," he said, comparing the Bush Administration's frequent attempts to attack his patriotism to McCarthyism. We need to remember our nation's "roots in liberty and democracy and rule of law," he said, emphasizing that sometimes "righteous anger" leads to change.[4]

"Change in America doesn't happen from the top down, it happens from the bottom up," Obama said, striking a populist tone that aligned him more with Dennis Kucinich than with Hillary Clinton. "Are you fired up? Ready to go? Fired up? Ready to go? Fired up? Ready to go?"[5]

After Obama's energetic call and response, the rally ended as it began, with a screaming crowd, pumping fists, and flashing lights. Secret service agents formed a wall in front of Obama as he waved, blew kisses to his adoring fans, and left the stage.

PULLING ON THE HOPE STRINGS

It is impossible to fully understand how Barack Obama journeyed from Chicago to Washington, from the Altgeld Gardens housing project to the White House, without understanding Obama's rhetoric of hope. From the earliest days of the campaign, Obama had a propensity for instilling in his listeners a sense that they were part of something great, something larger than themselves. The emotional appeal of Obama's positive rhetoric and eloquence, which always focused on inclusion, inspired millions to turn off the television and attend political rallies that often seemed more like religious revivals. Turning the dreams of citizens across the land into the rhetoric of hope, Obama reframed the debate in terms of the possibilities for change. By encouraging the nation's hopes for a political change and equating that change with himself and his campaign, Obama transcended the usual mudslinging and pulled on the nation's hope strings.

Describing his 2004 primary race for the United States Senate, Obama noted that he had been behind in the polls in January but that "for whatever reason, at some point my campaign began to generate that mysterious elusive quality of momentum, of buzz." Although Obama never actually came out and explained what permitted the "dark-horse" candidate to jump to first place, despite being outspent by a factor of six to one, the most obvious factor was the young Chicago lawyer's ability to inspire his listeners with his silver tongue. By way of negative explanation, he offered that "money can't guarantee victory—it can't buy passion, charisma, or the ability to tell a story."[6] Passion, charisma, and the ability to tell a story—these three characteristics of highly successful candidates have long cut across campaigns of all sorts, from city councilman to president of every nation on earth. These are keys to the kingdom.

Because most people like people who can get them excited, get them stamping their feet, get them clapping their hands, Obama had an instantaneous advantage going into his race for Senate against a candidate whose greatest strength appeared to be "the frightening efficiency with which his crews of paid volunteers could yank up everybody else's yard signs and replace them with [his] yard signs in the span of a single evening." It was during this campaign, Obama recalled, that he internalized the maxim that "signs don't vote," a maxim that the Obama campaign repeated endlessly to volunteers eager for non-existent, free yard signs during the 2008 presidential race. Obama realized at this early stage that yard signs just could not compete with passionate speeches and direct voter contact when it came to persuading someone to support him. The lessons of that 2004 primary campaign would surface again and again.[7]

Because Obama could tell a great story, both about himself and about others, he had an advantage over less eloquent candidates whose personal and public stories lacked oomph and passion. Obama's personal story resonated with hope and redemption: a story of a skinny kid without a home state, whose mother once qualified for food stamps, but who overcame adversity to become the first black president of the Harvard Law Review and then the third black man elected to the Senate since Reconstruction. They sensed that here was a man who had come from humble beginnings but now had a shot at becoming the most powerful man on earth. Here was a man who had fought his way up the political ladder with civility and humility, always deflecting attention from himself to the larger causes that he espoused. Obama's storytelling grew legendary, especially after he wrote his second book, a tome that applied the rhetoric of hope to his political ambitions.

Born into a multi-national, multi-racial household, Obama spent much of his college and post-college years searching for identity and explaining his identity to others. Consequently, he learned from a young age the value of telling his personal story, a trait that later helped him on the campaign trail. "Campaigns are a high-velocity duel of story versus story that stretches over months," explained Evan Cornog, a dean at the Columbia Graduate School of Journalism. "The successful candidate is the one whose stories connect with the largest number of voters."[8] Obama connected. He started by putting his personal story before the American public in a memoir about his racial exploration and inclination to learn about his father. "The single most vetted book in American politics right now," this book reflected Obama's inner conflicts about race and family.[9] In this way, Obama drew attention to his story even before his first campaign.

As Obama made his way up the political ladder in Illinois politics, he gathered followers who were always "reaching out to touch him."[10] After each debate, hand after hand shoved copies of *Dreams from My Father* and, later, *The Audacity of Hope*, toward the candidate to sign. By late 2006, everybody was talking about Obama. Because much of what was written about Obama during the freshman senator's early exposure to the national media either fell into the category of "savior" rhetoric or cynicism, however, Obama quickly felt overexposed.[11] "Andy Warhol said we all get our fifteen minutes of fame," Obama said in an interview that November. "I've already had an hour and a half. I'm so overexposed, I'm making Paris Hilton look like a recluse."[12] The cynicism of the pundits was no better, he said, emphasizing that "it's a cynicism that asks us to believe...that our motives in politics can never be pure."[13] Obama needed to speak for himself.

Understanding that Obama needed to cut through the cynicism of the pundits and to transcend the instincts of the celebrity-fed media to focus on Obama the man, the campaign deployed Obama to rallies across the country. Going public, Obama went to the American people directly to press his case. The campaign emphasized message control above all else, a strategy which amplified the rhetoric of Obama himself. The campaign would not allow individual organizers to speak to the press about the workings of the campaign or about Obama's platform. Since there were relatively few voices speaking publicly on Obama's behalf, Americans had little choice but to listen to Obama's own words. The use of carefully selected and groomed surrogate speakers, moreover, minimized the potential for the campaign to publicly contradict itself, a problem that Obama's opponents faced frequently. Obama's unprecedented "Wow!" factor, a phenomenon explained by Malcolm Gladwell in *Blink*, gave the candidate the link he needed to propagate his message of hope.

Never lacking crowds eager to hear the candidate's pronouncements, Obama decided to go public, sensing an opportunity to bypass the media in order to instill hope in his audience directly. He realized that the "unmediated campaign" offered him an outlet for his big ideas.[14] "Consistent with the requirements of a political community that is increasingly susceptible to the centrifugal forces of public opinion,"[15] Obama concentrated on retraining public attention from his personal story to the broader, public story of hope that he sought to make the centerpiece of his presidential campaign.[16] He clamped down on press access, leading a campaign "known for its discipline, which included limited and tightly controlled opportunities for journalists to interact with the candidate."[17] When he did speak publicly, it was usually at major rallies or on the set of major talk shows, such as that of the one person who seemed more popular than Obama—Oprah Winfrey.[18]

Unlike Bush, however, a president known for giving prepared "'town hall' speeches to people...handpicked for their affection for the president,"[19] Obama opened his rallies to anyone willing to stand in line for hours before standing for a few more hours until the candidate arrived to deliver a version of his latest major address. For Obama, the key to success lay in building a sense of hope through his eloquent addresses. But he also wanted to tell his audiences the truth about the challenges that the nation would face along the way. "When you listen to Barack Obama, when you really hear him, you witness a rare thing," Oprah observed as she stumped for Obama in Iowa. "You witness a politician who has an ear for eloquence and a tongue dipped in the unvarnished truth."[20] Oprah recognized in Obama an instantaneous eloquence that moved his listeners to wonder whether they could take their country back.

When Americans went to Obama's rallies, they formed "snap judgments" immediately, consistent with Malcolm Gladwell's theory of thin-slicing presented in *Blink*.[21] Long before most people who heard Obama speak could pinpoint why they felt moved by him, they felt a connection to him at once personal and inspirational. "He's a natural," one journalist felt immediately after meeting him.[22] "My American soul was stirred," a self-styled conservative columnist admitted, even though he later expressed a desire for more change in Obama's "golden rhetoric," a phenomenon which Gladwell described as the other side of thin-slicing.[23] Obama's enduring theme of hope made Governor Bill Richardson and others fed up with the politics of negativity and fear feel like Obama's campaign was about "hope and opportunity."[24] Hooked, listeners soon began to hear Obama's deeper message of "collective salvation."[25]

Through the rhetoric of hope, Obama shifted the language of politics toward a sense of hope for the nation as a community. He reframed the debate by replacing the language of fear with the language of hope. "Reframing is changing the way the public sees the world," explained prominent linguist George Lakoff. "Because language activates frames, new language is required for new frames. Thinking differently requires speaking differently."[26] Lakoff's theory of framing applies most aptly to the second phase of Obama's rhetoric, the conscious phase of employing rhetoric that spoke to the heart in order to shift listeners from a mind-set of fear of the challenges facing America to a mindset of hope for the opportunities that Americans could create. Recognizing the value of reframing in convincing Americans to shape their destiny, Obama observed that "there are moments in American history where there are opportunities to change the language of politics...and I think we're in one of those moments."[27]

With hope squarely at the center of Obama's rhetoric, the campaign also tackled the issue of race, initially out of necessity. From day one, many supporters, reporters, pundits, and historians expressed fear that Americans were not ready to elect a black man, even one of mixed-race origins. Both black and white supporters feared that a substantial number of white Americans would not be willing to pull the lever, fill in the bubble, or select the on-screen button for a man attacked by Republican opponents in ways reminiscent of Jim Crow and the segregationist degradation of black men. Obama's opponents, drawing on racist language and frames of reference, called Obama all sorts of names in an attempt to undermine his legitimacy as a candidate. Obama, however, did not falter and he did not fail. Cool and steady, Obama maintained his mission with a hopefulness that bodes well for the nation and its new president.

The rhetoric of hope and the rhetoric of race intersected multiple times during the 2008 presidential race. During his primary campaign season efforts to win South Carolina, and later in his efforts to win Georgia and Virginia, Obama gained enormous political clout from his ability to befriend African Americans in southern states where he needed to exceed the 2004 Democratic nominee's margins in order to have a shot at winning. "I believe America is ready," Obama told an aide months before announcing his bid for the White House. In South Carolina, Obama encouraged chants of "Race Doesn't Matter." At the same time, the campaign faced troubling racial problems that surfaced repeatedly until the general election. Questions about the Reverend Jeremiah A. Wright, Jr., discussed at length in Chapter 9—The New Faith, dogged Obama for more than a year. And Rep. John L. Lewis's defection to the Clinton camp did not make things any easier.[28]

Republican officials and operatives, meanwhile, resorted to the despicable language of Jim Crow in an attempt to intimidate the Obama campaign and push American politics back to a time when black children and white children were not permitted to attend school together or drink from the same fountain. Reminiscent of the mid-twentieth century era of legal, physical, and psychological intimidation against anyone who spoke in favor of equality between white people and black people, Rep. Lynn Westmoreland, a Republican from Georgia, called the Obama family "uppity" and refused to abandon his word choice when probed by the press. Rep. Geoff Davis, a Republican from Kentucky, said "that boy's finger does not need to be on the button," another blatant invocation of the language employed by white protectors of racism and segregation to demean and degrade African Americans. The McCain campaign even chimed in with more subtle race-baiting, "accusing Mr. Obama of being 'disrespectful' to Sarah Palin."[29]

Obama responded to the racism, the racial fears, and the racial divisions with rhetoric that both faced the problems in the country that stem from the nation's heritage of slavery and segregation and that turned the country toward a future without racism and inequality. Speaking in Philadelphia, Obama acknowledged that "at various stages in the campaign, some commentators have deemed me either 'too black' or 'not black enough.'...The press has scoured every exit poll for the latest evidence of racial polarization, not just in terms of white and black, but black and brown as well." He recognized that "so many of the disparities that exist in the African-American community today can be directly traced to inequalities passed on from an earlier generation that suffered under the brutal legacy of slavery and Jim Crow." But he also expressed his belief "that America can change," a belief vindicated by "the next generation—the young people whose attitudes and beliefs and openness to change have already made history."[30]

Declaring his "hope" that the union "can always be perfected,"[31] Obama won accolades and an endorsement from Richardson, who told the crowd, gathered for the endorsement, that Obama "addressed the issue of race with the eloquence and sincerity and decency and optimism we have come to expect of him. He did not seek to evade tough issues or to soothe us with comforting half-truths. Rather, he inspired us by reminding us of the awesome potential residing in our own responsibility."[32] Obama did not go out of his way to compare himself to the Reverend Dr. Martin Luther King, Jr., however, the civil rights leader who—had he not been tragically assassinated in the midst of his social justice and anti-war efforts—Oprah would undoubtedly have also said had "an ear for eloquence and a tongue dipped in the unvarnished truth."[33] Unlike King, Obama avoided assuming "the persona of Moses,"[34] preferring to offer himself as a presidential candidate who happened to be black rather than as a black presidential candidate.[35] By transcending but not avoiding race, Obama successfully infused a ray of hope into the national debate on race.

MAKING HISTORY

Just as Americans watching the returns come in on Election Day could not help but applaud Barack Obama for being the first black man to win the presidency, Americans who listened to Obama's addresses could not help but notice the similarities between the Chicago lawyer's unbounded optimism and the appeals to the "better angels of our nature"[36] by another young Illinois lawyer—the 16th president of the United States. Hearing Obama talk about how far the country had come since the founding and how far the country still had to go, Americans could not help but draw comparisons to the revolutionary rhetoric of Thomas Jefferson, the populist rhetoric of Andrew Jackson, and the unifying rhetoric of Abraham Lincoln. Listeners could not help but wonder if Obama's rhetoric would resurrect Franklin Delano Roosevelt's New Deal, inspiring a Green Deal in this century.

"Our pride is based on a very simple premise, summed up in a declaration made over two hundred years ago," Obama declared at the 2004 Democratic National Convention. "'We hold these truths to be self-evident, that all men are created equal. That they are endowed by their Creator with certain inalienable rights. That among these are life, liberty and the pursuit of happiness.'" With these words, Obama wrapped himself in the Declaration of Independence, a document penned by a patriot younger than the keynote speaker in Boston. Emphasizing that although "there are those who are preparing to divide us...there's not a liberal America and a conservative America—there's the United States of America," the Democratic Party's rising star cast himself as a post-partisan aspirant for higher office in a long tradition of post-partisan aspirants. Obama wanted to try things a new way. Hailing from the "land of Lincoln," Obama concluded with the hope that "out of this long political darkness a brighter day will come."[37]

When Obama declared that he had decided to pursue the presidency, he again cited his patron state's favorite president, mentioning that in "the shadow of the Old State Capitol, where Lincoln once called on a divided house to stand together, where common hopes and common dreams still live, I stand before you today to announce my candidacy for President of the United States." Fusing the legacies of Lincoln and Kennedy, Obama implored "a new generation" to answer the call to service that "a tall, gangly, self-made Springfield lawyer" had sounded a century earlier. He enlisted the "power of hope" that "organized the forces arrayed against slavery." The call to service for the nation sounded across the land as Obama aligned himself with Lincoln against the forces of entrenched power: "Together, starting today, let us finish the work that needs to be done, and usher in a new birth of freedom on this Earth."[38]

Once Obama accumulated enough delegates and won enough primaries to be virtually assured the Democratic nomination for president, he harked back once again to Philadelphia, where Jefferson pondered the best way to break the news to King George that the rebellious constitutionalists had convened to form "a more perfect union." He talked about those soldiers who died in order to make that union "more perfect."[39] Later, tens of thousands of Democrats, Republicans, and Independents filled a stadium and heard the Democratic nominee describe how "more Americans are out of work and more are working harder for less. More of you have lost your homes.... More of you have cars you can't afford to drive, credit card bills you can't afford to pay, and tuition that's beyond your reach." Here, in America, Obama emphasized, people were struggling to make ends meet as the economy headed downhill.[40]

Returning to his 2004 theme of unity under one flag, Obama reminded the tens of millions watching the 2008 convention on television that "the men and women who serve in our battlefields may be Democrats and Republicans and Independents, but they have fought together and bled together and some died together under the same proud flag. They have not served a Red America or a Blue America—they have served the United States of America."[41] Obama's lines about the divisions between Americans of different colors and creeds, different states and different cities, seemed to flow from the words of his speech in 2004, a rhetorical coincidence that had less to do with coincidence and more to do with history. In Berlin for an international speech, Obama told the world: "People of the world—look at Berlin!"[42] In this way, Obama offered a new generation both the rhetoric of history and the rhetoric of hope.

The Obama campaign recognized that Obama could enhance the movement for change, a movement spread by millions of people who called and canvassed their neighbors, by building on the rhetoric of both the campaigns and the presidencies of Thomas Jefferson, Andrew Jackson, Abraham Lincoln, Franklin Delano Roosevelt, and John Fitzgerald Kennedy. Constantly searching for new ideas while adhering to ancient ideals, the Obama campaign emphasized that an Obama White House would be a new generation's White House. Holding firmly to the egalitarian ideals that made the Obama campaign truly transformative, the organizers and volunteers who walked the streets every day branded the campaign as the beginning of a new day in American politics. The field campaigners, inspired by the rhetoric of a candidate whose speeches resonated with gravitas, passed the hope along to the world.

Obama's "soaring rhetoric became the touchstone of his campaign,"[43] encouraging historians and commentators to dust off their anthologies of speeches and to begin comparing Obama's rhetoric of hope with the rhetoric of history. Commentators, paid by the word, compared Obama to the entire pantheon of American orators and more, noting that in 2004 he "ripped off the rumpled suit of anonymous, mild-mannered state-senatorhood and squeezed into the gaudy cape and tights of our national oratorical superhero—a honey-tongued Frankenfusion of Lincoln, Gandhi, Cicero, Jesus, and all our most cherished national acronyms (MLK, JFK, RFK, FDR)."[44] Journalists looked at Obama's Web presence and the music video made by the Black Eyed Peas' will.i.am—which set Obama's speeches of hope against a hip-hop backdrop—and threw up their hands.[45] Historians, however, could follow the cyclical theory and pencil Obama in as the latest reconstructive president—next in line after Jefferson, Jackson, Lincoln, and FDR.[46]

Thirty-three years old when he drafted the Declaration of Independence at the request of a committee plagued by illness and ill-tempered men, Thomas Jefferson capitalized on his newfound fame to attain the governor's mansion in Virginia, a spot in the Continental Congress, an ambassadorship, the vice presidency, and finally the presidency. Ascending to the White House after a vicious campaign that featured a Federalist split between John Adams and Alexander Hamilton and accusations of rampant corruption, Jefferson promoted expansion of the suffrage and the polity. Leading a self-proclaimed "revolution,"[47] Jefferson announced in his first inaugural address that "we are all Republicans, we are all Federalists."[48] Inventing one of Obama's most famous phrases of unity, Jefferson entered office amid widespread support for a president eager to reinvigorate and reinvent the hopeful principles of the American Revolution.

Twenty-eight years later, an aging Andrew Jackson "restaged the drama of 1800. As the Jeffersonians had assaulted the monarchical designs of John Adams, so the Jacksonians assaulted his son. Like Jefferson before him, Jackson was a tried-and-true defender of American freedom committed to nothing so much as breaking a knot of aristocratic corruption and restoring integrity to republican institutions."[49] If Obama, the inclusive candidate, had been a graying war hero, he would have had much in common with Jackson, the presidential candidate. Jackson's defeat of the British in the Battle of New Orleans in 1815 undergirded Jackson's candidacy. As president, he planned to blot out "the public and private profligacy which a profuse expenditure of money by the government is but too apt to engender,"[50] a platform that would have aligned him with Obama's rhetorical emphasis on collective sacrifice and honest, open government.

In the late 1700s and early 1800s, transportation was difficult and populist rhetoric undignified, necessitating the printing and distribution of speeches rather than oral delivery. Early presidents intended their speeches to be read, not heard. By the mid-1800s, however, many states had expanded suffrage rights to all white men, including many who could not read. Illiteracy, coupled with interest, increased "campaign rallies, debates, and other opportunities for political oratory," just as new railways permitted candidates to "speak to a large number of voters by riding swiftly from town to town." In the land of Lincoln, a tall, gangly, self-made Springfield lawyer rode the rails to debate one of the most powerful politicians in the land over slavery and abolition— Stephen Douglas. Although he lost his bid for the Senate seat, he gained a reputation as a rising star. Abraham Lincoln's newfound fame earned him a spot on the Republican ticket in 1860.[51]

Just as Obama entered the 2008 presidential race with little to show for himself other than a stint as a state senator, a briefer stint as a United States senator, and two books, Lincoln entered the 1860 race as a dark horse lawyer from Illinois with little national exposure and only faint hopes of winning the nomination of his party. Similar to the way Obama's opponents savagely attacked his personal associations with racial overtones, Lincoln's opponents called him an "ass," a "chimpanzee," a "mobocrat," depicting him as "bent on destroying the [South's] most basic institutions."[52] Before southern states started seceding, Lincoln eloquently sought to unify the nation: "Though passion may have strained it must not break our bonds of affection. The mystic chords of memory, stretching from every battlefield and patriot grave to every living heart and hearthstone all over this broad land, will yet swell the chorus of the Union, when again touched, as surely they will be, by the better angels of our nature."[53]

Echoing Lincoln's calls to "repurify [our republican robe] and wash it white in the spirit, if not the blood of the Revolution,"[54] Franklin Delano Roosevelt set the gold standard for the rhetoric of hope in a presidential campaign. Overrun by crowds of screaming supporters when he arrived in Chicago on July 2, 1932, to accept the Democratic nomination, Roosevelt emphasized that "this is no time for fear, for reaction or for timidity."[55] Foreshadowing his famous assertion that "the only thing we have to fear is fear itself,"[56] Roosevelt forcefully proposed a New Deal for the American people to put Americans back to work, stimulate the economy, and assist struggling families. Even more significant from a rhetorical perspective, Roosevelt fostered in a broad swath of Americans—rich and poor, black and white, Jewish and Christian—hope for "a generation overdue in political and economic reconstruction."[57]

Obama's rhetorical entreaties to America during the 2008 presidential campaign paralleled Roosevelt's campaign pleas, setting him on the path of leading the next New Deal, or Green Deal, as is more likely. Like Roosevelt, Obama emphasized hope over fear and frequently targeted fear itself for lying at the root of many of society's problems. Like

Roosevelt, Obama spoke of a generation due for a political revolution. Like Roosevelt, Obama spurred widespread interest in his campaign not only by crisscrossing the nation but also through inspirational calls for Americans to take the country's destiny into their own hands. Like Roosevelt, Obama attacked the prior regime for muddying the political culture, allowing corruption to run wild, and for standing idle while the nation's economy disintegrated into a morass of broken dreams. Like Obama, Roosevelt urged the public to have "faith in America" and to remain hopeful.[58]

Despite these similarities to Roosevelt, Obama is compared to John F. Kennedy more frequently than he is to any other president. Obama is certainly a "political rock star on a scale not seen since the popularity of JFK, if ever."[59] Assessments of Obama's rhetoric that define Obama as the next Kennedy, however, ignore the implications of Obama's efforts to transcend partisanship, to overcome continuing racial divisions, and to draw upon the historical rhetoric of Jefferson, Jackson, Lincoln, and Roosevelt in order to reframe the political discourse. "The reason I'm involved in politics right now is not because I wanted to be JFK; it's because of the civil rights movement," Obama told public radio in 2004.[60] At the same time, Obama's campaign rhetoric matched Kennedy's campaign theme that "it is a time...for a new generation of leadership—new men to cope with new problems and new opportunities."[61] Moreover, Obama's rhetoric of hope paralleled Kennedy's announcement "that the torch has been passed to a new generation of Americans."[62]

Rejecting the cult of personality for the populism of humanity, Obama made history again and again, drawing increasingly large crowds to his rallies and increasingly large numbers of volunteers to his campaign offices. With his rhetoric of hope, Obama built up a following that took on a life of its own. Obama's rhetoric inspired Oprah to leave the set of her popular television show in order to join the young candidate in South Carolina, Iowa, and New Hampshire.[63] President John F. Kennedy's brother Ted, daughter Caroline, and aide Ted Sorensen, all inspired by Obama's positive campaign strategy, publicly endorsed Obama in newspaper columns and public speeches.[64] Never overshadowing the candidate, Obama's prominent backers drew still more people into the fold and solidified the historic nature of a new political movement powered by the historic rhetoric of hope and America's "better angels."[65]

EVOLVING RHETORICALLY

Understanding the need to evolve with the campaign, Barack Obama adapted his rhetoric to international and national events, shifting political contexts, and the nation's increasing anxiety about the economy. Ultimately implementing a policy of having Obama speak at major rallies after the early evening news, in order to avoid alienating Americans who prefer the quiet of an interview to the exuberance of a public gathering, the campaign recognized that Obama's hopefulness needed context. It is no longer possible for a candidate to write and deliver only one stump speech. Nestled in the context of campaign victories and upsets, Obama's rhetoric evolved to invoke deeper principles and to recognize broader challenges. Responding to concerns deeply rooted in the American psyche, Obama brought the nation full-circle—from the audacity of hope to hope for the future—over the course of the 10 quintessential speeches of the campaign, described below.

First, Obama stole the show in his "2004 Keynote Address" at the Democratic National Convention in Boston, Massachusetts. Outshining more prominent Democratic Party names like presidential nominee John Kerry and vice presidential nominee John Edwards, Obama gave the world a glimpse of his personal story and a taste of his rhetoric of hope. "It's the hope of slaves sitting around a fire singing freedom songs," Obama proclaimed, continuing, "the hope of a skinny kid with a funny name who believes that America has a place for him, too. The audacity of hope!"[66]

Second, Obama calmly broke into a crowded field of Democratic candidates with his "Declaration of Candidacy," delivered in Springfield, Illinois on February 10, 2007. "Each and every time, a new generation has risen up and done what's needed to be done," Obama declared, foreshadowing the campaign's focus on mobilizing excited young people in the field (see Chapter 5). "Today we are called once more—and it is time for our generation to answer that call. For that is our unyielding faith—that in the face of impossible odds, people who love their country can change it."[67]

Third, Obama established hope as the overriding theme of the campaign in his "Iowa Caucus Night" speech on January 3, 2008, in Des Moines. Having unpredictably emerged victorious, Obama gained momentum that inspired millions more Americans to get involved. "Hope—hope—is what led me here today—with a father from Kenya; a mother from Kansas; and a story that could only happen in the United States of America."[68] The Iowa caucus victory speech set high expectations for New Hampshire's primary elections, which occurred less than a week later.

Fourth, Obama turned an unexpected loss in the New Hampshire primary elections into a motivational "New Hampshire Primary Night" speech on January 8, 2008, in Nashua. Trying out a "Yes We Can" riff that became an international hit, Obama emphasized that "when we have faced down impossible odds; when we've been told that we're not ready, or that we shouldn't try, or that we can't, generations of Americans have responded with a simple creed that sums up the spirit of a people. Yes we can."[69] Obama originally thought "Yes We Can" too "corny" to use.[70]

Fifth, Obama transformed his disagreements with his pastor into a major speech, "A More Perfect Union," delivered on March 18, 2008. The Philadelphia speech on race in the United States became so popular that the campaign distributed the speech in pamphlet form in multiple states. "But I have asserted a firm conviction," Obama exhorted, "a conviction rooted in my faith in God and my faith in the American people—that working together we can move beyond some of our old racial wounds, and that in fact we have no choice if we are to continue on the path of a more perfect union."[71]

Sixth, Obama proved that he had the maturity necessary to run for and achieve the presidency in "Our Moment, Our Time," delivered on June 3, 2008, the night he clinched the nomination. "America, this is our moment. This is our time," Obama reiterated. "Our time to turn the page on the policies of the past. Our time to bring new energy and new ideas to the challenges we face. Our time to offer a new direction for the country we love."[72] Obama came across as more presidential and much more positive than Republican challenger Senator John McCain, who kept repeating—with a smirk on his face—that "that's not change we can believe in."

Seventh, Obama took his oratory to Europe in "A World that Stands as One." Speaking in Berlin, Germany on July 24, 2008, Obama was welcomed like an international rock star by upwards of 100,000 people. "Tonight, I speak to you not as a candidate for President, but as a citizen—a proud citizen of the United States, and a fellow citizen of the world."[73] Obama's speech demonstrated his appeal on the international stage, a critical step toward proving that he—not John McCain— would do a better job of restoring the nation's reputation and standing in the world. The speech would be frequently featured in McCain's attack ads, trying to show that Obama was too "European" or too much of a celebrity to work for the American people. Considering the votes Obama earned on Election Day, the American people clearly showed that they would appreciate a president willing to work with the rest of the world instead of against it.

Eighth, Obama spoke to some 75,000 Americans in his "The American Promise" Democratic National Convention speech in Denver, Colorado, on August 28, 2008. Accepting the Democratic nomination for president, Obama spoke in concrete terms about the future. "At defining moments," Obama said, "the change we need doesn't come from Washington. Change comes to Washington. Change happens because the American people demand it—because they rise up and insist on new ideas and new leadership, a new politics for a new time."[74]

Ninth, Obama delivered his "One Week" speech in cities all over the country, including in Canton, Ohio, on October 27, 2008. "Don't believe for a second this election is over," Obama warned his supporters. "Don't think for a minute that power concedes. We have to work like our future depends on it in this last week, because it does."[75] The final week of campaigning included a massive get-out-the-vote effort in every state. Learning from Iowa, the Obama campaign did not let up at all during the final days, even though polls showed Obama in the lead.

Finally, Obama addressed the nation in "Yes We Can," his victory speech in Chicago, Illinois, on November 4, 2008. Speaking to millions, Obama thanked his supporters and offered a hopeful outlook on the future: "This is our time—to put our people back to work and open doors of opportunity for our kids; to restore prosperity and promote the cause of peace; to reclaim the American Dream and reaffirm that fundamental truth—that out of many, we are one...and where we are met with cynicism...and those who tell us that we can't, we will respond with that timeless creed that sums up the spirit of a people: Yes We Can."[76]

Acknowledging that "there is a performance aspect to [public speaking] that I don't think came naturally to him at first," Robert Gibbs, who served as Obama's communication director for the campaign, underscored Obama's improvement in exuding emotion during his stump speeches.[77] Jason Green, the Obama campaign's national voter-registration director, and a personal friend, confirmed in a conversation in June of 2008 that Obama was not always the best public speaker. In fact, when he started out as a community organizer, he was apparently downright awful. Fortunately for Obama's presidential ambitions and for the nation, however, Obama maintained as his personal philosophy, "I need to get better."[78] After the Obama campaign failed dismally in its goal of winning the Pennsylvania primary, for instance, Obama began to incorporate more concrete details into his speeches. He was always eager to improve.

Even when the rhetoric of the Republican ticket—John McCain and Sarah Palin—unleashed venomous shouts of "Treason!" and "Terrorist!" and "Kill him!" and racial slurs directed toward Obama, the Democrat kept his cool.[79] Letting his vice presidential nominee, Delaware Senator Joe Biden, criticize Palin for not reprimanding members of her audience for their increasingly violent threats against her opponents, Obama remained calm. In the final presidential debate, McCain came across as immature and out of control while Obama "responded to Mr. McCain's lines of attacks by smiling and slightly shaking his head."[80] Only once did he slip up badly, before the Pennsylvania primary, when he described how bitter people end up clinging to their guns and religion. Learning from this mistake, however, Obama became more careful not to make seemingly derisive comments about any segment of the population, especially not segments of the population that ultimately helped him win Virginia, Florida, and North Carolina.

THE RHETORIC OF HOPE

With graceful optimism and extraordinary eloquence, Barack Obama carved out a space in modern politics for the rhetoric of hope. He pulled on the hope strings of millions of Americans desperately seeking a president who promised a return to democratic ideals, egalitarianism, and the principle that we can do better. With a faltering economy and an unpopular war, Americans demanded more than partisan attacks. Contrasted against his Republican opponent's refrain of "That's not change we can believe in," Obama's stump speeches exuded the hopefulness Americans sorely needed. More importantly, however, the Obama campaign made history by confidently facing and overcoming the specter of race that has haunted the American psyche from slavery to segregation to Senator Obama's entry into a predominantly white field of would-be presidents. Harking back to Jefferson, Jackson, Lincoln, Roosevelt, and Kennedy, Obama's rhetoric of hope moved millions toward a brighter future.

When Americans showed up at Obama's rallies, which had to be closely regulated because so many thousands of people showed up to each one, many of them felt an instantaneous connection with the Democratic nominee for president. This connection, explained by Malcolm Gladwell's theories of snap judgments and thin-slicing, allowed millions of people to feel like they were part of something bigger than themselves, something bound to change the world. To these individuals, the rhetoric of hope was uplifting and nearly spiritual, providing them with the opportunity to dream about a future where all Americans are created equal and where all Americans have the opportunities that they need. Sensing in Obama a deep yearning to organize a national community around shared values and common interests, millions of Americans heard Obama's rhetoric of hope and signed up to volunteer to talk to their neighbors.

Successfully reframing the debate, the Obama campaign put significant energy into controlling the discourse surrounding the campaign. By limiting press access to the candidate and making the candidate available primarily at large rallies, the campaign both protected the candidate from the dangers of savior status and provided the best opportunities for the rhetoric of hope to reach voters. Aware that the language of political discourse matters, the campaign carefully chose Obama's words while not limiting the hopeful style with which he was associated—language that reframed sensitive and controversial issues in more positive ways. On the issue of race, for example, Obama reframed the debate from a negative focus on his personal relationships with Wright and other controversial figures into a debate about the positive actions that Americans and the Obama Administration can take in the future.

On the walls of Obama's Senate office hung portraits of Abraham Lincoln and Martin Luther King, Jr., among others. "It's only when you hitch yourself up to something bigger than yourself that you realize your true potential," he said.[81] Reiterating a theme that pervaded his presidential campaign, Obama encouraged Americans to join together to restore the promise of democracy on which this nation was founded in 1776. The rhetoric of hope is not a one-way street, but a dialogue about the future. Speaking at the dedication of the Lincoln Museum in Springfield, Illinois, in the spring of 2005, Obama rhetorically revived the words of the nation's sixteenth president so that his wisdom might permeate the politics of the 21st century: "And as that man called once upon the better angels of our nature, so is he calling still, across the ages, to summon some measure of that character, his character, in each of us today."[82]

CHAPTER SEVEN

THE RHETORIC OF CHANGE

Nearly 10,000 South Central Pennsylvanians crowded into a gated space in front of the Pennsylvania Capitol on April 19, 2008, to catch a glimpse of Barack Obama and Senator Bob Casey, Jr., as they swept down the steps before Obama's final whistle-stop stump speech. Wearing matching black pants and white-collared shirts with rolled-up sleeves, the junior senator from Pennsylvania and the junior senator from Illinois looked like brothers—one black, one white.

Obama's speech, however, was long on generalities and short on specifics. The crowd wanted more than the rhetoric of hope. They wanted details about how Obama planned to give health insurance to millions of uninsured Americans. They wanted details about how Obama planned to prevent gasoline price gouging. They wanted details about how Obama planned to end the Iraq War without leaving Iraq worse off than before President George W. Bush ordered American soldiers to invade Baghdad. In short, they wanted the rhetoric of change.

The Harrisburg *Patriot-News* had endorsed Obama in an editorial remarkable for its lack of substance. Noting that Senator Hillary Clinton was "the first female candidate to have a serious chance to win the presidency," the newspaper criticized Clinton for being "the candidate of the past." And the editorial board praised "the candidate of the future" for having "won over young people...on a scale that may be unprecedented." But as a young person who had endorsed Obama before he decided to run, I knew that winning over people like me would not be enough.

For Obama to be successful in Pennsylvania, he would have to prove that he was the candidate of hope with practical solutions that would create change for blue-collar workers and struggling farmers. In a humorous and telling moment at the whistle-stop rally at the intersection of Third and State streets on Saturday evening, someone in the crowd responded to Obama's frustrations about the lack of progress on health care by yelling, "That's why we're bitter!"

"I'm not going to touch that," Obama said, and he and Casey chuckled. This small, unscripted moment in a tightly choreographed event involving dozens of organizers, hundreds of police and Secret Service officers, and thousands of local residents, underscored Obama's failure to fight back at a critical juncture before the Pennsylvania primary. All weekend, Obama supporters had inboxes filled with e-mails containing instructions to express their anger at attacks against Obama by Charles Gibson and George Stephanopoulos during the presidential debate in Philadelphia. But the candidate himself had yet to stand up and confront the professional pundits for rehashing divisive and distracting non-issues. Rich Lewis, a local columnist for the Carlisle *Sentinel*, put it bluntly when he wrote that although brushing off attacks is important, "a president also has to be forceful, demanding and hard on occasion—or risk being steamrolled by those who are." Lewis spoke for many in the mid-state concerned that Obama had not yet demonstrated that he could bury his opponents in their inadequacies in order to overcome the politics of inertia.

Having reached Harrisburg, the end of the line, Obama had to assert his moral leadership in order to convince Pennsylvanians that he had both the courage to remain cool under fire and the strength to stand up when necessary. Obama also had to hammer out the details of his policies and present those solutions to the teachers, laborers, and truck drivers who needed to know that Obama would do whatever it took to bring their voices to Washington.

Without the promise of change, charismatically instilled in Americans by a leader determined to fight to the bitter end, the rhetoric of hope would only carry Obama so far in South Central Pennsylvania and other areas hurting from Bush's failed economy. In order to win, Obama needed to use the power of the rhetoric of change. The nation needed the rhetoric of change—and more importantly, the nation needed change—more than ever.[1]

LEADING WITH CHARISMA

Barack Obama's eloquence and uplifting rhetoric of hope launched a new kind of political movement that empowered a people to build a brighter future. But without the promise of change, the movement would not have been able to bring people desperate for relief from the immediate hardships of Bush's failed economy into the Obama camp. Fortunately, the Obama campaign recognized the necessity of combining the rhetoric of hope with the rhetoric of change. Leading with charisma—that nebulous "it" factor that rhetoricians have argued about for thousands of years— Obama increasingly focused on the concrete changes that Americans from all walks of life needed their next president to advocate. He promised to lead with compassion and a post-partisan attitude that looks past the party labels to the changes that the American people need. Transcending partisanship, Obama led not only with hope but also with the courage to change.

Obama's critics, both black and white, accused him of lacking the courage of his convictions. "It was masking, not convictions, that brought Barack Obama forward in American life," wrote one black commentator. "He is decidedly not a conviction politician. His supporters do not look to him to *do* something; they look to him primarily to *be* something, to *represent* something."[2] Dubbing Obama's rise from obscure Chicago lawyer to leader of the free world "Obamamania," a black scholar described Obama as "the product of timing" in an atmosphere where "the political bar was lowered so low by missteps by both parties that Obama did not have to do much beyond deliver a cliché-filled, nonoffensive speech to endear himself to many disgruntled and desperate Americans."[3] Although such criticisms were derived from the style of Obama's rhetoric, they lack merit because Obama's rhetoric went far beyond mere clichés.

If the Obama campaign had been little more than clichés, the millions of Americans who volunteered to knock on doors and make telephone calls to their neighbors ought to have been gravely disappointed, or at least righteously indignant. Liberal satirist Maureen Dowd ought not to have denounced Democrats tempted to "dismiss a politically less experienced but personally more charismatic prospect as 'an empty vessel.'"[4] If the Obama campaign was all about Obamamania, why did so many followers talk incessantly about issues? Where did they get the idea that Obama knew anything about Iraq or taxes or oil dependence? Idolatry played some role in the campaign, as evinced by descriptions of Obama as the "Black Jesus," but not nearly to the extent portended by critics outside the campaign. We believed

Obama when he said, "My attitude is that you don't want to just be the president. You want to change the country."[5]

With so many people saying that Obama had "enormous charisma," however, the nagging question persisted on the campaign trail about what exactly gave Obama charisma and how it manifested itself. A political psychologist who said that Obama had enormous charisma also said, in the same sentence, that Obama had "all the nonverbal behaviors that portend political success and a first-rate intellect combined with an ability to talk to people where they live."[6] Presumably, this meant that Obama's charisma was not defined by his nonverbal language, intelligence, or extraverted persona. Coming closer to a working definition than most commentators, the progressive Barbara Ehrenreich called Obama "a fresh start," explaining that at least in terms of the war in Iraq, "that's what 'change' means right now: Get us out of here!"[7] The Black Eyed Peas' will.i.am, instead of providing a verbal answer, set Obama's "Yes We Can!" refrain from his New Hampshire primary speech to music—"the first U.S. political speech set to music."[8]

Charismatic political leadership, according to the author of *The Spellbinders: Charismatic Political Leadership*, is usually defined as "a combination of ambition, eloquence, and inspiration in a leader presented with a pivotal moment and potential follower to put under a spell."[9] "There seems to be relative consensus concerning the elements combining to produce political charisma and concerning their order and sequence," explained Ann Ruth Willner, "that is: (1) a crisis situation, (2) potential followers in distress, and (3) an aspirant leader with (4) a doctrine promising deliverance."[10] Under this definition, Obama would almost certainly qualify as charismatic. In a nation distressed from eight long years of George W. Bush, Obama arrived with ambitions of leading the nation out of a quagmire in Iraq and a morass at home. Although Obama did not personally promise deliverance, the savior-status comments of professional pundits notwithstanding, he did offer a doctrine of transformational change.

Pushing into action millions of people who had never before been involved in politics, the Obama campaign reached into long forgotten neighborhoods and found not just hope but also a fundamental belief that the country could change. Organizers, interns, and volunteers registered millions of Americans to vote who never bothered to register, either because they had lost hope in Washington or because they had never been asked to get involved. Using spirited e-mails and text messages to reinforce the connection between rhetoric and action, the Obama campaign turned the candidate's rhetoric into a means of networking with the entire nation. The campaign also raised more money, in relatively small denominations, than any presidential candidate in American history. Obama's leadership made it clear that though his candidacy and presidency were improbable, they were by no means impossible, instilling a desire to serve in the hearts of millions of Americans.

What made Obama a different kind of presidential candidate was not his ability to turn a phrase, even though he had a way with words. It was not his ability to provide insight on significant issues, even though he had a firm grasp of policy. It was not his ability to convince Americans to believe in him, even though he had the admiration of millions of Americans. It was his ability to inspire Americans to believe in themselves, their country, and their future. It was his ability to move millions to pick up the phone and call their neighbors or walk down dusty lanes to deliver information about the change that they believed in. It was his ability to promise transformational change—if his listeners were willing to fight for it. It was his ability to stand alone on a stage with the knowledge that he did not stand alone in the world. It was his ability to instill in almost every person he met or who heard him speak a sense that change was possible.

A five-and-a-half-year-old girl named Kade drew a picture of Obama with an American flag, surrounded by multitudes of stick figures, and sent it to my office in Gloucester, Virginia. The flag was waving. Obama was smiling. The people in the foreground of the picture had their arms in the air, cheering for the promise of change. Kade wrote at the top, "HI brok obama, I'm sorry becas I wanted to send you sum monny but then daddy found out that I'm not aloud to do it. If I could vote I would vote for you." After hanging Kade's drawing and letter on the window of the office, I thought about the implications of children barely old enough to attend kindergarten, let alone vote, feeling strongly enough about a political leader to offer everything they have in order to create change. And I realized that when commentators called Obama charismatic, they were talking about Kade and the millions of other children who felt moved by the promise of change.

At high schools and colleges all across the country, students felt compelled to take a stand in what was frequently heralded as the most important election in their lifetime. Sensing Obama's charisma, his ability to inspire millions of Americans to believe that they have the power to change the world, students played a particularly large role in fusing Obama's rhetoric with the action of the campaign. Accustomed to being ignored by nominees, students felt excited about the 2008 race because they knew that the stakes for change were high. "This is the election of our lifetime," wrote Ben Shaffer, president of the Yale College Democrats. "Our generation has more at stake than any other in the choice between a candidate who inspires us to look toward the future and one that remains stubbornly in the past." Looking past Obama's rhetoric, my cousin Ben implored Generation Change to focus on the "change our country needs."[11]

Where media observers and readers of his literary works once "had a tendency to give Obama a pass,"[12] they increasingly wanted answers. Where Obama lacked "detailed, real-world specifics"[13] in his early stump speeches and in *The Audacity of Hope*, he learned from the chilly reception in some quarters and began to ratchet up the emphasis on change. Shifting from the rhetoric of hope to the rhetoric of change over the course of the campaign, Obama increasingly backed up his hopeful themes with statistics, anecdotes, and policy proposals. Partly out of strategic vision and partly out of necessity, Obama moved to gain a foothold in the minds of the analytical proponents of change, the scholars and statisticians who drew conclusions not from snap judgments but from cool calculation. For the campaign, the shift meant reframing the discourse once again to emphasize the change that Obama asked Americans to believe in.

Eight decades ago, the famous political power broker Walter Lippmann wrote that "the leader knows by experience that only when symbols have done their work is there a handle he can use to move the crowd."[14] Charismatic leadership draws upon symbols, which combine to form pictures, which create emotion, which generates action. In this way, the charismatic political leader moves people to action not only by drawing upon previously instilled ideas and preconceptions but also by reframing the debate and instilling in the minds of the citizenry new symbols. For the Obama campaign, the basic logo remained the same, for instance, but the design and context changed. Starting with a simple circle with a blue cut-out semi-circle on top and red slanted lines across the bottom, the Obama 'O' "became one of the most recognizable political logos in recent history" after the campaign printed it on all kinds of paraphernalia.[15]

When the designers of the famous 'O' first began to design their logo, knowing it needed to encompass Obama's rhetoric of hope and plans for change, the designers "were struck by the ideas of hope, change and a new perspective on red and blue (not red and blue states, but one country). There was also a strong sense, from the start, that [Obama's] campaign represented something entirely new in American politics—'a new day,' so to speak." The designers wanted to create a logo that could withstand the pressures of the campaign trail while embodying the ideals of the campaign. They wanted something that would resonate with supporters and stick in the minds of opponents. Significantly, "the identity was for the campaign, not just for the candidate," the designers noted. "And to the degree that the campaign spoke to millions of people, it may have become a symbol of something broader—some have termed it a movement, a symbol of hope."[16]

As the rhetoric of hope evolved into the rhetoric of change, the Obama campaign recognized the necessity that "members of the public must not only receive [Obama's] message but understand it as well. Those who are unaware of a message are unlikely to know [Obama's] positions."[17] The campaign focused first on message dissemination, then message comprehension, then message response. Fusing the dissemination, comprehension, and response processes together, however, the campaign presented a seemingly well-oiled front in order to not contradict—even on a subconscious level—the message of change sparked by the campaign but developed by the public. The campaign also took advantage of "'pack journalism,' the tendency of many reporters to literally follow each other during the campaign,"[18] turning each appearance by the candidate into an opportunity for discourse in the press about the meaning of change.

Because charismatic leadership combines rhetoric and action, Obama's eloquent promises of post-partisanship and radical pragmatism drew the American people into much more than a campaign about hope. Obama's ability to move millions to tears with speeches filled with policy prescriptions demonstrated the candidate's devotion to finding innovative solutions to the problems plaguing the nation. Just as Obama successfully promoted ethical reforms that made lobbying efforts and pork-barrel spending more transparent, Obama's presidency promises to continue the candidate's commitment to doing what needs to be done without excessive concern for partisan political consequences. Because Obama appreciates the constitutional relationship between the executive branch and the other branches of government, his presidency has the potential to usher in a new era of charismatic leadership on issues that matter to all Americans.

PUSHING THE LIMITS OF LEADERSHIP

"I specifically remember a precinct captain training two weeks before Super Tuesday at the Santa Monica public library. We always started by telling our story, a quick anecdote about what inspired us to join the campaign. In front of 150 strangers, I told the story of how a friend of mine who had just left for Iraq had told me before he left, 'I like your boy (Obama), but I don't want him to leave us hangin'.' 'I know he would never do that,' I replied. The next day I received an e-mail from a young woman who had attended that meeting. She described to me how her closest friend had just been killed in Iraq only weeks earlier. She painted for me a picture of a young man who had been inspired greatly by Obama and his message of hope and change. She told me that she had attended the training to honor his memory, and how inspiring it had been for her to hear my story. That was the moment I realized just how strong this movement was becoming, and how much responsibility came with being a part of it."

My friend and co-worker BJ, a field organizer for the Campaign for Change, shared this story with me in part because of the enormous sense of responsibility he carried—and carries still—for all the people he met on the campaign trail who told him that they believed in Obama's rhetoric of change. It is undeniable that Obama stumbled several times on the road to the White House for exactly this reason. Because Obama's two best-selling books and early campaign speeches emphasized the rhetoric of hope without providing much of a roadmap for change, Obama fell short in some states where voters cared deeply about the specific challenges facing them and cared little for the generic rhetoric of hope.

Needing the rhetoric of change, they supported other candidates in the primary who were clearer about their willingness to bring the troops home from Iraq or their commitment to small family farmers or their understanding of the significance of faith in modern politics.

Obama's rally-oriented style of speaking fell on unreceptive ears in areas where voters wanted plain speaking about the challenges facing America and the world in the 21st century. Obama responded effectively, tackling immediate fears with clearer plans for a better world. At the same time, Obama sought to empower his listeners and his supporters to take ownership over exactly what the meaning of change would be in the campaign. He encouraged Americans to challenge their leaders and to challenge themselves to work harder and think more creatively about the nation's future. Embodying the charismatic political leader, Obama gave Washington a glimpse during the campaign of what a modern presidency—built on principles of community organizing and popular empowerment—might look like. He wanted the world to know that there was a fresh wind blowing in from the west that threatened the status quo.

"We are at a moment that is not familiar to Washington, of learning the difference between a transactional president and a transformational one," explained Andy Stern, the leader of one of the largest labor coalitions in the country. "What Barack Obama has created by this campaign was not only the idea that we can do big things—but we have to do big things."[19] At the campaign's low point, when it seemed like the odds of the Obama campaign doing big things seemed slim, Obama called his top lieutenants together to discuss how best to proceed. Despite calls for shake-ups from the top down, Obama did not fire anyone, preferring to have his inner circle adapt along with the rest of the campaign. As the campaign tinkered with strategy, shifting from the rhetoric of hope to the rhetoric of change, Obama emphasized that his team shared "a basic worldview [that] politics should be able to draw on our best and not our worst."[20]

Echoing the rhetoric of change of America's "most effective political leaders,"[21] Obama's rhetoric reached into history to find achievable goals and solutions. Obama's major addresses incorporated elements of the constitutional devotion of Thomas Jefferson, the people's presidency of Andrew Jackson, the commitment to unity through freedom of

Abraham Lincoln, and the programmatic pragmatism of Franklin Delano Roosevelt. Obama's best speeches during the campaign picked up on these past presidents' common themes of national unity, of sacrifice and salvation, and of collective courage and critical improvements. Obama implicated his predecessor and his Republican opponent in the failure to handle the forces that caused the nation's gravest problems and in the failure to remove longstanding barriers that have prevented generations of Americans from fulfilling their dreams and participating equally in politics.

Thomas Jefferson entered the White House with a profound belief in the ability of Americans to govern themselves. "Sometimes it is said that man cannot be trusted with the government of himself," Jefferson intoned in his first address as chief executive. "Can he, then, be trusted with the government of others? Or have we found angels in the forms of kings to govern him? Let history answer this question."[22] Compare this statement with Obama's answer on the night of his victory: "If there is anyone out there who still doubts that America is a place where all things are possible; who still wonders if the dream of our founders is alive in our time; who still questions the power of our democracy, tonight is your answer."[23] Following the same path of empowering a nation, Obama and Jefferson both encountered remarkably "little resistance" as they prepared for transition and change before occupying the Oval Office.[24] Obama has seemingly fulfilled Jefferson's promise of the power of democracy to achieve the improbable.

Andrew Jackson's "makings of an entirely new foundation for government and politics,"[25] stemming from his personal experiences on the frontier and aligning with his broad, popular support from both working-class members of society and rich members of the elite classes, held great sway in a world where the frontier seemed incredibly distant from the shore, where Washington, D.C., seemed so far away to little homes on the plains. To bridge the gap, Jackson called for "a spirit of liberal concession and compromise, and...partial sacrifices...for the preservation of the greater good."[26] Compare this request with Obama's request for "a new spirit of patriotism; of service and responsibility where each of us resolves to pitch in and work harder and look after not only ourselves, but each other."[27] Connecting collective sacrifice with patriotism, Obama and Jackson both called on their fellow Americans to look after each other.

Abraham Lincoln "was committed to overthrowing the slave power conspiracy and to reaffirming the principles of the Declaration of Independence, and he made clear that the latter was contingent on the former."[28] Like Obama, Lincoln wanted to overcome the racial divisions that had enslaved generations of African Americans and frayed the fabric of the American Dream. Firm yet forgiving, Lincoln pleaded: "With malice toward none, with charity toward all, with firmness in the right as God gives us to see the right, let us strive on to finish the work we are in...to do all which may achieve and cherish a just and lasting peace among ourselves and with all nations."[29]

Compare this promise of change and peace with Obama's call "to those Americans whose support I have yet to earn—I may not have won your vote, but I hear your voices, I need your help, and I will be your President too.... Our union can be perfected. And what we have already achieved gives us hope for what we can and must achieve tomorrow."[30] The promise of hard work to unify a polarizing nation defined the campaigns of both Obama and Lincoln.

Franklin Delano Roosevelt, who had pledged himself "to a new deal for the American people"[31] in accepting the Democratic presidential nomination in 1932, poignantly observed at the start of his second term that "I see one-third of the nation ill-housed, ill-clad, ill-nourished."[32] Recognizing the unfinished work of the New Deal, he called on all Americans to take care of their sisters and brothers, so that all might survive and prosper. Compare this recognition of the challenges facing the nation with Obama's recognition of the challenges that awaited him and the nation as he entered the White House: "Even as we celebrate tonight, we know the challenges that tomorrow will bring are the greatest of our lifetime—two wars, a planet in peril, the worst financial crisis in a century. Even as we stand here tonight, we know there are brave Americans waking up in the deserts of Iraq and the mountains of Afghanistan to risk their lives for us. There are mothers and fathers who will lie awake after their children fall asleep and wonder how they'll make the mortgage, or pay their doctor's bills, or save enough for college."[33] The two presidents share a common bond of inheriting a nation with a financial crisis, and each pledged themselves to work to ensure that no American suffers long in poverty.

Like Jefferson, Jackson, Lincoln, and Roosevelt, Obama enters office at "a moment...in which presidential authority is at its most compelling, a moment when opponents stand indicted in the court of public opinion and allies are not yet secure enough in their new positions of power to compete for authority." Like Jackson, Lincoln, and Roosevelt, Obama enters office with an extraordinary opportunity to "dislodge from government the residual institutional supports for the priorities of the past. Jackson's repudiation of entrenched elites took institutional form in the destruction of the Second National Bank; Lincoln's repudiation of the 'slave-power conspiracy' took institutional form in the destruction of slavery itself; and FDR's repudiation of 'economic royalists' took institutional form as a frontal assault on the independence of the U.S. Supreme Court."[34] Exactly how Obama will wield his new presidential powers remains to be seen.

What is known is that Obama enters the White House knowing that he will face enormous challenges and that those challenges will take the energies and sacrifices of not just the president but every American to overcome. Publicly recognizing just before the general election that "the next administration is going to be inheriting a host of really big problems,"[35] Obama demonstrated that he possessed—despite the inherent sleep deprivation of the campaign trail—the wisdom of foresight as well as hindsight. In this way, Obama proved repeatedly his charismatic leadership abilities. Adopting the rhetoric of change of Jefferson, Jackson, Lincoln, and Roosevelt, Obama demonstrated that he could not only shift deftly from the rhetoric of hope to the rhetoric of change but also incorporate the rhetoric of history into his outlook on the future. Obama's commitment to studying and learning from history also bodes well for his presidency.

Obama evinced a strong commitment to learning from his greatest predecessors on a *60 Minutes* interview shortly after the general election. Mentioning that he had read "a new book out about FDR's first 100 days," while not specifically identifying the title or author, Obama sparked a "scramble for the claim to First Reader rights all day" until the transition team cleared up the confusion. With four relatively new books published about Franklin Delano Roosevelt's presidency, and three of the four dealing explicitly with Roosevelt first hundred days in office, historians were understandably confused about which book Obama had read. More importantly, however, historians lauded Obama for his reading habits, explaining that "the idea that we now have a president-elect who is reading multiple books of history and is reading them to shape his presidency, I think is inspiring to historians everywhere and augurs well for his presidency."[36]

Having resurrected the rhetorical candidacy, Barack Obama has the potential to make the president's rhetoric once again a symbol of the nation's promise. In sharp contrast to George W. Bush's Orwellian rhetoric of denial and deception, Obama's rhetoric of positive change on the campaign trail bridged the gap between the rhetoric of the past and the rhetoric of the future. Pushing the limits of leadership, Obama called on every American to join a movement that stemmed from hope but pushed for change. Obama learned from his own experiences as a community organizer in Chicago that successful organizing requires concrete goals that community members strive to achieve. Obama's campaign was no different, setting goals for organizers that had to be met in order for the campaign to win. Similarly, Obama's rhetoric pushed beyond hope to change, setting significant goals for this great nation to achieve.

TRANSFORMING AMERICA

Barack Obama's democratic charisma pushed presidential campaign rhetoric to new heights, transforming each speech into an opportunity to motivate, mobilize, and inspire. His frequent calls for Americans to take their future into their own hands spurred millions to register to vote, contact their neighbors in person or via telephone, and hand out campaign literature at polling places on Election Day. Obama's transformative presence inspired a generation of young people to become organizers, interns, or volunteers. Other young people wrote blogs on MyBO or became journalists for Web-based outlets like *Scoop08*, following Obama and the campaign from state to state, county to county, and precinct to precinct. Obama's rhetoric of change transformed America in countless ways, moving a new generation to lead a revolution that has forever altered how presidential candidates campaign and how successful candidates win.

Obama's ability during the 2008 presidential campaign to deliver major address after major address with rarely a discernible drop-off in quality demonstrated the Democratic nominee's extraordinary eloquence and dedication to the cause. At least at the upper echelons of American politics, Obama proved the idea that "traditional political rhetoric is a declining art" outrageously false. Reviving popular politics and rhetorical persuasion, Obama took advantage of "the level of unrest in the culture. Great rhetoric often appeals to listeners who are hungry for vision, balm or—this year's unavoidable word—change." Recognizing the importance of highlighting the concrete, the immediate, and the urgent, as opposed to the intangible, the distant, and the esoteric, Obama moved from a rhetoric predominantly characterized by hope and boundless optimism to a rhetoric predominantly emphasizing the change Americans needed.[37]

Harking back to the rhetoric of other great orators, particularly those who preceded Obama in the White House, Obama's rhetoric received high praise from Democrats, Republicans, and Independents alike. With a precision-like ability to drill down to those fundamental American principles that made this nation what it is today and which all Americans would do well to remember, Obama's rhetoric of change constantly evoked images of Thomas Jefferson feverishly penning the Declaration of Independence, a band of patriots taking up arms against their British oppressors, and the "Common Sense" of Thomas Paine, whose pamphlets were distributed in a manner similar to the manner in which the Obama campaign printed and distributed "A More Perfect Union" in cities across the country. Obama also did not ignore the challenges the country has faced since 1776, some of which brought the nation to its knees.

The Civil War, a conflict that divided brother against brother and caused some states to form a Confederacy bent on defending the institution of slavery, generated the crisis over which Abraham Lincoln presided. Lincoln's messages to the Republican Party and to his fellow Americans have rung true long after the fighting ceased, giving Americans an example of what happens to a house divided. Lincoln's brevity, moreover, may eventually prove of use to Obama. Obama's appeals to our better angels, his insistence that the Civil War prompted a great reckoning for slavery that continued the march toward freedom in the United States, and his contextual placement of 20th and 21st century civil rights movements in the mid-19th century civil rights movements, demonstrated a profound understanding and appreciation for history that has the potential to make Obama one of the greatest presidents this nation has ever had.

Even John McCain recognized Obama's charismatic appeal during the course of the campaign, comparing Obama to John F. Kennedy, albeit in a negative fashion. More disturbing, however, is the fact that McCain's entire approach was apparently to tear down Obama and Biden as they canvassed, called, and rallied their way toward the White House. For most of the campaign, McCain fired at Obama with claims of "massive new tax increases" and "higher taxes," eliciting cries of "Obama sucks" and "He's a socialist!" On McCain's behalf, South Carolina Senator Lindsay Graham condemned Obama for being "the most liberal senator in the United States Senate." One audience member proudly reminded a reporter that he was the one screaming, "No socialist, not now, not ever." Generally speaking, the McCain approach demonstrated that race-baiting and red-baiting have, regrettably, yet to go out of fashion.[38]

The politics of fear, cynicism, and negativity, however, lost ground in the 2008 presidential election due in no small part to the Republican Party's insistence on bigoted, racial—bordering on racist—and culturally divisive language and issues. No longer fair game in this country, racist critiques of African Americans, Latinos, and other people of color now carry political consequences. Communities learned during the campaign to rally together in support of Barack Obama, and they will undoubtedly hold onto some of that organization in order to keep the progressive framework in place for the future. Critics of Obama's rhetorical abilities conceded that "it's not hard to hear...echoes of the moral urgency of Dr. King, the generational call to greatness in challenging times of John F. Kennedy and Robert Kennedy and the sunny vision of a unified America.... Part black church, part yes-we-can American positivism, Mr. Obama's speeches seem crafted to almost irresistibly hit some sweet spot in the American soul."[39]

On the foreign policy side, Obama's rhetoric of inclusion and outreach—not just domestically but also internationally— suggested that the Obama Administration will have enormous success at reconnecting the alliances that the Bush Administration severed or allowed to fall into disrepair. Fed up with the narrowing worldview of the Republican Party, former Secretary of State Colin Powell endorsed Obama less than three weeks before the election, carrying into the Obama camp refugees from the Republican Party as it existed under Bush's hawkish leadership. Within the Republican Party, "Mr. Powell's endorsement reflected the rift between the so-called pragmatists, many of whom have come to view the Iraq War or its execution as a mistake, and the neoconservatives, a competing camp whose thinking played a pivotal role in building the case for war." Explaining why he shifted to Obama, Powell said that Obama had a better chance "to fix the reputation that we've left with the rest of the world."[40]

The Obama Administration promises to transform the foreign policy of the United States from a policy of denial and deception, under Bush, to a policy "grounded in hope," as a Princeton Project on National Security study suggested.[41] Through the application of "soft power," a term used to describe foreign policy instruments other than violence, the United States can—and should—regain its position as a broker of peace treaties, a signer of environmental treaties, a supporter of fledgling democracies, and an opponent of genocide everywhere. With many qualified individuals nominated for cabinet positions, the Obama Administration stands poised to turn the clock forward to a time when Americans are no longer reviled for their president's propensity to invade under false pretenses. On a lighter note, Obama—unlike Bush—will probably not give foreign journalists cause to throw their shoes at our commander-in-chief.[42]

Looking toward the future, Obama's rhetoric of change promises to transform the presidency, returning the White House to the American people and giving ordinary citizens more opportunities to serve their country. With detailed policy proposals and plans for change etched into the memories of millions of Americans, the Obama presidency carries with it the support of more Americans than have ever voted for a presidential candidate in American history. Both at home and abroad, the Obama presidency promises to enhance America's reputation as a land of opportunity, a nation of inclusion, and a country of hope. Connecting world leadership and the reputation of the nation in foreign affairs, Obama recognized quickly the need to restore diplomacy as tool of peacemaking. Through the transformative promise of Obama's rhetoric of change, the United States will, once again, bring hope to the destitute and inspiration to democracies.

THE RHETORIC OF CHANGE

During the early phases of the 2008 presidential campaign, Barack Obama sometimes told the story of how he met a woman on the campaign trail who had lived for 109 years, a woman who had been the granddaughter of slaves. She told him that she was not tired. "If she's not tired," the presidential aspirant declared, "then I'm not tired." With so much cynicism and foot-dragging in politics today, it was heartening for Obama to meet a centenarian still willing to fight for the change that Obama's campaign represented. Adding plans for change to the rhetoric of hope, Obama charismatically sparked a movement that encouraged incredible numbers of people to talk about why and how they wanted to make the country better. Rejecting not only the politics of fear but also the politics of the status quo, Obama sensed that the country needed both the rhetoric of hope and the promise of change.

James MacGregor Burns, the noted political scientist, concluded in a study of leadership that the Achilles' heel of many presidencies is "running alone." Too many leaders avoid empowering their followers to become leaders in their own right. The rhetoric of change, however, bodes well for a president intent on "running together."[43] From the outset of the campaign, Obama empowered organizers, interns, and volunteers across the nation to play a leadership role in the new political movement and held out hope to a generation of Americans. After the election, he even created a new Web site—change.gov—to maintain connections with supporters. The site also urges supporters to stay involved in political campaigns and activism, or even to run for public office themselves.[44] To those ready to turn the page on the rhetoric of fear and the politics of division, Obama offered the rhetoric of hope, bolstered by the transformational promise of change.

Perhaps the "tipping point" offers a better analogy for the rhetoric of change. Like Obama's rhetoric of hope, Obama's rhetoric of change suggested that millions of Americans rallying together, promoting the change they seek in the world among their friends and neighbors, and holding house parties to talk about the future, will surely provide the impetus for change on a societal level. Obama urged Americans to look around and notice what can be improved, fixed, and solved. "With the slightest push—in just the right place—it can be tipped."[45]

"There will be setbacks and false starts," Obama emphasized in his victory speech on the evening of November 4, 2008. "There are many who won't agree with every decision or policy I make as President, and we know that government can't solve every problem. But I will always be honest with you about the challenges we face. I will listen to you, especially when we disagree. And above all, I will ask you to join in the work of remaking this nation the only way it's been done in America for two-hundred and twenty-one years—block by block, brick by brick, calloused hand by calloused hand."

Democracy was in the air, and Obama basked in the enormity of the nation's victory of hope over fear, of the rhetoric of change over the rhetoric of standing still. "What began twenty-one months ago in the depths of winter must not end on this autumn night. This victory alone is not the change we seek—it is only the chance for us to make that change. And that cannot happen if we go back to the way things were. It cannot happen without you."[46]

CHAPTER EIGHT

THE NEW FAITH

Barack Obama became a household name after the young senator delivered the keynote address at the Democratic National Convention in Boston on a hot July evening in 2004. Declaring that "the pundits like to slice-and-dice our country into Red States and Blue States; Red States for Republicans, Blue States for Democrats,"[1] but that "we worship an awesome God in the Blue States,"[2] Obama illuminated one of the most important questions of our time. How should Americans approach faith in the 21st century? Encompassed by this question are other questions that lie at the intersection of faith and politics. What is faith's role in modern politics? How should faith influence public policy? Where will Obama's faith lead this nation?

Obama's personal and public expressions of faith suggest that he believes in a loving and progressive God who inspires mere mortals to campaign for change. Obama's writings suggest that he carefully considers his most important decisions, often through prayer, and longs to lead a nation of believers who listen to those of different faith traditions and who consider the opinions of others before criticizing those with whom they disagree. Restoring and reviving the nation's faith in politics and the potential of Washington to change, Obama garnered an almost cultish following of Americans reawakened from their civic slumber. Leading a movement for change based on "hope mongering," Obama drew on the legacy and the rhetoric of the civil rights movements of the abolitionists, the suffragettes, and the Reverend Dr. Martin Luther King, Jr.

A member of the United Church of Christ, Obama seems to internalize the UCC motto: "God Is Still Speaking."[3] Reviving outreach through African-American churches and faith groups, Obama preached the gospel of hope and change constantly on the campaign trail. Though haunted by the false allegations that he is Muslim and that Obama's personal relationships with his former pastor, the Reverend Jeremiah Wright, should disqualify him from the presidency, Obama never faltered in defending himself without lending credibility to those who attacked him. He responded to each lie with the truth, and he responded to each smear with a rational explanation. He understood that to respond in kind would be to stoop to the level of those who want God solely on their side, those who would rather divide us than unite us.

The Obama Revolution is, in part, about instilling in people a new faith in a progressive vision of religion that can be a positive force in the world. Defining God as a nurturer of faith, Obama appropriated King's vision of the American Dream, a vision of a nation in which people of all colors, classes, and creeds join hands and walk together toward the Promised Land. Obama added gay and straight to the categories of people included within King's American Dream. By acknowledging the struggles of homosexual men and women to achieve equality and respect, Obama updated King's vision for the 21st century. Obama's vision of God melds with his vision of the American Dream, positing a new faith destined to "bridge our differences."[4]

Having dominated the discourse on faith and politics in this country for many years, differences of race, religion, class, color, and creed, have begun to fall away in favor a multi-race, multi-faith worldview that brings people together rather than breaking people apart. This chapter examines the dichotomies of negative cynicism versus positive faith, savior status versus communal redemption, and hatred toward those who are different versus faith in a God of inclusion. Drawing on various sources to depict a man at once in tune with his own faith and willing to learn about and learn from the faiths of others, this chapter looks at the role of faith in modern politics, the relationship between faith and public policy, and the implications that Obama's faith holds for the future of the American people.

HOPE MONGERING

When Obama slipped into the convention speech that made him famous the nine words, "we worship an awesome God in the Blue States,"[5] he invited Americans to reconsider the role of faith in the public square and the labels that have dogged dogma in this country for more than two decades. Since the creation of the Christian Coalition, the 500 Club, and FOX News, religion has been largely defined by right-wing fundamentalists, a segment of the population that has used religion as a cudgel to marginalize those of other faiths and beliefs. Anyone who did not adhere to Pat Robertson's particular brand of Christianity, they proclaimed, was not a true Christian. Anyone who did not accede to Jerry Falwell's particular brand of patriotism, they declared, was not a true American. Anyone who did not participate in George W. Bush's particular brand of compassionate conservatism, they announced, was neither compassionate nor conservative.

What the right-wing fundamentalists did to the discourse of faith and politics in this country was to polarize those who agreed with Robertson, Falwell, and Bush against those who abhorred the notions that to be inclusive was to not be faithful and that to be progressive was to not be American. The damage caused by those who constantly spewed hate cannot be measured. It can never be conveniently forgotten. But it can be overcome. "Martin Luther King Jr. did it best.... He reminded us all of God's purposes for justice, for peace, and for the 'beloved community' where those always left out and behind get a front-row seat. And he did it—bringing religion into public life—in a way that was always welcoming, inclusive, and inviting to all who cared about moral, spiritual, or religious values."[6]

King—working with Ella Baker, Jesse Jackson, and countless others—strove to bring together those of different races, religions, classes, colors, and creeds, in pursuit of justice for all people and affirmation of all faiths. He sought to restore dignity to those who toiled for low pay and less recognition. He sought to revive the conscience of millions of Americans who turned a blind eye to discrimination, degradation, and destruction. He sought to reinvigorate the moral authority of a nation compromised by a losing war, a floundering economy, and an addiction to foreign oil. He wanted Americans to stop using God to justify the bombing of cities, the torturing of people denied the right to defend themselves in court, and the maltreatment of African Americans, women, poor people, and immigrants. King knew that America would only live out its creed if it opened its borders and held aloft once again the torch of liberty and opportunity.

Obama began his rise to the highest public office in the land with the philosophy preached by Martin Luther King, Jr.—that it is better to include than to exclude. He replaced fear mongering with hope mongering, restoring the nation's faith in politics built around principles of positive change and hope for the future. Rejecting the notion that God is white, Republican, and rich, Obama shook the foundations of the nation's faith and came away with an appreciation for the diversity of the American people and the enduring mysteries of the country's theology. He recognized, "of course, [that] God is not partisan; God is not a Republican or a Democrat.... Both parties, and the nation, must let the prophetic voice of religion be heard. Faith must be free to challenge both right and left from a consistent moral ground."[7] In order to be meaningful in a rapidly changing world, faith must have a moral compass that continually points toward our better angels.

Faith without morality is like hope without change. It is crushed by the first defeat, destroyed by the first sign of failure, and easily manipulated to serve petty political agendas. It bends to serve the ends of fascism as easily as it bends to serve the ends of justice. And it swings from serving the poor to enriching the rich, from freeing the enslaved to enslaving the free, and from welcoming all to including none. Faith without morality is a faith devoid of feeling. Faith with morality, on the other hand, always has the potential to break the chains of oppression, to free the enslaved, and to permit the meek to inherit the earth. "Prophetic faith does not see the primary battle as the struggle between belief and secularism. It understands that the real battle [is the] choice between cynicism and hope. The prophets always begin in judgment, in a social critique of the status quo, but they end in hope—that these realities can and will be changed."[8]

At once individual and communal, hope mongering speaks to our better angels, the part of us that is unwilling to turn a blind eye to the oppression and hardship of our fellow human beings. Like the prophetic faith of those who risked death to free themselves and others from slavery in antebellum America, the prophetic faith of the 21st century has the potential to open the doors of opportunity in this nation ever wider. By lifting up the downtrodden from below, rather than from on high, hope mongering spreads faith in the American Dream. Hope inspires us to keep struggling, to keep fighting, to keep building on our communal strengths in order to create a better world. Hope mongering is the spreading of hope to those who might otherwise have none. That hope, in turn, sparks movements. And movements create change.

The change that Obama promised throughout the presidential race is bigger than the president. It cannot be achieved by one man or one woman. The change for which thousands of staff members and millions of volunteers worked comes out of a broad movement for change, a movement rooted in hope mongering. More than two years before Obama officially became the next president of the United States, he emphasized that public policy decisions should not be made lightly or carelessly. In an interview with *Time*, he said that "it's just not my style to go out of my way to offend people or to be controversial just for the sake of being controversial. That's offensive and counterproductive. It makes people feel defensive and more resistant to changes."[9] At the same time, Obama noted that politicians should also be willing to put their career prospects on the line for their principles when the situation demanded it.

Throughout the campaign, Obama pointed to his comments warning against rushing to war in Iraq as evidence that he possessed the political courage necessary to lead the nation. "When I spoke out against going to war in Iraq in 2002, Bush was at 60-65% in the polls," he said. "I was putting my viability as a U.S. Senate candidate at risk. It looks now like an easy thing to do, but it wasn't then."[10] Unlike most of the other candidates in the race for president—with the obvious exception of Ohio Congressman Dennis Kucinich and New Mexico Governor Bill Richardson, both proudly anti-war from the beginning—Obama spoke against Bush's misadventure in Iraq when it mattered most. While other Democratic candidates were busy voting for a vaguely worded authorization of force against a country which allegedly possessed weapons of mass destruction, Obama was critiquing the proposed invasion and occupation as reckless and immoral.

Part of a broad anti-Iraq War movement, but not necessarily part of an all-encompassing anti-war movement, Obama cast himself not as a savior but as a leader. Knowing that his every word would be read and re-read, he parsed his words carefully, reaching out to those across the aisle and across the cultural divide that has too often pitted preacher against preacher, parishioner against parishioner. "There's a core decency to the American people that doesn't get enough attention,"[11] Obama told a reporter in Chicago. The reporter, in turn, wrote that Obama is "liberal, but not a screechy partisan. Indeed, he seems obsessively eager to find common ground with conservatives."[12] Such descriptions are not anomalies. There is a quiet thoughtfulness about Obama that people of all persuasions recognized and applauded on the campaign trail.

Rather than being all-knowing or all-powerful, Obama sought to be all-including and all-listening. He understood that the most potent leaders inspire but do not force. They touch people's lives. They respect the opinions and ideologies of their opponents and affirm the faiths and beliefs of their followers. They are constantly "reaching out [and] saying the other side isn't evil."[13] And they convey strength not through fear but through hope. In his own way, Obama avoided the pitfalls of savior status. He would not, and could not, achieve change on his own. He needed people young and old to turn his message of faith in America's future into a movement for change. He needed the hopeful to exercise their right to believe, their right to speak, their right to publish, their right to assemble, and their right to vote in order to create a new kind of politics.

There were times, of course, when many of Obama's followers seemed more excited about Obama's youthful appearance, rock-star popularity, and dramatic eloquence, than about his message. Adults fainted at Obama rallies, not always from heat exhaustion. Children ate cotton candy and pulled the strings on talking Obama dolls as they entered arenas filled with audiences straining their necks for a glimpse of a black man in a suit about to make a speech. Older women and men recounted their own heady run-ins with celebrity figures like Marilyn Monroe and Jackie Robinson. Volunteers drew pictures, painted banners, and printed posters that portrayed Obama in a heavenly light, presumably with angels dancing at his side. Americans sometimes made Obama into more than a man—they sometimes made him into a god.

Yet most of the time, the believers chanted "Yes We Can" not because Obama led the chant but because Obama brought out in them a hopefulness that they had not known was there. Pushing Americans to rise up from the ashes of the past to brighten the world of the future, Obama downplayed effluent displays of idolatry and encouraged organic displays of hope. He constantly reminded his audiences that he was not the one who needed to fight. He was not the one who needed to believe. He was not the one who would make or break the campaign, the election, and his presidency. Obama reminded the faithful that he would not be president forever. The staffers, volunteers, and rally-goers knew that the presidency of Obama would eventually end but hoped that the vision of unity and change espoused by Obama would ultimately endure.

Sitting with several other organizers on the rooftop of the Obama headquarters in Pennsylvania on a cloudless night four months before the general election, I asked my colleagues whether they ever questioned their insomnia-inducing devotion to the campaign. My colleague Marty, a computer wiz, responded that he campaigned not so much for Obama himself but because we needed to "take our country back." He proceeded to tick off a laundry list of issues that mattered to him, ranging from ending the Iraq War to improving financial aid for college students. My colleague Nicole said that she, like Obama, struggled to balance her commitment to law school with her commitment to the cause. Ultimately, she decided to forgo an editorial position on her school's law review in order to organize house parties, canvasses, and phone banks in the most rural part of Dauphin County. Nicole later told me that unifying the country behind a campaign for change was more important than her personal career goals.

Though just one example, this story of one organizer's hope in a brighter future for the nation and another organizer's decision to sacrifice her personal career goals in order to become a professional hope mongerer is the story of a campaign guided by the gospel of hope and change. It is the story of a relatively young nation still figuring out how to welcome people from all nations and how to include people from all walks of life. It is the story of an anthropologist who encouraged her son to experience a little bit of many different religions and many different faiths before choosing his own path. And it is the story of how that young man developed his worldview, his perspective on faith, and his belief in a unifying, liberating God.

OBAMA'S GOD

Barack Obama's personal journey of faith ran the gamut from son of an anthropologist to spiritual seeker to baptized Christian. Restless, curious, and relentlessly probing, Obama grew up with a mother, raised by "two lapsed Christians," who embedded her children in traditions as diverse as Catholicism and Islam, Congregationalism and Buddhism, Agnosticism and American Baptism.[14] Ultimately finding a spiritual home at Trinity United Church of Christ, Obama preached the gospel of hope and change constantly on the campaign trail. He made outreach through African-American churches and interfaith groups central to his campaign. Hounded by right-wing pundits who spread lies and denounced Obama's closest relationships, Obama responded with grace and discipline. Obama's personal faith, however, largely remained a mystery—until now. This section examines Obama's God.

Obama devoted 32 pages in *The Audacity of Hope* to a discussion of faith, particularly his own. Characterizing American spirituality as "deepening," Obama pronounced himself an authority on faith journeys "because it's a road I have traveled." He acknowledged up-front that he "was not raised in a religious household," an admission that might have doomed his political aspirations, but did not.[15] Obama was too candid to be criticized for the religion of his parents and grandparents. He was too open about the intersection of faith and family to be condemned for lacking the certitude of faith that other presidential candidates felt compelled to create. He was too tolerant of other faiths to be attacked from the left for his spirituality and too spiritual to be considered devoid of faith. In fact, Obama spent much of his life sampling different religious traditions before finding a faith for his worldview.

Embracing the United Church of Christ's motto, "God Is Still Speaking,"[16] Obama landed at Trinity United Church of Christ after a lifetime of seeking, wandering, and questioning. Taught to remain detached from each of the traditions which formed a critical part of his development, Obama "was to live in a Muslim country but be taught by his stepfather's example to ignore the most fundamentalist teachings of Islam. He was to attend a Roman Catholic school, but regard Christianity as no more than superstition. And he was to love a mother who viewed all religion as nothing more than a man-made tool for contending with the mysteries of life."[17] He attended a parochial school in a secular state and a public school in a theocratic state. At different times and in different places, he ate "dog meat, snake meat and roasted grasshopper," celebrated Christmas, and learned that "Islam can be compatible with the modern world."[18]

Obama described how "the Bible, the Koran, and the Bhagavad-Gita sat on the shelf alongside books of Greek and Norse and African mythology" in his mother Ann's home. Obama did not have much to say in his second book about his father Barack, who left his mother when Obama was only two, but noted that "although my father had been raised a Muslim, by the time he met my mother he was a confirmed atheist, thinking religion to be so much superstition, like the mumbo-jumbo of witch doctors that he had witnessed in the Kenyan villages of his youth." He also noted that his Indonesian stepfather Lolo "saw religion as not particularly useful in the practical business of making one's way in the world, and...had grown up in a country that easily blended its Islamic faith with remnants of Hinduism, Buddhism, and ancient animist traditions." For morality, Obama looked to his mother's "abiding sense of wonder."[19]

Pulled in different directions by his grandfather's "restless soul," his grandmother's rational inability "to accept anything she couldn't see, feel, touch or count," his father's particular brand of Islamic atheism, and his mother's anthropological detachment, Obama passed nimbly over his childhood religions. He preferred to dwell on his personal conversion when possible and his mother's "inherited skepticism" when necessary. This is, of course, understandable in light of the complexity of faith and the penetrating stares of the political media circus. In a book published on the eve of Obama's announcement as a candidate, Obama chose not to dwell too much on his mother's sense that "organized religion too often dressed up closed-mindedness in the garb of piety, cruelty and oppression in the cloak of righteousness." While acknowledging his family's influence, Obama wanted readers to focus on his own faith.[20]

Faith, for Obama, provided an outlet for his practical philosophy, a community within which he could express his ideas about change. "I came to realize that without a vessel for my beliefs, without an unequivocal commitment to a particular community of faith, I would be consigned at some level to always remain apart,"[21] he wrote. He wanted to feel like he had a spiritual home where he could fit into a long tradition of prophetic activists. After transferring from Occidental College in Los Angeles, California, to Columbia University in New York City, Obama sporadically attended services at Abyssinian Baptist Church in Harlem. "I'd just sit in the back and I'd listen to the choir and I'd listen to the sermon," he told *Newsweek*. "There were times that I would just start tearing up listening to the choir and share that sense of release."[22]

Obama liked the "power of the African-American religious tradition to spur social change," the way in which African-American churches often integrated themselves into the religious, social, and economic lives of community members. Appreciating the "biblical call to feed the hungry and clothe the naked and challenge powers and principialities," Obama became acquainted with the cycle of sin, repentance, and redemption that characterizes evangelical Christian doctrine. He learned that "the typical black sermon freely acknowledged that all Christians (including the pastors) could expect to still experience the same greed, resentment, lust, and anger that everyone else experienced." Gospel songs and happy feet symbolized redemption, release from the sins of humanity and daily life. At the same time, Obama needed to know that salvation was communal and intertwined with social justice.[23]

"It was because of these newfound understandings— that religious commitment did not require me to suspend critical thinking, disengage from the battle for economic and social justice, or otherwise retreat from the world that I knew and loved—that I was finally able to walk down the aisle of Trinity United Church of Christ one day and be baptized,"[24] Obama later explained. His job as a community organizer made him recognize that he could not ignore the power of faith in some of the most impoverished neighborhoods in which he worked. Although he chose to join the Christian tradition, he never stopped believing that "there are many paths to the same place and that is a belief that there is a higher power, a belief that we are connected as a people."[25] Not wanting to alienate anyone, Obama recognized the shared notion of Christianity, Judaism, and Islam alike that faith is all about embracing our common humanity.

Blurring the line between what is religious and what is ethical, Obama ultimately developed a doctrine of faith that incorporated those who do not need religion to be ethical. Referencing the many stars in the constellation of American civic history, Obama connected thriving churches and faiths with the Jeffersonian separation of church and state. He pointed, particularly, to the expanding and multiplying faith traditions present in this country to dispel the notion that one particular religious tradition has a monopoly on faith. "Whatever we once were," he noted, "we are no longer just a Christian nation; we are also a Jewish nation, a Muslim nation, a Buddhist nation, a Hindu nation, and a nation of nonbelievers."[26] Because "Christianity is but one religious tree rooted in the common ethical soil of all human experience,"[27] Obama resisted the temptation to believe, as so many believers do, that he had finally found the one true religion.

Throughout the 2008 presidential race, Obama's critics spread rumors that Obama was secretly a Muslim, a Communist, and a terrorist, and used every trick in the book to prove Obama guilty by association. Repeatedly defamed by right-wing pundits who continually pointed to his relationship with the Reverend Jeremiah Wright, his former pastor at Trinity United Church of Christ, as proof of Obama's "black anger" or anti-Americanism, Obama responded with contemplation and respectful explanations. He always kept his cool and carefully refuted each attack in turn. The frequent attempts to prove Obama guilty by association, however, proved much more difficult to quash and dispel than one might have thought. Because so many of the allegations involved religion, Obama knew that he would eventually have to deal with the political problems directly. On March 18, 2008, Obama confronted the questions about Wright and his faith in a brilliant speech that discussed the implications of race in American politics.

Most of the criticism of Obama regarding Wright stemmed from Wright's incendiary sermons in which he denounced white oppression and called the nation to account for a checkered history of slavery, segregation, and exploitation. And although "Wright's political pronouncements have been so radical and his demeanor in YouTube clips so angry that it is hard for some, particularly evangelicals, to accept that the church [was] anything more than a black Marxist recruitment center,"[28] his most infamous statements were taken out of context. In the most widely viewed clip, Wright said "God damn America"[29] in a sermon in which he criticized the prison-industrial complex and crack sentencing guidelines in the same sentence. Wright's other sermons did not gain notoriety because they did not directly attack the government.

Right-wing authors published books with relatively innocuous names like *The Case Against Barack Obama* and *The Obama Nation*, that purported to provide meticulously documented proof that Obama's childhood experiences made him Muslim, Christian, or both, depending on the time of day. Even one of the most hardened critics admitted, however, that "it's absurd to believe that Barack Obama hates America," acknowledging that his writings are, "for the most part, very level-headed, even philosophical."[30] Another author, who happened to have written the best-selling book that made "swift boat" into a verb to describe unfounded political attacks (like those that debilitated Senator John Kerry's run for president in 2004,) concluded, albeit with qualifications, that "those of us who oppose Obama would make a mistake to claim he is secretly Islamic or that Obama professes Christianity only as a front."[31]

Directly confronting the questions about Wright in his speech about race on March 18, 2008, Obama effectively closed the book on his associations with Wright by renouncing Wright's use of "incendiary language to express views that have the potential not only to widen the racial divide, but views that denigrate both the greatness and the goodness of our nation; that rightly offend white and black alike." He expressed disagreement with many of Wright's views, but noted that disagreement with religious leaders is not unusual. He even sympathized with the general antipathy toward Wright, confessing that "if all that I knew of Reverend Wright were the snippets of those sermons that have run in an endless loop on the television and YouTube...there is no doubt that I would react in much the same way." Obama emphasized that he would not "justify or excuse comments that are simply inexcusable."[32]

But Obama, who ultimately severed ties with Wright and left Trinity United Church of Christ, poignantly expressed his ambivalence about the man who had welcomed him into the faith community in Chicago, married him and Michelle, and baptized his children. "I can no more disown him than I can disown the black community," Obama stated with quiet dignity and poise. "I can no more disown him than I can my white grandmother—a woman who helped raise me, a woman who sacrificed again and again for me, a woman who loves me as much as she loves anything in this world, but a woman who once confessed her fear of black men who passed by her on the street, and who on more than one occasion has uttered racial or ethnic stereotypes that made me cringe." Refocusing attention on the future of the nation, Obama intoned, "These people are a part of me. And they are a part of America, this country that I love."[33]

By focusing on all that is good about America, while not ignoring the bad, Obama called upon his faith for assistance in divining the path that the nation should take in order to feed the hungry, clothe the naked, care for the sick, and rehabilitate the imprisoned. His personal faith intertwined with his public devotion, Obama drew upon the African-American tradition of socially conscious faith in his efforts to reach out to evangelicals and nonbelievers alike. Unwilling to take sides against particular faiths, Obama emphasized the common ethical obligations that we all share and the role that faith can play in leading us to do the right thing. One of Obama's political opponents once said that "Christ would not vote for Barack Obama,"[34] but even Obama's fiercest critics acknowledged that he was deeply spiritual. His campaign, in fact, challenged the nation to have faith in themselves and in the ability of hope to change the world.

GOD'S POLITICS

Barack Obama declared on March 18, 2008, that "what we know—what we have seen—is that America can change," that "what we have already achieved gives us hope—the audacity to hope—for what we can and must achieve tomorrow," and that "what is called for is nothing more, and nothing less, than what all the world's great religions demand—that we do unto others as we would have them do unto us." The Obama Revolution is not only about hope but also about instilling in the people of this great nation a desire to "be our brother's keeper," to "be our sister's keeper," and to "let our politics reflect that spirit as well." It is about bringing the nation's politics in line with our faith—whether in God or in our fellow Americans—in such a way that we strengthen the foundations of the country's commitment to achieving religious liberty, equality of opportunity, and justice for all people everywhere.[35]

Cognizant of the implications of surveys showing that "95 percent of Americans believe in God, more than two-thirds belong to a church, 37 percent call themselves committed

Christians, and substantially more people believe in angels than believe in evolution,"[36] Obama built upon previously laid foundations for a progressive vision of religion that can be a positive force in the world. He picked up on the efforts of Jim Wallis, Cornel West, and Dr. Jim Forbes of Riverside Church to meld the politics of faith with a progressive consensus on critical issues. Obama raised the "banner of what he hopes will be the faith-based politics of a new generation," fueled by the belief that faith is not singular, not limited to the old, static politics of division and hatred. His unorthodox faith appealed to young people, in particular, who "think nothing of hammering together a personal faith from widely differing religious traditions."[37]

"We need to take faith seriously not simply to block the religious right but to engage all persons of faith in the larger project of American renewal," Obama wrote in *The Audacity of Hope*, commending megachurch leaders like T.D. Jakes and Rick Warren—whom Obama chose to deliver the invocation at his inauguration—for "wielding their enormous influence to confront AIDS, Third World debt relief, and the genocide in Darfur," and applauding Wallis and Tony Campolo for "lifting up the biblical injunction to help the poor as a means of mobilizing Christians against budget cuts to social programs and growing inequality." Obama's depiction of the Bible as "not a static text but the Living Word" sparked criticism from those who would prefer that segments of our society remained enslaved, that segments of our society remained disenfranchised and beholden to their husbands, and that humans stop evolving. But criticism from the right did not stop Obama from believing.[38]

Through his vision, similar to that of Martin Luther King, Jr., of a God tolerant of all religions, races, genders, and sexual orientations, Obama sought to include all people in his American Dream, his faith in humanity. Condemning the homophobia that has kept the nation from according the same rights to homosexuals that heterosexuals enjoy, Obama emphasized that he would not "have the state deny American citizens a civil union that confers equivalent rights on such basic matters as hospital visitation or health insurance coverage simply because the people they love are of the same sex—nor am I willing to accept a reading of the Bible that considers an obscure line in Romans to be more defining in Christianity than the Sermon on the Mount."[39]

Obama's vision of God melds with his vision of the American Dream in a new faith designed to "bridge our differences."[40] Supporting unity over bigotry, Obama's policy prescriptions fit well within the framework of a new faith built on inclusion, environmental conservation, peace, and social justice. At the heart of faith is a commitment to the Golden Rule. Treating others with respect, dignity, and kindness lies at the center of what Wallis termed "a progressive and prophetic vision of faith and politics." Wallis described his ideal candidate as "pro-family, pro-life [but not anti-choice], strong on personal responsibility and moral values," and also "an economic populist, pro-poor in social policy, tough on corporate corruption and power, clear in supporting...health care and education, an environmentalist, and committed to...international law and multilateral cooperation over preemptive and unilateral war."[41]

The notion that the God of Christians, Jews, and Muslims would not want humans to continue to destroy the planet through deforestation, pollution, and greenhouse gas emissions is a notion grounded in a faith that recognizes the sanctity of the earth. The notion that the God of children everywhere would not want humans to permit rampant excesses in the corporate suites of America while starvation and disease kill millions in developing countries is a notion grounded in a faith that recognizes the sanctity of all God's children. And the notion that the God of civilians in warring nations would not want Christians to ignore Jesus Christ's pronouncement that "blessed are the peacemakers" is a notion grounded in both religious and secular efforts to "find the alternatives to war and violence that are so desperately needed in a world full of terrorists, terrorist states, unilateralist superpowers, and weapons of mass destruction."[42]

God's politics are the politics of women and men in the context of broader moral themes and ethical dilemmas. God's politics include people of every gender, race, religion, sexual orientation, class, and nationality. Moreover, God's politics need not necessarily include God, just morality. As Obama astutely noted, "organized religion doesn't have a monopoly on virtue, and one not need be religious to make moral claims or appeal to a common good."[43] When Obama appeared with Republican presidential candidate Sam Brownback at a 2006 World AIDS Day summit sponsored by Rick Warren's Saddleback Church, Brownback referenced Obama by saying,

"Welcome to *my* house!" Obama, quick on his feet, responded when he took the stage, "There is one thing I have to say, Sam. This is my house, too. This is God's house." Obama's comment set the tone for the event, reinforcing Obama's theme of inclusion of all faiths.[44]

A new, progressive vision of God as inclusive, nurturing, pro-environment, anti-war, and open to change is a vision of God rapidly gaining support among progressive theologians, spiritual leaders, and political leaders seeking to bridge the divide between evangelical Protestants, socially conscious Catholics, progressive Jews, peace-minded Muslims, and secular humanists. How far Obama will push this multi-faith vision remains to be seen, but it is promising that Obama consistently urged his audiences on the campaign trail to find common ground, "some overlapping values that both religious and secular people share when it comes to the moral and material direction of our country." Obama continued, hoping that "we might realize that we have the ability to reach out to the evangelical community and engage millions of religious Americans in the larger project of American renewal."[45]

THE NEW FAITH

For those of us who believe that all men and women are created equal, the United States of America has granted us an extraordinary opportunity to reaffirm our commitment to fight for freedom for all the right reasons, to welcome the huddled masses who continue to look to the Statue of Liberty for inspiration, and to love all of God's children. Part of a "new, post-modern generation that picks and chooses its own truth from traditional faith,"[46] Barack Obama grew up in a multi-faith household in multiple nations and was deeply affected by the different traditions that he experienced. He met family and friends in Indonesia, Hawaii, Kenya, Los Angeles, Harlem, and Chicago with vastly different religious backgrounds. He learned that morality trumped organized religion and that faith did not require formality. At long last, he found a spiritual home at Trinity United Church of Christ, which combined redemption with social justice.

Even then, however, Obama's faith journey was incomplete. Although baptized into the Christian tradition, during the campaign Obama became the subject of scathing criticism concerning his former pastor. Without stooping to the level of indecency of some of his sharpest critics, Obama responded by telling the truth and explaining—in great detail—exactly how hard it was for him to renounce his former pastor and move forward in his faith. But he rose to the challenge and came out ahead. Obama "won because he offered decency instead of cynicism, because he seemed calm and steady under fire and because he held out the promise (evident in his often-featured genealogy) that America's many strands could come together as one," wrote Ellis Close for *Newsweek*. "So when his opponents in the general election suggested he was some wild-eyed, un-American extremist, many voters simply couldn't accept that."[47]

Americans would do well to learn from the long and dark history of slavery, segregation, and sermonizing in this country. "A frequent recourse to Scripture for grounding or garnishing political positions has been consistently present in American history."[48] Preachers in the late 1800s referred to Jesus as "colorless," saying that "'Christ Jesus came into the world to save sinners,' not white sinners, nor black sinners, nor red sinners, but sinners."[49] And the nation can never forget the second inaugural address of Abraham Lincoln, who had been publicly attacked as an "infidel:"[50] "Yet if God will that [the war] continue until all the wealth piled by the bondsman's two hundred and fifty years of unrequited toil shall be sunk, and until every drop of blood drawn with the lash, shall be paid with another drawn with the sword, as was said three thousand years ago, so still it must be said 'the judgments of the Lord are true and righteous altogether.'"[51]

The new, progressive faith reminds us that "the advance of hope"[52] begins with us, just as Obama began his journey not knowing that it would take him to the highest peak in American politics. Intertwined with politics, faith cries out for people willing to carry the banner of justice and peace, people willing to defend the environment and equal rights, and people willing to stand up for all that is right and good.

The new faith requires messengers to spread the word. "It's a calling the prophets knew and a lesson learned by every person of faith and conscience who has been used to build movements of spiritual and social change," Wallis explained. "It's a commission that can only be fulfilled by very human beings, but people who, because of faith and hope, believe that the world can be changed. And it is that very belief that changes the world. And if not us, who will believe? After all, we are the ones we have been waiting for."[53]

CHAPTER NINE

OBAMA'S AMERICA

Barack Obama's electoral victories and inauguration have been hailed as historic moments for African-Americans. And they are. But they are also historic moments for the "green generation"—green in years, green in our concern for our planet—that secured Obama's razor-thin edge over Hillary Clinton and decisive victory over John McCain. Young people led the way in Obama's presidential run in order to ensure that our issues would not be ignored and that our dreams would not be deferred. As Obama said repeatedly, "This is our time."[1]

With the snowcaps melting, gasoline prices soaring, and the economy collapsing, the daughters and sons of the baby boomers had never seen our nation in worse shape. Ashamed of a president whose idea of economic stimulation was corporate welfare and whose interest in climate change was limited to the change in Halliburton's stock price, the next generation of Americans—Generation Change—came together to take back our country.

We knew that our country could not afford to let the oceans rise. We knew that our country could not afford to pay four dollars for a gallon of gas and four dollars for a gallon of milk. We knew that our country could not afford to remain bogged down in Iraq for the next 100 years. The mothers and fathers and sisters and brothers of the teenagers returning from Iraq in flag-draped coffins deserve better. The struggling students working two jobs to support themselves and their families while trying to get an education deserve better. The laid-off factory workers left stranded without health insurance while their jobs moved overseas deserve better.

Watching Obama address a million people in Grant Park and over 70 million more via television the night he clinched the presidency, it was impossible to miss the intensity of a people excited about the new direction of a nation that had been mobilized for change.[2] It was encouraging to hear Obama return again and again to the same issues, the same themes and the same hope.

Strip away the lapel pins and the dueling slogans and we are all Americans. We all want to live in a nation where we are judged not on the color of our skin, or the God we worship, or the expression of our sexuality, but on the content of our character. We all want to grow up in a world where we can drink fresh water and breathe clean air. We all want to vote in a democracy where we can cast our ballots and know that they will count. This is the hope and the promise of a people who have struggled to overcome the sins of slavery and segregation and who have fought for freedom against long odds. This is why we must persevere.

Let us always remember that although we faced fierce opponents and seemingly insurmountable obstacles during the 2008 presidential race, generations before us opened the door for us to succeed by challenging fascism, McCarthyism and racism. We owe it to them and we owe it to ourselves to continue to fight for the change that our country needs. Our issues, including the Iraq War, climate change, education and health care, must not be ignored, and our dreams of change must not be postponed. The choice between half-heartedly maintaining the status quo and aggressively pursuing the change we wish to see in the world has never been clearer.

If we are to achieve the change we still believe in, we will have to rise to the challenge again and again. It is up to us to continue to reach out to those who have lost all hope and bring them back into the democratic process. It is up to us to prove that we are the generation that will end our oil addiction and solve our environmental problems. It is up to us to prove that we will stand up for the tired, the poor and the huddled masses yearning to breathe free. It is up to us to convince Americans from all walks of life that there was a reason we believed in change and a reason we stood with Barack Obama. This is our time.[3]

AMERICA'S PROMISE

Barack Obama's election on November 4, 2008, closed one chapter in American history and opened a new chapter in America's future. Through unprecedented voter registration efforts, volunteer mobilization, and rural outreach, a generation of believers motivated a people tired of do-nothing politicians to elect a do-something community organizer. Believing in the policy prescriptions of Obama's platform and implementing Obama's 50-State Strategy, the organizers, interns, and volunteers who fanned out to every village and every hamlet took Obama's case for change directly to the American people—one voter at a time. For millions of Americans, Obama's rhetoric of hope fostered new optimism for America's future and harkened back to the dreams propounded by Jefferson, Jackson, Lincoln, and Roosevelt. Obama's rhetoric of change made it real, transforming a generation's hopeful ideals into a movement for change.

Heading to Grant Park to deliver his victory speech, Barack Obama e-mailed his supporters to alert them that "we just made history." For the first time in American history, a presidential candidate who happened to be black received the nod of the Democratic Party. For the first time in American history, that candidate won. What turned the tide? A generation of believers, committed to creating a new kind of politics in America, started walking. They walked from door to door, driveway to driveway, dirt lane to dirt lane. They walked even though their feet ached. They walked even though they could have been earning more money per hour flipping burgers at McDonald's. They walked even though the pundits said that a black man could not win in rural Virginia or rural Pennsylvania or rural North Carolina. And they walked right up until Election Day, until Obama headed to Grant Park.

"America is ready to turn the page," Barack Obama whispered to America. "This is our time. A new generation is prepared to lead."[4] A new generation of believers heard Barack Obama whispering, and they left their jobs at insurance companies and investment banks, they put down their school books at Wellesley and William & Mary, and they hitched a ride to the nearest battleground state. They opened campaign offices in Carlisle and Camp Hill, Roanoke and Richmond, Williamsburg and Westchester. They called voters in Gloucester to invite them to watch the presidential debates, and they held house parties in Mechanicsburg. They registered students in State College, and they signed up volunteers to get-out-the-vote in Greensboro. They walked up rickety wood staircases in Harrisburg and down fire escapes in Philadelphia in order to register millions of new voters. And they turned the page on cynicism, smears, and robocalls.

"There is something happening in America," Barack Obama said to America. "There is something happening when

Americans who are young in age and in spirit—who have never before participated in politics—turn out in numbers we've never seen because they know in their hearts that this time must be different."[5] A new generation of believers heard Barack Obama speaking, and they wondered how many votes it would take to obliterate racism. They registered to vote in record numbers, and they defeated an opponent who openly mocked community organizing. They packed their bags, and they packed the polling places. They came out for information, and they stayed to help Obama win. They thought about the rhetoric of hope, and they talked about the rhetoric of change. And they painted banners with the Obama 'O' for rallies, and they realized that something was happening, something that they had never seen before.

"We cannot walk alone," Barack Obama shouted to America. "And as we walk, we must make the pledge that we shall always march ahead. We cannot turn back."[6] A new generation of believers heard Barack Obama shouting, and they drove to Mathews while the lightning cracked, they drove to Fredericksburg in the pouring rain, and they drove to Allison Hill after dark. They asked the shopkeepers to put up signs in their windows, and they asked retirees to manage the offices while they were out. They taught a young man on probation how to teach volunteers to make phone calls, and they spoke in broken Spanish to those who did not know English, but still wanted to vote. They wondered how many more doors they would knock on, how many more people they would call, how many more voters they would register, and they kept right on going. And they refused to walk alone, when they had the chance to walk together. They always marched ahead, eyes on the prize. And they never turned back.

AMERICA'S CHALLENGE

What turned a loose network of individuals who wanted to end the war in Iraq, begin to combat climate change and solve the world's environmental problems, and rejuvenate the country's failing economy, into a movement for change was the simple idea that one person talking to his or her neighbor can make a difference. Returning to the nation's founding principles of life, liberty, and the pursuit of happiness, a generation of Americans mobilized in support of a long-shot candidate virtually unknown before he was invited to give a brief speech at the 2004 Democratic National Convention. Generation Change—as we might be called—organized for that long-shot community organizer from Chicago in unprecedented numbers and with unprecedented energy, injecting new life into an old way of building communities. In the process, the organizers and the volunteers they recruited created a massive political revolution—the Obama Revolution.

Combining the rhetoric of hope with the promise of change, the Obama campaign spurred Americans from all walks of life—rich and poor, black and white, old and young, gay and straight, rural and urban—to think hard about the America in which they want to live and to do everything in their power to make that dream a reality. Obama's charismatic leadership inspired millions of Americans to unite around America's promise. Believing that America as it should be is America as it can be, Obama lifted Cesar Chavez' slogan of "Yes We Can" to pull all of Obama's different plans and supporters together. By uniting the world and all Americans behind a program to help the poor, the uninsured, and the unemployed by guaranteeing health insurance and creating green jobs, the Obama campaign sparked a wide-ranging discussion about America's future.

With the inauguration of Barack Obama as the 44th president of the United States on January 20, 2009, the nation opened a new chapter in America's future, a chapter that sets the stage for serious consideration of America's challenge. This nation, like all great nations, faces far-reaching problems that will require innovative solutions. Decaying infrastructure, a failure to combat genocide and abusive leaders abroad, corruption, and a lack of concern for the general welfare have marred Bush's presidency. Obama's post-partisan approach to solving the underlying problems that our nation faces promises to allow us to overcome the challenges that tear apart America's families, kill the world's children, and prevent other nations from viewing the United States as a leader in inspiring democracy and encouraging long-term planning. Obama's rhetoric of hope and the promise of change will surely sustain us along the way. By putting aside our differences of party label, Americans will have many new opportunities to restore diplomatic relations with ostracized former allies and to unite behind a new era of hope, help, and change. There is no time to waste.

As president of the most powerful nation in the world, Obama stands at the forefront of a national movement for change that promises to tackle, if not solve, the most pressing problems facing the nation. Having demonstrated during the campaign that it is possible to unite people from all different backgrounds and of all different political persuasions, Obama stands ready to face America's challenge with the support of a generation of Americans hopeful for change. A historic moment for America's youth, Obama's African-American supporters, and political progressives, this moment presents America with some of the nation's greatest challenges but also with enormous opportunity. Not constrained by the blinders of bigotry or the limits of partisanship, Obama has the opportunity to cast the money changers from the temple and to work with a public empowered by the campaign to create a new Green Deal for the American people.

OBAMA'S AMERICA

Supported by a new generation of believers committed to restoring our nation's place as a beacon of hope in an ever-changing world, President Barack Obama has an unprecedented opportunity to remake America in the image of the centenarian who told him that she was not tired, the college student who put her life on hold to organize canvasses and phone banks at her local campaign headquarters, and the former Republican with the Confederate flag on his truck who put an Obama sign in his yard. These disparate images of America provide a glimpse of what Obama's America is all about. More than a campaign, the Obama Revolution reawakened that spirit of inclusion for which many generations have struggled. Guided by hope for change and faith in Obama's America, the millions of Americans who came together to put a community organizer in the White House formed the first wave of a revolution that is sweeping America.

Mark Twain once wondered what made Americans American. "I think that there is but one specialty with us, only one thing that can be called by the wide name 'American.' That is the national devotion to ice-water."[7] Like ice water, the Obama Revolution transcends party affiliation, appealing to people of all colors and creeds. There may seem to be little in common between the man in Mathews who had never voted for a Democrat but put an Obama sign in his yard, and the woman in Harrisburg who registered all of her neighbors to vote. There may seem to be little in common between the young children who scampered after me in the housing projects on Allison Hill, eager for Obama stickers, and the Democrats in Westmoreland County who turned out in droves for rural action meetings. But below the surface, they all hope for a brighter future for their children, and they share a belief that America can—and will—change.

From red states to blue states, from sleepy towns to bustling metropolises, a generation of Americans eager to change the world turned off their televisions and turned on their computers. People of all ages followed the lead of the youth and connected with their fellow Obama fanatics through Facebook and MyBO, demonstrating how the Internet could be a place where Americans meet to discuss the nation's problems and to organize rallies for a lanky lawyer from Illinois with solutions to those problems. In high schools and on college campuses, students started talking about the rhetoric of hope and how to turn that hope into change. Empowered to serve as the backbone of Obama's well-organized, well-funded, quintessentially grassroots presidential campaign, young people left their jobs, their schools, and their homes, in order to recruit and mobilize an army of volunteers committed to positive change.

With President Barack Obama officially sworn in as the 44th president of the United States, the American people can eagerly look toward the rising sun, heralding the dawn of a new day for a nation of believers. What will the future hold? Will Obama launch a Green Deal for a nation addicted to oil and desperate for jobs that will pay a living wage? Will the United States finally stop the bloodletting in Iraq in order to focus on the threats that really matter? Will the American people unite behind a president who does not look like the presidents on the dollar bills? In the war for independence nearly two and a half centuries ago, a motley crew of future Americans expressed hope for a free nation where all citizens would be represented in the nation's highest councils. Only by continuing to hope will America achieve the change we wish to see in the world. For Generation Change, the Obama Revolution is just beginning.

For Charlotte Zainab Miller, words cannot describe the intensity of hope and the promise of change: "When I found out that Barack Obama won, I was in the library studying for an exam the next day. I dropped everything and started yelling. I think everybody forgot that they were in the library. Everyone was celebrating. I thought it was a dream—I kept turning to my friend and asking, 'Is this real?' My hands were shaking and it was hard to stand up. I just wanted to pray and say thank you. All of the struggles African Americans have faced in America—and we are finally here. From 40 acres and a mule—and we are finally here. And to know that working 15 hours a week for Barack Obama, I had somehow—in some small way—made a difference and turned Virginia blue, was the most powerful feeling in the world. Everyone came up to me and thanked me because they knew I had worked on the campaign, but I told them I should be thanking them. They are the ones who went out and voted. We did it and nobody, NOBODY! can take it from us. It was the happiest day of my life. I realized that anything is possible. I was so proud of America, and for the first time in my 21 years of existence, I was proud to be an American."

That is Obama's America. This is the Obama Revolution.

OBAMA'S SPEECHES
FOR CHANGE

2004 KEYNOTE ADDRESS
BOSTON, MASSACHUSETTS | JULY 27, 2004

DECLARATION OF CANDIDACY
SPRINGFIELD, ILLINOIS | FEBRUARY 10, 2007

IOWA CAUCUS NIGHT
DES MOINES, IOWA | JANUARY 3, 2008

NEW HAMPSHIRE PRIMARY NIGHT
NASHUA, NEW HAMPSHIRE | JANUARY 8, 2008

A MORE PERFECT UNION
PHILADELPHIA, PENNSYLVANIA | MARCH 18, 2008

OUR MOMENT, OUR TIME
ST. PAUL, MINNESOTA | JUNE 3, 2008

A WORLD THAT STANDS AS ONE
BERLIN, GERMANY | JULY 24, 2008

THE AMERICAN PROMISE
DENVER, COLORADO | AUGUST 28, 2008

ONE WEEK
CANTON, OHIO | OCTOBER 27, 2008

YES WE CAN
CHICAGO, ILLINOIS | NOVEMBER 4, 2008

On behalf of the great state of Illinois, crossroads of a nation, land of Lincoln, let me express my deep gratitude for the privilege of addressing this convention. Tonight is a particular honor for me because, let's face it, my presence on this stage is pretty unlikely. My father was a foreign student, born and raised in a small village in Kenya. He grew up herding goats, went to school in a tin-roof shack. His father, my grandfather, was a cook, a domestic servant.

But my grandfather had larger dreams for his son. Through hard work and perseverance my father got a scholarship to study in a magical place: America, which stood as a beacon of freedom and opportunity to so many who had come before. While studying here, my father met my mother. She was born in a town on the other side of the world, in Kansas. Her father worked on oil rigs and farms through most of the Depression. The day after Pearl Harbor he signed up for duty, joined Patton's army and marched across Europe. Back home, my grandmother raised their baby and went to work on a bomber assembly line. After the war, they studied on the GI Bill, bought a house through FHA, and moved west in search of opportunity.

And they, too, had big dreams for their daughter, a common dream, born of two continents. My parents shared not only an improbable love; they shared an abiding faith in the possibilities of this nation. They would give me an African name, Barack, or "blessed," believing that in a tolerant America your name is no barrier to success. They imagined me going to the best schools in the land, even though they weren't rich, because in a generous America you don't have to be rich to achieve your potential. They are both passed away now. Yet, I know that, on this night, they look down on me with pride.

I stand here today, grateful for the diversity of my heritage, aware that my parents' dreams live on in my precious daughters. I stand here knowing that my story is part of the larger American story, that I owe a debt to all of those who came before me, and that, in no other country on earth, is my story even possible. Tonight, we gather to affirm the greatness of our nation, not because of the height of our skyscrapers, or the power of our military, or the size of our economy. Our pride is based on a very simple premise, summed up in a declaration made over two hundred years ago, "We hold these truths to he self-evident, that all men are created equal. That they are endowed by their

Creator with certain inalienable rights. That among these are life, liberty and the pursuit of happiness."

That is the true genius of America, a faith in the simple dreams of its people, the insistence on small miracles. That we can tuck in our children at night and know they are fed and clothed and safe from harm. That we can say what we think, write what we think, without hearing a sudden knock on the door. That we can have an idea and start our own business without paying a bribe or hiring somebody's son. That we can participate in the political process without fear of retribution, and that our votes will he counted—or at least, most of the time.

This year, in this election, we are called to reaffirm our values and commitments, to hold them against a hard reality and see how we are measuring up, to the legacy of our forbearers, and the promise of future generations. And fellow Americans— Democrats, Republicans, Independents—I say to you tonight: we have more work to do. More to do for the workers I met in Galesburg, Illinois, who are losing their union jobs at the Maytag plant that's moving to Mexico, and now are having to compete with their own children for jobs that pay seven bucks an hour. More to do for the father I met who was losing his job and choking back tears, wondering how he would pay $4,500 a month for the drugs his son needs without the health benefits he counted on. More to do for the young woman in East St. Louis, and thousands more like her, who has the grades, has the drive, has the will, but doesn't have the money to go to college.

Don't get me wrong. The people I meet in small towns and big cities, in diners and office parks, they don't expect government to solve all their problems. They know they have to work hard to get ahead and they want to. Go into the collar counties around Chicago, and people will tell you they don't want their tax money wasted by a welfare agency or the Pentagon. Go into any inner city neighborhood, and folks will tell you that government alone can't teach kids to learn. They know that parents have to parent, that children can't achieve unless we raise their expectations and turn off the television sets and eradicate the slander that says a black youth with a book is acting white. No, people don't expect government to solve all their problems. But they sense, deep in their bones, that with just a change in priorities, we can make sure that every child in America has a decent shot at life, and that the doors of opportunity remain open to all. They know we can do better. And they want that choice.

In this election, we offer that choice. Our party has chosen a man to lead us who embodies the best this country has to offer.

That man is John Kerry. John Kerry understands the ideals of community, faith, and sacrifice, because they've defined his life. From his heroic service in Vietnam to his years as prosecutor and lieutenant governor, through two decades in the United States Senate, he has devoted himself to this country. Again and again, we've seen him make tough choices when easier ones were available. His values and his record affirm what is best in us.

John Kerry believes in an America where hard work is rewarded. So instead of offering tax breaks to companies shipping jobs overseas, he'll offer them to companies creating jobs here at home. John Kerry believes in an America where all Americans can afford the same health coverage our politicians in Washington have for themselves. John Kerry believes in energy independence, so we aren't held hostage to the profits of oil companies or the sabotage of foreign oil fields. John Kerry believes in the constitutional freedoms that have made our country the envy of the world, and he will never sacrifice our basic liberties nor use faith as a wedge to divide us. And John Kerry believes that in a dangerous world, war must be an option, but it should never he the first option.

A while back, I met a young man named Shamus at the VFW Hall in East Moline, Illinois. He was a good-looking kid, six-two or six-three, clear-eyed, with an easy smile. He told me he'd joined the Marines and was heading to Iraq the following week. As I listened to him explain why he'd enlisted, his absolute faith in our country and its leaders, his devotion to duty and service, I thought this young man was all any of us might hope for in a child. But then I asked myself: Are we serving Shamus as well as he was serving us? I thought of more than 900 service men and women, sons and daughters, husbands and wives, friends and neighbors, who will not be returning to their hometowns. I thought of families I had met who were struggling to get by without a loved one's full income, or whose loved ones had returned with a limb missing or with nerves shattered, but who still lacked long-term health benefits because they were reservists. When we send our young men and women into harm's way, we have a solemn obligation not to fudge the numbers or shade the truth about why they're going, to care for their families while they're gone, to tend to the soldiers upon their return, and to never ever go to war without enough troops to win the war, secure the peace, and earn the respect of the world.

Now let me be clear. We have real enemies in the world. These enemies must be found. They must be pursued and they must be defeated. John Kerry knows this. And just as Lieutenant Kerry did not hesitate to risk his life to protect the men who served with him in Vietnam, President Kerry will not hesitate one moment to use our military might to keep America safe and secure. John Kerry believes in America. And he knows it's not enough for just some of us to prosper. For alongside our famous individualism, there's another ingredient in the American saga.

A belief that we are connected as one people. If there's a child on the south side of Chicago who can't read, that matters to me, even if it's not my child. If there's a senior citizen somewhere who can't pay for her prescription and has to choose between medicine and the rent, that makes my life poorer, even if it's not my grandmother. If there's an Arab American family being rounded up without benefit of an attorney or due process, that threatens my civil liberties. It's that fundamental belief—I am my brother's keeper, I am my sister's keeper—that makes this country work. It's what allows us to pursue our individual dreams, yet still come together as a single American family. "E pluribus unum." Out of many, one.

Yet even as we speak, there are those who are preparing to divide us, the spin masters and negative ad peddlers who embrace the politics of anything goes. Well, I say to them tonight, there's not a liberal America and a conservative America—there's the United States of America. There's not a black America and white America and Latino America and Asian America; there's the United States of America. The pundits like to slice-and-dice our country into Red States and Blue States; Red States for Republicans, Blue States for Democrats. But I've got news for them, too. We worship an awesome God in the Blue States, and we don't like federal agents poking around our libraries in the Red States. We coach Little League in the Blue States and have gay friends in the Red States. There are patriots who opposed the war in Iraq and patriots who supported it. We are one people, all of us pledging allegiance to the stars and stripes, all of us defending the United States of America.

In the end, that's what this election is about. Do we participate in a politics of cynicism or a politics of hope? John Kerry calls on us to hope. John Edwards calls on us to hope. I'm not talking about blind optimism here—the almost willful ignorance that thinks unemployment will go away if we just don't talk about it, or the health care crisis will solve itself if we just ignore it. No, I'm talking about something more substantial. It's the hope of slaves sitting around a fire singing freedom songs; the hope of immigrants setting out for distant shores; the hope of a young naval lieutenant bravely patrolling the Mekong Delta; the hope of a millworker's son who dares to defy the odds; the hope of a skinny kid with a funny name who believes that America has a place for him, too. The audacity of hope!

In the end, that is God's greatest gift to us, the bedrock of this nation; the belief in things not seen; the belief that there are better days ahead. I believe we can give our middle class relief and provide working families with a road to opportunity. I believe we can provide jobs to the jobless, homes to the homeless, and reclaim young people in cities across America from violence and despair. I believe that as we stand on the crossroads of history, we can make the right choices, and meet the challenges that face us. America!

Tonight, if you feel the same energy I do, the same urgency I do, the same passion I do, the same hopefulness I do— if we do what we must do, then I have no doubt that all across the country, from Florida to Oregon, from Washington to Maine, the people will rise up in November, and John Kerry will be sworn in as president, and John Edwards will be sworn in as vice president, and this country will reclaim its promise, and out of this long political darkness a brighter day will come. Thank you and God bless you.

DECLARATION OF CANDIDACY
Springfield, Illinois | February 10, 2007

Let me begin by saying thanks to all you who've traveled, from far and wide, to brave the cold today.

We all made this journey for a reason. It's humbling, but in my heart I know you didn't come here just for me, you came here because you believe in what this country can be. In the face of war, you believe there can be peace. In the face of despair, you believe there can be hope. In the face of a politics that's shut you out, that's told you to settle, that's divided us for too long, you believe we can be one people, reaching for what's possible, building that more perfect union.

That's the journey we're on today. But let me tell you how I came to be here. As most of you know, I am not a native of this great state. I moved to Illinois over two decades ago. I was a young man then, just a year out of college; I knew no one in Chicago, was without money or family connections. But a group of churches had offered me a job as a community organizer for $13,000 a year. And I accepted the job, sight unseen, motivated then by a single, simple, powerful idea—that I might play a small part in building a better America.

My work took me to some of Chicago's poorest neighborhoods. I joined with pastors and lay-people to deal with communities that had been ravaged by plant closings. I saw that the problems people faced weren't simply local in nature—that the decision to close a steel mill was made by distant executives; that the lack of textbooks and computers in schools could be traced to the skewed priorities of politicians a thousand miles away; and that when a child turns to violence, there's a hole in his heart no government alone can fill.

It was in these neighborhoods that I received the best education I ever had, and where I learned the true meaning of my Christian faith.

After three years of this work, I went to law school, because I wanted to understand how the law should work for those in need. I became a civil rights lawyer, and taught constitutional law, and after a time, I came to understand that our cherished rights of liberty and equality depend on the active participation of an awakened electorate. It was with these ideas in mind that I arrived in this capital city as a state Senator.

It was here, in Springfield, where I saw all that is America converge—farmers and teachers, businessmen and laborers, all of them with a story to tell, all of them seeking a seat at the table, all of them clamoring to be heard. I made lasting friendships here—friends that I see in the audience today.

It was here we learned to disagree without being disagreeable—that it's possible to compromise so long as you know those principles that can never be compromised; and that so long as we're willing to listen to each other, we can assume the best in people instead of the worst.

That's why we were able to reform a death penalty system that was broken. That's why we were able to give health insurance to children in need. That's why we made the tax system more fair and just for working families, and that's why we passed ethics reforms that the cynics said could never, ever be passed.

It was here, in Springfield, where North, South, East and West come together that I was reminded of the essential decency of the American people—where I came to believe that through this decency, we can build a more hopeful America.

And that is why, in the shadow of the Old State Capitol, where Lincoln once called on a divided house to stand together, where common hopes and common dreams still, I stand before you today to announce my candidacy for President of the United States.

I recognize there is a certain presumptuousness—a certain audacity—to this announcement. I know I haven't spent a lot of time learning the ways of Washington. But I've been there long enough to know that the ways of Washington must change.

The genius of our founders is that they designed a system of government that can be changed. And we should take heart, because we've changed this country before. In the face of tyranny, a band of patriots brought an Empire to its knees. In the face of secession, we unified a nation and set the captives free. In the face of Depression, we put people back to work and lifted millions out of poverty. We welcomed immigrants to our shores, we opened railroads to the west, we landed a man on the moon, and we heard a King's call to let justice roll down like water, and righteousness like a mighty stream.

Each and every time, a new generation has risen up and done what's needed to be done. Today we are called once more—and it is time for our generation to answer that call.

For that is our unyielding faith—that in the face of impossible odds, people who love their country can change it.

That's what Abraham Lincoln understood. He had his doubts. He had his defeats. He had his setbacks. But through his will and his words, he moved a nation and helped free a people. It is because of the millions who rallied to his cause that we are no longer divided, North and South, slave and free. It is because men and women of every race, from every walk of life, continued to march for freedom long after Lincoln was laid to rest, that today we have the chance to face the challenges of this millennium together, as one people—as Americans.

All of us know what those challenges are today—a war with no end, a dependence on oil that threatens our future, schools where too many children aren't learning, and families struggling paycheck to paycheck despite working as hard as they can. We know the challenges. We've heard them. We've talked about them for years.

What's stopped us from meeting these challenges is not the absence of sound policies and sensible plans. What's stopped us is the failure of leadership, the smallness of our politics—the ease with which we're distracted by the petty and trivial, our chronic avoidance of tough decisions, our preference for scoring cheap political points instead of rolling up our sleeves and building a working consensus to tackle big problems.

For the last six years we've been told that our mounting debts don't matter, we've been told that the anxiety Americans feel about rising health care costs and stagnant wages are an illusion, we've been told that climate change is a hoax, and that tough talk and an ill-conceived war can replace diplomacy, and strategy, and foresight. And when all else fails, when Katrina happens, or the death toll in Iraq mounts, we've been told that our crises are somebody else's fault. We're distracted from our real failures, and told to blame the other party, or gay people, or immigrants.

And as people have looked away in disillusionment and frustration, we know what's filled the void. The cynics, and the lobbyists, and the special interests who've turned our government into a game only they can afford to play. They write the checks and you get stuck with the bills, they get the access while you get to write a letter, they think they own this government, but we're here today to take it back. The time for that politics is over. It's time to turn the page.

We've made some progress already. I was proud to help lead the fight in Congress that led to the most sweeping ethics reform since Watergate.

But Washington has a long way to go. And it won't be easy. That's why we'll have to set priorities. We'll have to make hard choices. And although government will play a crucial role in bringing about the changes we need, more money and programs alone will not get us where we need to go. Each of us, in our own lives, will have to accept responsibility—for instilling an ethic of achievement in our children, for adapting to a more competitive economy, for strengthening our communities, and sharing some measure of sacrifice. So let us begin. Let us begin this hard work together. Let us transform this nation.

Let us be the generation that reshapes our economy to compete in the digital age. Let's set high standards for our schools and give them the resources they need to succeed. Let's recruit a new army of teachers, and give them better pay and more support in exchange for more accountability. Let's make college more affordable, and let's invest in scientific research, and let's lay down broadband lines through the heart of inner cities and rural towns all across America.

And as our economy changes, let's be the generation that ensures our nation's workers are sharing in our prosperity. Let's protect the hard-earned benefits their companies have promised. Let's make it possible for hardworking Americans to save for retirement. And let's allow our unions and their organizers to lift up this country's middle-class again.

Let's be the generation that ends poverty in America. Every single person willing to work should be able to get job training that leads to a job, and earn a living wage that can pay the bills, and afford child care so their kids have a safe place to go when they work. Let's do this.

Let's be the generation that finally tackles our health care crisis. We can control costs by focusing on prevention, by providing better treatment to the chronically ill, and using technology to cut the bureaucracy. Let's be the generation that says right here, right now, that we will have universal health care in America by the end of the next president's first term.

Let's be the generation that finally frees America from the tyranny of oil. We can harness homegrown, alternative fuels like ethanol and spur the production of more fuel-efficient cars. We can set up a system for capping greenhouse gases. We can turn this crisis of global warming into a moment of opportunity for innovation, and job creation, and an incentive for businesses that will serve as a model for the world. Let's be the generation that makes future generations proud of what we did here.

Most of all, let's be the generation that never forgets what happened on that September day and confront the terrorists with everything we've got. Politics doesn't have to divide us on this anymore—we can work together to keep our country safe. I've worked with Republican Senator Dick Lugar to pass a law that will secure and destroy some of the world's deadliest, unguarded weapons. We can work together to track terrorists down with a stronger military, we can tighten the net around their finances, and we can improve our intelligence capabilities. But let us also understand that ultimate victory against our enemies will come only by rebuilding our alliances and exporting those ideals that bring hope and opportunity to millions around the globe.

But all of this cannot come to pass until we bring an end to this war in Iraq. Most of you know I opposed this war from the start. I thought it was a tragic mistake. Today we grieve for the families who have lost loved ones, the hearts that have been broken, and the young lives that could have been. America, it's time to start bringing our troops home. It's time to admit that no amount of American lives can resolve the political disagreement that lies at the heart of someone else's civil war. That's why I have a plan that will bring our combat troops home by March of 2008. Letting the Iraqis know that we will not be there forever is our last, best hope to pressure the Sunni and Shia to come to the table and find peace.

Finally, there is one other thing that is not too late to get right about this war—and that is the homecoming of the men and women—our veterans—who have sacrificed the most. Let us honor their valor by providing the care they need and rebuilding the military they love. Let us be the generation that begins this work.

I know there are those who don't believe we can do all these things. I understand the skepticism. After all, every four years, candidates from both parties make similar promises, and I expect this year will be no different. All of us running for president will travel around the country offering ten-point plans and making grand speeches; all of us will trumpet those qualities we believe make us uniquely qualified to lead the country. But too many times, after the election is over, and the confetti is swept away, all those promises fade from memory, and the lobbyists and the special interests move in, and people turn away, disappointed as before, left to struggle on their own.

That is why this campaign can't only be about me. It must be about us—it must be about what we can do together. This campaign must be the occasion, the vehicle, of your hopes, and your dreams. It will take your time, your energy, and your advice—to push us forward when we're doing right, and to let us know when we're not. This campaign has to be about reclaiming the meaning of citizenship, restoring our sense of common purpose, and realizing that few obstacles can withstand the power of millions of voices calling for change.

By ourselves, this change will not happen. Divided, we are bound to fail.

But the life of a tall, gangly, self-made Springfield lawyer tells us that a different future is possible.

He tells us that there is power in words.

He tells us that there is power in conviction.

That beneath all the differences of race and region, faith and station, we are one people.

He tells us that there is power in hope.

As Lincoln organized the forces arrayed against slavery, he was heard to say: "Of strange, discordant, and even hostile elements, we gathered from the four winds, and formed and fought to battle through."

That is our purpose here today.

That's why I'm in this race.

Not just to hold an office, but to gather with you to transform a nation.

I want to win that next battle—for justice and opportunity.

I want to win that next battle—for better schools, and better jobs, and health care for all.

I want us to take up the unfinished business of perfecting our union, and building a better America.

And if you will join me in this improbable quest, if you feel destiny calling, and see as I see, a future of endless possibility stretching before us; if you sense, as I sense, that the time is now to shake off our slumber, and slough off our fear, and make good on the debt we owe past and future generations, then I'm ready to take up the cause, and march with you, and work with you. Together, starting today, let us finish the work that needs to be done, and usher in a new birth of freedom on this Earth.

IOWA CAUCUS NIGHT
Des Moines, Iowa | January 3, 2008

Thank you, Iowa.

You know, they said this day would never come.

They said our sights were set too high.

They said this country was too divided; too disillusioned to ever come together around a common purpose.

But on this January night—at this defining moment in history—you have done what the cynics said we couldn't do. You have done what the state of New Hampshire can do in five days. You have done what America can do in this New Year, 2008. In lines that stretched around schools and churches; in small towns and big cities; you came together as Democrats, Republicans and Independents to stand up and say that we are one nation; we are one people; and our time for change has come.

You said the time has come to move beyond the bitterness and pettiness and anger that's consumed Washington; to end the political strategy that's been all about division and instead make it about addition—to build a coalition for change that stretches through Red States and Blue States. Because that's how we'll win in November, and that's how we'll finally meet the challenges that we face as a nation.

We are choosing hope over fear. We're choosing unity over division, and sending a powerful message that change is coming to America.

You said the time has come to tell the lobbyists who think their money and their influence speak louder than our voices that they don't own this government, we do; and we are here to take it back.

The time has come for a President who will be honest about the choices and the challenges we face; who will listen to you and learn from you even when we disagree; who won't just tell you what you want to hear, but what you need to know. And in New Hampshire, if you give me the same chance that Iowa did tonight, I will be that president for America.

Thank you.

I'll be a President who finally makes health care affordable and available to every single American the same way I expanded health care in Illinois—by bringing Democrats and Republicans together to get the job done.

I'll be a President who ends the tax breaks for companies that ship our jobs overseas and put a middle-class tax cut into the pockets of the working Americans who deserve it.

I'll be a President who harnesses the ingenuity of farmers and scientists and entrepreneurs to free this nation from the tyranny of oil once and for all.

And I'll be a President who ends this war in Iraq and finally brings our troops home; who restores our moral standing; who understands that 9/11 is not a way to scare up votes, but a challenge that should unite America and the world against the common threats of the 21st century; common threats of terrorism and nuclear weapons; climate change and poverty; genocide and disease.

Tonight, we are one step closer to that vision of America because of what you did here in Iowa. And so I'd especially like to thank the organizers and the precinct captains; the volunteers and the staff who made this all possible.

And while I'm at it, on "thank yous," I think it makes sense for me to thank the love of my life, the rock of the Obama family, the closer on the campaign trail; give it up for Michelle Obama.

I know you didn't do this for me. You did this—you did this because you believed so deeply in the most American of ideas—that in the face of impossible odds, people who love this country can change it.

I know this—I know this because while I may be standing here tonight, I'll never forget that my journey began on the streets of Chicago doing what so many of you have done for this campaign and all the campaigns here in Iowa—organizing, and working, and fighting to make people's lives just a little bit better.

I know how hard it is. It comes with little sleep, little pay, and a lot of sacrifice. There are days of disappointment, but sometimes, just sometimes, there are nights like this—a night—a night that, years from now, when we've made the changes we believe in; when more families can afford to see a doctor; when our children—when Malia and Sasha and your children—inherit a planet that's a little cleaner and safer; when the world sees America differently, and America sees itself as a nation less divided and more united; you'll be able to look back with pride and say that this was the moment when it all began.

This was the moment when the improbable beat what Washington always said was inevitable.

This was the moment when we tore down barriers that have divided us for too long—when we rallied people of all parties and ages to a common cause; when we finally gave Americans who'd never participated in politics a reason to stand up and to do so.

This was the moment when we finally beat back the politics of fear, and doubt, and cynicism; the politics where we tear each other down instead of lifting this country up. This was the moment.

Years from now, you'll look back and you'll say that this was the moment—this was the place—where America remembered what it means to hope.

For many months, we've been teased, even derided for talking about hope.

But we always knew that hope is not blind optimism. It's not ignoring the enormity of the task ahead or the roadblocks that stand in our path. It's not sitting on the sidelines or shirking from a fight. Hope is that thing inside us that insists, despite all evidence to the contrary, that something better awaits us if we have the courage to reach for it, and to work for it, and to fight for it.

Hope is what I saw in the eyes of the young woman in Cedar Rapids who works the night shift after a full day of college and still can't afford health care for a sister who's ill; a young woman who still believes that this country will give her the chance to live out her dreams.

Hope is what I heard in the voice of the New Hampshire woman who told me that she hasn't been able to breathe since her nephew left for Iraq; who still goes to bed each night praying for his safe return.

Hope is what led a band of colonists to rise up against an empire; what led the greatest of generations to free a continent and heal a nation; what led young women and young men to sit at lunch counters and brave fire hoses and march through Selma and Montgomery for freedom's cause.

Hope—hope—is what led me here today—with a father from Kenya; a mother from Kansas; and a story that could only happen in the United States of America. Hope is the bedrock of this nation; the belief that our destiny will not be written for us, but by us; by all those men and women who are not content to settle for the world as it is; who have the courage to remake the world as it should be.

That is what we started here in Iowa, and that is the message we can now carry to New Hampshire and beyond; the same message we had when we were up and when we were down; the one that can change this country brick by brick, block by block, calloused hand by calloused hand—that together, ordinary people can do extraordinary things; because we are not a collection of Red States and Blue States, we are the United States of America; and at this moment, in this election, we are ready to believe again. Thank you, Iowa.

New Hampshire Primary Night
Nashua, New Hampshire | January 8, 2008

I want to congratulate Senator Clinton on a hard-fought victory here in New Hampshire.

A few weeks ago, no one imagined that we'd have accomplished what we did here tonight. For most of this campaign, we were far behind, and we always knew our climb would be steep.

But in record numbers, you came out and spoke up for change. And with your voices and your votes, you made it clear that at this moment—in this election—there is something happening in America.

There is something happening when men and women in Des Moines and Davenport; in Lebanon and Concord come out in the snows of January to wait in lines that stretch block after block because they believe in what this country can be.

There is something happening when Americans who are young in age and in spirit—who have never before participated in politics—turn out in numbers we've never seen because they know in their hearts that this time must be different.

There is something happening when people vote not just for the party they belong to but the hopes they hold in common— that whether we are rich or poor; black or white; Latino or Asian; whether we hail from Iowa or New Hampshire, Nevada or South Carolina, we are ready to take this country in a fundamentally new direction. That is what's happening in America right now. Change is what's happening in America.

You can be the new majority who can lead this nation out of a long political darkness—Democrats, Independents and Republicans who are tired of the division and distraction that has clouded Washington; who know that we can disagree without being disagreeable; who understand that if we mobilize our voices to challenge the money and influence that's stood in our way and challenge ourselves to reach for something better, there's no problem we can't solve—no destiny we cannot fulfill.

Our new American majority can end the outrage of unaffordable, unavailable health care in our time. We can bring doctors and patients; workers and businesses, Democrats and Republicans together; and we can tell the drug and insurance industry that while they'll get a seat at the table, they don't get to buy every chair. Not this time. Not now.

Our new majority can end the tax breaks for corporations that ship our jobs overseas and put a middle-class tax cut into the pockets of the working Americans who deserve it.

We can stop sending our children to schools with corridors of shame and start putting them on a pathway to success. We can stop talking about how great teachers are and start rewarding them for their greatness. We can do this with our new majority.

We can harness the ingenuity of farmers and scientists; citizens and entrepreneurs to free this nation from the tyranny of oil and save our planet from a point of no return.

And when I am President, we will end this war in Iraq and bring our troops home; we will finish the job against al Qaeda in Afghanistan; we will care for our veterans; we will restore our moral standing in the world; and we will never use 9/11 as a way to scare up votes, because it is not a tactic to win an election, it is a challenge that should unite America and the world against the common threats of the 21st century: terrorism and nuclear weapons; climate change and poverty; genocide and disease.

All of the candidates in this race share these goals. All have good ideas. And all are patriots who serve this country honorably.

But the reason our campaign has always been different is because it's not just about what I will do as President, it's also about what you, the people who love this country, can do to change it.

That's why tonight belongs to you. It belongs to the organizers and the volunteers and the staff who believed in our improbable journey and rallied so many others to join.

We know the battle ahead will be long, but always remember that no matter what obstacles stand in our way, nothing can withstand the power of millions of voices calling for change.

We have been told we cannot do this by a chorus of cynics who will only grow louder and more dissonant in the weeks to come. We've been asked to pause for a reality check. We've been warned against offering the people of this nation false hope.

But in the unlikely story that is America, there has never been anything false about hope. For when we have faced down impossible odds; when we've been told that we're not ready, or that we shouldn't try, or that we can't, generations of Americans have responded with a simple creed that sums up the spirit of a people.

Yes we can.

It was a creed written into the founding documents that declared the destiny of a nation.

Yes we can.

It was whispered by slaves and abolitionists as they blazed a trail toward freedom through the darkest of nights.

Yes we can.

It was sung by immigrants as they struck out from distant shores and pioneers who pushed westward against an unforgiving wilderness.

Yes we can.

It was the call of workers who organized; women who reached for the ballot; a President who chose the moon as our new frontier; and a King who took us to the mountaintop and pointed the way to the Promised Land.

Yes we can to justice and equality. Yes we can to opportunity and prosperity. Yes we can heal this nation. Yes we can repair this world. Yes we can.

And so tomorrow, as we take this campaign South and West; as we learn that the struggles of the textile worker in Spartanburg are not so different than the plight of the dishwasher in Las Vegas; that the hopes of the little girl who goes to a crumbling school in Dillon are the same as the dreams of the boy who learns on the streets of LA; we will remember that there is something happening in America; that we are not as divided as our politics suggests; that we are one people; we are one nation; and together, we will begin the next great chapter in America's story with three words that will ring from coast to coast; from sea to shining sea—Yes. We. Can.

A More Perfect Union
Philadelphia, Pennsylvania | March 18, 2008

"We the people, in order to form a more perfect union."

Two hundred and twenty one years ago, in a hall that still stands across the street, a group of men gathered and, with these simple words, launched America's improbable experiment in democracy. Farmers and scholars; statesmen and patriots who had traveled across an ocean to escape tyranny and persecution finally made real their declaration of independence at a Philadelphia convention that lasted through the spring of 1787.

The document they produced was eventually signed but ultimately unfinished. It was stained by this nation's original sin of slavery, a question that divided the colonies and brought the convention to a stalemate until the founders chose to allow the slave trade to continue for at least twenty more years, and to leave any final resolution to future generations.

Of course, the answer to the slavery question was already embedded within our Constitution—a Constitution that had at is very core the ideal of equal citizenship under the law; a Constitution that promised its people liberty, and justice, and a union that could be and should be perfected over time.

And yet words on a parchment would not be enough to deliver slaves from bondage, or provide men and women of every color and creed their full rights and obligations as citizens of the United States. What would be needed were Americans in successive generations who were willing to do their part—through protests and struggle, on the streets and in the courts, through a civil war and civil disobedience and always at great risk—to narrow that gap between the promise of our ideals and the reality of their time

This was one of the tasks we set forth at the beginning of this campaign—to continue the long march of those who came before us, a march for a more just, more equal, more free, more caring and more prosperous America. I chose to run for the presidency at this moment in history because I believe deeply that we cannot solve the challenges of our time unless we solve them together—unless we perfect our union by understanding that we may have different stories, but we hold common hopes; that we may not look the same and we may not have come from the same place, but we all want to move in the same direction—towards a better future for our children and our grandchildren.

This belief comes from my unyielding faith in the decency and generosity of the American people. But it also comes from my own American story.

I am the son of a black man from Kenya and a white woman from Kansas. I was raised with the help of a white grandfather who survived a Depression to serve in Patton's Army during World War II and a white grandmother who worked on a bomber assembly line at Fort Leavenworth while he was overseas. I've gone to some of the best schools in America and lived in one of the world's poorest nations. I am married to a black American who carries within her the blood of slaves and slaveowners—an inheritance we pass on to our two precious daughters. I have brothers, sisters, nieces, nephews, uncles and cousins, of every race and every hue, scattered across three continents, and for as long as I live, I will never forget that in no other country on Earth is my story even possible.

It's a story that hasn't made me the most conventional candidate. But it is a story that has seared into my genetic makeup the idea that this nation is more than the sum of its parts—that out of many, we are truly one.

Throughout the first year of this campaign, against all predictions to the contrary, we saw how hungry the American people were for this message of unity. Despite the temptation to view my candidacy through a purely racial lens, we won commanding victories in states with some of the whitest populations in the country. In South Carolina, where the Confederate Flag still flies, we built a powerful coalition of African Americans and white Americans.

This is not to say that race has not been an issue in the campaign. At various stages in the campaign, some commentators have deemed me either "too black" or "not black enough." We saw racial tensions bubble to the surface during the week before the South Carolina primary. The press has scoured every exit poll for the latest evidence of racial polarization, not just in terms of white and black, but black and brown as well.

And yet, it has only been in the last couple of weeks that the discussion of race in this campaign has taken a particularly divisive turn.

On one end of the spectrum, we've heard the implication that my candidacy is somehow an exercise in affirmative action; that it's based solely on the desire of wide-eyed liberals to purchase racial reconciliation on the cheap. On the other end, we've heard my former pastor, Reverend Jeremiah Wright, use incendiary language to express views that have the potential not only to widen the racial divide, but views that denigrate both the greatness and the goodness of our nation; that rightly offend white and black alike.

I have already condemned, in unequivocal terms, the statements of Reverend Wright that have caused such controversy. For some, nagging questions remain. Did I know him to be an occasionally fierce critic of American domestic and foreign policy? Of course. Did I ever hear him make remarks that could be considered controversial while I sat in church? Yes. Did I strongly disagree with many of his political views? Absolutely— just as I'm sure many of you have heard remarks from your pastors, priests, or rabbis with which you strongly disagreed.

But the remarks that have caused this recent firestorm weren't simply controversial. They weren't simply a religious leader's effort to speak out against perceived injustice. Instead, they expressed a profoundly distorted view of this country—a view that sees white racism as endemic, and that elevates what is wrong with America above all that we know is right with America; a view that sees the conflicts in the Middle East as rooted primarily in the actions of stalwart allies like Israel, instead of emanating from the perverse and hateful ideologies of radical Islam.

As such, Reverend Wright's comments were not only wrong but divisive, divisive at a time when we need unity; racially charged at a time when we need to come together to solve a set of monumental problems—two wars, a terrorist threat, a falling economy, a chronic health care crisis and potentially devastating climate change; problems that are neither black or white or Latino or Asian, but rather problems that confront us all.

Given my background, my politics, and my professed values and ideals, there will no doubt be those for whom my statements of condemnation are not enough. Why associate myself with Reverend Wright in the first place, they may ask? Why not join another church? And I confess that if all that I knew of Reverend Wright were the snippets of those sermons that have run in an endless loop on the television and You Tube, or if Trinity United Church of Christ conformed to the caricatures being peddled by some commentators, there is no doubt that I would react in much the same way

But the truth is, that isn't all that I know of the man. The man I met more than twenty years ago is a man who helped introduce me to my Christian faith, a man who spoke to me about our obligations to love one another; to care for the sick and lift up the poor. He is a man who served his country as a U.S. Marine; who has studied and lectured at some of the finest universities and seminaries in the country, and who for over thirty years led a church that serves the community by doing God's work here on Earth—by housing the homeless, ministering to the needy, providing day care services and scholarships and prison ministries, and reaching out to those suffering from HIV/AIDS.

In my first book, Dreams From My Father, I described the experience of my first service at Trinity: "People began to shout, to rise from their seats and clap and cry out, a forceful wind carrying the reverend's voice up into the rafters.... And in that single note—hope!—I heard something else; at the foot of that cross, inside the thousands of churches across the city, I imagined the stories of ordinary black people merging with the stories of David and Goliath, Moses and Pharaoh, the Christians in the lion's den, Ezekiel's field of dry bones. Those stories—of survival, and freedom, and hope—became our story, my story; the blood that had spilled was our blood, the tears our tears; until this black church, on this bright day, seemed once more a vessel carrying the story of a people into future generations and into a larger world. Our trials and triumphs became at once unique and universal, black and more than black; in chronicling our journey, the stories and songs gave us a means to reclaim memories that we didn't need to feel shame about...memories that all people might study and cherish—and with which we could start to rebuild."

That has been my experience at Trinity. Like other predominantly black churches across the country, Trinity embodies the black community in its entirety—the doctor and the welfare mom, the model student and the former gang-banger. Like other black churches, Trinity's services are full of raucous laughter and sometimes bawdy humor. They are full of dancing, clapping, screaming and shouting that may seem jarring to the untrained ear. The church contains in full the kindness and cruelty, the fierce intelligence and the shocking ignorance, the struggles and successes, the love and yes, the bitterness and bias that make up the black experience in America.

And this helps explain, perhaps, my relationship with Reverend Wright. As imperfect as he may be, he has been like family to me. He strengthened my faith, officiated my wedding, and baptized my children. Not once in my conversations with him have I heard him talk about any ethnic group in derogatory terms, or treat whites with whom he interacted with anything but courtesy and respect. He contains within him the contradictions—the good and the bad—of the community that he has served diligently for so many years.

I can no more disown him than I can disown the black community. I can no more disown him than I can my white grandmother—a woman who helped raise me, a woman who sacrificed again and again for me, a woman who loves me as much as she loves anything in this world, but a woman who once confessed her fear of black men who passed by her on the street, and who on more than one occasion has uttered racial or ethnic stereotypes that made me cringe.

These people are a part of me. And they are a part of America, this country that I love.

Some will see this as an attempt to justify or excuse comments that are simply inexcusable. I can assure you it is not. I suppose the politically safe thing would be to move on from this episode and just hope that it fades into the woodwork. We can dismiss Reverend Wright as a crank or a demagogue, just as some have dismissed Geraldine Ferraro, in the aftermath of her recent statements, as harboring some deep-seated racial bias.

But race is an issue that I believe this nation cannot afford to ignore right now. We would be making the same mistake that Reverend Wright made in his offending sermons about America—to simplify and stereotype and amplify the negative to the point that it distorts reality.

The fact is that the comments that have been made and the issues that have surfaced over the last few weeks reflect the complexities of race in this country that we've never really worked through—a part of our union that we have yet to perfect. And if we walk away now, if we simply retreat into our respective corners, we will never be able to come together and solve challenges like health care, or education, or the need to find good jobs for every American.

Understanding this reality requires a reminder of how we arrived at this point. As William Faulkner once wrote, "The past isn't dead and buried. In fact, it isn't even past." We do not need to recite here the history of racial injustice in this country. But we do need to remind ourselves that so many of the disparities that exist in the African-American community today can be directly traced to inequalities passed on from an earlier generation that suffered under the brutal legacy of slavery and Jim Crow.

Segregated schools were, and are, inferior schools; we still haven't fixed them, fifty years after Brown v. Board of Education, and the inferior education they provided, then and now, helps explain the pervasive achievement gap between today's black and white students.

Legalized discrimination—where blacks were prevented, often through violence, from owning property, or loans were not granted to African-American business owners, or black homeowners could not access FHA mortgages, or blacks were excluded from unions, or the police force, or fire departments—meant that black families could not amass any meaningful wealth to bequeath to future generations. That history helps explain the wealth and income gap between black and white, and the concentrated pockets of poverty that persists in so many of today's urban and rural communities.

A lack of economic opportunity among black men, and the shame and frustration that came from not being able to provide for one's family, contributed to the erosion of black families—a problem that welfare policies for many years may have worsened. And the lack of basic services in so many urban black neighborhoods—parks for kids to play in, police walking the beat, regular garbage pick-up and building code enforcement—all helped create a cycle of violence, blight and neglect that continue to haunt us.

This is the reality in which Reverend Wright and other African-Americans of his generation grew up. They came of age in the late fifties and early sixties, a time when segregation was still the law of the land and opportunity was systematically constricted. What's remarkable is not how many failed in the face of discrimination, but rather how many men and women overcame the odds; how many were able to make a way out of no way for those like me who would come after them.

But for all those who scratched and clawed their way to get a piece of the American Dream, there were many who didn't make it—those who were ultimately defeated, in one way or another, by discrimination. That legacy of defeat was passed on to future generations—those young men and increasingly young women who we see standing on street corners or languishing in our prisons, without hope or prospects for the future. Even for those blacks who did make it, questions of race, and racism, continue to define their worldview in fundamental ways. For the men and women of Reverend Wright's generation, the memories of humiliation and doubt and fear have not gone away; nor has the anger and the bitterness of those years. That anger may not get expressed in public, in front of white co-workers or white friends. But it does find voice in the barbershop or around the kitchen table. At times, that anger is exploited by politicians, to gin up votes along racial lines, or to make up for a politician's own failings.

And occasionally it finds voice in the church on Sunday morning, in the pulpit and in the pews. The fact that so many people are surprised to hear that anger in some of Reverend Wright's sermons simply reminds us of the old truism that the most segregated hour in American life occurs on Sunday morning. That anger is not always productive; indeed, all too often it distracts attention from solving real problems; it keeps us from squarely facing our own complicity in our condition, and prevents the African-American community from forging the alliances it needs to bring about real change. But the anger is real; it is powerful; and to simply wish it away, to condemn it without understanding its roots, only serves to widen the chasm of misunderstanding that exists between the races.

In fact, a similar anger exists within segments of the white community. Most working-class and middle-class white Americans don't feel that they have been particularly privileged by their race. Their experience is the immigrant experience—as far as they're concerned, no one's handed them anything, they've built it from scratch. They've worked hard all their lives, many times only to see their jobs shipped overseas or their pension dumped after a lifetime of labor. They are anxious about their futures, and feel their dreams slipping away; in an era of stagnant wages and global competition, opportunity comes to be seen as a zero sum game, in which your dreams come at my expense. So when they are told to bus their children to a school across town; when they hear that an African American is getting an advantage in landing a good job or a spot in a good college because of an injustice that they themselves never committed; when they're told that their fears about crime in urban neighborhoods are somehow prejudiced, resentment builds over time.

Like the anger within the black community, these resentments aren't always expressed in polite company. But they have helped shape the political landscape for at least a generation. Anger over welfare and affirmative action helped forge the Reagan Coalition. Politicians routinely exploited fears of crime for their own electoral ends. Talk show hosts and conservative commentators built entire careers unmasking bogus claims of racism while dismissing legitimate discussions of racial injustice and inequality as mere political correctness or reverse racism.

Just as black anger often proved counterproductive, so have these white resentments distracted attention from the real culprits of the middle class squeeze—a corporate culture rife with inside dealing, questionable accounting practices, and short-term greed; a Washington dominated by lobbyists and special interests; economic policies that favor the few over the many. And yet, to wish away the resentments of white Americans, to label them as misguided or even racist, without recognizing they are grounded in legitimate concerns—this too widens the racial divide, and blocks the path to understanding.

This is where we are right now. It's a racial stalemate we've been stuck in for years. Contrary to the claims of some of my critics, black and white, I have never been so naïve as to believe that we can get beyond our racial divisions in a single election cycle, or with a single candidacy—particularly a candidacy as imperfect as my own.

But I have asserted a firm conviction—a conviction rooted in my faith in God and my faith in the American people—that working together we can move beyond some of our old racial wounds, and that in fact we have no choice if we are to continue on the path of a more perfect union.

For the African-American community, that path means embracing the burdens of our past without becoming victims of our past. It means continuing to insist on a full measure of justice in every aspect of American life. But it also means binding our particular grievances—for better health care, and better schools, and better jobs—to the larger aspirations of all Americans—the white woman struggling to break the glass ceiling, the white man whose been laid off, the immigrant trying to feed his family. And it means taking full responsibility for own lives—by demanding more from our fathers, and spending more time with our children, and reading to them, and teaching them that while they may face challenges and discrimination in their own lives, they must never succumb to despair or cynicism; they must always believe that they can write their own destiny.

Ironically, this quintessentially American—and yes, conservative—notion of self-help found frequent expression in Reverend Wright's sermons. But what my former pastor too often failed to understand is that embarking on a program of self-help also requires a belief that society can change.

The profound mistake of Reverend Wright's sermons is not that he spoke about racism in our society. It's that he spoke as if our society was static; as if no progress has been made; as if this country—a country that has made it possible for one of his own members to run for the highest office in the land and build a coalition of white and black; Latino and Asian, rich and poor, young and old—is still irrevocably bound to a tragic past. But what we know—what we have seen—is that America can change. That is true genius of this nation. What we have already achieved gives us hope—the audacity to hope—for what we can and must achieve tomorrow.

In the white community, the path to a more perfect union means acknowledging that what ails the African-American community does not just exist in the minds of black people; that the legacy of discrimination—and current incidents of discrimination, while less overt than in the past—are real and must be addressed. Not just with words, but with deeds—by investing in our schools and our communities; by enforcing our civil rights laws and ensuring fairness in our criminal justice system; by providing this generation with ladders of opportunity that were unavailable for previous generations. It requires all Americans to realize that your dreams do not have to come at the expense of my dreams; that investing in the health, welfare, and education of black and brown and white children will ultimately help all of America prosper.

In the end, then, what is called for is nothing more, and nothing less, than what all the world's great religions demand— that we do unto others as we would have them do unto us. Let us be our brother's keeper, Scripture tells us. Let us be our sister's keeper. Let us find that common stake we all have in one another, and let our politics reflect that spirit as well.

For we have a choice in this country. We can accept a politics that breeds division, and conflict, and cynicism. We can tackle race only as spectacle—as we did in the OJ trial—or in the wake of tragedy, as we did in the aftermath of Katrina—or as fodder for the nightly news. We can play Reverend Wright's sermons on every channel, every day and talk about them from now until the election, and make the only question in this campaign whether or not the American people think that I somehow believe or sympathize with his most offensive words. We can pounce on some gaffe by a Hillary supporter as evidence that she's playing the race card, or we can speculate on whether white men will all flock to John McCain in the general election regardless of his policies.

We can do that.

But if we do, I can tell you that in the next election, we'll be talking about some other distraction. And then another one. And then another one. And nothing will change.

That is one option. Or, at this moment, in this election, we can come together and say, "Not this time." This time we want to talk about the crumbling schools that are stealing the future of black children and white children and Asian children and Hispanic children and Native American children. This time we want to reject the cynicism that tells us that these kids can't learn; that those kids who don't look like us are somebody else's problem. The children of America are not those kids, they are our kids, and we will not let them fall behind in a 21st century economy. Not this time.

This time we want to talk about how the lines in the Emergency Room are filled with whites and blacks and Hispanics who do not have health care; who don't have the power on their own to overcome the special interests in Washington, but who can take them on if we do it together.

This time we want to talk about the shuttered mills that once provided a decent life for men and women of every race, and the homes for sale that once belonged to Americans from every religion, every region, every walk of life. This time we want to talk about the fact that the real problem is not that someone who doesn't look like you might take your job; it's that the corporation you work for will ship it overseas for nothing more than a profit

This time we want to talk about the men and women of every color and creed who serve together, and fight together, and bleed together under the same proud flag. We want to talk about how to bring them home from a war that never should've been authorized and never should've been waged, and we want to talk about how we'll show our patriotism by caring for them, and their families, and giving them the benefits they have earned.

I would not be running for President if I didn't believe with all my heart that this is what the vast majority of Americans want for this country. This union may never be perfect, but generation after generation has shown that it can always be perfected. And today, whenever I find myself feeling doubtful or cynical about this possibility, what gives me the most hope is the next generation—the young people whose attitudes and beliefs and openness to change have already made history in this election.

There is one story in particularly that I'd like to leave you with today—a story I told when I had the great honor of speaking on Dr. King's birthday at his home church, Ebenezer Baptist, in Atlanta.

There is a young, twenty-three year old white woman named Ashley Baia who organized for our campaign in Florence, South Carolina. She had been working to organize a mostly African-American community since the beginning of this campaign, and one day she was at a roundtable discussion where everyone went around telling their story and why they were there.

And Ashley said that when she was nine years old, her mother got cancer. And because she had to miss days of work, she was let go and lost her health care. They had to file for bankruptcy, and that's when Ashley decided that she had to do something to help her mom.

She knew that food was one of their most expensive costs, and so Ashley convinced her mother that what she really liked and really wanted to eat more than anything else was mustard and relish sandwiches. Because that was the cheapest way to eat.

She did this for a year until her mom got better, and she told everyone at the roundtable that the reason she joined our campaign was so that she could help the millions of other children in the country who want and need to help their parents too.

Now Ashley might have made a different choice. Perhaps somebody told her along the way that the source of her mother's problems were blacks who were on welfare and too lazy to work, or Hispanics who were coming into the country illegally. But she didn't. She sought out allies in her fight against injustice.

Anyway, Ashley finishes her story and then goes around the room and asks everyone else why they're supporting the campaign. They all have different stories and reasons. Many bring up a specific issue. And finally they come to this elderly black man who's been sitting there quietly the entire time. And Ashley asks him why he's there. And he does not bring up a specific issue. He does not say health care or the economy. He does not say education or the war. He does not say that he was there because of Barack Obama. He simply says to everyone in the room, "I am here because of Ashley."

"I'm here because of Ashley." By itself, that single moment of recognition between that young white girl and that old black man is not enough. It is not enough to give health care to the sick, or jobs to the jobless, or education to our children.

But it is where we start. It is where our union grows stronger. And as so many generations have come to realize over the course of the two-hundred and twenty one years since a band of patriots signed that document in Philadelphia, that is where the perfection begins.

OUR MOMENT, OUR TIME
St. Paul, Minnesota | June 3, 2008

Tonight, after fifty-four hard-fought contests, our primary season has finally come to an end.

Sixteen months have passed since we first stood together on the steps of the Old State Capitol in Springfield, Illinois. Thousands of miles have been traveled. Millions of voices have been heard. And because of what you said—because you decided that change must come to Washington; because you believed that this year must be different than all the rest; because you chose to listen not to your doubts or your fears but to your greatest hopes and highest aspirations, tonight we mark the end of one historic journey with the beginning of another—a journey that will bring a new and better day to America. Tonight, I can stand before you and say that I will be the Democratic nominee for President of the United States.

I want to thank every American who stood with us over the course of this campaign—through the good days and the bad; from the snows of Cedar Rapids to the sunshine of Sioux Falls. And tonight I also want to thank the men and woman who took this journey with me as fellow candidates for President.

At this defining moment for our nation, we should be proud that our party put forth one of the most talented, qualified field of individuals ever to run for this office. I have not just competed with them as rivals, I have learned from them as friends, as public servants, and as patriots who love America and are willing to work tirelessly to make this country better. They are leaders of this party, and leaders that America will turn to for years to come.

That is particularly true for the candidate who has traveled further on this journey than anyone else. Senator Hillary Clinton has made history in this campaign not just because she's a woman who has done what no woman has done before, but because she's a leader who inspires millions of Americans with her strength, her courage, and her commitment to the causes that brought us here tonight.

We've certainly had our differences over the last sixteen months. But as someone who's shared a stage with her many times, I can tell you that what gets Hillary Clinton up in the morning—even in the face of tough odds—is exactly what sent her and Bill Clinton to sign up for their first campaign in Texas all those years ago; what sent her to work at the Children's Defense Fund and made her fight for health care as First Lady;

what led her to the United States Senate and fueled her barrier-breaking campaign for the presidency—an unyielding desire to improve the lives of ordinary Americans, no matter how difficult the fight may be. And you can rest assured that when we finally win the battle for universal health care in this country, she will be central to that victory. When we transform our energy policy and lift our children out of poverty, it will be because she worked to help make it happen. Our party and our country are better off because of her, and I am a better candidate for having had the honor to compete with Hillary Rodham Clinton.

There are those who say that this primary has somehow left us weaker and more divided. Well I say that because of this primary, there are millions of Americans who have cast their ballot for the very first time. There are Independents and Republicans who understand that this election isn't just about the party in charge of Washington, it's about the need to change Washington. There are young people, and African-Americans, and Latinos, and women of all ages who have voted in numbers that have broken records and inspired a nation.

All of you chose to support a candidate you believe in deeply. But at the end of the day, we aren't the reason you came out and waited in lines that stretched block after block to make your voice heard. You didn't do that because of me or Senator Clinton or anyone else. You did it because you know in your hearts that at this moment—a moment that will define a generation—we cannot afford to keep doing what we've been doing. We owe our children a better future. We owe our country a better future. And for all those who dream of that future tonight, I say—let us begin the work together. Let us unite in common effort to chart a new course for America.

In just a few short months, the Republican Party will arrive in St. Paul with a very different agenda. They will come here to nominate John McCain, a man who has served this country heroically. I honor that service, and I respect his many accomplishments, even if he chooses to deny mine. My differences with him are not personal; they are with the policies he has proposed in this campaign.

Because while John McCain can legitimately tout moments of independence from his party in the past, such independence has not been the hallmark of his presidential campaign.

It's not change when John McCain decided to stand with George Bush ninety-five percent of the time, as he did in the Senate last year.

It's not change when he offers four more years of Bush economic policies that have failed to create well-paying jobs, or insure our workers, or help Americans afford the skyrocketing cost of college—policies that have lowered the real incomes of the average American family, widened the gap between Wall Street and Main Street, and left our children with a mountain of debt.

And it's not change when he promises to continue a policy in Iraq that asks everything of our brave men and women in uniform and nothing of Iraqi politicians—a policy where all we look for are reasons to stay in Iraq, while we spend billions of dollars a month on a war that isn't making the American people any safer.

So I'll say this—there are many words to describe John McCain's attempt to pass off his embrace of George Bush's policies as bipartisan and new. But change is not one of them.

Change is a foreign policy that doesn't begin and end with a war that should've never been authorized and never been waged. I won't stand here and pretend that there are many good options left in Iraq, but what's not an option is leaving our troops in that country for the next hundred years—especially at a time when our military is overstretched, our nation is isolated, and nearly every other threat to America is being ignored.

We must be as careful getting out of Iraq as we were careless getting in—but start leaving we must. It's time for Iraqis to take responsibility for their future. It's time to rebuild our military and give our veterans the care they need and the benefits they deserve when they come home. It's time to refocus our efforts on al Qaeda's leadership and Afghanistan, and rally the world against the common threats of the 21st century—terrorism and nuclear weapons; climate change and poverty; genocide and disease. That's what change is.

Change is realizing that meeting today's threats requires not just our firepower, but the power of our diplomacy—tough, direct diplomacy where the President of the United States isn't afraid to let any petty dictator know where America stands and what we stand for. We must once again have the courage and conviction to lead the free world. That is the legacy of Roosevelt, and Truman, and Kennedy. That's what the American people want. That's what change is.

Change is building an economy that rewards not just wealth, but the work and workers who created it. It's understanding that the struggles facing working families can't be solved by spending billions of dollars on more tax breaks for big corporations and wealthy CEOs, but by giving a the middle-class a tax break, and investing in our crumbling infrastructure, and transforming how we use energy, and improving our schools, and renewing our commitment to science and innovation. It's understanding that fiscal responsibility and shared prosperity can go hand-in-hand, as they did when Bill Clinton was President.

John McCain has spent a lot of time talking about trips to Iraq in the last few weeks, but maybe if he spent some time taking trips to the cities and towns that have been hardest hit by this economy—cities in Michigan, and Ohio, and right here in Minnesota—he'd understand the kind of change that people are looking for.

Maybe if he went to Iowa and met the student who works the night shift after a full day of class and still can't pay the medical bills for a sister who's ill, he'd understand that she can't afford four more years of a health care plan that only takes care of the healthy and wealthy. She needs us to pass health care plan that guarantees insurance to every American who wants it and brings down premiums for every family who needs it. That's the change we need.

Maybe if he went to Pennsylvania and met the man who lost his job but can't even afford the gas to drive around and look for a new one, he'd understand that we can't afford four more years of our addiction to oil from dictators. That man needs us to pass an energy policy that works with automakers to raise fuel standards, and makes corporations pay for their pollution, and oil companies invest their record profits in a clean energy future—an energy policy that will create millions of new jobs that pay well and can't be outsourced. That's the change we need.

And maybe if he spent some time in the schools of South Carolina or St. Paul or where he spoke tonight in New Orleans, he'd understand that we can't afford to leave the money behind for No Child Left Behind; that we owe it to our children to invest in early childhood education; to recruit an army of new teachers and give them better pay and more support; to finally decide that in this global economy, the chance to get a college education should not be a privilege for the wealthy few, but the birthright of every American. That's the change we need in America. That's why I'm running for President.

The other side will come here in September and offer a very different set of policies and positions, and that is a debate I look forward to. It is a debate the American people deserve. But what you don't deserve is another election that's governed by fear, and innuendo, and division. What you won't hear from this campaign or this party is the kind of politics that uses religion as a wedge, and patriotism as a bludgeon—that sees our opponents not as competitors to challenge, but enemies to demonize. Because we may call ourselves Democrats and Republicans, but we are Americans first. We are always Americans first.

Despite what the good Senator from Arizona said tonight, I have seen people of differing views and opinions find common cause many times during my two decades in public life, and I have brought many together myself. I've walked arm-in-arm with community leaders on the South Side of Chicago and watched tensions fade as black, white, and Latino fought together for good jobs and good schools. I've sat across the table from law enforcement and civil rights advocates to reform a criminal justice system that sent thirteen innocent people to death row. And I've worked with friends in the other party to provide more children with health insurance and more working families with a tax break; to curb the spread of nuclear weapons and ensure that the American people know where their tax dollars are being spent; and to reduce the influence of lobbyists who have all too often set the agenda in Washington.

In our country, I have found that this cooperation happens not because we agree on everything, but because behind all the labels and false divisions and categories that define us; beyond all the petty bickering and point-scoring in Washington, Americans are a decent, generous, compassionate people, united by common challenges and common hopes. And every so often, there are moments which call on that fundamental goodness to make this country great again.

So it was for that band of patriots who declared in a Philadelphia hall the formation of a more perfect union; and for all those who gave on the fields of Gettysburg and Antietam their last full measure of devotion to save that same union.

So it was for the Greatest Generation that conquered fear itself, and liberated a continent from tyranny, and made this country home to untold opportunity and prosperity.

So it was for the workers who stood out on the picket lines; the women who shattered glass ceilings; the children who braved a Selma bridge for freedom's cause.

So it has been for every generation that faced down the greatest challenges and the most improbable odds to leave their children a world that's better, and kinder, and more just.

And so it must be for us.

America, this is our moment. This is our time. Our time to turn the page on the policies of the past. Our time to bring new energy and new ideas to the challenges we face. Our time to offer a new direction for the country we love.

The journey will be difficult. The road will be long. I face this challenge with profound humility, and knowledge of my own limitations. But I also face it with limitless faith in the capacity of the American people. Because if we are willing to work for it, and fight for it, and believe in it, then I am absolutely certain that generations from now, we will be able to look back and tell our children that this was the moment when we began to provide care for the sick and good jobs to the jobless; this was the moment when the rise of the oceans began to slow and our planet began to heal; this was the moment when we ended a war and secured our nation and restored our image as the last, best hope on

Earth. This was the moment—this was the time—when we came together to remake this great nation so that it may always reflect our very best selves, and our highest ideals. Thank you, God Bless you, and may God Bless the United States of America.

A WORLD THAT STANDS AS ONE
Berlin, Germany | July 24, 2008

Thank you to the citizens of Berlin and to the people of Germany. Let me thank Chancellor Merkel and Foreign Minister Steinmeier for welcoming me earlier today. Thank you Mayor Wowereit, the Berlin Senate, the police, and most of all thank you for this welcome.

I come to Berlin as so many of my countrymen have come before. Tonight, I speak to you not as a candidate for President, but as a citizen—a proud citizen of the United States, and a fellow citizen of the world.

I know that I don't look like the Americans who've previously spoken in this great city. The journey that led me here is improbable. My mother was born in the heartland of America, but my father grew up herding goats in Kenya. His father—my grandfather—was a cook, a domestic servant to the British.

At the height of the Cold War, my father decided, like so many others in the forgotten corners of the world, that his yearning—his dream—required the freedom and opportunity promised by the West. And so he wrote letter after letter to universities all across America until somebody, somewhere answered his prayer for a better life.

That is why I'm here. And you are here because you too know that yearning. This city, of all cities, knows the dream of freedom. And you know that the only reason we stand here tonight is because men and women from both of our nations came together to work, and struggle, and sacrifice for that better life.

Ours is a partnership that truly began sixty years ago this summer, on the day when the first American plane touched down at Templehof.

On that day, much of this continent still lay in ruin. The rubble of this city had yet to be built into a wall. The Soviet shadow had swept across Eastern Europe, while in the West, America, Britain, and France took stock of their losses, and pondered how the world might be remade.

This is where the two sides met. And on the twenty-fourth of June, 1948, the Communists chose to blockade the western part of the city. They cut off food and supplies to more than two million Germans in an effort to extinguish the last flame of freedom in Berlin.

The size of our forces was no match for the much larger Soviet Army. And yet retreat would have allowed Communism to march across Europe. Where the last war had ended, another

World War could have easily begun. All that stood in the way was Berlin.

And that's when the airlift began—when the largest and most unlikely rescue in history brought food and hope to the people of this city.

The odds were stacked against success. In the winter, a heavy fog filled the sky above, and many planes were forced to turn back without dropping off the needed supplies. The streets where we stand were filled with hungry families who had no comfort from the cold.

But in the darkest hours, the people of Berlin kept the flame of hope burning. The people of Berlin refused to give up. And on one fall day, hundreds of thousands of Berliners came here, to the Tiergarten, and heard the city's mayor implore the world not to give up on freedom. "There is only one possibility," he said. "For us to stand together united until this battle is won...The people of Berlin have spoken. We have done our duty, and we will keep on doing our duty. People of the world: now do your duty... People of the world, look at Berlin!"

People of the world—look at Berlin!

Look at Berlin, where Germans and Americans learned to work together and trust each other less than three years after facing each other on the field of battle.

Look at Berlin, where the determination of a people met the generosity of the Marshall Plan and created a German miracle; where a victory over tyranny gave rise to NATO, the greatest alliance ever formed to defend our common security.

Look at Berlin, where the bullet holes in the buildings and the somber stones and pillars near the Brandenburg Gate insist that we never forget our common humanity.

People of the world—look at Berlin, where a wall came down, a continent came together, and history proved that there is no challenge too great for a world that stands as one.

Sixty years after the airlift, we are called upon again. History has led us to a new crossroad, with new promise and new peril. When you, the German people, tore down that wall—a wall that divided East and West; freedom and tyranny; fear and hope—walls came tumbling down around the world. From Kiev to Cape Town, prison camps were closed, and the doors of democracy were opened. Markets opened too, and the spread of information and technology reduced barriers to opportunity and prosperity. While the 20th century taught us that we share a common destiny, the 21st has revealed a world more intertwined than at any time in human history.

The fall of the Berlin Wall brought new hope. But that very closeness has given rise to new dangers—dangers that cannot be contained within the borders of a country or by the distance of an ocean.

The terrorists of September 11th plotted in Hamburg and trained in Kandahar and Karachi before killing thousands from all over the globe on American soil.

As we speak, cars in Boston and factories in Beijing are melting the ice caps in the Arctic, shrinking coastlines in the Atlantic, and bringing drought to farms from Kansas to Kenya.

Poorly secured nuclear material in the former Soviet Union, or secrets from a scientist in Pakistan could help build a bomb that detonates in Paris. The poppies in Afghanistan become the heroin in Berlin. The poverty and violence in Somalia breeds the terror of tomorrow. The genocide in Darfur shames the conscience of us all.

In this new world, such dangerous currents have swept along faster than our efforts to contain them. That is why we cannot afford to be divided. No one nation, no matter how large or powerful, can defeat such challenges alone. None of us can deny these threats, or escape responsibility in meeting them. Yet, in the absence of Soviet tanks and a terrible wall, it has become easy to forget this truth. And if we're honest with each other, we know that sometimes, on both sides of the Atlantic, we have drifted apart, and forgotten our shared destiny.

In Europe, the view that America is part of what has gone wrong in our world, rather than a force to help make it right, has become all too common. In America, there are voices that deride and deny the importance of Europe's role in our security and our future. Both views miss the truth—that Europeans today are bearing new burdens and taking more responsibility in critical parts of the world; and that just as American bases built in the last century still help to defend the security of this continent, so does our country still sacrifice greatly for freedom around the globe.

Yes, there have been differences between America and Europe. No doubt, there will be differences in the future. But the burdens of global citizenship continue to bind us together. A change of leadership in Washington will not lift this burden. In this new century, Americans and Europeans alike will be required to do more—not less. Partnership and cooperation among nations is not a choice; it is the one way, the only way, to protect our common security and advance our common humanity.

That is why the greatest danger of all is to allow new walls to divide us from one another.

The walls between old allies on either side of the Atlantic cannot stand. The walls between the countries with the most and those with the least cannot stand. The walls between races and tribes; natives and immigrants; Christian and Muslim and Jew cannot stand. These now are the walls we must tear down.

We know they have fallen before. After centuries of strife, the people of Europe have formed a Union of promise and prosperity. Here, at the base of a column built to mark victory in war, we meet in the center of a Europe at peace. Not only have walls come down in Berlin, but they have come down in Belfast, where Protestant and Catholic found a way to live together; in the Balkans, where our Atlantic alliance ended wars and brought savage war criminals to justice; and in South Africa, where the struggle of a courageous people defeated apartheid.

So history reminds us that walls can be torn down. But the task is never easy. True partnership and true progress requires constant work and sustained sacrifice. They require sharing the burdens of development and diplomacy; of progress and peace. They require allies who will listen to each other, learn from each other and, most of all, trust each other.

That is why America cannot turn inward. That is why Europe cannot turn inward. America has no better partner than Europe. Now is the time to build new bridges across the globe as strong as the one that bound us across the Atlantic. Now is the time to join together, through constant cooperation, strong institutions, shared sacrifice, and a global commitment to progress, to meet the challenges of the 21st century. It was this spirit that led airlift planes to appear in the sky above our heads, and people to assemble where we stand today. And this is the moment when our nations—and all nations—must summon that spirit anew.

This is the moment when we must defeat terror and dry up the well of extremism that supports it. This threat is real and we cannot shrink from our responsibility to combat it. If we could create NATO to face down the Soviet Union, we can join in a new and global partnership to dismantle the networks that have struck in Madrid and Amman; in London and Bali; in Washington and New York. If we could win a battle of ideas against the communists, we can stand with the vast majority of Muslims who reject the extremism that leads to hate instead of hope.

This is the moment when we must renew our resolve to rout the terrorists who threaten our security in Afghanistan, and the traffickers who sell drugs on your streets. No one welcomes war. I recognize the enormous difficulties in Afghanistan. But my country and yours have a stake in seeing that NATO's first mission beyond Europe's borders is a success. For the people of Afghanistan, and for our shared security, the work must be done. America cannot do this alone. The Afghan people need our troops and your troops; our support and your support to defeat the Taliban and al Qaeda, to develop their economy, and to help them rebuild their nation. We have too much at stake to turn back now.

This is the moment when we must renew the goal of a world without nuclear weapons. The two superpowers that faced each other across the wall of this city came too close too often to destroying all we have built and all that we love. With that wall gone, we need not stand idly by and watch the further spread of the deadly atom. It is time to secure all loose nuclear materials; to stop the spread of nuclear weapons; and to reduce the arsenals from another era. This is the moment to begin the work of seeking the peace of a world without nuclear weapons.

This is the moment when every nation in Europe must have the chance to choose its own tomorrow free from the shadows of yesterday. In this century, we need a strong European Union that deepens the security and prosperity of this continent, while extending a hand abroad. In this century—in this city of all cities—we must reject the Cold War mind-set of the past, and resolve to work with Russia when we can, to stand up for our values when we must, and to seek a partnership that extends across this entire continent.

This is the moment when we must build on the wealth that open markets have created, and share its benefits more equitably. Trade has been a cornerstone of our growth and global development. But we will not be able to sustain this growth if it favors the few, and not the many. Together, we must forge trade that truly rewards the work that creates wealth, with meaningful protections for our people and our planet. This is the moment for trade that is free and fair for all.

This is the moment we must help answer the call for a new dawn in the Middle East. My country must stand with yours and with Europe in sending a direct message to Iran that it must abandon its nuclear ambitions. We must support the Lebanese who have marched and bled for democracy, and the Israelis and Palestinians who seek a secure and lasting peace. And despite past differences, this is the moment when the world should support the millions of Iraqis who seek to rebuild their lives, even as we pass responsibility to the Iraqi government and finally bring this war to a close.

This is the moment when we must come together to save this planet. Let us resolve that we will not leave our children a world where the oceans rise and famine spreads and terrible storms devastate our lands. Let us resolve that all nations—including my own—will act with the same seriousness of purpose as has your nation, and reduce the carbon we send into our atmosphere. This is the moment to give our children back their future. This is the moment to stand as one.

And this is the moment when we must give hope to those left behind in a globalized world. We must remember that the Cold War born in this city was not a battle for land or treasure. Sixty years ago, the planes that flew over Berlin did not drop bombs; instead they delivered food, and coal, and candy to grateful children. And in that show of solidarity, those pilots won more than a military victory. They won hearts and minds; love and loyalty and trust—not just from the people in this city, but from all those who heard the story of what they did here.

Now the world will watch and remember what we do here—what we do with this moment. Will we extend our hand to the people in the forgotten corners of this world who yearn for lives marked by dignity and opportunity; by security and justice? Will we lift the child in Bangladesh from poverty, shelter the refugee in Chad, and banish the scourge of AIDS in our time?

Will we stand for the human rights of the dissident in Burma, the blogger in Iran, or the voter in Zimbabwe? Will we give meaning to the words "never again" in Darfur?

Will we acknowledge that there is no more powerful example than the one each of our nations projects to the world? Will we reject torture and stand for the rule of law? Will we welcome immigrants from different lands, and shun discrimination against those who don't look like us or worship like we do, and keep the promise of equality and opportunity for all of our people?

People of Berlin—people of the world—this is our moment. This is our time.

I know my country has not perfected itself. At times, we've struggled to keep the promise of liberty and equality for all of our people. We've made our share of mistakes, and there are times when our actions around the world have not lived up to our best intentions.

But I also know how much I love America. I know that for more than two centuries, we have strived—at great cost and great sacrifice—to form a more perfect union; to seek, with other nations, a more hopeful world. Our allegiance has never been to any particular tribe or kingdom—indeed, every language is spoken in our country; every culture has left its imprint on ours; every point of view is expressed in our public squares. What has always united us—what has always driven our people; what drew my father to America's shores—is a set of ideals that speak to aspirations shared by all people: that we can live free from fear and free from want; that we can speak our minds and assemble with whomever we choose and worship as we please.

These are the aspirations that joined the fates of all nations in this city. These aspirations are bigger than anything that drives us apart. It is because of these aspirations that the airlift began. It is because of these aspirations that all free people—everywhere—became citizens of Berlin. It is in pursuit of these aspirations that a new generation—our generation—must make our mark on the world.

People of Berlin—and people of the world—the scale of our challenge is great. The road ahead will be long. But I come before you to say that we are heirs to a struggle for freedom. We are a people of improbable hope. With an eye toward the future, with resolve in our hearts, let us remember this history, and answer our destiny, and remake the world once again.

THE AMERICAN PROMISE
Denver, Colorado | August 28, 2008

To Chairman Dean and my great friend Dick Durbin, and to all my fellow citizens of this great nation: With profound gratitude and great humility, I accept your nomination for the presidency of the United States.

Let me express my thanks to the historic slate of candidates who accompanied me on this journey, and especially the one who traveled the farthest—a champion for working Americans and an inspiration to my daughters and to yours—Hillary Rodham Clinton. To President Clinton, who last night made the case for change as only he can make it; to Ted Kennedy, who embodies the spirit of service; and to the next Vice President of the United States, Joe Biden, I thank you. I am grateful to finish this journey with one of the finest statesmen of our time, a man at ease with everyone from world leaders to the conductors on the Amtrak train he still takes home every night.

To the love of my life, our next First Lady, Michelle Obama, and to Sasha and Malia—I love you so much, and I'm so proud of all of you.

Four years ago, I stood before you and told you my story—of the brief union between a young man from Kenya and a young woman from Kansas who weren't well-off or well-known, but shared a belief that in America, their son could achieve whatever he put his mind to.

It is that promise that has always set this country apart—that through hard work and sacrifice, each of us can pursue our individual dreams but still come together as one American family, to ensure that the next generation can pursue their dreams as well.

That's why I stand here tonight. Because for two hundred and thirty two years, at each moment when that promise was in jeopardy, ordinary men and women—students and soldiers, farmers and teachers, nurses and janitors—found the courage to keep it alive.

We meet at one of those defining moments—a moment when our nation is at war, our economy is in turmoil, and the American promise has been threatened once more.

Tonight, more Americans are out of work and more are working harder for less. More of you have lost your homes and even more are watching your home values plummet. More of you have cars you can't afford to drive, credit card bills you can't afford to pay, and tuition that's beyond your reach.

These challenges are not all of government's making. But the failure to respond is a direct result of a broken politics in Washington and the failed policies of George W. Bush.

America, we are better than these last eight years. We are a better country than this.

This country is more decent than one where a woman in Ohio, on the brink of retirement, finds herself one illness away from disaster after a lifetime of hard work.

This country is more generous than one where a man in Indiana has to pack up the equipment he's worked on for twenty years and watch it shipped off to China, and then chokes up as he explains how he felt like a failure when he went home to tell his family the news.

We are more compassionate than a government that lets veterans sleep on our streets and families slide into poverty; that sits on its hands while a major American city drowns before our eyes.

Tonight, I say to the American people, to Democrats and Republicans and Independents across this great land—enough! This moment—this election—is our chance to keep, in the 21st century, the American promise alive. Because next week, in Minnesota, the same party that brought you two terms of George Bush and Dick Cheney will ask this country for a third. And we are here because we love this country too much to let the next four years look like the last eight. On November 4th, we must stand up and say: "Eight is enough."

Now let there be no doubt. The Republican nominee, John McCain, has worn the uniform of our country with bravery and distinction, and for that we owe him our gratitude and respect. And next week, we'll also hear about those occasions when he's broken with his party as evidence that he can deliver the change that we need.

But the record's clear: John McCain has voted with George Bush ninety percent of the time. Senator McCain likes to talk about judgment, but really, what does it say about your judgment when you think George Bush has been right more than ninety percent of the time? I don't know about you, but I'm not ready to take a ten percent chance on change.

The truth is, on issue after issue that would make a difference in your lives—on health care and education and the economy—Senator McCain has been anything but independent. He said that our economy has made "great progress" under this President. He said that the fundamentals of the economy are strong. And when one of his chief advisors—the man who wrote his economic plan—was talking about the anxiety Americans are feeling, he said that we were just suffering from a "mental recession," and that we've become, and I quote, "a nation of whiners." A nation of whiners? Tell that to the proud auto workers at a Michigan plant who, after they found out it was closing, kept showing up every day and working as hard as ever, because they knew there were people who counted on the brakes that they made. Tell that to the military families who shoulder their burdens silently as they watch their loved ones leave for their third or fourth or fifth tour of duty. These are not whiners. They work hard and give back and keep going without complaint. These are the Americans that I know.

Now, I don't believe that Senator McCain doesn't care what's going on in the lives of Americans. I just think he doesn't know. Why else would he define middle-class as someone making under five million dollars a year? How else could he propose hundreds of billions in tax breaks for big corporations and oil companies but not one penny of tax relief to more than one hundred million Americans? How else could he offer a health care plan that would actually tax people's benefits, or an education plan that would do nothing to help families pay for college, or a plan that would privatize Social Security and gamble your retirement?

It's not because John McCain doesn't care. It's because John McCain doesn't get it.

For over two decades, he's subscribed to that old, discredited Republican philosophy—give more and more to those with the most and hope that prosperity trickles down to everyone else. In Washington, they call this the Ownership Society, but what it really means is—you're on your own. Out of work? Tough luck. No health care? The market will fix it. Born into poverty? Pull yourself up by your own bootstraps - even if you don't have boots. You're on your own.

Well it's time for them to own their failure. It's time for us to change America.

You see, we Democrats have a very different measure of what constitutes progress in this country.

We measure progress by how many people can find a job that pays the mortgage; whether you can put a little extra money away at the end of each month so you can someday watch your child receive her college diploma. We measure progress in the 23 million new jobs that were created when Bill Clinton was President—when the average American family saw its income go up $7,500 instead of down $2,000 like it has under George Bush.

We measure the strength of our economy not by the number of billionaires we have or the profits of the Fortune 500, but by whether someone with a good idea can take a risk and start a new business, or whether the waitress who lives on tips can take a day off to look after a sick kid without losing her job—an economy that honors the dignity of work.

The fundamentals we use to measure economic strength are whether we are living up to that fundamental promise that has made this country great—a promise that is the only reason I am standing here tonight.

Because in the faces of those young veterans who come back from Iraq and Afghanistan, I see my grandfather, who signed up after Pearl Harbor, marched in Patton's Army, and was rewarded by a grateful nation with the chance to go to college on the GI Bill.

In the face of that young student who sleeps just three hours before working the night shift, I think about my mom, who raised my sister and me on her own while she worked and earned her degree; who once turned to food stamps but was still able to send us to the best schools in the country with the help of student loans and scholarships.

When I listen to another worker tell me that his factory has shut down, I remember all those men and women on the South Side of Chicago who I stood by and fought for two decades ago after the local steel plant closed.

And when I hear a woman talk about the difficulties of starting her own business, I think about my grandmother, who worked her way up from the secretarial pool to middle-management, despite years of being passed over for promotions because she was a woman. She's the one who taught me about hard work. She's the one who put off buying a new car or a new dress for herself so that I could have a better life. She poured everything she had into me. And although she can no longer travel, I know that she's watching tonight, and that tonight is her night as well.

I don't know what kind of lives John McCain thinks that celebrities lead, but this has been mine. These are my heroes. Theirs are the stories that shaped me. And it is on their behalf that I intend to win this election and keep our promise alive as President of the United States.

What is that promise?

It's a promise that says each of us has the freedom to make of our own lives what we will, but that we also have the obligation to treat each other with dignity and respect.

It's a promise that says the market should reward drive and innovation and generate growth, but that businesses should live up to their responsibilities to create American jobs, look out for American workers, and play by the rules of the road.

Ours is a promise that says government cannot solve all our problems, but what it should do is that which we cannot do for ourselves—protect us from harm and provide every child a decent education; keep our water clean and our toys safe; invest in new schools and new roads and new science and technology.

Our government should work for us, not against us. It should help us, not hurt us. It should ensure opportunity not just for those with the most money and influence, but for every American who's willing to work.

That's the promise of America—the idea that we are responsible for ourselves, but that we also rise or fall as one nation; the fundamental belief that I am my brother's keeper; I am my sister's keeper.

That's the promise we need to keep. That's the change we need right now. So let me spell out exactly what that change would mean if I am President.

Change means a tax code that doesn't reward the lobbyists who wrote it, but the American workers and small businesses who deserve it.

Unlike John McCain, I will stop giving tax breaks to corporations that ship jobs overseas, and I will start giving them to companies that create good jobs right here in America.

I will eliminate capital gains taxes for the small businesses and the start-ups that will create the high-wage, high-tech jobs of tomorrow.

I will cut taxes—cut taxes—for 95% of all working families. Because in an economy like this, the last thing we should do is raise taxes on the middle-class.

And for the sake of our economy, our security, and the future of our planet, I will set a clear goal as President: in ten years, we will finally end our dependence on oil from the Middle East.

Washington's been talking about our oil addiction for the last thirty years, and John McCain has been there for twenty-six of them. In that time, he's said no to higher fuel-efficiency standards for cars, no to investments in renewable energy, no to renewable fuels. And today, we import triple the amount of oil as the day that Senator McCain took office.

Now is the time to end this addiction, and to understand that drilling is a stop-gap measure, not a long-term solution. Not even close.

As President, I will tap our natural gas reserves, invest in clean coal technology, and find ways to safely harness nuclear power. I'll help our auto companies re-tool, so that the fuel-efficient cars of the future are built right here in America. I'll make it easier for the American people to afford these new cars. And I'll invest 150 billion dollars over the next decade in affordable, renewable sources of energy—wind power and solar power and the next generation of biofuels; an investment that will lead to new industries and five million new jobs that pay well and can't ever be outsourced.

America, now is not the time for small plans.

Now is the time to finally meet our moral obligation to provide every child a world-class education, because it will take nothing less to compete in the global economy. Michelle and I are only here tonight because we were given a chance at an education. And I will not settle for an America where some kids don't have that chance. I'll invest in early childhood education. I'll recruit an army of new teachers, and pay them higher salaries and give them more support. And in exchange, I'll ask for higher standards and more accountability. And we will keep our promise to every young American—if you commit to serving your community or your country, we will make sure you can afford a college education.

Now is the time to finally keep the promise of affordable, accessible health care for every single American. If you have health care, my plan will lower your premiums. If you don't, you'll be able to get the same kind of coverage that members of Congress give themselves. And as someone who watched my mother argue with insurance companies while she lay in bed dying of cancer, I will make certain those companies stop discriminating against those who are sick and need care the most.

Now is the time to help families with paid sick days and better family leave, because nobody in America should have to choose between keeping their jobs and caring for a sick child or ailing parent.

Now is the time to change our bankruptcy laws, so that your pensions are protected ahead of CEO bonuses; and the time to protect Social Security for future generations.

And now is the time to keep the promise of equal pay for an equal day's work, because I want my daughters to have exactly the same opportunities as your sons.

Now, many of these plans will cost money, which is why I've laid out how I'll pay for every dime—by closing corporate loopholes and tax havens that don't help America grow. But I will also go through the federal budget, line by line, eliminating programs that no longer work and making the ones we do need work better and cost less—because we cannot meet 21st century challenges with a twentieth century bureaucracy.

And Democrats, we must also admit that fulfilling America's promise will require more than just money. It will require a renewed sense of responsibility from each of us to recover what John F. Kennedy called our "intellectual and moral strength." Yes, government must lead on energy independence, but each of us must do our part to make our homes and businesses more efficient. Yes, we must provide more ladders to success for young men who fall into lives of crime and despair. But we must also admit that programs alone can't replace parents; that government can't turn off the television and make a child do her homework; that fathers must take more responsibility for providing the love and guidance their children need.

Individual responsibility and mutual responsibility—that's the essence of America's promise.

And just as we keep our keep our promise to the next generation here at home, so must we keep America's promise abroad. If John McCain wants to have a debate about who has the temperament, and judgment, to serve as the next Commander-in-Chief, that's a debate I'm ready to have.

For while Senator McCain was turning his sights to Iraq just days after 9/11, I stood up and opposed this war, knowing that it would distract us from the real threats we face. When John McCain said we could just "muddle through" in Afghanistan, I argued for more resources and more troops to finish the fight against the terrorists who actually attacked us on 9/11, and made clear that we must take out Osama bin Laden and his lieutenants if we have them in our sights. John McCain likes to say that he'll follow bin Laden to the Gates of Hell—but he won't even go to the cave where he lives.

And today, as my call for a time frame to remove our troops from Iraq has been echoed by the Iraqi government and even the Bush Administration, even after we learned that Iraq has a $79 billion surplus while we're wallowing in deficits, John McCain stands alone in his stubborn refusal to end a misguided war.

That's not the judgment we need. That won't keep America safe. We need a President who can face the threats of the future, not keep grasping at the ideas of the past.

You don't defeat a terrorist network that operates in eighty countries by occupying Iraq. You don't protect Israel and deter Iran just by talking tough in Washington. You can't truly stand up for Georgia when you've strained our oldest alliances. If John McCain wants to follow George Bush with more tough talk and bad strategy, that is his choice—but it is not the change we need.

We are the party of Roosevelt. We are the party of Kennedy. So don't tell me that Democrats won't defend this country. Don't tell me that Democrats won't keep us safe. The Bush-McCain foreign policy has squandered the legacy that generations of Americans—Democrats and Republicans—have built, and we are here to restore that legacy.

As Commander-in-Chief, I will never hesitate to defend this nation, but I will only send our troops into harm's way with a clear mission and a sacred commitment to give them the equipment they need in battle and the care and benefits they deserve when they come home.

I will end this war in Iraq responsibly, and finish the fight against al Qaeda and the Taliban in Afghanistan. I will rebuild our military to meet future conflicts. But I will also renew the tough, direct diplomacy that can prevent Iran from obtaining nuclear weapons and curb Russian aggression. I will build new partnerships to defeat the threats of the 21st century: terrorism and nuclear proliferation; poverty and genocide; climate change and disease. And I will restore our moral standing, so that America is once again that last, best hope for all who are called to the cause of freedom, who long for lives of peace, and who yearn for a better future.

These are the policies I will pursue. And in the weeks ahead, I look forward to debating them with John McCain.

But what I will not do is suggest that the Senator takes his positions for political purposes. Because one of the things that we have to change in our politics is the idea that people cannot disagree without challenging each other's character and patriotism.

The times are too serious, the stakes are too high for this same partisan playbook. So let us agree that patriotism has no party. I love this country, and so do you, and so does John McCain. The men and women who serve in our battlefields may be Democrats and Republicans and Independents, but they have fought together and bled together and some died together under the same proud flag. They have not served a Red America or a Blue America—they have served the United States of America.

So I've got news for you, John McCain. We all put our country first.

America, our work will not be easy. The challenges we face require tough choices, and Democrats as well as Republicans will need to cast off the worn-out ideas and politics of the past. For part of what has been lost these past eight years can't just be measured by lost wages or bigger trade deficits. What has also been lost is our sense of common purpose—our sense of higher purpose. And that's what we have to restore.

We may not agree on abortion, but surely we can agree on reducing the number of unwanted pregnancies in this country. The reality of gun ownership may be different for hunters in rural Ohio than for those plagued by gang-violence in Cleveland, but don't tell me we can't uphold the Second Amendment while keeping AK-47s out of the hands of criminals. I know there are differences on same-sex marriage, but surely we can agree that our gay and lesbian brothers and sisters deserve to visit the person they love in the hospital and to live lives free of discrimination. Passions fly on immigration, but I don't know anyone who benefits when a mother is separated from her infant child or an employer undercuts American wages by hiring illegal workers. This too is part of America's promise—the promise of a democracy where we can find the strength and grace to bridge divides and unite in common effort.

I know there are those who dismiss such beliefs as happy talk. They claim that our insistence on something larger, something firmer and more honest in our public life is just a Trojan Horse for higher taxes and the abandonment of traditional values. And that's to be expected. Because if you don't have any fresh ideas, then you use stale tactics to scare the voters. If you don't have a record to run on, then you paint your opponent as someone people should run from.

You make a big election about small things.

And you know what—it's worked before. Because it feeds into the cynicism we all have about government. When Washington doesn't work, all its promises seem empty. If your hopes have been dashed again and again, then it's best to stop hoping, and settle for what you already know.

I get it. I realize that I am not the likeliest candidate for this office. I don't fit the typical pedigree, and I haven't spent my career in the halls of Washington.

But I stand before you tonight because all across America something is stirring. What the nay-sayers don't understand is that this election has never been about me. It's been about you.

For eighteen long months, you have stood up, one by one, and said enough to the politics of the past. You understand that in this election, the greatest risk we can take is to try the same old politics with the same old players and expect a different result. You have shown what history teaches us—that at defining moments like this one, the change we need doesn't come from Washington. Change comes to Washington. Change happens because the American people demand it—because they rise up and insist on new ideas and new leadership, a new politics for a new time.

America, this is one of those moments.

I believe that as hard as it will be, the change we need is coming. Because I've seen it. Because I've lived it. I've seen it in Illinois, when we provided health care to more children and moved more families from welfare to work. I've seen it in Washington, when we worked across party lines to open up government and hold lobbyists more accountable, to give better care for our veterans and keep nuclear weapons out of terrorist hands.

And I've seen it in this campaign. In the young people who voted for the first time, and in those who got involved again after a very long time. In the Republicans who never thought they'd pick up a Democratic ballot, but did. I've seen it in the workers who would rather cut their hours back a day than see their friends lose their jobs, in the soldiers who re-enlist after losing a limb, in the good neighbors who take a stranger in when a hurricane strikes and the floodwaters rise.

This country of ours has more wealth than any nation, but that's not what makes us rich. We have the most powerful military on Earth, but that's not what makes us strong. Our universities and our culture are the envy of the world, but that's not what keeps the world coming to our shores.

Instead, it is that American spirit—that American promise—that pushes us forward even when the path is uncertain; that binds us together in spite of our differences; that makes us fix our eye not on what is seen, but what is unseen, that better place around the bend.

That promise is our greatest inheritance. It's a promise I make to my daughters when I tuck them in at night, and a promise that you make to yours—a promise that has led immigrants to cross oceans and pioneers to travel west; a promise that led workers to picket lines, and women to reach for the ballot.

And it is that promise that forty five years ago today, brought Americans from every corner of this land to stand together on a Mall in Washington, before Lincoln's Memorial, and hear a young preacher from Georgia speak of his dream.

The men and women who gathered there could've heard many things. They could've heard words of anger and discord. They could've been told to succumb to the fear and frustration of so many dreams deferred.

But what the people heard instead—people of every creed and color, from every walk of life—is that in America, our destiny is inextricably linked. That together, our dreams can be one.

"We cannot walk alone," the preacher cried. "And as we walk, we must make the pledge that we shall always march ahead. We cannot turn back."

America, we cannot turn back. Not with so much work to be done. Not with so many children to educate, and so many veterans to care for. Not with an economy to fix and cities to rebuild and farms to save. Not with so many families to protect and so many lives to mend. America, we cannot turn back. We cannot walk alone. At this moment, in this election, we must pledge once more to march into the future. Let us keep that promise—that American promise—and in the words of Scripture hold firmly, without wavering, to the hope that we confess.

Thank you, God Bless you, and God Bless the United States of America.

ONE WEEK

Canton, Ohio | October 27, 2008

One week.

After decades of broken politics in Washington, eight years of failed policies from George Bush, and twenty-one months of a campaign that has taken us from the rocky coast of Maine to the sunshine of California, we are one week away from change in America.

In one week, you can turn the page on policies that have put the greed and irresponsibility of Wall Street before the hard work and sacrifice of folks on Main Street.

In one week, you can choose policies that invest in our middle-class, create new jobs, and grow this economy from the bottom-up so that everyone has a chance to succeed; from the CEO to the secretary and the janitor; from the factory owner to the men and women who work on its floor.

In one week, you can put an end to the politics that would divide a nation just to win an election; that tries to pit region against region, city against town, Republican against Democrat; that asks us to fear at a time when we need hope.

In one week, at this defining moment in history, you can give this country the change we need.

We began this journey in the depths of winter nearly two years ago, on the steps of the Old State Capitol in Springfield, Illinois. Back then, we didn't have much money or many endorsements. We weren't given much of a chance by the polls or the pundits, and we knew how steep our climb would be.

But I also knew this. I knew that the size of our challenges had outgrown the smallness of our politics. I believed that Democrats and Republicans and Americans of every political stripe were hungry for new ideas, new leadership, and a new kind of politics—one that favors common sense over ideology; one that focuses on those values and ideals we hold in common as Americans.

Most of all, I believed in your ability to make change happen. I knew that the American people were a decent, generous people who are willing to work hard and sacrifice for future generations. And I was convinced that when we come together, our voices are more powerful than the most entrenched lobbyists, or the most vicious political attacks, or the full force of a status quo in Washington that wants to keep things just the way they are.

Twenty-one months later, my faith in the American people has been vindicated. That's how we've come so far and so close—because of you. That's how we'll change this country—with your help. And that's why we can't afford to slow down, sit back, or let up for one day, one minute, or one second in this last week. Not now. Not when so much is at stake.

We are in the middle of the worst economic crisis since the Great Depression. 760,000 workers have lost their jobs this year. Businesses and families can't get credit. Home values are falling. Pensions are disappearing. Wages are lower than they've been in a decade, at a time when the cost of health care and college have never been higher. It's getting harder and harder to make the mortgage, or fill up your gas tank, or even keep the electricity on at the end of the month.

At a moment like this, the last thing we can afford is four more years of the tired, old theory that says we should give more to billionaires and big corporations and hope that prosperity trickles down to everyone else. The last thing we can afford is four more years where no one in Washington is watching anyone on Wall Street because politicians and lobbyists killed common-sense regulations. Those are the theories that got us into this mess. They haven't worked, andit's time for change. That's why I'm running for President of the United States.

Now, Senator McCain has served this country honorably. And he can point to a few moments over the past eight years where he has broken from George Bush—on torture, for example. He deserves credit for that. But when it comes to the economy—when it comes to the central issue of this election—the plain truth is that John McCain has stood with this President every step of the way. Voting for the Bush tax cuts for the wealthy that he once opposed. Voting for the Bush budgets that spent us into debt. Calling for less regulation twenty-one times just this year. Those are the facts.

And now, after twenty-one months and three debates, Senator McCain still has not been able to tell the American people a single major thing he'd do differently from George Bush when it comes to the economy. Senator McCain says that we can't spend the next four years waiting for our luck to change, but you understand that the biggest gamble we can take is embracing the same old Bush-McCain policies that have failed us for the last eight years.

It's not change when John McCain wants to give a $700,000 tax cut to the average Fortune 500 CEO. It's not change when he wants to give $200 billion to the biggest corporations or $4 billion to the oil companies or $300 billion to the same Wall

Street banks that got us into this mess. It's not change when he comes up with a tax plan that doesn't give a penny of relief to more than 100 million middle-class Americans. That's not change.

Look—we've tried it John McCain's way. We've tried it George Bush's way. Deep down, Senator McCain knows that, which is why his campaign said that "if we keep talking about the economy, we're going to lose." That's why he's spending these last weeks calling me every name in the book. Because that's how you play the game in Washington. If you can't beat your opponent's ideas, you distort those ideas and maybe make some up. If you don't have a record to run on, then you paint your opponent as someone people should run away from. You make a big election about small things.

Ohio, we are here to say "Not this time. Not this year. Not when so much is at stake." Senator McCain might be worried about losing an election, but I'm worried about Americans who are losing their homes, and their jobs, and their life savings. I can take one more week of John McCain's attacks, but this country can't take four more years of the same old politics and the same failed policies. It's time for something new.

The question in this election is not "Are you better off than you were four years ago?" We know the answer to that. The real question is, "Will this country be better off four years from now?"

I know these are difficult times for America. But I also know that we have faced difficult times before. The American story has never been about things coming easy—it's been about rising to the moment when the moment was hard. It's about seeing the highest mountaintop from the deepest of valleys. It's about rejecting fear and division for unity of purpose. That's how we've overcome war and depression. That's how we've won great struggles for civil rights and women's rights and worker's rights. And that's how we'll emerge from this crisis stronger and more prosperous than we were before—as one nation; as one people.

Remember, we still have the most talented, most productive workers of any country on Earth. We're still home to innovation and technology, colleges and universities that are the envy of the world. Some of the biggest ideas in history have come from our small businesses and our research facilities. So there's no reason we can't make this century another American century. We just need a new direction. We need a new politics.

Now, I don't believe that government can or should try to solve all our problems. I know you don't either. But I do believe that government should do that which we cannot do for ourselves—protect us from harm and provide a decent education for our children; invest in new roads and new science and technology. It should reward drive and innovation and growth in the free market, but it should also make sure businesses live up to their responsibility to create American jobs, and look out for American workers, and play by the rules of the road. It should ensure a shot at success not only for those with money and power and influence, but for every single American who's willing to work. That's how we create not just more millionaires, but more middle-class families. That's how we make sure businesses have customers that can afford their products and services. That's how we've always grown the American economy—from the bottom-up. John McCain calls this socialism. I call it opportunity, and there is nothing more American than that.

Understand, if we want get through this crisis, we need to get beyond the old ideological debates and divides between left and right. We don't need bigger government or smaller government. We need a better government—a more competent government—a government that upholds the values we hold in common as Americans.

We don't have to choose between allowing our financial system to collapse and spending billions of taxpayer dollars to bail out Wall Street banks. As President, I will ensure that the financial rescue plan helps stop foreclosures and protects your money instead of enriching CEOs. And I will put in place the common-sense regulations I've been calling for throughout this campaign so that Wall Street can never cause a crisis like this again. That's the change we need.

The choice in this election isn't between tax cuts and no tax cuts. It's about whether you believe we should only reward wealth, or whether we should also reward the work and workers who create it. I will give a tax break to 95% of Americans who work every day and get taxes taken out of their paychecks every week. I'll eliminate income taxes for seniors making under $50,000 and give homeowners and working parents more of a break. And I'll help pay for this by asking the folks who are making more than $250,000 a year to go back to the tax rate they were paying in the 1990s. No matter what Senator McCain may claim, here are the facts—if you make under $250,000, you will not see your taxes increase by a single dime—not your income taxes, not your payroll taxes, not your capital gains taxes. Nothing. Because the last thing we should do in this economy is raise taxes on the middle-class.

When it comes to jobs, the choice in this election is not between putting up a wall around America or allowing every job to disappear overseas. The truth is, we won't be able to bring back every job that we've lost, but that doesn't mean we should follow John McCain's plan to keep giving tax breaks to corporations that send American jobs overseas. I will end those breaks as President, and I will give American businesses a $3,000 tax credit for every job they create right here in the United States of America. I'll eliminate capital gains taxes for small businesses and start-up companies that are the engine of job creation in this country. We'll create two million new jobs by rebuilding our crumbling roads, and bridges, and schools, and by laying broadband lines to reach every corner of the country. And I will invest $15 billion a year in renewable sources of energy to create five million new energy jobs over the next decade—jobs that pay well and can't be outsourced; jobs building solar panels and wind turbines and a new electricity grid; jobs building the fuel-efficient cars of tomorrow, not in Japan or South Korea but here in the United States of America; jobs that will help us eliminate the oil we import from the Middle East in ten years and help save the planet in the bargain. That's how America can lead again.

When it comes to health care, we don't have to choose between a government-run health care system and the unaffordable one we have now. If you already have health insurance, the only thing that will change under my plan is that we will lower premiums. If you don't have health insurance, you'll be able to get the same kind of health insurance that Members of Congress get for themselves. We'll invest in preventative care and new technology to finally lower the cost of health care for families, businesses, and the entire economy. And as someone who watched his own mother spend the final months of her life arguing with insurance companies because they claimed her cancer was a pre-existing condition and didn't want to pay for treatment, I will stop insurance companies from discriminating against those who are sick and need care most.

When it comes to giving every child a world-class education so they can compete in this global economy for the jobs of the 21st century, the choice is not between more money and more reform—because our schools need both. As President, I will invest in early childhood education, recruit an army of new teachers, pay them more, and give them more support. But I will also demand higher standards and more accountability from our teachers and our schools. And I will make a deal with every American who has the drive and the will but not the money to go to college: if you commit to serving your community or your country, we will make sure you can afford your tuition. You invest in America, America will invest in you, and together, we will move this country forward.

And when it comes to keeping this country safe, we don't have to choose between retreating from the world and fighting a war without end in Iraq. It's time to stop spending $10 billion a month in Iraq while the Iraqi government sits on a huge surplus. As President, I will end this war by asking the Iraqi government to step up, and finally finish the fight against bin Laden and the al Qaeda terrorists who attacked us on 9/11. I will never hesitate to defend this nation, but I will only send our troops into harm's way with a clear mission and a sacred commitment to give them the equipment they need in battle and the care and benefits they deserve when they come home. I will build new partnerships to defeat the threats of the 21st century, and I will restore our moral standing, so that America is once again that last, best hope for all who are called to the cause of freedom, who long for lives of peace, and who yearn for a better future.

I won't stand here and pretend that any of this will be easy—especially now. The cost of this economic crisis, and the cost of the war in Iraq, means that Washington will have to tighten its belt and put off spending on things we can afford to do without. On this, there is no other choice. As President, I will go through the federal budget, line-by-line, ending programs that we don't need and making the ones we do need work better and cost less.

But as I've said from the day we began this journey all those months ago, the change we need isn't just about new programs and policies. It's about a new politics—a politics that calls on our better angels instead of encouraging our worst instincts; one that reminds us of the obligations we have to ourselves and one another.

Part of the reason this economic crisis occurred is because we have been living through an era of profound irresponsibility. On Wall Street, easy money and an ethic of "what's good for me is good enough" blinded greedy executives to the danger in the decisions they were making. On Main Street, lenders tricked people into buying homes they couldn't afford. Some folks knew they couldn't afford those houses and bought them anyway. In Washington, politicians spent money they didn't have and allowed lobbyists to set the agenda. They scored political points instead of solving our problems, and even after the greatest attack on American soil since Pearl Harbor, all we were asked to do by our President was to go out and shop.

That is why what we have lost in these last eight years cannot be measured by lost wages or bigger trade deficits alone. What has also been lost is the idea that in this American story, each of us has a role to play. Each of us has a responsibility to work hard and look after ourselves and our families, and each of us has a responsibility to our fellow citizens. That's what's been lost these last eight years—our sense of common purpose; of higher purpose. And that's what we need to restore right now.

Yes, government must lead the way on energy independence, but each of us must do our part to make our homes and our businesses more efficient. Yes, we must provide more ladders to success for young men who fall into lives of crime and despair. But all of us must do our part as parents to turn off the television and read to our children and take responsibility for providing the love and guidance they need. Yes, we can argue and debate our positions passionately, but at this defining moment, all of us must summon the strength and grace to bridge our differences and unite in common effort—black, white, Latino, Asian, Native American; Democrat and Republican, young and old, rich and poor, gay and straight, disabled or not.

In this election, we cannot afford the same political games and tactics that are being used to pit us against one another and make us afraid of one another. The stakes are too high to divide us by class and region and background; by who we are or what we believe.

Because despite what our opponents may claim, there are no real or fake parts of this country. There is no city or town that is more pro-America than anywhere else—we are one nation, all of us proud, all of us patriots. There are patriots who supported this war in Iraq and patriots who opposed it; patriots who believe in Democratic policies and those who believe in Republican policies. The men and women who serve in our battlefields may be Democrats and Republicans and Independents, but they have fought together and bled together and some died together under the same proud flag. They have not served a Red America or a Blue America—they have served the United States of America.

It won't be easy, Ohio. It won't be quick. But you and I know that it is time to come together and change this country. Some of you may be cynical and fed up with politics. A lot of you may be disappointed and even angry with your leaders. You have every right to be. But despite all of this, I ask of you what has been asked of Americans throughout our history.

I ask you to believe—not just in my ability to bring about change, but in yours.

I know this change is possible. Because I have seen it over the last twenty-one months. Because in this campaign, I have had the privilege to witness what is best in America.

I've seen it in lines of voters that stretched around schools and churches; in the young people who cast their ballot for the first time, and those not so young folks who got involved again after a very long time. I've seen it in the workers who would rather cut back their hours than see their friends lose their jobs; in the neighbors who take a stranger in when the floodwaters rise; in the soldiers who re-enlist after losing a limb. I've seen it in the faces of the men and women I've met at countless rallies and town halls across the country, men and women who speak of their struggles but also of their hopes and dreams.

I still remember the e-mail that a woman named Robyn sent me after I met her in Ft. Lauderdale. Sometime after our event, her son nearly went into cardiac arrest, and was diagnosed with a heart condition that could only be treated with a procedure that cost tens of thousands of dollars. Her insurance company refused to pay, and their family just didn't have that kind of money.

In her e-mail, Robyn wrote, "I ask only this of you—on the days where you feel so tired you can't think of uttering another word to the people, think of us. When those who oppose you have you down, reach deep and fight back harder."

Ohio, that's what hope is—that thing inside us that insists, despite all evidence to the contrary, that something better is waiting around the bend; that insists there are better days ahead. If we're willing to work for it. If we're willing to shed our fears and our doubts. If we're willing to reach deep down inside ourselves when we're tired and come back fighting harder.

Hope! That's what kept some of our parents and grandparents going when times were tough. What led them to say, "Maybe I can't go to college, but if I save a little bit each week my child can; maybe I can't have my own business but if I work really hard my child can open one of her own." It's what led immigrants from distant lands to come to these shores against great odds and carve a new life for their families in America; what led those who couldn't vote to march and organize and stand for freedom; that led them to cry out, "It may look dark tonight, but if I hold on to hope, tomorrow will be brighter."

That's what this election is about. That is the choice we face right now.

Don't believe for a second this election is over. Don't think for a minute that power concedes. We have to work like our future depends on it in this last week, because it does.

In one week, we can choose an economy that rewards work and creates new jobs and fuels prosperity from the bottom-up.

In one week, we can choose to invest in health care for our families, and education for our kids, and renewable energy for our future.

In one week, we can choose hope over fear, unity over division, the promise of change over the power of the status quo.

In one week, we can come together as one nation, and one people, and once more choose our better history.

That's what's at stake. That's what we're fighting for. And if in this last week, you will knock on some doors for me, and make some calls for me, and talk to your neighbors, and convince your friends; if you will stand with me, and fight with me, and give me your vote, then I promise you this—we will not just win Ohio, we will not just win this election, but together, we will change this country and we will change the world. Thank you, God bless you, and may God bless America.

YES WE CAN

If there is anyone out there who still doubts that America is a place where all things are possible; who still wonders if the dream of our founders is alive in our time; who still questions the power of our democracy, tonight is your answer.

It's the answer told by lines that stretched around schools and churches in numbers this nation has never seen; by people who waited three hours and four hours, many for the very first time in their lives, because they believed that this time must be different; that their voice could be that difference.

It's the answer spoken by young and old, rich and poor, Democrat and Republican, black, white, Latino, Asian, Native American, gay, straight, disabled and not disabled—Americans who sent a message to the world that we have never been a collection of Red States and Blue States: we are, and always will be, the United States of America.

It's the answer that led those who have been told for so long by so many to be cynical, and fearful, and doubtful of what we can achieve to put their hands on the arc of history and bend it once more toward the hope of a better day.

It's been a long time coming, but tonight, because of what we did on this day, in this election, at this defining moment, change has come to America.

I just received a very gracious call from Senator McCain. He fought long and hard in this campaign, and he's fought even longer and harder for the country he loves. He has endured sacrifices for America that most of us cannot begin to imagine, and we are better off for the service rendered by this brave and selfless leader. I congratulate him and Governor Palin for all they have achieved, and I look forward to working with them to renew this nation's promise in the months ahead.

I want to thank my partner in this journey, a man who campaigned from his heart and spoke for the men and women he grew up with on the streets of Scranton and rode with on that train home to Delaware, the Vice President-elect of the United States, Joe Biden.

I would not be standing here tonight without the unyielding support of my best friend for the last sixteen years, the rock of our family and the love of my life, our nation's next First Lady, Michelle Obama. Sasha and Malia, I love you both so much, and you have earned the new puppy that's coming with us to the White House. And while she's no longer with us, I know my grandmother is watching, along with the family that made me who I am. I miss them tonight, and know that my debt to them is beyond measure.

To my campaign manager David Plouffe, my chief strategist David Axelrod, and the best campaign team ever assembled in the history of politics—you made this happen, and I am forever grateful for what you've sacrificed to get it done.

But above all, I will never forget who this victory truly belongs to—it belongs to you.

I was never the likeliest candidate for this office. We didn't start with much money or many endorsements. Our campaign was not hatched in the halls of Washington—it began in the backyards of Des Moines and the living rooms of Concord and the front porches of Charleston.

It was built by working men and women who dug into what little savings they had to give five dollars and ten dollars and twenty dollars to this cause. It grew strength from the young people who rejected the myth of their generation's apathy; who left their homes and their families for jobs that offered little pay and less sleep; from the not-so-young people who braved the bitter cold and scorching heat to knock on the doors of perfect strangers; from the millions of Americans who volunteered, and organized, and proved that more than two centuries later, a government of the people, by the people and for the people has not perished from this Earth. This is your victory.

I know you didn't do this just to win an election and I know you didn't do it for me. You did it because you understand the enormity of the task that lies ahead. For even as we celebrate tonight, we know the challenges that tomorrow will bring are the greatest of our lifetime—two wars, a planet in peril, the worst financial crisis in a century. Even as we stand here tonight, we know there are brave Americans waking up in the deserts of Iraq and the mountains of Afghanistan to risk their lives for us. There are mothers and fathers who will lie awake after their children fall asleep and wonder how they'll make the mortgage, or pay their doctor's bills, or save enough for college. There is new energy to harness and new jobs to be created; new schools to build and threats to meet and alliances to repair.

The road ahead will be long. Our climb will be steep. We may not get there in one year or even one term, but America—I have never been more hopeful than I am tonight that we will get there. I promise you—we as a people will get there.

There will be setbacks and false starts. There are many who won't agree with every decision or policy I make as President, and we know that government can't solve every problem. But I will always be honest with you about the challenges we face. I will listen to you, especially when we disagree. And above all, I will ask you join in the work of remaking this nation the only way it's been done in America for two-hundred and twenty-one years—block by block, brick by brick, calloused hand by calloused hand.

What began twenty-one months ago in the depths of winter must not end on this autumn night. This victory alone is not the change we seek—it is only the chance for us to make that change. And that cannot happen if we go back to the way things were. It cannot happen without you.

So let us summon a new spirit of patriotism; of service and responsibility where each of us resolves to pitch in and work harder and look after not only ourselves, but each other. Let us remember that if this financial crisis taught us anything, it's that we cannot have a thriving Wall Street while Main Street suffers—in this country, we rise or fall as one nation; as one people.

Let us resist the temptation to fall back on the same partisanship and pettiness and immaturity that has poisoned our politics for so long. Let us remember that it was a man from this state who first carried the banner of the Republican Party to the White House—a party founded on the values of self-reliance, individual liberty, and national unity. Those are values we all share, and while the Democratic Party has won a great victory tonight, we do so with a measure of humility and determination to heal the divides that have held back our progress. As Lincoln said to a nation far more divided than ours, "We are not enemies, but friends...though passion may have strained it must not break our bonds of affection." And to those Americans whose support I have yet to earn—I may not have won your vote, but I hear your voices, I need your help, and I will be your President too.

And to all those watching tonight from beyond our shores, from parliaments and palaces to those who are huddled around radios in the forgotten corners of our world—our stories are singular, but our destiny is shared, and a new dawn of American leadership is at hand. To those who would tear this world down— we will defeat you. To those who seek peace and security—we support you. And to all those who have wondered if America's beacon still burns as bright—tonight we proved once more that the true strength of our nation comes not from our the might of our arms or the scale of our wealth, but from the enduring power of our ideals: democracy, liberty, opportunity, and unyielding hope.

For that is the true genius of America—that America can change. Our union can be perfected. And what we have already achieved gives us hope for what we can and must achieve tomorrow.

This election had many firsts and many stories that will be told for generations. But one that's on my mind tonight is about a woman who cast her ballot in Atlanta. She's a lot like the millions of others who stood in line to make their voice heard in this election except for one thing—Ann Nixon Cooper is 106 years old.

She was born just a generation past slavery; a time when there were no cars on the road or planes in the sky; when someone like her couldn't vote for two reasons—because she was a woman and because of the color of her skin.

And tonight, I think about all that she's seen throughout her century in America—the heartache and the hope; the struggle and the progress; the times we were told that we can't, and the people who pressed on with that American creed: Yes we can.

At a time when women's voices were silenced and their hopes dismissed, she lived to see them stand up and speak out and reach for the ballot. Yes we can.

When there was despair in the dust bowl and depression across the land, she saw a nation conquer fear itself with a New Deal, new jobs and a new sense of common purpose. Yes we can.

When the bombs fell on our harbor and tyranny threatened the world, she was there to witness a generation rise to greatness and a democracy was saved. Yes we can.

She was there for the buses in Montgomery, the hoses in Birmingham, a bridge in Selma, and a preacher from Atlanta who told a people that "We Shall Overcome." Yes we can.

A man touched down on the moon, a wall came down in Berlin, a world was connected by our own science and imagination. And this year, in this election, she touched her finger to a screen, and cast her vote, because after 106 years in America, through the best of times and the darkest of hours, she knows how America can change. Yes we can.

America, we have come so far. We have seen so much. But there is so much more to do. So tonight, let us ask ourselves—if our children should live to see the next century; if my daughters should be so lucky to live as long as Ann Nixon Cooper, what change will they see? What progress will we have made?

This is our chance to answer that call. This is our moment. This is our time—to put our people back to work and open doors of opportunity for our kids; to restore prosperity and promote the cause of peace; to reclaim the American Dream and reaffirm that fundamental truth—that out of many, we are one; that while we breathe, we hope, and where we are met with cynicism, and doubt, and those who tell us that we can't, we will respond with that timeless creed that sums up the spirit of a people:

Yes We Can. Thank you, God bless you, and may God Bless the United States of America.

NOTES

INTRODUCTION—President Barack Obama

[1] Jim Nolan, "Full Coliseum plus 7,000 turn out to hear Obama," *Times Dispatch*, October 23, 2008, www.inrich.com.

[2] "'That One,' McCain Calls Obama in Debate (VIDEO)," *Huffington Post*, October 7, 2008, www.huffingtonpost.com.

[3] Barack, Obama, "Remarks of Senator Barack Obama (Richmond, Virginia)," Obama for America, October 22, 2008, www.barackobama.com.

[4] Keynote Address by Senator Barack Obama, Richmond, Virginia, February 17, 2007, based on author's notes.

[5] *Adapted from* Alan Kennedy-Shaffer, "The Obama Revolution: Just the Beginning," *Scoop08*, November 6, 2008, www.scoop08.com. Reprinted with permission of Scoop Media.

[6] Barack Obama, "Remarks of President-Elect Barack Obama: Election Night," Obama for America, November 4, 2008, www.barackobama.com.

[7] Ibid.

[8] Ibid.

Robert Barnes and Michael D. Shear, "Obama Makes History: U.S. Decisively Elects First Black President, Democrats Expand Control of Congress, *Washington Post*, November 5, 2008, A1.

[10] Barack Obama, "Remarks of President-Elect Barack Obama: Election Night," Obama for America, November 4, 2008, www.barackobama.com.

[11] Ibid.

[12] Ibid.

[13] Gail Collins, "Time for Him to Go," *New York Times*, November 22, 2008, Opinion, www.nytimes.com.

[14] Ethan Bronner, "The Promise: For Many Abroad, An Ideal Renewed," *New York Times*, November 5, 2008, A1.

[15] Barack Obama, "Remarks of President-Elect Barack Obama: Election Night," Obama for America, November 4, 2008, www.barackobama.com.

[16] Jim Nolan, "Full Coliseum plus 7,000 turn out to hear Obama," *Richmond Times-Dispatch*, October 23, 2008, www.inrich.com.

[17] Barack Obama, "Remarks of President-Elect Barack Obama: Election Night," Obama for America, November 4, 2008, www.barackobama.com.

[18] Ibid.

[19] Kevin Sack, "After Decades, A Time to Reap," *New York Times*, November 5, 2008, A1.

[20] Barack Obama, "Remarks of President-Elect Barack Obama: Election Night," Obama for America, November 4, 2008, www.barackobama.com.

[21] Ibid.

[22] Ibid.

[23] "Why Barack Obama Could Be The Next President," *Time*, October 23, 2006, Cover.

[24] Richard Cohen, "Why Not Obama?," *Washington Post*, October 24, 2006, A19.

[25] David Brooks, "Run, Barack, Run," *New York Times*, October 19, 2006, Opinion.

[26] See Lisa Rogak, ed., *In His Own Words* (New York: Caroll & Graf, 2007), 113.

[27] Barack Obama, "Keynote Address at the 2004 Democratic National Convention," Obama for America, July 27, 2004, www.barackobama.com.

[28] Shailagh Murray and Chris Cillizza, "Obama Jumps Into Presidential Fray," *Washington Post*, January 17, 2007, A1.

[29] Barack Obama, "Remarks of Illinois State Sen. Barack Obama Against Going to War with Iraq," Obama for America, October 2, 2002, www.barackobama.com.

CHAPTER ONE—Change We Still Believe In

[1] Keynote Address by Senator Barack Obama, Richmond, Virginia, February 17, 2007, based on author's notes.

[2] Ibid.

[3] Ibid.

[4] Ibid.

[5] Ibid.

[6] "President Bush Announces Combat Operations in Iraq Have Ended," United States Department of State, May 1, 2003, www.state.gov.

[7] "Iraq Insurgency in 'Last Throes,' Cheney Says," CNN, June 20, 2005, www.cnn.com.

[8] "'Can I Quit Now?' FEMA Chief Wrote as Katrina Raged," CNN, November 4, 2005, www.cnn.com.

[9] Christine Hauser, "Concession in Virginia Race Tips Balance," *New York Times*, November 9, 2006, Politics, www.nytimes.com.

[10] "President Bush Delivers State of the Union Address," The White House, January 23, 2007, www.whitehouse.gov.

[11] Ibid.

[12] Ibid.

[13] "Democratic Response to the State of the Union Address," *Washington Post*, January 23, 2007, www.washingtonpost.com.

[14] Ibid.

[15] Barack Obama, "Remarks of Senator Barack Obama: The American Promise," Obama for America, August 28, 2008, www.barackobama.com.

[16] Barack Obama, "Remarks of Illinois State Sen. Barack Obama Against Going to War with Iraq," Obama for America, October 2, 2002, www.barackobama.com.

[17] Barack Obama, foreword to *Change We Can Believe In: Barack Obama's Plan to Renew America's Promise*, by Obama for America (New York: Three Rivers Press, 2008), 3.

[18] Ibid., at 3-4.

[19] Ibid., at 4.

[20] Obama for America, *Change We Can Believe In: Barack Obama's Plan to Renew America's Promise* (New York: Three Rivers Press, 2008), 29.

[21] Ibid., at 33-4.
[22] Ibid., at 36-9.
[23] Ibid., at 42, 46.
[24] Ibid., at 47-8.
[25] Ibid., at 55-8.
[26] Ibid., at 64-5.
[27] Ibid., at 65-70.
[28] Ibid., at 75.
[29] Ibid., at 79-81.
[30] Ibid., at 84-8.
[31] Ibid., at 89-90.
[32] Ibid., at 93-5.
[33] Ibid., at 96-9.
[34] Ibid., at 104.
[35] Ibid., at 106-7.
[36] Ibid., at 109-113.
[37] Ibid., at 122.
[38] Ibid., at 122, 145-7.
[39] Ibid., at 148-9.
[40] Ibid., at 154-7.
[41] "Plan to Strengthen Retirement Security," Obama for America, www.barackobama.com.
[42] Obama for America, *Change We Can Believe In: Barack Obama's Plan to Renew America's Promise* (New York: Three Rivers Press, 2008), 160-1.
[43] Ibid., at 162-4.
[44] Ibid., at 169.
[45] Ibid., at 171.
[46] Ibid., at 175-6.

CHAPTER TWO—A Green Deal

[1] "Exit Surveys: In the End, the Economy," *New York Times*, November 5, 2008, A1.
[2] Paul Krugman, "The Lame-Duck Economy," *New York Times*, November 21, 2008, Opinion, www.nytimes.com.
[3] Ibid.
[4] William Kristol, "George W. Hoover?," *New York Times*, November 17, 2008, Opinion, www.nytimes.com.
[5] Barack Obama, *The Audacity of Hope: Thoughts on Reclaiming the American Dream* (New York: Crown Publishers, 2006), 148.
[6] Obama for America, *Change We Can Believe In: Barack Obama's Plan to Renew America's Promise* (New York: Three Rivers Press, 2008), 31, 37.
[7] John R. Talbott, *Obamanomics: How Bottom-Up Prosperity Will Replace Trickle-Down Economics* (New York: Seven Stories Press, 2008), 33-34.
[8] Barack Obama, *The Audacity of Hope: Thoughts on Reclaiming the American Dream* (New York: Crown Publishers, 2006), 146.
[9] David Brooks, "Change I Can Believe In," *New York Times*, November 7, 2008, Opinion, www.nytimes.com.

[10] Obama for America, *Change We Can Believe In: Barack Obama's Plan to Renew America's Promise* (New York: Three Rivers Press, 2008), 55-6.

[11] John R. Talbott, *Obamanomics: How Bottom-Up Prosperity Will Replace Trickle-Down Economics* (New York: Seven Stories Press, 2008), 70.

[12] "Civilian Conservation Corps Introduction," Oregon State Archives, www.sos.state.or.us.

[13] "Works Progress Administration," Lilly Library of Indiana University at Bloomington, www.indiana.edu.

[14] "An Inconvenient Truth Official Site: Global Warming Science, Climate Change Science, Facts & Evidence," Official Web site of *An Inconvenient Truth*, www.climatecrisis.net.

[15] See Al Gore, *An Inconvenient Truth*, www.climatecrisis.net.

[16] Thomas L. Friedman, "The Power of Green," *New York Times*, April 15, 2007, Magazine, www.nytimes.com.

[17] Ibid.

[18] Ibid.

[19] John M. Broder, "Obama Affirms Climate Change Goals," *New York Times*, November 19, 2008, Politics, www.nytimes.com.

[20] John M. Broder, "Obama Affirms Climate Change Goals," *New York Times*, November 19, 2008, Politics, www.nytimes.com; Andrew C. Revkin, "Obama: Climate Plan Firm Amid Economic Woes," *New York Times*, November 18, 2008, Dot Earth, dotearth.blogs.nytimes.com.

[21] Andrew C. Revkin, "Obama: Climate Plan Firm Amid Economic Woes," *New York Times*, November 18, 2008, Dot Earth, dotearth.blogs.nytimes.com.

[22] Obama for America, *Change We Can Believe In: Barack Obama's Plan to Renew America's Promise* (New York: Three Rivers Press, 2008), 65-74.

[23] Ibid., at 70.

[24] John R. Talbott, *Obamanomics: How Bottom-Up Prosperity Will Replace Trickle-Down Economics* (New York: Seven Stories Press, 2008), 129.

[25] Obama for America, *Change We Can Believe In: Barack Obama's Plan to Renew America's Promise* (New York: Three Rivers Press, 2008), 70.

[26] Ibid., at 71.

[27] John R. Talbott, *Obamanomics: How Bottom-Up Prosperity Will Replace Trickle-Down Economics* (New York: Seven Stories Press, 2008), 130.

[28] Ibid., at 191.

[29] Craig Timberg, "In Darfur's Death Grip," *Washington Post*, September 6, 2006. The included exchange comes directly from Timberg's account.

[30] Ibid. The included exchange comes directly from Timberg's account.

[31] See, e.g., Craig Timberg, "Sudan's Offensive Comes at Key Time," *Washington Post*, September 5, 2006; Eric Reeves, "Accommodating Genocide," *Washington Post*, September 3, 2006; Glen Kessler & Craig Timberg, "Sudan Says No As US Backs UN Force in Darfur," *Washington Post*, September 1, 2006.

[32] Ibid.

[33] Ibid.

[34] Alan Kennedy-Shaffer, "The World Watches as Genocide Unfolds," *New York Times*, March 21, 2006, Letter to the Editor, www.nytimes.com.

[35] Alan Kennedy-Shaffer, "Ready to Serve in Darfur," *Washington Post*, January 16, 2008, Letter to the Editor, A14, www.washingtonpost.com.

36 Ibid.
37 Barack Obama, "Remarks of Senator Barack Obama: A World that Stands as One," Obama for America, July 24, 2008, www.barackobama.com.
38 Ibid.
39 Stephanie McCrummen and Colum Lynch, "Sudan's Leaders Brace for U.S. Shift: Obama Team Seen As Tough on Darfur," *Washington Post*, December 8, 2008, A1, www.washingtonpost.com.
40 Ibid.

CHAPTER THREE—50-State Strategy

1 *Adapted from* Alan Kennedy-Shaffer, "The View from Mechanicsburg, Pa.," *Scoop08*, April 19, 2008, www.scoop08.com. Reprinted with permission of Scoop Media.
2 William Saletan, "Conclusion," in *Divided States of America: The Slash and Burn Politics of the 2004 Presidential Election*, ed. Larry J. Sabato (New York: Pearson Longman, 2006), 277.
3 David Lublin, *The Republican South: Democratization and Partisan Change* (Princeton: Princeton University Press, 2004), 218.
4 Ibid.
5 Tom Hamburger and Peter Wallsten, *One Party Country: The Republican Plan for Dominance in the 21st Century* (Hoboken, NJ: John Wiley & Sons, 2006), 233.
6 Thomas B. Edsall, *Building Red America: The New Conservative Coalition and the Drive for Permanent Power* (New York: Basic Books, 2006), 248.
7 David Lublin, *The Republican South: Democratization and Partisan Change* (Princeton: Princeton University Press, 2004), 218.
8 Mark Crispin Miller, *Fooled Again: How the Right Stole the 2004 Election and Why They'll Steal the Next One Too (Unless We Stop Them)* (New York: Basic Books, 2005), 274.
9 Andrew Gumbel, *Steal This Vote: Dirty Elections and the Rotten History of Democracy in America* (New York: Nation Books, 2005), 315-316.
10 Thomas B. Edsall, *Building Red America: The New Conservative Coalition and the Drive for Permanent Power* (New York: Basic Books, 2006), 214.
11 William Saletan, "Conclusion," in *Divided States of America: The Slash and Burn Politics of the 2004 Presidential Election*, ed. Larry J. Sabato (New York: Pearson Longman, 2006), 271.
12 Thomas Frank, *What's the Matter with Kansas?: How Conservatives Won the Heart of America* (New York: Henry Holt), 247.
13 Thomas B. Edsall, *Building Red America: The New Conservative Coalition and the Drive for Permanent Power* (New York: Basic Books, 2006), 77.
14 William Saletan, "Conclusion," in *Divided States of America: The Slash and Burn Politics of the 2004 Presidential Election*, ed. Larry J. Sabato (New York: Pearson Longman, 2006), 273.
15 Ibid., at 277.
16 Thomas B. Edsall, *Building Red America: The New Conservative Coalition and the Drive for Permanent Power* (New York: Basic Books, 2006), 214.
17 The Democratic Party, "A 50-State Strategy," DNC Services Corporation, www.democrats.org.

[18] Ibid.

[19] "NBC News' Meet the Press," MSNBC.com, May 22, 2005, www.msnbc.com.

[20] Ibid.

[21] Bob Moser, "Purple America", *Nation*, July 25, 2007, www.thenation.com.

[22] Ibid.

[23] Dan Gilgoff, "Dean's List," *U.S. News & World Report*, July 16, 2006, www.usnews.com.

[24] Chris Cillizza, "Dean Defends the 50-State Strategy," *Washington Post*, The Fix, blog.washingtonpost.com.

[25] Dan Gilgoff, "Dean's List," *U.S. News & World Report*, July 16, 2006, www.usnews.com.

[26] Ibid.

[27] Bob Moser, "Purple America, *Nation*, July 25, 2007, www.thenation.com.

[28] Ibid.

[29] Ibid.

[30] The Democratic Party, "50-State Strategy: More Competitive Races," DNC Services Corporation, October 18, 2006, www.democrats.org.

[31] Bob Moser, "Purple America, *Nation*, July 25, 2007, www.thenation.com.

[32] Dan Gilgoff, "Dean's List," *U.S. News & World Report*, July 16, 2006, www.usnews.com.

[33] Ibid.

[34] Margaret Weir and Marshall Ganz, "Reconnecting People and Politics," in *The New Majority: Toward a Popular Progressive Politics*, ed. Stanley B. Greenberg and Theda Skocpol (New Haven: Yale University Press, 1997), 151.

[35] Paul Starr, "An Emerging Democratic Majority," in *The New Majority: Toward a Popular Progressive Politics*, ed. Stanley B. Greenberg and Theda Skocpol (New Haven: Yale University Press, 1997), 236.

[36] John B. Judis and Ruy Teixeira, The Emerging Democratic Majority (New York: A Lisa Drew Book/Scribner, 2002), 6.

[37] The Democratic Party, "How we can win," DNC Services Corporation, www.democrats.org.

[38] Jay Newton-Small, "Obama Scales Back His 50-State Strategy," *Time*, September 23, 2008, www.time.com.

[39] Roland Martin, "Commentary: Dean's 50-state strategy is a plus for Obama," CNN.com, www.cnn.com.

[40] Jay Newton-Small, "Obama Scales Back His 50-State Strategy," *Time*, September 23, 2008, www.time.com.

[41] Bob Moser, *Blue Dixie: Awakening the South's Democratic Majority* (New York: Times Books, 2008), 233.

[42] Ibid., at 235-6.

[43] Roland Martin, "Commentary: Dean's 50-state strategy is a plus for Obama," CNN.com, www.cnn.com.

[44] Mike Madden, "Obama's debt to Howard Dean," *Salon.com*, November 12, 2008, www.salon.com.

[45] Adam Nagourney, "Dean argues his 50-state strategy helped Obama win," *International Herald Tribune*, November 11, 2008, Americas, www.iht.com.

[46] Sam Stein, "DNC Memo: This is the 50-State Strategy Realized," *Huffington Post*, November 6, 2008, www.huffingtonpost.com.

[47] "Election Results 2008: President: Map," *New York Times*, elections.nytimes.com.

[48] "Election Results 2008: President: Big Board," *New York Times*, elections.nytimes.com.

CHAPTER FOUR—Community Organizing

[1] Frank Rich, "In Defense of White Americans," *New York Times*, Opinion, www.nytimes.com.

[2] Ibid.

[3] *Adapted from* Alan Kennedy-Shaffer, "The Real Virginia," *Scoop08*, October 23, 2008, www.scoop08.com. Reprinted with permission of Scoop Media.

[4] Barack Obama, "Full Text of Senator Barack Obama's Announcement for President," Obama for America, February 10, 2007, www.barackobama.com.

[5] Frank Rich, "In Defense of White Americans," *New York Times*, Opinion, www.nytimes.com.

[6] Barack Obama, *Dreams from My Father: A Story of Race and Inheritance* (New York: Crown Publishers, 2004 [originally published 1995]), 134.

[7] Ibid., at 155.

[8] Ibid., at 135.

[9] Ibid., at 162.

[10] Howard Dean and Judith Warner, *You Have the Power: How to Take Back Our Country and Restore Democracy in America* (New York: Simon & Schuster, 2004), 174.

[11] Barack Obama, "Full Text of Senator Barack Obama's Announcement for President," Obama for America, February 10, 2007, www.barackobama.com.

[12] Nancy Gibbs, "How Obama Rewrote the Book," *Time*, November 5, 2008, www.time.com.

[13] Richard J. Semiatin, "Voter Mobilization—Into the Future," in *Campaigns on the Cutting Edge*, ed. Richard J. Semiatin (Washington, D.C.: CQ Press, 2008), 94.

[14] See Malcolm Gladwell, *The Tipping Point: How Little Things Can Make a Big Difference* (New York: Back Bay, 2002 [originally published 2000]); *see also* Malcolm Gladwell, *Outliers: The Story of Success* (New York: Little, Brown, 2008).

[15] Donald P. Green and Alan S. Gerber, *Get Out the Vote: How to Increase Voter Turnout* (Washington, D.C.: Brookings Institution Press, 2008), 89.

[16] Serge Kovaleski, "The Long Run: Obama's Organizing Years, Guiding Others and Finding Himself," *New York Times*, July 7, 2008, Politics, www.nytimes.com.

[17] Ibid.

[18] See Colston Newton, "Consider politician's accessibility," *Northern Neck News*, August 20, 2008, Opinion, A9.

[19] David Sirota, *The Uprising: An Unauthorized Tour of the Populist Revolt Scaring Wall Street and Washington* (New York: Crown Publishing, 2008), 330.

[20] Adam Nagourney, Jim Rutenberg, and Jeff Zeleny, "Near-Flawless Run Is Credited in Victory," *New York Times*, November 5, 2008, Politics, www.nytimes.com.

21 Nancy Gibbs, "How Obama Rewrote the Book," *Time*, November 5, 2008, www.time.com.

22 Christopher C. Hull, *Grassroots Rules: How the Iowa Caucus Helps Elect American Presidents* (Stanford, California: Stanford University Press, 2008), 148.

23 Stephen E. Frantzich, *Citizen Democracy: Political Activists in a Cynical Age* (Lanham, Maryland: Rowman & Littlefield, 2008), 3rd. ed., 229.

24 Frank Rich, "In Defense of White Americans," *New York Times*, Opinion, www.nytimes.com.

25 Ibid.

26 "National Exit Polls Table," *New York Times*, November 5, 2008, Election Results 2008, elections.nytimes.com.

27 John F. Kirn III, "College students jump on campaign trail," *Flat Hat*, September 23, 2008, 1.

28 Ibid.

CHAPTER FIVE—Generation Change

1 Address by Senator Hillary Clinton and Reactions, Richmond, Virginia, February 9, 2008, based on author's notes.

2 Address by Senator Barack Obama, Richmond, Virginia, February 9, 2008, based on author's notes.

3 Ibid.

4 *Adapted from* Alan Kennedy-Shaffer, "Clinton, Obama Battle for Virginia: Divided Democrats Duel Down to the Wire," *Scoop08*, February 12, 2008, www.scoop08.com. Reprinted with permission of Scoop Media.

5 Megan Thee-Brenan, "Election Drew Highest Turnout in 40 Years," *New York Times*, December 15, 2008, The Caucus, thecaucus.blogs.nytimes.com.

6 "National Exit Polls Table," *New York Times*, November 5, 2008, Election Results 2008, elections.nytimes.com.

7 "Exit Polls," CNN.com, November 5, 2008, Election Center 2008, www.cnn.com; "National Exit Polls Table," *New York Times*, November 5, 2008, Election Results 2008, elections.nytimes.com.

8 Compare "National Exit Polls Table," *New York Times*, November 5, 2008, Election Results 2008, elections.nytimes.com, and "Electoral Explorer," *New York Times*, November 5, 2008, Election Results 2008, elections.nytimes.com.

9 "Electoral Explorer," *New York Times*, November 5, 2008, Election Results 2008, elections.nytimes.com; "National Exit Polls Table," *New York Times*, November 5, 2008, Election Results 2008, elections.nytimes.com.

10 Compare "National Exit Polls Table," *New York Times*, November 5, 2008, Election Results 2008, elections.nytimes.com, and "Electoral Explorer," *New York Times*, November 5, 2008, Election Results 2008, elections.nytimes.com.

11 "National Exit Polls Table," *New York Times*, November 5, 2008, Election Results 2008, elections.nytimes.com.

12 Katharine Q. Seelye, "Record Number of Pa. Democrats Registered," *New York Times*, March 24, 2008, The Caucus, thecaucus.blogs.nytimes.com.

13 Ibid.

14 Ibid.

15 Reggie Sheffield, "GOP aims to regain Dauphin County majority: GOP arrives a little late to the registration party," *Patriot-News*, July 6, 2008, www.pennlive.com.

16 Ibid.

17 "Election Results 2008: President: Map," *New York Times*, elections.nytimes.com.

18 Obama for America Field Manual, based on author's notes.

19 Steven Heller, "The 'O' in Obama," *New York Times*, November 20, 2008, Campaign Stops, campaignstops.blogs.nytimes.com.

20 Barack Obama, *Dreams from My Father: A Story of Race and Inheritance* (New York: Crown Publishers, 2004 [1995]), 135.

21 Ibid., at 156.

22 Martin P. Wattenberg, *Where Have All the Voters Gone?* (Cambridge, Mass.: Harvard University Press, 2002), 93.

23 Ibid., at 87.

24 Ibid., at 88.

25 David E. Campbell, *Why We Vote: How Schools and Communities Shape Our Civic Life* (Princeton: Princeton University Press, 2006), 1.

26 Miles S. Rapoport and Marc Caplan, "Championing Democracy Reforms," in *The New Majority: Toward a Popular Progressive Politics*, ed. Stanley B. Greenberg and Theda Skocpol (New Haven: Yale University Press, 1997), 199.

27 Megan Thee-Brenan, "Election Drew Highest Turnout in 40 Years," *New York Times*, December 15, 2008, The Caucus, thecaucus.blogs.nytimes.com.

28 Frances Fox Piven and Richard A. Cloward, *Why Americans Still Don't Vote: And Why Politicians Want It That Way* (Boston: Beacon Press, 2000), 271.

29 Frank Newport, "Early Voting Up to 18%," *Gallup Daily*, October 28, 2008, www.gallup.com.

30 Ibid.

31 Nancy Gibbs, "How Obama Rewrote the Book," *Time*, November 5, 2008, www.time.com.

32 "Virginia Election Results: York County: Dare Precinct," *PilotOnline.com*, hamptonroads.com (accessed December 17, 2008).

33 Stephen Kaufman, "2008 U.S. Voter Turnout on Course to Set Record: Signs point to highly energized voters eager for change," U.S. Department of State, November 4, 2008, www.america.gov.

34 Isshin Teshima and Felicia Tsung, "Students helped swing Va. to Obama: Stryker precinct, where most students voted, went strongly for Democrats," *Flat Hat*, November 7, 2008, 1.

35 Ibid.

36 Adam Nagourney, Jim Rutenberg, and Jeff Zeleny, "Near-Flawless Run Is Credited in Victory," *New York Times*, November 5, 2008, Politics, www.nytimes.com.

37 Jessica Ramirez, "How Accepting Are American Voters?," *Newsweek*, July 16, 2007, 25.

38 Steve Cobble and Joe Velasquez, "Obama's Latino Vote Mandate, *Nation*, November 18, 2008, www.thenation.com.

39 Ibid.

40 Ibid.

[41] Ibid.

[42] Miles S. Rapoport and Marc Caplan, "Championing Democracy Reforms," in *The New Majority: Toward a Popular Progressive Politics*, ed. Stanley B. Greenberg and Theda Skocpol (New Haven: Yale University Press, 1997), 200.

[43] Steve Cobble and Joe Velasquez, "Obama's Latino Vote Mandate, *Nation*, November 18, 2008, www.thenation.com.

[44] David Lublin, *The Republican South: Democratization and Partisan Change* (Princeton: Princeton University Press), 228.

[45] Steve Cobble and Joe Velasquez, "Obama's Latino Vote Mandate, *Nation*, November 18, 2008, www.thenation.com.

[46] Frank Newport, "Americans See Obama Election as Race Relations Milestone," *Gallup Daily*, November 7, 2008, www.gallup.com.

[47] Ibid.

[48] Tim Root, *Love, Empowerment and Social Justice: Personal Relationships and Citizen Action* (London: Open Gate Press, 2005), 231.

[49] Jay R. Mandle, *Democracy, America, and the Age of Globalization* (Cambridge: Cambridge University Press, 2008), 146.

[50] "MyBO," Obama for America, my.barackobama.com.

[51] Joseph Graf, "New Media—The Cutting Edge of Campaign Communications," in *Campaigns on the Cutting Edge*, ed. Richard J. Semiatin (Washington, D.C.: CQ Press, 2008), 94.

[52] Lowell Feld and Nate Wilcox, *Netroots Rising: How a Citizen Army of Bloggers and Online Activists Is Changing American Politics* (Westport, Connecticut: Praeger, 2008), 167.

[53] Ibid.

[54] Kirsten A. Foot and Steven M. Schneider, *Web Campaigning* (Cambridge, Mass.: MIT Press, 2006), 203.

[55] Dennis W. Johnston, *No Place for Amateurs: How Political Consultants Are Reshaping American Democracy* (New York: Routledge, 2007), 142.

[56] Melvin Delgado and Lee Staples, *Youth-Led Community Organizing: Theory and Action* (Oxford: Oxford University Press, 2008), 134.

[57] Ibid.

CHAPTER SIX—The Rhetoric of Hope

[1] Address by Senator Barack Obama, Charlottesville, Virginia, October 27, 2007, based on author's notes.

[2] Ibid.

[3] Ibid.

[4] Ibid.

[5] Ibid.

[6] Barack Obama, *The Audacity of Hope: Thoughts on Reclaiming the American Dream* (New York: Crown Publishers, 2006), 109, 113.

[7] Ibid., at 112.

[8] Evan Cornog, *The Power and the Story: How the Crafted Presidential Narrative Has Determined Presidential Success from George Washington to George W. Bush* (New York: Penguin Press, 2004), 91.

9 Janny Scott, "The Story of Obama, Written by Obama," *New York Times*, May 18, 2008, Politics, www.nytimes.com.

10 Deborah Willis and Kevin Merida, *Obama: The Historic Campaign in Photographs* (New York: Amistad, 2008), 68.

11 Ibid., at 150.

12 Lisa Rogak, ed., *In His Own Words* (New York: Caroll & Graf, 2007), 121.

13 John K. Wilson, *Barack Obama: This Improbable Quest* (Boulder: Paradigm Publishers, 2008), 17.

14 William L. Benoit, *Communication in Political Campaigns* (New York: Peter Lang, 2007), 189.

15 Samuel Kernell, *Going Public: New Strategies of Presidential Leadership* (Washington: CQ Press, 1997), 249.

16 Adam Nagourney, Jim Rutenberg, and Jeff Zeleny, "Near-Flawless Run Is Credited in Victory," *New York Times*, November 5, 2008, Politics, www.nytimes.com.

17 Deborah Willis and Kevin Merida, *Obama: The Historic Campaign in Photographs* (New York: Amistad, 2008), 44.

18 See Lisa Rogak, ed., *In His Own Words* (New York: Caroll & Graf, 2007), 113.

19 Zephyr Teachout and Thomas Streeter, "The Legacies of Dean's Internet Campaign," in *Mousepads, Shoe Leather, and Hope: Lessons from the Howard Dean Campaign for the Future of Internet Politics*, ed. Zephyr Teachout and Thomas Streeter, et al. (Boulder: Paradigm Publishers, 2008), 241.

20 Jeff Zeleny, "Oprah Winfrey Hits Campaign Trail for Obama," *New York Times*, December 9, 2007, Politics, www.nytimes.com.

21 Malcolm Gladwell, *Blink: The Power of Thinking Without Thinking* (New York: Back Bay Books, 2005), 50.

22 Pete Souza, *The Rise of Barack Obama* (Chicago: Triumph Books, 2008), 6.

23 David Brooks, "Playing Innocent Abroad," *New York Times*, July 25, 2008, Opinion, www.nytimes.com.

24 Jeff Zeleny, "Richardson Endorses Obama," *New York Times*, March 21, 2008, Politics, www.nytimes.com.

25 Steve Dougherty, *Hopes and Dreams: The Story of Barack Obama* (New York: Black Dog & Leventhal, 2007), 64.

26 George Lakoff, *Don't Think of an Elephant!: Know Your Values and Frame the Debate* (White River Junction, Vermont: Chelsea Green, 2004), xv.

27 Steve Dougherty, *Hopes and Dreams: The Story of Barack Obama* (New York: Black Dog & Leventhal, 2007), 99.

28 Ginger Thompson, "Seeking Unity, Obama Feels Pull of Racial Divide," *New York Times*, February 12, 2008, Politics, www.nytimes.com.

29 Brent Staples, "Barack Obama, John McCain and the Language of Race," *New York Times*, September 22, 2008, Opinion, www.nytimes.com.

30 Barack Obama, "Remarks of Senator Barack Obama: 'A More Perfect Union,'" Obama for America, March 18, 2008, www.barackobama.com.

31 Ibid.

32 Jeff Zeleny, "Richardson Endorses Obama," *New York Times*, March 21, 2008, Politics, www.nytimes.com.

33 Jeff Zeleny, "Oprah Winfrey Hits Campaign Trail for Obama," *New York Times*, December 9, 2007, Politics, www.nytimes.com.

34 Gary S. Selby, *Martin Luther King and the Rhetoric of Freedom: The Exodus Narrative in America's Struggle for Civil Rights* (Waco, Texas: Baylor University Press, 2008), 125.

[35] Nick Bryant, "How Barack Obama Defied History," *BBC News*, November 5, 2008, news.bbc.co.uk.

[36] Abraham Lincoln, "First Inaugural Address: March 4, 1861," in *Fellow Citizens: The Penguin Book of U.S. Presidential Inaugural Addresses*, ed. Robert V. Remini and Terry Golway (New York: Penguin Books, 2008), 175.

[37] Barack Obama, "Keynote Address at the 2004 Democratic National Convention," Obama for America, July 27, 2004, www.barackobama.com.

[38] Barack Obama, "Full Text of Senator Barack Obama's Announcement for President," Obama for America, February 10, 2007, www.barackobama.com.

[39] Barack Obama, "Remarks of Senator Barack Obama: Final Primary Night," Obama for America, June 3, 2008, www.barackobama.com.

[40] Barack Obama, "Remarks of Senator Barack Obama: The American Promise," Obama for America, August 28, 2008, www.barackobama.com.

[41] Ibid.

[42] Barack Obama, "Remarks of Senator Barack Obama: A World that Stands as One," Obama for America, July 24, 2008, www.barackobama.com.

[43] Michael A. Cohen: *Live from the Campaign Trail: The Greatest Presidential Campaign Speeches of the Twentieth Century and How They Shaped Modern America* (New York: Walker & Company, 2008), 494.

[44] David Olive, *An American Story: The Speeches of Barack Obama* (Toronto: ECW Press, 2008), 87.

[45] Deborah Willis and Kevin Merida, *Obama: The Historic Campaign in Photographs* (New York: Amistad, 2008), 142.

[46] See Stephen Skowronek, *The Politics Presidents Make: Leadership from John Adams to Bill Clinton* (Cambridge, Mass.: Belknap Press, 1993).

[47] Ibid., at 63.

[48] Thomas Jefferson, "First Inaugural Address: March 4, 1801," in *Fellow Citizens: The Penguin Book of U.S. Presidential Inaugural Addresses*, ed. Robert V. Remini and Terry Golway (New York: Penguin Books, 2008), 23.

[49] Stephen Skowronek, *The Politics Presidents Make: Leadership from John Adams to Bill Clinton* (Cambridge, Mass.: Belknap Press, 1993), 131.

[50] Andrew Jackson, "First Inaugural Address: March 4, 1829," in *Fellow Citizens: The Penguin Book of U.S. Presidential Inaugural Addresses*, ed. Robert V. Remini and Terry Golway (New York: Penguin Books, 2008), 85.

[51] Evan Cornog, *The Power and the Story: How the Crafted Presidential Narrative Has Determined Presidential Success from George Washington to George W. Bush* (New York: Penguin Press, 2004), 22.

[52] Stephen Skowronek, *The Politics Presidents Make: Leadership from John Adams to Bill Clinton* (Cambridge, Mass.: Belknap Press, 1993), 201.

[53] Abraham Lincoln, "First Inaugural Address: March 4, 1861," in *Fellow Citizens: The Penguin Book of U.S. Presidential Inaugural Addresses*, ed. Robert V. Remini and Terry Golway (New York: Penguin Books, 2008), 175.

[54] Stephen Skowronek, *The Politics Presidents Make: Leadership from John Adams to Bill Clinton* (Cambridge, Mass.: Belknap Press, 1993), 206.

[55] Michael A. Cohen: *Live from the Campaign Trail: The Greatest Presidential Campaign Speeches of the Twentieth Century and How They Shaped Modern America* (New York: Walker & Company, 2008), 106.

56 Franklin Delano Roosevelt, "First Inaugural Address: March 4, 1933," in *Fellow Citizens: The Penguin Book of U.S. Presidential Inaugural Addresses*, ed. Robert V. Remini and Terry Golway (New York: Penguin Books, 2008), 334.

57 Stephen Skowronek, *The Politics Presidents Make: Leadership from John Adams to Bill Clinton* (Cambridge, Mass.: Belknap Press, 1993), 292.

58 Michael A. Cohen: *Live from the Campaign Trail: The Greatest Presidential Campaign Speeches of the Twentieth Century and How They Shaped Modern America* (New York: Walker & Company, 2008), 124.

59 John K. Wilson, *Barack Obama: This Improbable Quest* (Boulder: Paradigm Publishers, 2008), 165.

60 Lisa Rogak, ed., *In His Own Words* (New York: Caroll & Graf, 2007), 113.

61 Michael A. Cohen: *Live from the Campaign Trail: The Greatest Presidential Campaign Speeches of the Twentieth Century and How They Shaped Modern America* (New York: Walker & Company, 2008), 258.

62 John Fitzgerald Kennedy, "First Inaugural Address: January 20, 1961," in *Fellow Citizens: The Penguin Book of U.S. Presidential Inaugural Addresses*, ed. Robert V. Remini and Terry Golway (New York: Penguin Books, 2008), 386.

63 Jeff Zeleny, "Oprah Winfrey Hits Campaign Trail for Obama," *New York Times*, December 9, 2007, Politics, www.nytimes.com.

64 Jeff Zeleny and Carl Hulse, "Kennedy Chooses Obama, Spurning Plea by Clintons," *New York Times*, January 28, 2008, Politics, www.nytimes.com; Caroline Kennedy, "A President Like My Father," *New York Times*, January 27, 2008, Opinion, www.nytimes.com; Adam Nagourney, "Kennedy Aide Back in Iowa for Obama," *New York Times*, October 2, 2007, The Caucus, thecaucus.blogs.nytimes.com.

65 Pete Souza, *The Rise of Barack Obama* (Chicago: Triumph Books, 2008), 37.

66 Barack Obama, "Keynote Address at the 2004 Democratic National Convention," Obama for America, July 27, 2004, www.barackobama.com.

67 Barack Obama, "Full Text of Senator Barack Obama's Announcement for President," Obama for America, February 10, 2007, www.barackobama.com.

68 Barack Obama, "Remarks of Senator Barack Obama: Iowa Caucus Night," Obama for America, January 3, 2008, www.barackobama.com.

69 Barack Obama, "Remarks of Senator Barack Obama: New Hampshire Caucus Night," Obama for America, January 8, 2008, www.barackobama.com.

70 Jodi Kantor, "For a New Political Age, a Self-Made Man," *New York Times*, August 28, 2008, Politics, www.nytimes.com.

71 Barack Obama, "Remarks of Senator Barack Obama: 'A More Perfect Union,'" Obama for America, March 18, 2008, www.barackobama.com.

72 Barack Obama, "Remarks of Senator Barack Obama: Final Primary Night," Obama for America, June 3, 2008, www.barackobama.com.

73 Barack Obama, "Remarks of Senator Barack Obama: A World that Stands as One," Obama for America, July 24, 2008, www.barackobama.com.

74 Barack Obama, "Remarks of Senator Barack Obama: The American Promise," Obama for America, August 28, 2008, www.barackobama.com.

[75] Barack Obama, "Senator Barack Obama's Closing Argument Speech: 'One Week,'" Obama for America, October 27, 2008, www.barackobama.com.

[76] Barack Obama, "Remarks of President-Elect Barack Obama: Election Night," Obama for America, November 4, 2008, www.barackobama.com.

[77] Michael Powell, "Obama, Awaiting a New Title, Carefully Hones His Partisan Image," *New York Times*, June 3, 2008, Politics, www.nytimes.com.

[78] Ibid.

[79] Frank Rich, "The Terrorist Barack Hussein Obama," *New York Times*, October 12, 2008, Opinion, www.nytimes.com.

[80] Patrick Healy, "McCain Attacks, but Obama Stays Steady," *New York Times*, October 16, 2008, Politics, www.nytimes.com.

[81] Steve Dougherty, *Hopes and Dreams: The Story of Barack Obama* (New York: Black Dog & Leventhal, 2007), 70.

[82] Pete Souza, *The Rise of Barack Obama* (Chicago: Triumph Books, 2008), 37.

CHAPTER SEVEN—The Rhetoric of Change

[1] *Adapted from* Alan Kennedy-Shaffer, "At the End of the Line, We Need Someone to Fight for Us," *Scoop08*, April 22, 2008, www.scoop08.com. Reprinted with permission of Scoop Media.

[2] Shelby Steele, *A Bound Man: Why We Are Excited About Obama and Why He Can't Win* (New York: Free Press, 2008), 133.

[3] Ricky L. Jones, *What's Wrong with Obamamania?: Black America, Black Leadership, and the Death of Political Imagination* (Albany: State University of New York Press, 2008), 16.

[4] Maureen Dowd, "What's Better? His Empty Suit or Her Baggage?" *New York Times*, March 15, 2006, Opinion, select.nytimes.com.

[5] David Mendell, *Obama: From Promise to Power* (New York: Amistad, 2007), 376.

[6] Drew Westen, *The Political Brain: The Role of Emotion in Deciding the Fate of the Nation* (New York: PublicAffairs, 2007), 246.

[7] David Olive, *An American Story: The Speeches of Barack Obama* (Toronto: ECW Press, 2008), 28.

[8] Ibid., at 90.

[9] Alan Kennedy-Shaffer, *Denial and Deception: A Study of the Bush Administration's Rhetorical Case for Invading Iraq* (Boca Raton, Florida: Universal Publishers, 2006), 19.

[10] Ibid.

[11] Ben Shaffer, "Obama is Better for Young Americans," *Politic*, October 29, 2008, thepolitic.org.

[12] David Mendell, Obama: *From Promise to Power* (New York: Amistad, 2007), 376.

[13] Ibid., at 379.

[14] Walter Lippmann, *Public Opinion* (New York: Free Press Paperbacks, 1997 [originally published 1922]), 150.

[15] Steven Heller, "The 'O' in Obama," *New York Times*, November 20, 2008, Campaign Stops, campaignstops.blogs.nytimes.com.

[16] Ibid.

[17] George C. Edwards III, *On Deaf Ears: The Limits of the Bully Pulpit* (New Haven: Yale University Press, 2003), 216.

[18] Elizabeth A. Skewes, *Message Control: How News Is Made on the Presidential Campaign Trail* (Lanham, Maryland: Rowman & Littlefield, 2007), 97.

[19] John Harwood, "Change Is Landing in Old Hands," *New York Times*, November 23, 2008, Week in Review, www.nytimes.com.

[20] Jeff Zeleny, "Long by Obama's Side, an Adviser Fills a Role That Exceeds His Title," *New York Times*, October 27, 2008, Politics, www.nytimes.com.

[21] Stephen Skowronek, *Presidential Leadership in Political Time: Reprise and Reappraisal* (Lawrence, Kansas: University Press of Kansas, 2008), 93.

[22] Thomas Jefferson, "First Inaugural Address: March 4, 1801," in *Fellow Citizens: The Penguin Book of U.S. Presidential Inaugural Addresses*, ed. Robert V. Remini and Terry Golway (New York: Penguin Books, 2008), 24.

[23] Barack Obama, "Remarks of President-Elect Barack Obama: Election Night," Obama for America, November 4, 2008, www.barackobama.com.

[24] Stephen Skowronek, *The Politics Presidents Make: Leadership from John Adams to Bill Clinton* (Cambridge, Mass.: Belknap Press, 1993), 70.

[25] Ibid., at 131.

[26] Andrew Jackson, "Second Inaugural Address: March 4, 1833," in *Fellow Citizens: The Penguin Book of U.S. Presidential Inaugural Addresses*, ed. Robert V. Remini and Terry Golway (New York: Penguin Books, 2008), 92.

[27] Barack Obama, "Remarks of President-Elect Barack Obama: Election Night," Obama for America, November 4, 2008, www.barackobama.com.

[28] Stephen Skowronek, *The Politics Presidents Make: Leadership from John Adams to Bill Clinton* (Cambridge, Mass.: Belknap Press, 1993), 208.

[29] Abraham Lincoln, "Second Inaugural Address: March 4, 1865," in *Fellow Citizens: The Penguin Book of U.S. Presidential Inaugural Addresses*, ed. Robert V. Remini and Terry Golway (New York: Penguin Books, 2008), 180.

[30] Barack Obama, "Remarks of President-Elect Barack Obama: Election Night," Obama for America, November 4, 2008, www.barackobama.com.

[31] Michael A. Cohen, *Live from the Campaign Trail: The Greatest Presidential Campaign Speeches of the Twentieth Century and How They Shaped Modern America* (New York: Walker & Company, 2008), 113.

[32] Franklin Delano Roosevelt, "Second Inaugural Address: January 20, 1937," in *Fellow Citizens: The Penguin Book of U.S. Presidential Inaugural Addresses*, ed. Robert V. Remini and Terry Golway (New York: Penguin Books, 2008), 345.

[33] Barack Obama, "Remarks of President-Elect Barack Obama: Election Night," Obama for America, November 4, 2008, www.barackobama.com.

[34] Stephen Skowronek, *Presidential Leadership in Political Time: Reprise and Reappraisal* (Lawrence, Kansas: University Press of Kansas, 2008), 94, 97.

[35] Jeff Zeleny, "Obama Chides Biden Over Remark About a World Crisis Testing His Presidency," *New York Times*, October 23, 2008, Politics, www.nytimes.com.

[36] Motoko Rich, "For Books, Is Obama New Oprah?," *New York Times*, November 18, 2008, Books, www.nytimes.com.

[37] Peter Applebome, "Is Eloquence Overrated?," *New York Times*, January 13, 2008, Week in Review, www.nytimes.com.

[38] Rebecca Traister, "McCain Gets Mean," *Salon.com*, November 2, 2008, Politics & Democrats, www.salon.com.

[39] Peter Applebome, "Is Eloquence Overrated?," *New York Times*, January 13, 2008, Week in Review, www.nytimes.com.

[40] Elisabeth Bumiller, "Powell's Endorsement Puts Spotlight on His Legacy," *New York Times*, October 20, 2008, Politics, www.nytimes.com.

[41] James Traub, "Is (His) Biography (Our) Destiny?," *New York Times*, November 4, 2007, Magazine, www.nytimes.com.

[42] Dan Froomkin, "The Sole of a Nation," *WashingtonPost.com*, December 15, 2008, White House Watch, www.washingtonpost.com.

[43] James MacGregor Burns, *Running Alone: Presidential Leadership from JFK to Bush II: Why It Has Failed and How We Can Fix It* (New York, Basic Books, 2007), 199.

[44] "The Office of the President-Elect," Obama-Biden Transition Team, www.change.gov (accessed December 22, 2008).

[45] Malcolm Gladwell, *The Tipping Point: How Little Things Can Make a Big Difference* (New York: Little, Brown, 2002 [originally published in 2000]), 259.

[46] Barack Obama, "Remarks of President-Elect Barack Obama: Election Night," Obama for America, November 4, 2008, www.barackobama.com.

CHAPTER EIGHT—The New Faith

[1] Barack Obama, "Keynote Address at the 2004 Democratic National Convention," Obama for America, July 27, 2004, www.barackobama.com.

[2] Ibid.

[3] "God is still speaking," United Church of Christ, www.ucc.org.

[4] Barack Obama, "Senator Barack Obama's Closing Argument Speech: 'One Week,'" Obama for America, www.barackobama.com.

[5] Barack Obama, "Keynote Address at the 2004 Democratic National Convention," Obama for America, July 27, 2004, www.barackobama.com.

[6] Jim Wallis, *God's Politics: Why the Right Gets It Wrong and the Left Doesn't Get It* (New York: HarperSanFrancisco, 2005), xviii.

[7] Ibid.

[8] Ibid., at 346.

[9] Joe Klein, "The Fresh Face," *Time*, October 23, 2006, 49.

[10] Ibid.

[11] Ibid., at 47.

[12] Ibid., at 46.

[13] Ibid., at 46.

[14] Lisa Miller and Richard Wolffe, "Finding His Faith," *Newsweek*, July 21, 2008, 28.

[15] Barack Obama, *The Audacity of Hope: Thoughts on Reclaiming the American Dream* (New York: Crown Publishers, 2006), 202.

[16] "God is still speaking," United Church of Christ, www.ucc.org.

[17] Stephen Mansfield, *The Faith of Barack Obama* (Nashville: Thomas Nelson, 2008), 16.

[18] Lisa Miller and Richard Wolffe, "Finding His Faith," *Newsweek*, July 21, 2008, 28.

[19] Barack Obama, *The Audacity of Hope: Thoughts on Reclaiming the American Dream* (New York: Crown Publishers, 2006), 203-5.

[20] Ibid., at 203.

[21] Ibid., at 206.

[22] Lisa Miller and Richard Wolffe, "Finding His Faith," *Newsweek*, July 21, 2008, 27.

[23] Barack Obama, *The Audacity of Hope: Thoughts on Reclaiming the American Dream* (New York: Crown Publishers, 2006), 207.

[24] Ibid., at 208.

[25] Stephen Mansfield, *The Faith of Barack Obama* (Nashville: Thomas Nelson, 2008), 55.

[26] Barack Obama, *The Audacity of Hope: Thoughts on Reclaiming the American Dream* (New York: Crown Publishers, 2006), 218.

[27] Stephen Mansfield, *The Faith of Barack Obama* (Nashville: Thomas Nelson, 2008), 55.

[28] Ibid., at 52.

[29] David Freddoso, *The Case Against Barack Obama: The Unlikely Rise and Unexamined Agenda of the Media's Favorite Candidate* (Washington, D.C.: Regnery, 2008), 152.

[30] Ibid., at 157.

[31] Jerome R. Corsi, *The Obama Nation: Leftist Politics and the Cult of Personality* (New York: Threshold Editions, 2008), 302.

[32] Barack Obama, "Remarks of Senator Barack Obama: 'A More Perfect Union,'" Obama for America, March 18, 2008, www.barackobama.com.

[33] Ibid.

[34] Barack Obama, *The Audacity of Hope: Thoughts on Reclaiming the American Dream* (New York: Crown Publishers, 2006), 209.

[35] Barack Obama, "Remarks of Senator Barack Obama: 'A More Perfect Union,'" Obama for America, March 18, 2008, www.barackobama.com.

[36] Barack Obama, *The Audacity of Hope: Thoughts on Reclaiming the American Dream* (New York: Crown Publishers, 2006), 198.

[37] Stephen Mansfield, *The Faith of Barack Obama* (Nashville: Thomas Nelson, 2008), xix.

[38] Barack Obama, *The Audacity of Hope: Thoughts on Reclaiming the American Dream* (New York: Crown Publishers, 2006), 216, 224.

[39] Ibid., at 222.

[40] Barack Obama, "Senator Barack Obama's Closing Argument Speech: 'One Week,'" Obama for America, www.barackobama.com.

[41] Jim Wallis, *God's Politics: Why the Right Gets It Wrong and the Left Doesn't Get It* (New York: HarperSanFrancisco, 2005), xxiii, 73.

[42] Ibid., at 160-1.

[43] Barack Obama, *The Audacity of Hope: Thoughts on Reclaiming the American Dream* (New York: Crown Publishers, 2006), 214.

[44] Stephen Mansfield, *The Faith of Barack Obama* (Nashville: Thomas Nelson, 2008), 29-30.

[45] Ibid., at 88.

[46] Ibid., at 52.

[47] Ellis Close, "An Epic Moment, Yes. But Transcendent? No," *Newsweek*, November 17, 2008, 30.

[48] Mark A. Noll, *God and Race in American Politics: A Short History* (Princeton: Princeton University Press, 2008), 2.

[49] Ibid., at 53.

[50] Stephen Mansfield, *The Faith of Barack Obama* (Nashville: Thomas Nelson, 2008), 79.

[51] Abraham Lincoln, "Second Inaugural Address: March 4, 1865," in *Fellow Citizens: The Penguin Book of U.S. Presidential Inaugural Addresses*, ed. Robert V. Remini and Terry Golway (New York: Penguin Books, 2008), 179-180.

[52] William Sloane Coffin, *The Heart is a Little to the Left* (Hanover: Dartmouth College, 1999), 81.

[53] Jim Wallis, *God's Politics: Why the Right Gets It Wrong and the Left Doesn't Get It* (New York: HarperSanFrancisco, 2005), 374.

CHAPTER NINE—Obama's America

[1] E.g., Barack Obama, "Remarks of Senator Barack Obama: Final Primary Night," Obama for America, June 3, 2008, www.barackobama.com; Barack Obama, "Remarks of Senator Barack Obama: A World that Stands as One," Obama for America, July 24, 2008, www.barackobama.com; Barack Obama, "Remarks of President-Elect Barack Obama: Election Night," Obama for America, November 4, 2008, www.barackobama.com.

[2] Jill Sergeant, "Election climax drew 71.4 million TV viewers," *Reuters*, November 6, 2008, www.reuters.com.

[3] *Adapted from* Alan Kennedy-Shaffer, "Taking a Stand," *Patriot-News*, August 10, 2008, F1. Reprinted with permission of the *Patriot-News*.

[4] Lisa Rogak, ed., *In His Own Words* (New York: Caroll & Graf, 2007), 125.

[5] Barack Obama, "Remarks of Senator Barack Obama: New Hampshire Caucus Night," Obama for America, January 8, 2008, www.barackobama.com.

[6] Barack Obama, "Remarks of Senator Barack Obama: The American Promise," Obama for America, August 28, 2008, www.barackobama.com.

[7] Shelley Fisher Fishkin, "Crossroads of Cultures: The Transnational Turn in American Studies—Presidential Address to the American Studies Association," *American Quarterly* (2004): 17.

SELECTED BIBLIOGRAPHY

Applebome, Peter. "Is Eloquence Overrated?" *New York Times*, January 13, 2008, Week in Review, www.nytimes.com.

Barnes, Robert, and Michael D. Shear. "Obama Makes History: U.S. Decisively Elects First Black President, Democrats Expand Control of Congress." *Washington Post*, November 5, 2008, A1.

Benoit, William L. *Communication in Political Campaigns*. New York: Peter Lang, 2007.

Broder, John M. "Obama Affirms Climate Change Goals." *New York Times*, November 19, 2008, Politics, www.nytimes.com.

———. "Change I Can Believe In." *New York Times*, November 7, 2008, Opinion, www.nytimes.com.

———. "Playing Innocent Abroad." *New York Times*, July 25, 2008, Opinion, www.nytimes.com.

———. "Run, Barack, Run." *New York Times*, October 19, 2006, Opinion, select.nytimes.com.

Bronner, Ethan. "The Promise: For Many Abroad, an Ideal Renewed." *New York Time*, November 5, 2008, A1.

Bryant, Nick. "How Barack Obama Defied History." *BBC News*, November 5, 2008, news.bbc.co.uk.

Bumiller, Elisabeth. "Powell's Endorsement Puts Spotlight on His Legacy." *New York Times*, October 20, 2008, Politics, www.nytimes.com.

Burns, James MacGregor. *Running Alone: Presidential Leadership from JFK to Bush II: Why It Has Failed and How We Can Fix It*. New York: Basic Books, 2007.

Campbell, David E. *Why We Vote: How Schools and Communities Shape Our Civic Life*. Princeton: Princeton University Press, 2006.

"'Can I Quit Now?' FEMA Chief Wrote as Katrina Raged." CNN, November 4, 2005, www.cnn.com.

Cillizza, Chris. "Dean Defends the 50-State Strategy." *Washington Post*, The Fix, blog.washingtonpost.com.

"Civilian Conservation Corps Introduction." Oregon State Archives, www.sos.state.or.us.

ClimateCrisis.net. www.climatecrisis.net/thescience.

Close, Ellis. "An Epic Moment, Yes. But Transcendent? No." *Newsweek*, November 17, 2008, 30.

Cobble, Steve, and Joe Velasquez. "Obama's Latino Vote Mandate." *Nation*, November 18, 2008, www.thenation.com.

Coffin, William Sloane. *The Heart is a Little to the Left*. Hanover: Dartmouth College, 1999.

Cohen, Michael A. *Live from the Campaign Trail: The Greatest Presidential Campaign Speeches of the Twentieth Century and How They Shaped Modern America*. New York: Walker & Company, 2008.

Cohen, Richard. "Why Not Obama?" *Washington Post*, October 24, 2006, A19.

Collins, Gail. "Time for Him to Go." *New York Times*, November 22, 2008, Opinion, www.nytimes.com.

Cornog, Evan. *The Power and the Story: How the Crafted Presidential Narrative Has Determined Presidential Success from George Washington to George W. Bush*. New York: Penguin Press, 2004.

Corsi, Jerome R. *The Obama Nation: Leftist Politics and the Cult of Personality*. New York: Threshold Editions, 2008.

Dean, Howard, and Judith Warner. *You Have the Power: How to Take Back Our Country and Restore Democracy in America*. New York: Simon & Schuster, 2004.

Delgado, Melvin, and Lee Staples. *Youth-Led Community Organizing: Theory and Action*. Oxford: Oxford University Press, 2008.

The Democratic Party. "50-State Strategy: More Competitive Races." DNC Services Corporation, October 18, 2006, www.democrats.org.

———. "A 50-State Strategy." DNC Services Corporation, www.democrats.org.

———. "How we can win." DNC Services Corporation, www.democrats.org.

"Democratic Response to the State of the Union Address." *Washington Post*, January 23, 2007, www.washingtonpost.com.

Dougherty, Steve. *Hopes and Dreams: The Story of Barack Obama.* New York: Black Dog & Leventhal, 2007.

Dowd, Maureen. "What's Better? His Empty Suit or Her Baggage?" *New York Times*, March 15, 2006, Opinion, select.nytimes.com.

Edsall, Thomas B. *Building Red America: The New Conservative Coalition and the Drive for Permanent Power.* New York: Basic Books, 2006.

Edwards, George C. III. *On Deaf Ears: The Limits of the Bully Pulpit.* New Haven: Yale University Press, 2003.

Election Results 2008, elections.nytimes.com.

"Exit Surveys: In the End, the Economy," *New York Times*, November 5, 2008.

Feld, Lowell, and Nate Wilcox. *Netroots Rising: How a Citizen Army of Bloggers and Online Activists Is Changing American Politics.* Westport, Connecticut: Praeger, 2008.

Fishkin, Shelley Fisher. "Crossroads of Cultures: The Transnational Turn in American Studies—Presidential Address to the American Studies Association." *American Quarterly* (2004): 17.

Foot, Kirsten A., and Steven M. Schneider. *Web Campaigning.* Cambridge, Mass.: MIT Press, 2006.

Frank, Thomas. *What's the Matter with Kansas?: How Conservatives Won the Heart of America.* New York: Henry Holt.

Frantzich, Stephen E. *Citizen Democracy: Political Activists in a Cynical Age.* Lanham, Maryland: Rowman & Littlefield, 2008), 3rd. ed.

Freddoso, David. *The Case Against Barack Obama: The Unlikely Rise and Unexamined Agenda of the Media's Favorite Candidate.* Washington, D.C.: Regnery, 2008.

Friedman, Thomas L. "The Power of Green." *New York Times*, April 15, 2007, Magazine, www.nytimes.com.

Froomkin, Dan. "The Sole of a Nation." *WashingtonPost.com*, December 15, 2008, White House Watch, www.washingtonpost.com.

Gibbs, Nancy. "How Obama Rewrote the Book." *Time*, November 5, 2008, www.time.com.

Gilgoff, Dan. "Dean's List." *U.S. News & World Report*, July 16, 2006, www.usnews.com.

Gladwell, Malcolm. *Blink: The Power of Thinking Without Thinking*. New York: Back Bay Books, 2005.

———. *Outliers: The Story of Success*. New York: Little, Brown, 2008.

———. *The Tipping Point: How Little Things Can Make a Big Difference*. New York: Back Bay, 2002 [originally published 2000].

Gore, Al. *An Inconvenient Truth: The Planetary Emergency of Global Warming and What We Can Do About It*. New York: Rodale, 2006.

Graf, Joseph. "New Media—The Cutting Edge of Campaign Communications." In *Campaigns on the Cutting Edge*, edited by Richard J. Semiatin. Washington, D.C.: CQ Press, 2008.

Green, Donald P., and Alan S. Gerber. *Get Out the Vote: How to Increase Voter Turnout*. Washington, D.C.: Brookings Institution Press, 2008.

Gumbel, Andrew. *Steal This Vote: Dirty Elections and the Rotten History of Democracy in America*. New York: Nation Books, 2005.

Hamburger, Tom, and Peter Wallsten. *One Party Country: The Republican Plan for Dominance in the 21st Century*. Hoboken, NJ: John Wiley & Sons, 2006.

Harwood, John. "Change Is Landing in Old Hands." *New York Times*, November 23, 2008, Week in Review, www.nytimes.com.

Hauser, Christine. "Concession in Virginia Race Tips Balance." *New York Times*, November 9, 2006, Politics, www.nytimes.com.

Healy, Patrick. "McCain Attacks, but Obama Stays Steady." *New York Times*, October 16, 2008, Politics, www.nytimes.com.

Heller, Steven. "The 'O' in Obama." *New York Times*, November 20, 2008, Campaign Stops, campaignstops.blogs.nytimes.com.

Hull, Christopher C. *Grassroots Rules: How the Iowa Caucus Helps Elect American Presidents*. Stanford, California: Stanford University Press, 2008.

"Iraq Insurgency in 'Last Throes,' Cheney Says." CNN, June 20, 2005, www.cnn.com.

Jackson, Andrew. "First Inaugural Address: March 4, 1829." In *Fellow Citizens: The Penguin Book of U.S. Presidential Inaugural Addresses*, edited by Robert V. Remini and Terry Golway. New York: Penguin Books, 2008.

———. "Second Inaugural Address: March 4, 1833." In *Fellow Citizens: The Penguin Book of U.S. Presidential Inaugural Addresses*, edited by Robert V. Remini and Terry Golway. New York: Penguin Books, 2008.

Jefferson, Thomas. "First Inaugural Address: March 4, 1801." In *Fellow Citizens: The Penguin Book of U.S. Presidential Inaugural Addresses*, edited by Robert V. Remini and Terry Golway. New York: Penguin Books, 2008.

Johnston, Dennis W. *No Place for Amateurs: How Political Consultants Are Reshaping American Democracy*. New York: Routledge, 2007.

Jones, Ricky L. *What's Wrong with Obamamania?: Black America, Black Leadership, and the Death of Political Imagination*. Albany: State University of New York Press, 2008.

Judis, John B., and Ruy Teixeira. *The Emerging Democratic Majority*. New York: A Lisa Drew Book/Scribner, 2002.

Kantor, Jodi. "For a New Political Age, a Self-Made Man." *New York Times*, August 28, 2008, Politics, www.nytimes.com.

Kaufman, Stephen. "2008 U.S. Voter Turnout on Course to Set Record: Signs point to highly energized voters eager for change." U.S. Department of State, November 4, 2008, www.america.gov.

Kennedy, Caroline. "A President Like My Father." *New York Times*, January 27, 2008, Opinion, www.nytimes.com.

Kennedy, John Fitzgerald. "First Inaugural Address: January 20, 1961." In *Fellow Citizens: The Penguin Book of U.S. Presidential Inaugural Addresses*, edited by Robert V. Remini and Terry Golway. New York: Penguin Books, 2008.

Kennedy-Shaffer, Alan. "At the End of the Line, We Need Someone to Fight for Us." *Scoop08*, April 22, 2008, www.scoop08.

———. "Broken Promises." *William & Mary Advocate*, September 6, 2006.

———. "Clinton, Obama Battle for Virginia: Divided Democrats Duel Down to the Wire." *Scoop08*, February 12, 2008, www.scoop08.com.

———. *Denial and Deception: A Study of the Bush Administration's Rhetorical Case for Invading Iraq*. Boca Raton, Florida: Universal Publishers, 2006.

———. "Dying for Peace in Darfur." *William & Mary Advocate*, September 20, 2006.

———. "Hope Mongering: Barack Obama Stirs Supporters with Promises of Change." *William & Mary Advocate*, November 7, 2007.

———. "The Obama Revolution: Just the Beginning." *Scoop08*, November 6, 2008, www.scoop08.com.

———. "Ready to Serve in Darfur." *Washington Post*, January 16, 2008, Letters to the Editor.

———. "The Real State of the Union: Alan Kennedy-Shaffer Evaluates the President's Speech." *William & Mary Advocate*, January 31, 2007.

———. "The Real Virginia." *Scoop08*, October 23, 2008, www.scoop08.com.

———. "The Real World of Virginia: Alan Kennedy-Shaffer Reports from Richmond on the Jefferson Jackson Dinner." *William & Mary Advocate*, February 28, 2007.

———. "Run, Obama, Run: Alan Kennedy-Shaffer's Presidential Predilections." *William & Mary Advocate*, November 8, 2006.

———. "Tackling Global Warming: Alan Kennedy-Shaffer's Take on Climate Change." *William & Mary Advocate*, March 28, 2007.

———. "Taking a Stand." *Patriot-News*, August 10, 2008, Review & Opinion.

———. "The View from Mechanicsburg, Pa." *Scoop08*, April 19, 2008, www.scoop08.com.

———. "The World Watches as Genocide Unfolds," *New York Times*, March 21, 2006, Letters to the Editor.

———. "The Year of the Democrats: Alan Kennedy-Shaffer's Victory Special." *William & Mary Advocate*, November 22, 2006.

Kernell, Samuel, *Going Public: New Strategies of Presidential Leadership*. Washington: CQ Press, 1997.

Kessler, Glen, and Craig Timberg. "Sudan Says No As US Backs UN Force in Darfur." *Washington Post*, September 1, 2006.

Kirn, John F. III. "College students jump on campaign trail." *Flat Hat*, September 23, 2008, News.

Klein, Joe. "The Fresh Face." *Time*, October 23, 2006.

Kovaleski, Serge. "The Long Run: Obama's Organizing Years, Guiding Others and Finding Himself." *New York Times*, July 7, 2008, Politics, www.nytimes.com.

Kristol, William. "George W. Hoover?" *New York Times*, November 17, 2008, Opinion, www.nytimes.com.

Krugman, Paul. "The Lame-Duck Economy," *New York Times*, November 21, 2008, Opinion, www.nytimes.com.

Lakoff, George. *Don't Think of an Elephant!: Know Your Values and Frame the Debate*. White River Junction, Vermont: Chelsea Green, 2004.

Lincoln, Abraham. "First Inaugural Address: March 4, 1861." In *Fellow Citizens: The Penguin Book of U.S. Presidential Inaugural Addresses*, edited by Robert V. Remini and Terry Golway. New York: Penguin Books, 2008.

———. "Second Inaugural Address: March 4, 1865." In *Fellow Citizens: The Penguin Book of U.S. Presidential Inaugural Addresses*, edited by Robert V. Remini and Terry Golway. New York: Penguin Books, 2008.

Lippmann, Walter. *Public Opinion*. New York: Free Press Paperbacks, 1997 [originally published 1922].

Lublin, David. *The Republican South: Democratization and Partisan Change*. Princeton: Princeton University Press, 2004.

Madden, Mike. "Obama's debt to Howard Dean." *Salon*, November 12, 2008, www.salon.com.

Mandle, Jay R. *Democracy, America, and the Age of Globalization*. Cambridge: Cambridge University Press, 2008.

Mansfield, Stephen. *The Faith of Barack Obama*. Nashville: Thomas Nelson, 2008.

Martin, Roland. "Commentary: Dean's 50-state strategy is a plus for Obama." CNN, www.cnn.com.

McCrummen, Stephanie, and Colum Lynch. "Sudan's Leaders Brace for U.S. Shift: Obama Team Seen As Tough on Darfur." *Washington Post*, December 8, 2008, www.washingtonpost.com.

Mendell, David. *Obama: From Promise to Power*. New York: Amistad, 2007.

Miller, Lisa, and Richard Wolffe. "Finding His Faith." *Newsweek*, July 21, 2008.

Miller, Mark Crispin. *Fooled Again: How the Right Stole the 2004 Election and Why They'll Steal the Next One Too (Unless We Stop Them)*. New York: Basic Books, 2005.

Moser, Bob. *Blue Dixie: Awakening the South's Democratic Majority*. New York: Times Books, 2008.

———. "Purple America." *Nation*, July 25, 2007, www.thenation.com.

Murray, Shailagh, and Chris Cillizza. "Obama Jumps Into Presidential Fray." *Washington Post*, January 17, 2007.

MyBO. my.barackobama.com.

Nagourney, Adam. "Dean argues his 50-state strategy helped Obama win." *International Herald Tribune*, November 11, 2008, Americas, www.iht.com.

———. "Kennedy Aide Back in Iowa for Obama." *New York Times*, October 2, 2007, The Caucus, thecaucus.blogs.nytimes.com.

Nagourney, Adam, Jim Rutenberg, and Jeff Zeleny. "Near-Flawless Run Is Credited in Victory." *New York Times*, November 5, 2008, Politics, www.nytimes.com.

"NBC News' Meet the Press." MSNBC, May 22, 2005, www.msnbc.com.

Newport, Frank. "Americans See Obama Election as Race Relations Milestone." *Gallup Daily*, November 7, 2008, www.gallup.com.

———. "Early Voting Up to 18%." *Gallup Daily*, October 28, 2008, www.gallup.com.

Newton, Colston. "Consider politician's accessibility." *Northern Neck News*, August 20, 2008, Opinion.

Newton-Small, Jay. "Obama Scales Back His 50-State Strategy." *Time*, September 23, 2008, www.time.com.

Nolan, Jim. "Full Coliseum plus 7,000 turn out to hear Obama." *Richmond Times-Dispatch*, October 23, 2008,www.inrich.com.

Noll, Mark A. *God and Race in American Politics: A Short History*. Princeton: Princeton University Press, 2008.

Obama, Barack. *The Audacity of Hope: Thoughts on Reclaiming the American Dream*. New York: Crown Publishers, 2006.

———. *Dreams from My Father: A Story of Race and Inheritance*. New York: Crown Publishers, 2004 [1995].

———. Foreword to *Change We Can Believe In: Barack Obama's Plan to Renew America's Promise*, by Obama for America. New York: Three Rivers Press, 2008.

———. "Full Text of Senator Barack Obama's Announcement for President." February 10, 2007.

———. "Keynote Address at the 2004 Democratic National Convention." July 27, 2004.

———. "Remarks of Senator Barack Obama: 'A More Perfect Union.'" March 18, 2008.

———. "Remarks of Senator Barack Obama: A World that Stands as One." July 24, 2008.

———. "Remarks of President-Elect Barack Obama: Election Night." November 4, 2008.

———. "Remarks of Senator Barack Obama: Final Primary Night." June 3, 2008.

———. "Remarks of Senator Barack Obama: Iowa Caucus Night." January 3, 2008.

———. "Remarks of Senator Barack Obama: New Hampshire Caucus Night." January 8, 2008.

———. "Remarks of Senator Barack Obama: The American Promise." August 28, 2008.

———. "Senator Barack Obama's Closing Argument Speech: 'One Week.'" October 27, 2008.

Obama-Biden Transition Team. www.change.gov.

Obama for America. *Change We Can Believe In: Barack Obama's Plan to Renew America's Promise*. New York: Three Rivers Press, 2008.

Obama for America. www.barackobama.com.

Olive, David. *An American Story: The Speeches of Barack Obama*. Toronto: ECW Press, 2008.

Piven, Frances Fox, and Richard A. Cloward. *Why Americans Still Don't Vote: And Why Politicians Want It That Way*. Boston: Beacon Press, 2000.

Powell, Michael. "Obama, Awaiting a New Title, Carefully Hones His Partisan Image." *New York Times*, June 3, 2008, Politics, www.nytimes.com.

"President Bush Announces Combat Operations in Iraq Have Ended," United States Department of State, May 1, 2003, www.state.gov.

"President Bush Delivers State of the Union Address," The White House, January 23, 2007, www.whitehouse.gov.

Ramirez, Jessica. "How Accepting Are American Voters?" *Newsweek*, July 16, 2007.

Rapoport, Miles S., and Marc Caplan. "Championing Democracy Reforms." In *The New Majority: Toward a Popular Progressive Politics*, edited by Stanley B. Greenberg and Theda Skocpol. New Haven: Yale University Press, 1997.

Reeves, Eric. "Accommodating Genocide." *Washington Post*, September 3, 2006.

Revkin, Andrew C. "Obama: Climate Plan Firm Amid Economic Woes." *New York Times*, November 18, 2008, Dot Earth, dotearth.blogs.nytimes.com.

Rich, Frank. "In Defense of White Americans." *New York Times*, Opinion, www.nytimes.com.

———. "The Terrorist Barack Hussein Obama." *New York Times*, October 12, 2008, Opinion, www.nytimes.com.

Rich, Motoko. "For Books, Is Obama New Oprah?" *New York Times*, November 18, 2008, Books, www.nytimes.com.

Rogak, Lisa ed. *In His Own Words*. New York: Caroll & Graf, 2007.

Roosevelt, Franklin Delano. "First Inaugural Address: March 4, 1933." In *Fellow Citizens: The Penguin Book of U.S. Presidential Inaugural Addresses*, edited by Robert V. Remini and Terry Golway. New York: Penguin Books, 2008.
———. "Second Inaugural Address: January 20, 1937." In *Fellow Citizens: The Penguin Book of U.S. Presidential Inaugural Addresses*, edited by Robert V. Remini and Terry Golway. New York: Penguin Books, 2008.

Root, Tim. *Love, Empowerment and Social Justice: Personal Relationships and Citizen Action*. London: Open Gate Press, 2005.

Sack, Kevin. "After Decades, A Time to Reap." *New York Times*, November 5, 2008.

Saletan, William. "Conclusion." In *Divided States of America: The Slash and Burn Politics of the 2004 Presidential Election*, edited by Larry J. Sabato. New York: Pearson Longman, 2006.

Scott, Janny. "The Story of Obama, Written by Obama." *New York Times*, May 18, 2008, Politics, www.nytimes.com.

Seelye, Katharine Q. "Record Number of Pa. Democrats Registered." *New York Times*, March 24, 2008, The Caucus, thecaucus.blogs.nytimes.com.

Selby, Gary S. *Martin Luther King and the Rhetoric of Freedom: The Exodus Narrative in America's Struggle for Civil Rights*. Waco, Texas: Baylor University Press, 2008.

Semiatin, Richard J. "Voter Mobilization—Into the Future." In *Campaigns on the Cutting Edge*, edited by Richard J. Semiatin. Washington, D.C.: CQ Press, 2008.

Sergeant, Jill. "Election climax drew 71.4 million TV viewers." *Reuters*, November 6, 2008, www.reuters.com.

Shaffer, Ben. "Obama is Better for Young Americans." *Politic*, October 29, 2008, thepolitic.org

Sheffield, Reggie. "GOP aims to regain Dauphin County majority: GOP arrives a little late to the registration party." *Patriot-News*, July 6, 2008, www.pennlive.com.

Sirota, David. *The Uprising: An Unauthorized Tour of the Populist Revolt Scaring Wall Street and Washington.* New York: Crown Publishing, 2008.

Skewes, Elizabeth A. *Message Control: How News Is Made on the Presidential Campaign Trail.* Lanham, Maryland: Rowman & Littlefield, 2007.

Skowronek, Stephen. *The Politics Presidents Make: Leadership from John Adams to Bill Clinton.* Cambridge, Mass.: Belknap Press, 1993.

———. *Presidential Leadership in Political Time: Reprise and Reappraisal.* Lawrence, Kansas: University Press of Kansas, 2008.

Souza, Pete. *The Rise of Barack Obama.* Chicago: Triumph Books, 2008.

Staples, Brent. "Barack Obama, John McCain and the Language of Race." *New York Times*, September 22, 2008, Opinion, www.nytimes.com.

Starr, Paul. "An Emerging Democratic Majority." In *The New Majority: Toward a Popular Progressive Politics*, edited by Stanley B. Greenberg and Theda Skocpol. New Haven: Yale University Press, 1997.

Steele, Shelby. *A Bound Man: Why We Are Excited About Obama and Why He Can't Win.* New York: Free Press, 2008.

Stein, Sam. "DNC Memo: This is the 50-State Strategy Realized." *Huffington Post*, November 6, 2008, www.huffingtonpost.com.

Talbott, John R. *Obamanomics: How Bottom-Up Prosperity Will Replace Trickle-Down Economics.* New York: Seven Stories Press, 2008.

Teachout, Zephyr, and Thomas Streeter. "The Legacies of Dean's Internet Campaign." In *Mousepads, Shoe Leather, and Hope: Lessons from the Howard Dean Campaign for the Future of Internet Politics*, edited by Zephyr Teachout and Thomas Streeter, et al. Boulder: Paradigm Publishers, 2008.

"'That One,' McCain Calls Obama in Debate (VIDEO)." *Huffington Post*, October 7, 2008, www.huffingtonpost.com.

Thee-Brenan, Megan. "Election Drew Highest Turnout in 40 Years." *New York Times*, December 15, 2008, The Caucus, thecaucus.blogs.nytimes.com.

Thompson, Ginger. "Seeking Unity, Obama Feels Pull of Racial Divide." *New York Times*, February 12, 2008, Politics, www.nytimes.com.

Timberg, Craig. "In Darfur's Death Grip." *Washington Post*, September 6, 2006.

———. "Sudan's Offensive Comes at Key Time." *Washington Post*, September 5, 2006.

Teshima, Isshin, and Felicia Tsung. "Students helped swing Va. to Obama: Stryker precinct, where most students voted, went strongly for Democrats." *Flat Hat*, November 7, 2008, News.

Traister, Rebecca. "McCain Gets Mean." *Salon.com*, November 2, 2008, Politics & Democrats, www.salon.com.

Traub, James. "Is (His) Biography (Our) Destiny?" *New York Times*, November 4, 2007, Magazine, www.nytimes.com.

United Church of Christ. www.ucc.org.

"Virginia Election Results: York County: Dare Precinct." *PilotOnline.com*, hamptonroads.com.

Wallis, Jim. *God's Politics: Why the Right Gets It Wrong and the Left Doesn't Get It.* New York: HarperSanFrancisco, 2005.

Wattenberg, Martin P. *Where Have All the Voters Gone?* Cambridge, Mass.: Harvard University Press, 2002.

Weir, Margaret, and Marshall Ganz. "Reconnecting People and Politics." In *The New Majority: Toward a Popular Progressive Politics*, edited by Stanley B. Greenberg and Theda Skocpol. New Haven: Yale University Press, 1997.

Westen, Drew. *The Political Brain: The Role of Emotion in Deciding the Fate of the Nation.* New York: PublicAffairs, 2007.

"Why Barack Obama Could Be the Next President," *Time*, October 23, 2006.

Willis, Deborah, and Kevin Merida. *Obama: The Historic Campaign in Photographs.* New York: Amistad, 2008.

Wilson, John K. *Barack Obama: This Improbable Quest.* Boulder: Paradigm Publishers, 2008.

"Works Progress Administration." Lilly Library of Indiana University at Bloomington, www.indiana.edu.

Zeleny, Jeff. "Long by Obama's Side, an Adviser Fills a Role That Exceeds His Title." *New York Times*, October 27, 2008, Politics, www.nytimes.com.

———. "Obama Chides Biden Over Remark About a World Crisis Testing His Presidency." *New York Times*, October 23, 2008, Politics, www.nytimes.com.

———. "Oprah Winfrey Hits Campaign Trail for Obama." *New York Times*, December 9, 2007, Politics, www.nytimes.com.

———. "Richardson Endorses Obama." *New York Times*, March 21, 2008, Politics, www.nytimes.com.

Zeleny, Jeff, and Carl Hulse. "Kennedy Chooses Obama, Spurning Plea by Clintons." *New York Times*, January 28, 2008, Politics, www.nytimes.com.

ACKNOWLEDGMENTS

First and foremost, President Barack Obama deserves credit for inspiring me to write this book. I thank my colleagues from the Obama campaign in Pennsylvania: Alex Kragie, Nicole Comstock, Marty Santalucia, Mawuli Dake, Chris Holder-Ross, Roku Fukui, Keara McKenna, Jeff Kayer, Alicia Gurdus, Jade Gibbs, Tim Scott, and many others. I also thank my colleagues from the Campaign for Change and Coordinated campaigns in Virginia: Yohannes Abraham, Matt Robinson, Frank Sedita, Keauna Gregory, Jessica Bowman, Victoria McCullough, Micah Fergenson, Ian Ferguson, Keeley Houlahan, Casey Emmett, and, above all, William J. Donovan. I owe a debt of gratitude to Cynthia Burton-Shackelford and Raymond Shackelford for their hospitality and advice regarding rural organizing. Bill Day deserves accolades for running a superb campaign and, more importantly, for trusting me as his personal aide. From Bill Day's staff, I thank Strat Cavros, Sam Eure, Paul Savitz, and the legendary Charles Mason. I especially thank my interns for their boundless energy and unwavering devotion: Katelyn Andell, Cassandra Bauco, Molly Bulman, Tyler Crowe, Cat Dame, Breton Harned, John Hill, Erik Houser, Sarah Maguire, Charlotte Miller, Jennifer Odom, Nicole Roussell, Sadie Shea, and Sarah Turcotte. I also thank Emily Hogge, Dianne Carter, Debbie Taylor, Stephen Bennett, Bud Ward, the Hoods, the Kenleys, the Renners, and the countless other volunteers who contributed in innumerable ways to the campaign. Also deserving thanks are the Tidewater county chairs, notably Diane Waltrip, Maggie Sacra, and Donna Thompson. At Phoenix Books, I thank Darby Connor. At Scoop Media, I thank Alexander Heffner. For editing the manuscript, I thank Aaron Garrett and Brian Mahoney, as well as my amazing brother Lee. At William & Mary Law School, I thank Professor Neal Devins for his indulgence, along with William Smith and the Law School Democrats. In the American Studies department, I thank Professor Charlie McGovern for his early feedback and ongoing guidance. For her emotional support and boundless affection, I thank Leila Tubbeh. For his wisdom and enduring friendship, I thank Zach Ulrich.

Finally, I deeply appreciate the unconditional love of my entire family. I am particularly grateful to my grandfather Donald Shaffer for standing behind this project from day one and for recruiting Ken Norwick to represent me. And, of course, this book would not have been possible without the extraordinary love of my brothers, Ross and Lee, and Mom and Dad—the best parents in the world.